CRAZY PAVING

Paving succeeds. For the humour entertains swingingly throughout so that only in the final chapter are you made aware of any serious issue at stake here. Together, these elements create an amusingly thoughtful first novel'
LITERARY REVIEW

'I read with a mixture of awe and fascination Louise Doughty's brilliant first novel . . . If [it] does not get her onto the list of the Booker Prize or some other prestigious award this year I shall cease to harbour what residual faith I still have in a higher justice'
JACK TINKER, DAILY MAIL

'Set mostly either in the office or travelling to and from it, Miss Doughty's wryly observed tale is based on her own secretarial experiences where petty bureaucracy, sexual intrigue and subtle power shifts are the source of gossip over coffee. Where the book departs from an everyday story of office life is in the sharp streak of black comedy that pervades . . . A spirited first novel full of fun yet tinged with sadness'
SUNDAY EXPRESS

'The cardinal rule of travelling on public transport . . . is to go as far as you can on whatever happens to be available. Her tragi-comic novel of urban life is companionable reading for the journey. The tribulations of commuting are a satisfying source of recognition humour; so too is office life, and here the revenge factor comes into play . . . Gratifyingly, this is a novel with a plot, ably

managed by Doughty, a lively writer who does not press her metaphors too far'
DAILY TELEGRAPH

'[Doughty's] strategy is clever; she sets up an elaborate plot involving blackmail, office corruption, sexual intrigue and double dealing, only to have it rendered obsolete by the final, shattering bomb attack. In this way, she makes it uncomfortably clear that, however hard we labour to control our destinies, we are really at the mercy of more random forces'
JONATHAN COE, SUNDAY TIMES

'Louise Doughty loathed her job with London Transport but gets her revenge with her blackly humourous first novel, *Crazy Paving*'
COSMOPOLITAN

'*Crazy Paving* should be approached with caution by anyone in senior management'
ALISON BURNS, THE TIMES

'What makes *Crazy Paving* an original and compulsive read is Doughty's power to make you care about what happens to these people you don't actually like. She also creates an eerie sense of time and place. The at-times cruelly witty dialogue, the details of crass and egotistical behaviour, the intrigue fomenting around the coffee machine . . . it's like every office I've every worked in and yet in a world of its own. This book is a must for anyone who's ever plotted

Louise Doughty has worked as a journalist and critic for a wide variety of newspapers and radio programmes and has an M.A. in Creative Writing from the University of East Anglia. In 1990, she was the recipient of an Ian St. James Award for a short story and a *Radio Times* Drama Award for her first play, *Maybe*, later broadcast on Radio Three. Her second play, *The Koala Bear Joke*, was broadcast on Radio Four in 1994.

Crazy Paving is her first novel.

CRAZY PAVING

Louise Doughty

T O U C H S T O N E

LONDON · SYDNEY · NEW YORK · TOKYO · SINGAPORE · TORONTO

First published in Great Britain in hardback by Touchstone, 1995
This paperback edition first published by Touch stone, 1995
An imprint of Simon & Schuster Ltd
A Paramount Communications Company

Simon & Schuster Ltd
West Garden Place
Kendal Street
London W2 2AQ

Simon & Schuster of Australia Pty Ltd
Sydney

A CIP catalogue record for this book is available from the British Library.

ISBN 0-671-718797

Typeset in Century Old Style 10/11.5 by
Hewer Text Composition Services, Edinburgh
Printed and bound in Great Britain by
HarperCollins*Manufacturing*, Glasgow

For

Jessie Edna Milnes Fellows

1901–1993

Chaos umpire sits
And by decision more embroils the fray
By which he reigns: next him high arbiter
Chance governs all.

John Milton
Paradise Lost
1.907

By the year 2,000, 6.6 million passengers' journeys will take
place every day on London's tubes, buses and trains.

Official estimate from the
office of the London Transport
Director of Planning

Accidents will happen.

Elvis Costello

1

*A*s the train pulled out of Waterloo East, Annette realised she was about to vomit.

She began to breathe deeply, concentrating on the large turning mass that was her stomach, trying to force it down. She was sitting next to the aisle. A businessman was squeezed between her and the window, his legs planted firmly either side of a black Samsonite briefcase. In front of her, hanging onto the luggage rack, was a woman in a pale mac. I am thirty-one, thought Annette. I have spent most of my adult life on public transport of one sort or another but this is the first time I have heaved my breakfast onto a fellow commuter. Shame the woman's mac was so pale.

The train lurched to a halt. Annette's stomach lurched with it. They had come to a stop on Hungerford Bridge. She gazed past the businessman, still breathing deeply. Snow was falling over London, down onto the upright slabs of office blocks and the gleaming dome of St Paul's. A light sun was filtering its way through the thick white air. The Thames was a shifting pattern of grey and brown and silver. Low tide, Annette observed. Odd that the Thames was subject to tides; more appropriate if it was subject to delays caused by staff shortages or a rise in interest rates.

The woman leant forward and lowered the window. There was a small whoosh of cold air into the crowded carriage. The businessman next to Annette flexed his shoulders back against the seat and wriggled from side to side, making himself more comfortable and cramming Annette further back against the armrest. His left shoulder was pressed up against her and she could feel the heat of his body through her own thin coat. If I *was* going to vomit, thought Annette, I would do it over you, you inconsiderate toad.

At Charing Cross another train had arrived simultaneously on a nearby platform. She joined the throng of passengers shuffling towards the exit. Her legs felt a little unsteady. She belched discreetly. Out on the concourse, she headed for the ladies, winding her way through other commuters and fumbling in her handbag for a twenty pence piece.

At the top of the stairs that led down into the toilets, she saw two policemen. They were half-way down, bending over a figure that was slumped across the steps. She hesitated.

One of the policemen looked up and smiled. 'Alright miss,' he said, waving her down. 'Mind how you go.'

She edged her way past the group. The policeman had returned to the prone figure and was saying jovially, 'Shift your arse double quick you smelly old git or we're going to shift it for you.'

In the dank toilet cubicle, Annette wound her knickers

2

and tights over her hips and lifted her skirt. As she sat, she put her head between her legs and let it hang down, breathing in. Monday morning. Hell. The toes of her shoes were scuffed; black suede, not that old either. Have to get the felt tip pen out tonight, she thought aimlessly. Maybe I'll have a shoe cleaning evening. Get them all out. Line them up like soldiers. Outside the cubicle, she could hear the cleaner whistling, 'How much is that doggie in the window . . .'

Joan was the fourth person to arrive at the bus stop. The others were also middle-aged women: one wearing a large pair of glasses was at the front of the queue, and behind her were two Asian women, coats buttoned over their saris, talking to each other and nodding. Joan checked her watch. The number 36 bus was supposed to run every ten to twelve minutes during peak hours but seeing as it travelled in threes this could mean anything up to half an hour. Half the commuter traffic of London met at Camberwell Green, on its way to the West End up the Walworth Road or to the south west along Camberwell New Road. Cars and lorries sat in sullen queues at the traffic lights, chugging out clouds of grey dirt. The shopkeepers on Denmark Hill were beginning to open up. On Camberwell Green, the usual group of men and women were gathering, inmates from the Maudsley Hospital let out for the day. From where she was standing, Joan could see a regular sitting in the centre of the group. He had a lampshade on his head.

Within ten minutes the bus queue had grown and dissolved into a mob. The snow had started to fall again. A dozen people were crammed beneath the shelter. Handfuls of others were huddled together under the shop doorways by the bus stop. Those who had arrived too late to find shelter stood around, shoulders hunched, eyeing each other suspiciously.

When the bus appeared at the other side of the traffic lights, a murmur ran through the crowd. They craned their necks and edged forwards. Umbrellas were optimistically collapsed and shoved into bags.

The bus swept to a halt beside the stop. The chaos began. The conductor, a middle-aged man with a huge stomach, began bellowing as they pushed forward: 'Two inside and three upstairs! Two inside and three upstairs! That's all I'm taking!'

Joan shuffled along anxiously. The two Asian women were in front of her but a small gang of schoolboys had wriggled their way ahead. She felt an elbow barge into her ribs. Behind her, a young white man in a smart mac was pushing forward saying, 'Hey! I was here before them! Hey!' Two of the schoolboys stepped onto the platform and the conductor lifted an arm to let them in. One of their classmates who was left behind shouted gleefully, 'Johnny, man!' and grabbed at the back of his friend's jacket to pull himself up. The schoolboy yelped and fell backwards, arms flailing. Joan stepped back to avoid him and trod on someone's foot. The young man with the briefcase took advantage of the calamity to clear the crowd and get a foot up on the platform. He ducked under the conductor's arm and started up the stairs to the top deck. 'One more upstairs!' hollered the conductor.

4

Joan had a foot raised when the schoolboy darted past her. 'That's it!' screamed the conductor, reaching out to give the starting signal. Another schoolboy had been left behind and was cramming forward. The conductor leant out of the bus, placed a large hand in the centre of his chest and gave him a neat little shove, sending him reeling back into the crowd. 'Full up now!'

A communal groan went up as the bus pulled away. Joan stepped back onto the pavement. The bus's arrival had disorganised the crowd and more people had turned up in the interim. She had lost her place beneath the shelter.

'You know what your problem is?' Helly Rawlins said to her mother. Her mother did not respond. 'You're full of shit.'

Helly stood with her hands on her hips, regarding her mother's supine figure as it lay on the settee. Her mother was not responding for a good reason. She was drunk. Again. Helly was dressed in her short skirt and baggy suede jacket. Her canvas bag was slung over her shoulder. She was late for work. She was late because she had been looking for her shoes, the navy ones with the buckle.

She had turned her bedroom upside-down. She had stormed around the kitchen. She had despaired. While she was brushing her teeth, she had heard the front door slam. Her mother was home. Godammit, she had thought, now she would have to speak to her. She hated talking to her mother. Helly had gone back to her bedroom and put on her lipstick. Then she had taken her coat and bag and had gone to her bedroom door. She had listened.

5

Downstairs, there was silence. After a few moments, she had crept down. She had peered into the kitchen. It was empty, the debris of her breakfast still scattered across the red formica table.

Her mother was in the front room, where she had collapsed onto the settee with her head against the armrest which forced it forward at an unnatural angle. One arm was bent across her body and the other hung down off the edge of the settee. The ends of her fingers brushed the floor. She hadn't even taken off her coat. At the end of her long thin legs, squeezed onto her long thin feet, were Helly's shoes.

Helly pulled the shoes off her mother's feet and dropped them to the floor. She turned one over with a stockinged foot, exploring. It felt warm and soft. With a grimace, she slipped them on. Then she turned and left the house, banging the front door as loudly as she could.

The tube train was pulling in as Helly clattered onto the platform. She edged her way into the middle of a gang of commuters waiting to pile on board. As soon as the doors slid open, the pushing and shoving began. An announcer pleaded with them to let the passengers off the train first. In front of Helly, an elderly man wearing a brown suit was trying to get his foot up onto the train. She pushed past him. The hanging straps were all occupied so she wriggled past another woman into the corner of the door and glass panel. As the doors began to judder shut, three young men came leaping down the stairs and dived into her carriage. She was jammed backwards. The shoulder of one of them brushed past her nose. The train began to pull forward in short, jerky movements. The passengers bumped together like ninepins. The man in front of Helly trod on her foot. 'Sorry,' he said over his shoulder. She scowled at the back of his neck, at the dark curls which twisted over a white shirt collar. The small red bump of a spot was just visible, peeping from between two locks of hair.

In the middle of the tunnel, just after Vauxhall, the train stopped. There was often a pause at this point, to remind commuters that they were travelling hundreds of feet underground, beneath tons of water. The passengers edged around uneasily. Helly stared gloomily ahead, then sighed. She had some mints in her bag but it was impossible to get at them in this scrum. They waited.

Eventually, the train began to move. At Pimlico, it seemed impossible that any more passengers would try to get on, but they did. The young man stepped back onto Helly's foot again and this time she snapped, 'D'you *mind?*', pushing at him with her elbow.

He glanced at her, registered that she was not worth arguing with and turned back to his friends. 'Bleedin' hell,' one of them was saying, 'this is so packed I'm scared I'm going to get someone pregnant.'

Annette's detour via the Ladies at Charing Cross made her late. She trotted up the steps of John Blow House and past the security guard, who was sitting glumly behind Reception reading the *Daily Mail* and chewing the ends of his fingers. She stabbed the lift button with one finger and then, while she waited, continued to stab.

Joan had already arrived. She was watering the plants that had colonised the window sill, peering over an uncontrollable ivy and chuckling to herself.

'Morning Joan,'

'Morning. How are you?'

'Fine. Slight delay on Hungerford Bridge.'

'You won't believe what happened to me.' Joan turned from the plants. 'Really. Good grief, I haven't quite calmed down.' She put down the plastic watering jug, withdrew a tissue from her blouse sleeve and wiped her eyes. 'It gets better every day, doesn't it?'

Annette was hanging up her coat. 'Let me guess. The bus driver fainted at the wheel and one of the passengers took over.'

'Not quite. They made everyone get off at Vauxhall. Two inspectors got on at the Oval. When they came down from the top deck, they stopped the bus and said we all had to get off because there was a suspicious handbag upstairs. They had completely straight faces as well. Oh dear . . .' She blew her nose.

Helly strolled in at nine thirty-two. 'Alright?' she asked Annette and Joan rhetorically as she swaggered past their desks.

Annette sighed. She pulled a small notepad out of her desk drawer and flicked through a list of numbers. At the bottom of the list she added the date, then a dash, then the figure 32. Annette was keeping an eye on Helly. She still had two months of her probationary period to go.

'Helly!' Annette called, as her small plump figure disappeared round the corner. Helly turned on one foot, a sulky expression on her soft round features. A lot of the surveyors fancied Helly, although Annette could not comprehend why. She spent most of her time eating biscuits and the rest scowling. She was just five feet tall and had a figure like a jelly baby. Her light brown hair was straight on the left hand side and tucked behind her ear. On the right, it fell in unnaturally stiffened curls around her face. She swore. She had good skin for a seventeen-year-old but even that could not, in Annette's view, compensate for the fundamental unpleasantness that lay beneath it. Younger men in the office seemed prepared to overlook this because she wore short skirts and developed dimples on the rare occasions that she smiled. Annette despised the boys. Helly was not employed to dimple. Helly was employed to work. She was murder: the Office Junior from Hell.

'What?' *What* was Helly's favourite word.

Annette looked down and flicked through the contents of her in-tray while she spoke, to demonstrate that however discourteous Helly might be she was just as capable of being discourteous back.

'Can you go through the stationery cupboard for me please and do a list? I'm going over to Wimperton's later on.'

Helly turned to go without response, which meant, *What? Bloody hell, alright then*.

Joan was looking at her diary and frowning. 'It is February, isn't it?' she asked Annette.

''Fraid so,' Annette replied.

'Oh, I'm looking at the wrong month,' Joan said. 'Silly me – I did tell you April, didn't I?'

'Yes. Where are you going?'

'Spain.'

'Will it be hot enough by then?' Annette was making a list of the jobs to do that day which she would stick onto the front of her computer. It was divided into three groups: Urgent, Non-Urgent and If Possible.

'Well, Alun said so,' Joan replied, 'I'm really looking forward to it. It's the first time we've been abroad for six years. I'll have to buy a swimsuit.'

Helly appeared round the corner. She was holding a box of paperclips. 'Here, look at this,' she said, grinning and chewing a biscuit at the same time. 'Do you know what paperclips are called in Europe?' She rattled the box.

'What?' asked Joan.

'Trombones.'

'Oh stop it,' Joan replied.

'No straight up. That's what it says here. Large-lipped paperclips. *Long ourles trombones*.' She twisted her mouth as she spoke. 'If we join Europe we'll have to clip memos together with trombones.'

'And people in brass bands will have to play paperclips,' muttered Annette.

Helly removed a large paperclip from the box and put it on her lower lip. Then she went back to the stationery cupboard.

Annette glanced up at the clock: nine fifty-six. Richard was even later than usual. She turned on her computer and reached for the mouse. As the hard disk span up, she ran her eye down her list of tasks for that day, sighing.

10

Richard sat in the passenger seat while his wife drove. They were silent. Their three golden retrievers sat in the back. Two of them were lying down and one was resting his head over the back of Gillian's seat with his snout on her right shoulder. Gillian had tied a patterned silk headscarf tight under her chin and pulled it forward so that it obscured most of her face. Glancing sideways, Richard could see only the small angle of her nose. He glanced sideways several times, trying to guess her demeanour from her posture and the movements of her hands on the wheel. It was always hard to tell with Gillian.

As they rounded the bend past The Jolly Huntsman, they passed David Harton on his bicycle. David Harton was their neighbour and had taken to cycling only recently. He was wearing a yellow waterproof cape over his suit and had wrapped his briefcase in clear plastic and placed it in a white wire basket clipped to the front of the handlebars. Bicycle clips restrained his trouser legs. It had stopped snowing but the air was still damp. Harton wobbled as he pedalled slowly through the deep brown slush, his knees sticking out at thirty-degrees angles. He glanced over his shoulder and waved at them as their car swished past. They both waved back.

'David is taking this fitness campaign seriously then,' commented Gillian.

Richard felt relieved. 'Juanita has put him on a diet,' he said. 'Avocados and brown rice. It's a new thing.'

They came to the village high street.

'Did he get planning permission for the heli-pad?' Gillian asked.

'I think there's a problem. He may not be able to put it on the roof after all. They're thinking about the paddock.'

'Oh *no*. Really?'

'That's what he said.' Richard felt pleased with himself. If Gillian became annoyed about their neighbours' plans for a helicopter pad in the paddock then she would forget about last night's little problem. Gillian was a woman who could only be annoyed about one thing at a time.

Gillian sighed heavily. Richard took a risk. 'What about dinner?'

Her response disappointed him. She barked. The dog on her shoulder jumped.

'Dinner?' she added, dismissively. They drove in silence for the rest of the journey.

As they pulled into the station car park, Richard checked his watch. He had seven minutes to spare; time to try and make things right before he got his train. He hated going to work with things all wrong. It ruined his entire day.

She switched off the engine and he turned to her. Then he reached out and took her hand. She was wearing string-backed driving gloves. His were black leather. 'Gillian,' he said, looking down at her hand, 'I am sorry about last night. I am sure we can get it fixed . . .'

'We? You mean *I*, Richard. You are sure *I* can get it fixed.'

'I could ring Benson's from work.'

'No,' Gillian replied quickly. 'Leave it to me. Last

time we had Benson & Sons in their apprentice ruined the carpet.'

'I did get him sacked.'

'That's hardly the point, is it?'

He began to rub one of her fingers between two of his. 'No, Gillian.'

She sighed. 'I will call out the plumbers and the engineers. I will sort everything out – and there will be dinner.'

He knew he was forgiven. He leant towards her.

She waited until his face was close to hers and then put her free gloved hand over his mouth. 'But you have to promise me,' she said evenly, 'that you will never try and fix the boiler again.' She took her hand away.

'Promise,' he said.

He leant forward again and their lips brushed briefly. The retriever on Gillian's right shoulder watched them, unmoved.

Richard drew back slightly, paused, then risked placing a hand on her knee. She looked at him.

'I've been very bad . . .' he suggested hopefully.

She kept her gaze level. Then she said softly, 'Yes, Richard, you have. And tonight you will be punished.'

His carriage was half full. All of its occupants were men and most were reading bits of paper. The only problem with first class travel was that it obliged you to pretend to work. Richard always carried a calculator in his pocket. Once seated, he would withdraw it and press its buttons at random. Occasionally, when he knew himself to be

13

observed by the man sitting opposite, he would pause and frown at it, shaking his head slightly.

Today, he tapped in the numbers 01134 and turned the calculator upside-down. It said hEllO.

At Victoria, he remained seated for a few minutes to allow the scrambling mob on the platform to clear. Then he strolled towards the concourse. Half-way there he stopped, put down his briefcase and lit a cigarette. He blew smoke into the air in a manner which a casual observer would have considered confident, derisive. There are days, thought Richard, when it occurs to you that in comparison with many people you have made a success of your life and have much to be proud of.

He headed for the bank of telephones in the corner of the station, the ones tucked out of sight. There were some in the middle of the concourse, but he couldn't risk being spotted by any of his staff who might be running late. In the alcove, he took out his phonecard and a small book bound in plum coloured leather which he kept tucked in the inside pocket of his jacket. He had one or two calls to make before he got to the office.

The first person to greet him as he stepped out of the lift was his new surveyor, William Bennett.

'Richard,' William observed. Then stopped.

'Yes?' said Richard as he walked down the open-plan department, William in pursuit.

'Sutton Street,' said William. 'Compulsory purchase

order on Rosewood Cottage. Need to talk. Might be a problem.'

Richard grunted. By now they had reached his office. He slung his briefcase on his desk, opened it and began unloading sheafs of paper.

'Had to take the Sports Ground specs home over the weekend,' he muttered. 'No overtime in this job you know.'

William looked a little frustrated. 'I really do think we need to sort this out,' he said. 'I thought it would be straightforward after the Royal Assent. To be honest, Richard, I'm not sure. I need some back-up.'

William Bennett was twenty-seven. He had worked for Richard Leather for six weeks but had already surmised that the only way to get him to do anything was to appear helpless.

Richard was looking pleased. He came round to William's side of the desk and slapped a fatherly hand on his shoulder. 'Don't worry. We've got the project meeting on Friday. It will all get sorted out then.'

Annette stepped into the office swiftly and silently and placed a cup of freshly poured black coffee on Richard's desk. Silently, she left.

Richard was guiding William towards the door. 'The thing to do is to move fast, before the other side have time to get organised. They haven't employed a solicitor or anything, have they?'

'The old couple? No, I don't think so.'

'When are you going round?'

'I don't know.'

15

'Well, I tell you what.' Richard dropped his voice. 'Pop round, next week maybe, after the meeting, do a few measurements and have a sniff about, okay?'

By now they had reached the door. William looked at Richard, confused. Richard smiled, winked, and closed the door in his face.

When Richard turned from the door, his smile had disappeared.

It happened at eleven sixteen a.m. Annette knew because as soon as she heard the blast, she checked her watch. It was a deep, unmistakable boom, short but sonorous, as if a roll of thunder had been compressed into a box and then burst free. The window next to her rattled. For a minute there was silence, then the sirens began. Opposite her Joan looked up, her gaze questioning. Annette nodded, then reached for the phone.

It rang twice before her mother answered. 'Yes?'

'Mum, it's me. I thought I'd better ring. A bomb's gone off. I'm fine.'

'A bomb?'

'Yes. There's been an explosion. It rattled the windows of our office.'

'Are you at work? Are you okay? How near was it?'

'I don't know. Whitehall, maybe. It's hard to tell. It seemed quite distant.'

'I'll put the radio on. Did you get my note about the jumper?'

'Mum I can't talk now, I'm at work. I just wanted to

let you know, so you wouldn't hear it on the news and worry . . .'

Raymond came round the corner. He was the senior surveyor and Richard's deputy. He wore a bow-tie. He wrote his draft memos in green ink and complained to Annette that young surveyors these days didn't understand the past participle. 'Was that what I thought it was?' he asked.

'Yes,' replied Annette.

'I'd hang them,' spat Raymond. 'They should all be hanged. Every one of them. Bloody Irish.'

Annette returned to the Schedule of Dilapidations she was typing. The vehemence of Raymond's opinions irritated her even when she agreed with him, and in this case she did not.

Joan picked up the phone. It would not have occurred to her to ring Alun, but seeing Annette so considerate about her mother, she wondered if her husband might be concerned.

Alun was on shifts that week so he was at home. 'Hello?'

'Oh hello Alun, it's only me. I just thought I would tell you, a bomb's gone off.'

'Oh.'

'But I'm alright. I'm fine in fact. I'm in the office. I'm at work.'

'Yes I know.' Hearing his irritation made Joan feel stupid. She often felt stupid when she spoke to her husband.

Richard had emerged and was conferring with Raymond.

He too thought that bombers should be hanged. Then he went back to his office.

'There's no excuse for it,' pronounced Raymond to Joan and Annette, 'no excuse for it at all.' Having no audience for his opinions never bothered Raymond, any more than he would worry if nobody was listening to his jokes. If no one thought them funny, he was more than happy to provide the laughter on his own. If no one agreed with him that those who planted bombs should be strung up, then he was perfectly content to agree with himself.

'Oh dear,' said Joan as she put down the phone. 'I suppose they'll close all the stations. The traffic will be terrible.'

'It'll be alright by tonight,' said Annette, without looking up from her work.

'There was a bus crash up my way last week,' said Joan. 'A bus went over on its side going round a corner. It ended up leaning up against a lamp-post. Imagine sitting on a bus that was leaning up a lamp-post.'

Annette kept her head down. 'I suppose you would slope rather a lot.'

'I mean,' Joan continued amiably, 'if you get a train you crash, if you get a bus you end up sloping. If you walk down the street a litter bin blows up.'

Raymond had turned to go but turned back and rounded on Joan. 'It's not the same thing!' he exploded furiously. 'Honestly Joan, how can you say that!'

Annette looked up. Raymond was usually polite to Joan. She was fifty-four and Raymond regarded himself as a gentleman.

He continued. 'It's just that kind of immorality that lets the IRA get away with this sort of thing.'

Joan was looking at him. She blinked.

Raymond sighed. 'A bomb exploding in the street,' he explained patiently, 'is not the same as a car crash or a train derailment. It is not an accident. It is something that someone has done deliberately. It is not something to be merely regretted. We need to take action!' He concluded this speech by thumping the air with his fist, turning smartly on his heel and striding off down the office. Joan looked at Annette.

'Raymond doesn't have a member of the IRA handy,' said Annette, 'so it looks as though you're the next best thing.'

'But I didn't mean it like that,' said Joan.

'I know,' said Annette with a sigh. One of these days, she thought, I am going to push something unpleasant up Raymond's left nostril.

Joan stood and went to the filing cabinet. 'Actually,' she said as she returned to her desk, 'I think maybe I did mean it like that.'

Annette looked up again.

Joan plonked the day file on her lap and unclipped it. She picked up a handful of papers from her in-tray and began to sort them into date order. 'The fact is,' she continued, 'as far as we're concerned, it might as well be like a bus crash. We have no control over it. It could happen any time. We just have to think about statistics and cross our fingers.

'Someone might have died in that bomb we just heard,' she added as she began to insert the pages into the file. 'And

19

as far as he or she is concerned, the important thing was that they walked down that street at that time, instead of stopping to buy a newspaper or taking another route. They went past the bomb. The bomb didn't go past them.'

No one had died in the blast. The bomb had gone off down a side-street near Lambeth Bridge, in a rubbish skip. Two homeless people sleeping in a doorway opposite had been slightly injured. Several windows had been blown out. The *Evening Standard* headline pasted to the newspaper sellers' kiosks read, 'LONDONERS DEFY BOMB TERROR'. Annette bought a late edition to read while she waited in a pub off Broadway. She was having dinner with an old schoolfriend.

Later, she walked down Birdcage Walk and up Horse Guards Parade, to catch her train home. Whitehall was still cordoned off, even though the bomb had been streets away. There was a nice pub on Whitehall, she remembered, with snugs and wooden floorboards. It probably got evacuated nightly now.

The snow had been falling all day and by early evening it had settled. Now it floated sparsely in huge flakes which swung from side to side as they descended. Trafalgar Square was empty. The occasional bus or car drove slowly through the slush. Orange street-lamps lit up an inky sky. As she crossed the square she made deep, fresh prints in the ankle-deep snow. The only sounds were the distant hum of traffic from the Strand and the soft swoosh of a passing black cab as it ploughed gently past the National Gallery. London, thought Annette with a sigh, is the most beautiful place on earth.

By Friday the snow had gone rotten; melted into a deep brown dampness. Walking along a pavement was a treacherous business. Trying to cross the road was hell. Intermittently it drizzled or the wind blew but the weather couldn't make its mind up. Commuters found its indecision irritating.

Annette was visiting her mother that weekend and struggled into work with an overnight bag and a carrier full of old tights. Annette's mother collected old tights.

It had been a busy week. Richard had been in a panic over the Sports Grounds' specifications. Raymond had had an urgent schedule. Expecting Joan to do anything complicated on the computer was out of the question. Annette had buckled down with grim determination, allowing herself a glimmer of satisfaction in the knowledge that without her the entire department would grind to a halt.

Friday was a quiet day, thank God. Most of the boys were out on site visits. Richard had a project meeting at two thirty. It would be nice with him shut in his office for a couple of hours. He had been hurling dictation work at her all week with mounting frenzy. By Thursday, he had taken to emerging from his office, whistling, then tossing a tape at her from the door. It would sail over her computer to land in her in-tray or, once, on her head.

She was half-way through the first memo when the telephone on Helly's desk rang. She couldn't see Helly from where she sat but knew she was supposed to be at her desk. Joan was out at a dental appointment. Annette let the phone ring six times before muttering, picking up the receiver on her desk and pressing seven. It was Reception; some more of Richard's visitors were here.

'Helly?' Annette stood in front of Helly's desk. Helly had her arms resting on it and her forehead on her arms. She was trying to go to sleep.

'What?' Helly responded, without lifting her head.

'Richard's visitors have arrived. Go and meet them at the lift or you'll be sacked.'

Annette returned to her desk and replaced her audio headphones. She pressed the foot pedal. Richard's crisp tones pronounced, *'In addition, and furthermore, I draw your attention to my memo of . . .'*

Helly rose to her feet so slowly she nearly fell over. By the time she was half-way down the office, the gentlemen from Arnold & Sons had emerged from the lift and were standing in front of the swing doors, blinking.

'Hello. This way,' said Helly from approximately twenty paces. She turned smartly on her heel and led them back down the office at some speed. The two men trotted after her.

At the door to Richard's office, she paused. Then she tapped and opened it, standing back and gesturing for the men to go in. They moved forward hesitantly. She heard Richard greet them. She tried to close the door behind them but it caught on the second one's heel. 'Sorry,' she said as he looked back. She went to pull the door shut but it was too late.

'Helen!' Richard's voice called from inside the office. She rolled her eyes, fixed a smile on her face and opened the door.

Richard was standing behind his desk. William, the new surveyor, sat on his right. Raymond sat on his left. One of the contractors and an architect were sitting in front of the desk. The two men from Arnold & Sons were struggling with plastic chairs which they were trying to fit into the small remaining space next to the architect. One of them had decided to sit on his chair first, grasp the edges with both hands and nudge it sideways.

'We'll have coffee thank you Helen,' said Richard in a tone of voice that suggested politeness within the context of total command.

The contractor was called Mr Robinson. He had a pitted, bulging nose which he blew often into handkerchiefs the size of cushion covers. 'Ah, Helen,' he declared, grinning at her. 'The face that launched a thousand tea trolleys!'

'What?' said Helly.

'Oh never mind,' he said. The men laughed.

She looked at them expectantly. 'Tea for me,' said Mr Robinson. 'One sugar.'

'Coffee,' said the architect.

'Coffee, black please,' said one of the men from Arnold & Sons and his companion added, 'Same.'

'White coffee,' said Raymond.

'Did I say white?' asked the architect.

'Usual,' said Richard.

'Oh, I'll have a tea please,' said William.

'Gosh,' said Mr Robinson, cheerily. 'Will you remember all that?'

While the kettle boiled, Helly rummaged through the cupboard to find the family selection tin of biscuits which was reserved for visitors. A memo had recently gone round reminding staff that the contents of this particular tin were for consumption at meetings only. While she arranged some of them on a plate and poured the drinks, she stuck the end of a pink wafer between her lips and sucked at it. As she leant over the tray to reach the sugar bowl, the remaining end fell off and landed with a small splash in one of the cups of tea. She fished it out with a spoon.

When she reached Richard's door, she tapped it lightly with one foot. A voice called, 'Come in.'

Stupid gits, she thought, and tapped again.

There was a small rumpus from inside and the door opened. They parted to allow her to set down the tray on Richard's desk. The two men from Arnold & Sons had to jump up and pull back the chairs that they had arranged with such care. There was shuffling, murmurs. Eventually there was just room for Helly to make her way through. She edged sideways past the architect's chair and leant forward. As she did, her shirt tightened against the front of her body and her skirt rode higher up her thighs. The seven men observed her in silence.

The tray slipped as she put it down and the plate of biscuits slid dangerously towards the edge. The men all leant forward. Richard took the plate of biscuits from the tray and set it down in front of himself. Helly negotiated the tray and stood back to allow them to take their drinks. 'Thank you Helen,' Richard said. William and Mr Robinson nodded their agreement. She waited for them to help themselves so that she could remove the tray.

There was a white coffee left. The architect was looking at Richard. 'I think I said black.'

'Helen,' Richard said, lifting the tray up with a tight little smile, 'Mr Smallwood said black.' Helly took it from him.

The filter jug was almost empty. Helly poured the architect the dregs. Some grounds were still stuck in the bottom so she scraped them out with a teaspoon and added them to the cup. Then she topped it up with cold water from the tap, stirring well. She put some fresh coffee on to brew.

By the time she had returned to Richard's office, the meeting was under way. Mr Robinson was talking. As he spoke, the biscuit plate was being passed slowly round the group. His eyes were fixed on it. 'I'm not sure that's the point really,' he was saying as he observed William helping himself to a jammy dodger. 'The point is, do we want to be reactive or proactive? Like, just complaining or really sorting these guys out? Do we want them to do the job properly or do we want a custard cream?' There was a pause. 'I mean, do we want them to come up with the yum-yums? I mean, the goodies – er, goods,' he ended in confusion.

'Quite,' said Richard.

Helly took advantage of the pause to hand the architect his very black coffee.

25

Helly returned to her corner and slumped back into her chair. She put her elbows on her desk and chin in her hands, listening to the hum of the wall heater behind her desk and the intermittent click and whirr of Annette's audio machine.

Then she leant back and pulled some filing onto her lap so that it would look as if she was working if anyone walked past. While she shuffled the papers around, she prepared her little speech for Richard. About ten to five should do it. His visitors would have gone. Friday night. He wouldn't have long to argue or he would miss his train.

Annette had completed the first tape by half past three, in time to look up from her desk and see that Philip Woodrow from Commercial was sweeping round the corner with a paper plate on which sat three fresh cream éclairs. He was also holding a partially consumed bottle of dessert wine. He put down the paper plate and waved the bottle. 'Mugs?' he enquired cheerily.

'In the coffee alcove,' said Annette. 'What's the occasion?'

He was gone before she had finished but when he came back he said, slightly indignantly, 'Roger's birthday!' He poured wine into three mugs. 'Where's Joan?'

'At the dentist,' said Annette. 'I don't think she's going to want a cream cake.'

'You'll have to eat two then,' he said and strode off, swinging the bottle.

Helly had appeared.

'Cake,' said Annette, indicating the plate.

26

'What for?' said Helly, 'I don't like éclairs.'

'Roger's birthday,' said Annette.

'Who?'

Annette shrugged.

Helly picked up one of the mugs of dessert wine and took a contemplative swig. She pulled a face. 'Bleeding hell Annette, even I can't drink this shit!'

'I'll deal with it.'

Annette took the three mugs and poured the wine down the sink. She rinsed them and placed them back in the cupboard, upside-down. When she returned, Helly had gone back to her desk but the éclairs were still sitting on the paper plate next to Annette's computer. She stopped and gazed at them. Calmly, despairingly, she felt the sweep of destiny. She checked her watch. Richard would be in his meeting for a while yet. There was time.

She opened the bottom drawer on the right hand side of her desk and withdrew a small key. With that, she opened the top drawer on the left, which contained her personal belongings: hand cream, a box of tampons and a diskette containing her CV. At the back, there were a number of carefully folded paper bags. You never knew when you might need a paper bag. She drew one out and unfolded it. Then she slid the plate with the éclairs inside and re-locked the drawer.

She took the back staircase. The ladies' toilet was on the landing. Inside, she nudged the door of each cubicle gently with her foot to make sure she was alone. She, Joan and Helly were the only women on their floor so it was unlikely she would be interrupted. She went into a cubicle and locked the door. She lowered the toilet seat and sat down. She pulled the éclairs out of the paper bag and set the plate down in front of her.

Then, leaning forward, she picked up an éclair and stuffed it almost whole into her mouth. Cream spurted over her chin. She leant further forward so that it would not plop down onto her skirt, which was all wool and needed dry cleaning. A crust of chocolate fell onto the floor and she picked it up, adding it to the thick sweet mush already in her mouth. She chewed as little as possible before she swallowed.

She sat up, breathing deeply.

Then she repeated the process with the next éclair. Then she did it again.

Eating the three éclairs took her less than five minutes. She picked up the paper plate and placed it back in the bag. Then she folded it stiffly and placed it on the tray of the sanitary towel bin to her right. She pulled some toilet paper from the dispenser and wiped her face. As she did, she began to sweat. It always started with sweating. Then she began to feel dizzy. She slipped from the toilet and lifted the lid. She held her hair back from her face with one hand and grasped the side of the seat with the other. Then she waited for the huge, heaving, glorious rush – the push towards cleanliness, her punishment, her just deserts.

While his visitors rose and put on their coats, Richard shuffled the papers on his desk. William was fidgeting at his elbow. He looked up at him.

'It's just that . . .' William began.

Richard held his hand up, half closed his eyes, pursed his lips and nodded. As far as he was concerned, the meeting was over. They hadn't quite got around to the points William had wanted to cover but there were a few things Richard had to check out first. Young William was proving to be a bit slow on the uptake.

The men from Arnold & Sons were chatting with the architect and making their way to the door. Richard said goodbye, rising from his chair and checking his watch. The others were leaving too.

As he ushered them out, he caught a glimpse of Helly hovering nearby, waiting to clear the cups. He had some phone calls to make, so he shut the door and returned to his desk. It was ten to five. He didn't want to be late tonight.

He had only just sat down when there was a light tap and Helly entered. He looked up with a frown, ready to suggest that she left the crockery until after he had gone, but instead of going to gather it up she closed the door behind her, sat down in a chair freshly unoccupied by Mr J F Liver of Arnold & Sons Limited and crossed her legs. She looked at him with an expression he had never seen on her face before; it was a mixture of calmness, arrogance and purpose. He realised that he had never really thought of her as having a range of facial expressions at her disposal, until now.

'Can I have a word,' she said, after a pause. It was not phrased as a question.

29

He raised his eyebrows and blinked. 'Monday would be more convenient.'

'Not for me.'

He looked at her. He reminded himself that she was still a probationer and wondered if he ought to remind her too. This girl had an unfortunate manner. There were plenty of jobless youngsters out there who did not have unfortunate manners. He waited for her to continue.

'It's like this Richard,' she spoke lightly but without flippancy. 'I know you're bent.'

He paused. Then he said, 'What?'

'Bent. Bent double. As crooked as they come. You've been taking backhanders from Arnold & Sons; from Summerton Limited as well. A few others probably but those are the two I know about. I suppose they could turn up a few other worms if they looked into it. If someone told them to look into it that is.'

Their gazes met.

Helly looked down at her lap and then back up. 'I suppose you're wondering what I want. Now you might be thinking I want money and you'd be wrong. Also, I'm not going to start acting up and all that. I only want one thing and I'm not going to explain why either. It's very simple and should be easy; mind you, I don't know what you decided this afternoon.'

Richard kept his face impassive.

'If you gave Arnold & Sons the go ahead then you're in a bit of trouble. However, you won't have had time to do a Letter of Intent so I'm sure you can come up with something. Say there's been a budget problem or something like that.'

She paused, looking down again at her hands which, for once, were folded demurely in her lap. She was giving him the opportunity to ask her what the hell she was talking about but he remained silent. Eventually, she looked up again and continued.

'The compulsory purchase order on Rosewood Cottage in Deptford, to make way for the South-East Line Extension Plan. I want it stopped.'

Richard stared. The phone rang. They both jumped.

Richard grabbed it. There was a pause. Then he said, 'Tell him I'm tied up. Tell him I'm still in the meeting. It'll have to wait until Monday . . . yes.' He put down the phone.

Helly continued. 'How you do it is up to you. I don't much care. Tell them that it isn't necessary after all, or tell them that you've heard there might be a local campaign. You're worried about bad publicity. You can swing it. You're a lot cleverer than people round here think.' She gave a small smile. 'You can work around Rosewood Cottage, no problem. It's a clear three hundred yards from the main site and there's no statutory minimum. You can put the workman's portakabin on the wasteground to the east. You could use Melford Road for daytime access; you don't even need to go down Sutton Street.'

Richard took a deep breath. Helly checked her watch. 'Look Richard. I understand you're a bit taken aback so I'll give you the weekend to think about it. I really don't give a damn how much money you're making on the side. In your position I would probably want to screw the shit out of this bunch of bastards too. Good luck to you. All you have to do is think of an excuse to drop the compulsory purchase and I'll never mention this again. I'll just forget everything I know, unless you try and give me the boot of course in which case I go straight to the top. And by the way, I do have proof. Mind you, if you've got any sense you won't want to get rid of me. It's much better to have me who knows and doesn't care than someone who might find out.' She rose from her chair. 'I'm not going to milk this Richard. You'll be able to forget this conversation happened. Except just this once. Sorry, but clear away your own coffee cups.'

Annette explained to Mr Javed that Richard was still in his meeting, although she knew full well that he was not. Mr Javed had been trying to get through all afternoon and was not pleased. He left a number for Richard to try first thing on Monday. She wrote it down and then took the note to Richard.

She rounded the corner in time to see him storming away down the office, briefcase in one hand, pulling his mac on over his suit with the other. The belt from his mac was hanging from one loop, down to the floor, and the buckle clattered after him as he hurried off, as if a tiny dog was snapping at his heels.

2

*A*nnette caught the eight eighteen from Hither Green. It was a twelve minute walk to the station so she left the house between eight o'clock and five past; never later or earlier. She was always on Platform 1 in time, but the train rarely rewarded her punctuality. Sometimes it rained; sometimes the sun shone; sometimes a rainbow flew across the sky and took a suicidal dive into the backstreets of Catford; but at eight eighteen the eight eighteen to Charing Cross was always stuck in the wilds of Kent, trawling its way towards her through swathes of ever solid, unoptimistic south-east London travellers.

Her alarm went off at six thirty. First, there was the stagger to the bathroom to run the bath, then the groggy clamber downstairs to make tea. Breakfast was a single slice of fine brown bread, toasted to a crisp and smeared with Marmite. She would climb the stairs again and sit on the toilet in her bathrobe while she ate, watching her bath froth and fill.

She washed her hair every morning, leaving her towel wrapped round her head while she dried her long pale body. Then came the ritual inspection of her face, the peering

33

and prodding, the squeezing here and there. She used a magnifying mirror for each square inch, avoiding the overall picture. Thirty-one, she sometimes thought; I am thirty-one and have the oily, bumpy skin of an adolescent. Soon I will have wrinkles. I will be the only woman in the history of cosmetics to go straight from Clearasil to Oil of Ulay.

Then she would apply moisturiser, and make herself another cup of black tea. Sometimes she would pause in the kitchen, sipping and glancing round at the bare, gleaming surfaces. She kept all her crockery and utensils in a cupboard, out of sight. She hated clutter. A stranger coming into her home might assume she had only just moved in.

Upstairs, it was time for foundation, powder and blush. She paid particular attention to her eyes, knowing them to be the most prominent feature in an otherwise small, rather flat face. They were wide-spaced, dark, clear. She applied base tint on the lids, then powder, liner, translucent mascara followed by the eyelash curler and then, coloured mascara – not too much, otherwise it smeared. The eyes alone took ten minutes.

After her hair was gelled and blow-dried, she plugged in her curling tongs while she dressed. Recently, she had taken to wearing men's shirts: crisp billowing cotton which crunched when she put on her coat. She loved white, brilliant white, white so white it made her teeth look slightly yellow. When she was dressed, she would sit on the edge of her bed and curl the ends of her hair, watching herself in the full length mirror on the wardrobe.

Her hair was brown, straight, layered and very fine. No matter how often she had it trimmed it always looked to her as though she was growing it out. Each morning she would flick and twist and spray, in hope. Each day at work she would go to the Ladies as soon as she got the chance, with a handbag-sized canister of hairspray, to flick and twist again.

By seven fifty-five, the process was complete and she had five minutes to check the contents of her handbag, find her gloves and button her coat. Mostly, she looked in the mirror again and felt pleased. It was impossible not to feel pleased after all that effort. She would turn this way and that, slightly, and shake her head. She would imagine herself being glimpsed.

Occasionally, she would despair. Once in a while, as she observed her slim, competent figure, she would be overcome with misery, an existential longing for short hair and good skin, for a look that looked the same in the middle of the day as in the middle of the night. She would settle for being less attractive if only she could always look the same, regardless of primping or preening or lotions or devices. Those she met saw careful make-up and gently hanging waves of hair. When she looked at her reflection she saw bad skin and flat, droopy locks – a look guaranteed to give a fresh surprise each morning.

Any man who takes me on, she sometimes thought, is in for a bit of a shock when he gets up close.

Richard was almost on time. She heard him unlocking his office door and went to pour his coffee.

He looked up as she entered and extended a hand for
the cup. 'Thanks,' he said.

Then, as she was turning, he added, 'Take a seat. I
need a word.' She was half-way to the seat when he said,
'Shut the door.'

Richard called her in for a word two or three times
a month. He always asked her to shut the door. The
word was usually about a suggested name change for the
department or an adjustment to memo format. It would last
ten to fifteen minutes and would involve Annette nodding
and frowning slightly while Richard talked. He called it,
bouncing ideas off her.

He seemed more relaxed than usual. He did not look
as though he wanted to bounce an idea. He took his time,
leaning back in his seat sipping from his coffee while she
waited. Eventually, he put down his cup, leant over the
desk towards her, and stared.

Annette felt uncomfortable when people met her gaze.
It made her wonder if she had plucked her eyebrows
recently.

'How's Helen getting on?' Richard said, at last.

Annette frowned slightly. 'Alright. Timekeeping isn't
brilliant but she does the work okay.'

Richard said, 'Hmm . . .'

'Is there a problem?'

Richard sighed. 'To be honest, Annette, I'm not
sure. Something a little tricky has come up and I need
your help. I need to take you into my confidence. I
know I don't have to tell you that confidentiality is very
important.'

Annette found the thought of being told something important rather refreshing.

'I've been contacted by Personnel. Helen's references didn't come through for a while. I can't really go into details – I'm sure you'll appreciate. Anyway, I will be locking my office from now on. I want you to have a quiet word with Joan, but do it discreetly. Don't mention Helen's name.' Annette nodded. 'It would be very unfair on Helen,' Richard continued, 'if her name was mentioned. I don't think we should discriminate against a person because of a few mistakes they may or may not have made in the past.'

'No, yes,' said Annette, thinking, this does not surprise me. This does not surprise me at all.

Richard rose from his chair and went over to the window. He tucked his hands in his pockets and shrugged. 'After all, we all make mistakes.'

By his tone of voice, she knew that 'the word' was over. She rose from her seat. She saw that his coffee cup was drained so she reached out for it.

'I appreciate your discretion Annette, I really do,' Richard said. 'It's not often you find a personal secretary as trustworthy as you are, even in this current job climate. I'm very glad I am able to keep you on.'

William was standing in front of Helly's desk, running one hand absent-mindedly through his wiry brown hair and scratching his scalp. He was explaining to her that the Liverpool Street specification had to be photocopied by three, in time to catch the post. They were only giving the contractors a week to price the job. Helly had her feet on her desk. She did not look overly concerned.

She brought her feet down smartly as Richard approached. She swivelled her chair to face William and said brightly, 'Okey dokey. Do you want them bound?'

'Er . . . no,' said William. 'Stapled will do.'

'William.' Richard came and stood beside him. He was smoking. As he talked, he paused occasionally to flick ash into the metal wastepaper basket next to Helly's desk. 'We need to have a chat about Rosewood Cottage. We are going to have to put the brakes on the purchase.'

'Planning problem?' William dropped the Liverpool Street spec onto Helly's desk.

Richard shook his head. 'Budget. I did some sums over the weekend. We'll manage though. We can put the portakabin on the wasteground to the east.'

'Oh, okay.'

Richard noticed that his cigarette had gone out. He rummaged through his pockets and pulled out a small platinum lighter. 'Take a seat,' he said, nodding his head in the direction of his office as he re-lit his cigarette. 'I'll just get a coffee.'

When William had gone, Richard paused for a moment in front of Helly's desk. She had picked up William's specification and was flicking through it, slowly. Richard took a deep drag from his cigarette and exhaled. Then he reached out a hand and picked up a red stapler that was sitting on Helly's desk. She did not look up. He turned the stapler over in his hand. Then he leant forward and put it back down, gently, in a different position. He patted

38

it twice, lightly. Then he tossed his cigarette into her bin, without stubbing it out, and went to get his coffee.

Mr Arthur Robinson had not always been a building contractor. He had originally trained as a chef. Pastry had been his speciality; no one could coax a choux bun to rise the way he had. 'Feeling hands,' his supervisor at the Grand Hotel in Maidstone had told him, 'your hands can feel, Robinson.' He thought about it sometimes, his sensitive past. But there was more money in bricks and mortar. It was solid, and solidity was what was required of a man with three teenage daughters and elderly parents.

Arthur Robinson raised his bulk and wandered over to the window. Outside his portakabin, his lads were on their lunch break, sitting in companionable silence around the new cement mixer. They were good lads, his lads. It had taken him years to put together a team like the one he had now. Most builders didn't give a toss; easy come, easy go – operatives were two a penny. Arthur liked to treat his employees properly. He took them out for drinks. He gave them bonuses. Once a year he took them racing and paid for the first bets. Jim the Chippie had won six hundred quid last time, on a horse called Smiling Esmerelda. From the look on his face as it had crossed the line, Arthur Robinson knew that Jim the Chippie had never won a penny in his life. Working for Robinson Builders was lucky for you, he liked to make them think. They were his boys.

He returned to his desk and opened the right-hand drawer. From it he withdrew a little plastic packet. He opened it and slid the contents out onto his desk. Small round sweets in different colours toppled out: red, orange, green, yellow and mauve. Arthur Robinson rubbed his hands together and smiled.

As Richard approached the portakabin, it began to rain. The group of men around the cement mixer looked up at the sky. One of them swore. As they rose to their feet, Richard called over, 'Alright lads?' He raised the flat of his left hand in greeting.

The men glanced across. Most of them knew him by sight. The nearest to him nodded neutrally. The others stared.

Richard tripped up the cement block steps and knocked on the door of the portakabin. He opened the door to see Arthur Robinson beaming at several piles of sweets which he had arranged on his desk according to colour; a pile of red, a pile of green, a pile of orange . . .

As Richard came in, Arthur scattered them with his hand and leant forward, placing an arm over them protectively. 'Oh, hello Richard,' he said hastily. 'Surprise.'

Richard brushed at the shoulders of his coat. 'Raining,' he said. He went over to a free-standing gas heater which sat burbling beneath the window. Outside, the men had disappeared. One of them had left an open tupperware box on the ground next to the cement mixer.

'I don't have much time,' Richard said. 'Supposed to be on my way to Hammersmith. You got anyone you really trust?'

Arthur Robinson had pushed his sweets to one side while Richard was talking. Now he selected a mauve one, popped it into his mouth and rolled it around while he talked. 'Well you know me,' he replied genially. 'I trust all my boys. You know the way I like to work. It's not everybody's way but that's how I do things.'

'Yes I know,' replied Richard. He was still looking out of the window at the deserted yard. The tall wooden gates opposite stood open and traffic rushed and zoomed up the Kennington Road. 'I mean really trust. For something tricky.'

'Arnolds?'

Richard shook his head. 'Uh-uh. There can't be a connection. Just in case.' He turned. 'It's serious. Either this gets done right or we all get blown out of the water.'

Arthur Robinson held Richard's gaze. I have never liked you, you weasel-faced git, he thought to himself. Richard was smaller than Arthur, but compact. Arthur was all soft belly and fleshy face. Richard had muscles that began on his forearm and seemed to make their way up across his shoulders to his neck in one thin, taut line, like steel cables. His hair was a light grey and always combed with an immaculate side parting. His face was narrow, with sharp hollows, whereas Arthur had rounded red cheeks. In a fair fist fight Arthur could beat him, but Richard was not a man to get into a fist fight, fair or otherwise. He's like a panther, Arthur thought, or the devil, or a spy – and he's got me by the balls.

'What do you need?' asked Arthur, keeping his tone light.

'Someone who can hang around on street corners,' Richard replied.

41

Arthur got to his feet and went to the door of the portakabin. In the far corner of the yard there was a huge pile of second-hand tyres. They had been laid in alternate rows, like bricks, to form an igloo shape. At the bottom was a hole just big enough for a small man to climb through.

'Benny!' Arthur called across the yard.

A head appeared in the opening. A wide face with smooth skin and black hair looked out. Arthur beckoned. A man clambered out, looked up at the sky, wrapped his arms about his body and trotted through the rain across the yard.

Arthur turned away from the door and said to Richard, 'Benny's here on a six-month visitor's pass that ran out three years ago. Where he comes from, he was going to be a vet. Good at plastering. Can't stand thunderstorms.' He returned to his seat.

'No names,' said Richard quickly as Benny entered.

'Benny . . .' said Arthur. 'Have a seat.'

A light drizzle misted the darkening countryside as Richard drove. The line between the landscape and the sky was blurred, smeared here and there with a gloomy smudge of tree. He had the heating turned up high and Fauré blaring full blast. *Libera me, Domine*: his favourite bit of the *Requiem*. He sang along, softly, gripping the wheel. He had spent the afternoon on site visits, ringing in to Annette to pick up messages. He had stayed out until it wasn't worth his while going back to the office before he went home. It would be a good idea to spend a lot of time out and about this week, he had thought. Give Helen time

42

to settle down. Let her relax a bit. He sighed. He had done what he should have done that day. It was a question of stitching really, stitching everything into place, so that no unforeseen event could interfere with his plans. That had been his mistake; not anticipating. He had learnt. Nothing unexpected could happen to him now.

A white BMW overtook him in the fast lane and then nipped in between him and the lorry ahead. He eased off the accelerator, allowing the BMW room. Some people; some people had a lot to prove. *Libera me, Domine, de morte eterna* . . . The chorus was joining in, softly, whispering their plea: Free me, oh Lord, from eternal death – then the push and swell as their voices rose – Free me, oh Lord . . . The great cry of the human race, a huge, wrenching shout of pain: free me . . .

Suddenly, the clouds caved in. There was a huge tearing sound, as if God had been listening and was standing over the world, pulling the sky apart. Even as Richard thought – thunder – his foot was shooting out to the brake. Directly ahead was the white BMW, but side on. Looming over it was the dark hulk of the lorry. The driver of the car was facing out to Richard's right. His hands were lifted from the wheel and his face was a mask of open-mouthed, wide-eyed horror. Richard stared, frozen, as the side of the BMW rushed towards him. In the same moment, he heard the bang of the impact and the blare of his car horn as his hand came down on it. Then there was another huge crunch from behind which seemed to echo and shudder through his seat. Another horn was blaring in discordant unison with his, then came two more successive crumping noises. There was a moment of blackness. *Libera me, Domine* . . .

When he opened his eyes, he found that he was pushed back in his seat with the car wheel very close to his chest. The windscreen had shattered and there was glass everywhere, over the dashboard, in his lap. Directly in front of him, sitting sideways, was the driver of the BMW, his car crumpled around him like cooking foil. His head was twisted forwards against the wheel and blood cleaved a neat line down the centre of his forehead and along his nose. His eyes and mouth were open.

Richard tried to turn in his seat. He couldn't move. The door on his side had folded inwards and his arm was trapped. His legs could move two inches either way but no further. It was raining harder now. He could hear shouts, a groaning sound and, from somewhere, a woman's voice calling weakly for help.

He thought to himself, very clearly, I must breathe deeply. That is the important thing, to stay still and take deep breaths. He began, but it seemed to make his chest shudder alarmingly. He could feel air rushing past the back of his throat. He tried to work out if the sensation was one caused by physical injury or panic.

Gradually, his breath subsided. I am alive, he thought distinctly, I am alive.

Gillian. He spoke the word silently to himself. There was nothing else he wanted to say. He just wanted to hear her name articulated, as if conjuring it up would procure her warmth, her steadiness, her hands calming him. Gillian. Now that he was certain that he was alive, he found himself already noting how he felt, so that he could tell her later.

A face appeared at the side window, which was still intact but somehow skewed out of place. 'Are you alright?' asked the face.

Richard nodded. He pointed towards the BMW driver with his free hand.

'He's had it mate,' said the face. 'Someone will be here bloody quick. I think they'll have to cut you out. Oh, hello Richard.'

Richard turned his head slightly. The face had broken into a warm smile of recognition. He blinked and his sight became a little clearer. It was only then that he realised it had been blurred. The face belonged to Nobbie Patterson, a leading member of the clay pigeon club where Richard and Gillian had gone for a shoot last Whitsun weekend. Gillian and Nobbie were distantly related.

'Nobbie,' said Richard.

'Well I never,' said Nobbie, shaking his head with a would-you-credit-it grin. 'Fancy meeting you like this. You never know do you . . .'

Richard was still struggling to free his trapped arm. He was afraid to pull too hard amongst the glass and twisted metal. 'Er . . . Nobbie . . .' he began.

Nobbie was still shaking his head. 'I was on my way home, about a hundred yards back,' he said. 'I had to skid to avoid the guy behind you. He's alright so I thought I'd come up here and see what I could do. And here you are. Amazing.' He chuckled, then made a clicking noise with his tongue against the roof of his mouth. He shook his head again. 'Amazing . . .'

It was nearly an hour before Richard was cut out of the wreckage. The emergency services arrived in a flurry of wailing sirens and spinning lights. An ambulance man rushed over and asked him questions. Was there any pain? Could he feel his legs? He put his hands either side of Richard's neck and asked him to turn his head. Then he told him not to move and ran off.

Nobbie chatted to him while they waited. He was glad that he and Gillian had enjoyed the shoot. Why didn't they come again? Richard listened and nodded occasionally, watching the dead face of the dead driver of the BMW. He had never seen a dead man before.

Nobbie was saying, 'You wouldn't believe what I found out yesterday Richard. Do you know, there is a company somewhere in Essex that makes the British Standard turd? Honest, honest to God.'

Richard recalled that Nobbie was in fixtures and fittings and had talked of crossing over to bathroom and sanitary equipment.

'The toilets all have to be tested of course, and to conform to the Standards inspectorate they have to be able to flush a turd of a certain size, shape and density. Sawdust, I think. I hope so, anyway.' He chuckled. 'So yesterday we had to ring up this place in Essex that manufactures the standard British turd and order a box. Now, what I'd like to know is . . .'

'Excuse me sir,' an authoritative voice came from somewhere out of Richard's field of vision. A fireman stepped forward. A group of others was surrounding the BMW and examining the point at which it was jammed into Richard's car.

'Oh sorry,' said Nobbie, stepping back.

'My arm . . .' grimaced Richard at the fireman.

'Right-o sir,' said the fireman, and worked a heavily-gloved hand into the gap between the window and the buckled door frame, feeling around Richard's trapped arm. Nobbie was leaning over the fireman's shoulder and calling, 'How do they get the measurements? That's what I'd like to know.'

Gillian was listening to reports of the crash when the hospital rang. The radio announcer was telling her, with admirable calm, that it was one of the worst pile-ups in the history of the M23. Four dead and as many as twenty injured. Gillian was in the middle of polishing a set of six stainless steel dessert dishes and continued her work, determinedly. A policeman on the radio informed her that people these days found it impossible to keep their distance.

When the phone rang, she dropped a dish and it landed on her tiled floor with a metallic clatter that echoed around the kitchen.

Richard was completely uninjured. A young lady doctor informed him, with some venom, that he had had a remarkable escape. There was bruising to the right forearm and he had wrenched his back; nothing that a couple of days' rest wouldn't cure. She saw no reason to keep him in hospital overnight.

47

When they reached home, Gillian saw him up to bed and then went down to the kitchen to make hot drinks. Horlicks, they had decided. There was an old tin in the pantry somewhere. They would normally be drinking whisky at this time but Horlicks somehow had the right sound. The tin was so old it was rusty around the seam. Gillian peeled back the blue plastic lid and peered in. The Horlicks had got slightly damp but other than that it seemed fine. She began to cry with relief.

Richard was in bed when she took the drinks up. She had arranged some fruit cake on a plate. Settled beside him, on top of the coverlet with the tray on her lap, she broke off small pieces of cake and began to feed them to him until he shook his head. They drank their drinks in silence. Richard cradled his cup between his hands. 'You know,' he said eventually, 'I saw dying today.'

'You had a very lucky escape . . .' murmured Gillian, lifting a hand to stroke his head.

'No, I don't mean that.' Richard frowned.

'You mean when you were watching the dead man, when Nobbie was talking to you?'

'No. Before that even.' Richard turned the mug round in his hands. 'I mean just before his car hit mine, when it was swinging round. I saw him, his hands up in the air, mouth open, the look on his face. It must have lasted only a split second, but in that split second . . .' Richard coughed, wincing at the stiffness in his back, '. . .in that second, that man knew he was about to die.'

Gillian reached out a hand and took the mug from his grasp. She placed it on the tray and then lifted the tray to the bedside table. Then she turned back to Richard and took his hand. She held it between both of hers, tightly.

'I never want to see that moment, Gillian,' Richard said. 'I'm not afraid of dying, not really, but I am afraid of that – that split second. Some people might be curious I suppose, wonder what it's like. I'm not. I couldn't stand it, all that defeat, knowing you have lost everything . . .'

'Sshh,' said Gillian, stroking his hand. 'Sshh . . . you never will. I promise, you never will.'

They lapsed into silence and Richard closed his eyes. Gillian watched his face, stroked his hand.

Rosewood Cottage sat on the edge of a patch of wasteground, a small, squat building at the end of a street surrounded by a wide expanse of earth, concrete and scrubby grass. Sutton Street had once been a thriving row of cottages on the very edge of pre-First World War London. Then the city had swallowed it whole. Tower blocks and factories had sprung up around it. The cottages had crumbled, one by one. Rosewood was the sole survivor in a wide patch of dereliction, the last molar in a broken, ruined mouth.

William stood at the top of the street, looking down to where the cottage sat alone. To the left, the wasteground stretched away. On the other side, an informal rubbish tip had sprung up: cardboard boxes, prams, a blue mattress with a burnt and blackened hole. Beyond it was the railway line embankment, punctuated by arches. Commuters coming in from Kent were able to look down on Rosewood Cottage every day. Behind the embankment was the main road, cutting a swathe through Deptford. Sutton Street itself was inaccessible. If you exited from the road at the wrong place you were stranded in the wilds of Rotherhithe. The nearest BR station was twenty minutes' walk away. William had got badly lost and tramped around the quiet backstreets for over half an hour.

It was a heavy day, with solid wads of cloud in grey folds overhead; so dark it almost seemed that night could fall at any minute. After he had turned out of the station, a brown mongrel had picked up his trail. When William paused to consult the list of directions he had copied down from the A-Z in the office, the dog paused too, pretending to snuffle in the verge. As William moved on, so did the dog. When William stopped again, the dog trotted to a halt, lifted its leg and urinated.

In the end, William stopped and said loudly, 'Piss off, dog.'

The dog lifted his head and regarded him blankly, then turned and lolloped off down the road. William felt bad.

The door to Rosewood Cottage had been painted pink a great many years ago but was cracked and peeling now, set in a small porch of crumbling brickwork. From the front of the porch, someone had used a piece of frayed string to hang an oval-shaped, porcelain sign with the name of the cottage painted in curling letters and a sprig of flowers enamelled underneath. It swung lightly in the wind. William had to duck underneath it to step into the porch and ring the bell.

If the bell was working, it made no sound. He waited. He sighed. He stepped back from the house and peered upwards. He thought he saw a net curtain twitch at an upstairs window but it was hard to tell. It was beginning to rain. He went back into the porch and pressed the bell again, then knocked lightly.

Eventually, there was the sound of shuffling behind the door. A voice mumbled. Then, very slowly, the door opened a crack. William tipped his head to one side, clutching an orange wallet file to his chest. He felt suddenly aware that he was wearing a suit. 'Mrs Appleton?' he asked, hesitantly.

No reply.

'I'm William Bennett. I'm a surveyor for the Capital Transport Authority. I have come to talk to you about the cottage. The compulsory purchase . . .' Thinking that the door was about to slam shut, William began to talk very quickly. 'There have been a few developments Mrs Appleton we thought we would have to demolish the cottage due to site works as you know but it now appears that it might not be necessary . . .'

Very slowly, the door opened. A woman of indeterminate age was revealed – late sixties perhaps. What was left of her hair was scraped back from her forehead into a green rubber band that held a topknot on the crown of her head. She wore thick bi-focal glasses. She regarded him. William tried to keep his eyes on her face while being unable to avoid noticing that she wore huge slippers which were rimmed with bright purple fur.

Mrs Appleton held his gaze for some time. 'Better come in,' she said eventually. As she turned and stepped back into the hall, he noticed that she waddled slightly.

The feet in the purple fur-rimmed slippers dragged along the carpet. He was reminded of some creature he had read about in an encyclopaedia when he was a child. He struggled to remember its name. Then it came to him: a duck-billed platypus.

The hall was dark and very narrow. He squeezed past a mock-wooden coat rack on which were hung various macs in slightly different shades of beige or navy blue. Mrs Duck-billed Platypus gestured into the living room.

Sitting in a chair beside an unlit gas fire was Mr Duck-billed Platypus. At least William presumed that it was he. They were not introduced. Mrs Appleton said shortly, 'I'll put the kettle on.'

William had taken a seat opposite Mr Appleton. He turned. 'I shan't take up too much of your time Mrs Duckapple, really there's no . . .' but she had already gone. William turned to face the old man. He smiled uncertainly. The old man did not respond.

Mrs Appleton was gone for a very long time. At first, William tried to keep smiling but the old man met him with the same unnervingly blank stare that the dog had given. So he occupied himself by opening the orange wallet file and withdrawing his papers, then shuffling them around and flicking through. Gradually, he became aware of a noise – a dull, regular thumping from the ceiling above. He looked up, and then across at Mr Appleton. The noise stopped. Then it began again. Mr Appleton lifted a fist and shook it slowly at the ceiling. The noise stopped. Mr Appleton returned to his immobile, stony state. William looked down at his papers.

Mrs Appleton shuffled back into the room carrying a kitchen tray with wicker handles. On it sat a large brown mug and two jam jars, all filled with weak grey tea. Next to them was a plate on which three Digestive biscuits had been neatly arranged.

'He has to have his mug,' said Mrs Appleton as she put down the tray. She picked up the mug and placed it on the coffee table at her husband's side. Still he did not move.

'Sugar?' she asked, as she picked up one of the jam jars and handed it to William.

William watched as the jam jar made its way inexorably towards him. Around the rim he could see a few remnants of pink jam, encrusted. He managed to shake his head and say, 'Thank you.'

He took the jam jar from her and placed it on the carpet at his feet. Mrs Appleton sat on the sofa and picked up her jar. She sipped from it at intervals while he talked.

'Well, I've good news of a sort . . .' William began. He explained to them that the compulsory purchase had been suspended due to an unforeseen difficulty. It seemed likely that they would not now have to move. He couldn't offer them any guarantees, however, and there would be some disruption when the building work began.

The couple listened in silence. Eventually, Mrs Appleton said, 'So will you be coming back?'

William paused. 'I don't know, Mrs Appleton. Probably not for a long while. I think you can relax.'

At that, Mr Appleton made a sudden movement. William jumped. Mr Appleton was waving his left arm wildly. Mrs Appleton rose, shuffled across to him and handed him a stick that was lying beside the chair. As she helped him out of the chair, he began to cough, softly at first, then in great harrumphing gulps that shook his body. He was leaning his full weight on the stick and it wobbled frantically, even though his wife still had hold of his arm. 'Careful, dear,' she shouted into his ear, 'you'll have one of your turns!'

Mr Appleton was coughing so hard he began to turn slightly blue. Eventually he stopped, on the cusp of one huge gasp – and froze. He hung there while his wife explained, 'It's news of any sort, good or bad, doesn't matter what, always turns him a bit funny.'

William was concerned that Mr Appleton appeared not to be breathing. At what point should he insist that an ambulance be called, and how? There was no phone.

'I've tried to tell him not to get excited. One of these days . . .' Mrs Appleton continued. Her husband had still not moved.

'Er, do you think perhaps . . .' William began.

Then, Mr Appleton, still without moving, began to tip slowly backwards into the chair. Mrs Appleton let go of his arm and he fell, frozen, appearing to have suffered instant rigor mortis. William jumped to his feet.

'Oh, Mr Bent!' his wife exclaimed. 'You can't go yet. You haven't finished your tea.'

William looked down at the jam jar in alarm. 'Oh dear, I really must go,' he said. 'That is, if you don't have any questions? I hope.'

'Just a minute now,' Mrs Appleton said firmly, lifting a finger. She shuffled over to where he stood and picked up the jam jar, then she shuffled out of the room. William glanced over anxiously at Mr Appleton, who still showed no signs of life. He picked up the orange wallet file and stepped out into the hall.

Mrs Appleton was making her way towards him holding the jam jar. She had found a lid and screwed it on. 'There you are,' she said proudly, extending the jar, 'you can finish it later.'

William took the jar from her. 'Thank you,' he said. 'Goodbye.'

As he turned to open the front door, he heard the thumping noise from upstairs again, more distinct this time, three separate banging noises in sharp succession. Mrs Appleton rolled her eyes and leant forward. 'That's my mother,' she murmured to William, confidentially. 'We keep her upstairs. She's a little eccentric, you know.'

Outside, the sky had cleared slightly. It was brighter. William walked briskly down Sutton Street, the folder under his arm, the lukewarm jar of tea in his hand. As he reached the corner of the street, he turned and looked back at Rosewood Cottage. Mrs Appleton was standing in front of the porch, waving. He waved back.

Half-way to the main road, he realised he was going to have to sit on the train holding a jam jar of tea. He looked around for a rubbish bin, saw one screwed to a lamp-post and went over. It had no bottom. People had dropped rubbish in anyway and underneath there was a small pile of crisp packets, drinks cartons and cigarette ends. He knelt down and placed the jam jar amongst the heap, carefully pushing rubbish around it to conceal it. When he had finished, he looked up to see that he was being observed by the brown dog, which stood on the pavement a few feet away.

'Shoo!' said William, waving an arm. The dog tipped its head to one side.

Joanna Appleton closed the door and turned to her husband, who now stood by her side, recovered. They looked at each other, then their faces began to crack. Joanna spluttered. Her husband bent over and slapped his thigh. They roared.

'I can't believe it!' Joanna squeaked. 'Oooh . . . oooh . . . I can't believe it. Works every time . . .'

Bob Appleton was bending over. He had dropped his walking stick and was holding both arms across his stomach. 'The look – on his –' He was laughing so much that he began to snort and cough.

'Careful dear,' said his wife, squeakily, 'you might have one of your turns!'

'Here,' Bob Appleton bent and picked up his stick, 'put that thing back in the cupboard.'

Joanna turned and opened the cupboard door behind her. It was only then that she heard the voice from upstairs, calling crankily, 'Joanna! Joanna!'

'Oh dear,' said Joanna, withdrawing a yellow cotton hankie from her sleeve and wiping the tears from her cheeks.

'Do you really think we're in the clear now?' Bob asked, standing up and straightening his cardigan. 'Or will they be back next week?'

'Oh I don't know, love.' Joanna's face became softer and more serious. 'I don't think we've heard the last, do you?'

'No, me neither.'

'Joanna! Joanna!' The voice came from upstairs.

'Do you want me to go?' asked Bob.

Joanna kicked off the purple slippers and pulled the green rubber band out of her hair. 'No. You put the kettle on. I'll be down in a minute. Let's discuss it over a cappuccino.'

Joanna's mother was sitting up in bed, gnashing her gums. Her pink hairnet had slid sideways and hung down over her forehead at a rakish angle.

'What's all that racket for?' she demanded. Many afflictions of the aged had come to Joanna's mother. Deafness was not among them.

'Oh nothing, Mum,' Joanna replied. 'We were just having a bit of a laugh, that's all.'

'A laugh?'

Joanna pulled the bedclothes up around her mother's loose little body. She had taken to wearing pyjamas instead of her nightie but she was so tiny that even the smallest of men's sizes hung off her shoulders. Joanna had had to buy seven sets in boys' sizes, as incontinence was the one elderly habit her mother had embraced with enthusiasm. Mrs Hawthorne's favourite top was a lurid dead-blood colour and had small grey helicopters flying from sleeve to sleeve. Joanna drew it across and did up one of the buttons. Then she reached up to adjust the pink hairnet.

'Stop fussing Joanna, for God's sake,' said her mother.

'I'm not fussing . . .'

'Don't take it off. I've told you, I like it.'

'I'm not taking it off Mum, I'm just putting it straight. It is a nuisance you know, pinning your hair and putting this thing on. I don't know why we bother.'

'Just because I'm your mother it doesn't mean I can't look my best.'

Mrs Hawthorne had been living with them for eighteen months. It had not been an easy time. Until six years ago, she had occupied a ground floor flat on a nearby housing estate, alone but for a tiny mongrel with spiky brown fur who skittered from room to room, barking at shadows. Joanna had visited regularly with food and air freshener. The dog was called Pip. While Joanna and her mother drank tea in the kitchen Pip would stand in front of them with his fur on end and his tiny dripping penis erect, panting for a biscuit.

Then Mrs Hawthorne took to turning on the gas ring but forgetting to light it and tripping over the pattern in the carpet. One day, Joanna visited and discovered her mother pottering around with one hand tucked inside her cardigan. After some persuasion, she permitted her to withdraw it and look. A dirty handkerchief was wrapped around the index finger which was swollen and blackened with dried blood. Under pressure, Mrs Hawthorne confessed that she had cut it on a tin can. When a doctor was called, he admitted her to hospital immediately where the finger was found to be gangrenous. When the hospital doctor discovered she had not visited a GP for seventeen years, he decided to give her a full examination. This resulted

58

in a furious battle during which the doctor had sustained a small nose-bleed. 'What are you playing at?' Joanna had heard her mother shriek from behind the curtain, 'I only want a plaster for me finger!'

The finger was amputated and the doctor told Joanna that her mother was lucky not to have lost her hand. The examination revealed a variety of other complications. A hysterectomy was found to be necessary and the removal of other items of intestine were considered. Joanna went home to Bob and informed him sadly, 'My mother is imploding.'

Mrs Hawthorne took the interference with bad grace. Her theory, which she expounded to anyone who would listen – and several who wouldn't – was that having been denied the opportunity to mutilate her for so many years, the medical profession was making up for lost time. Several operations later, she was admitted to the Restview Home for the Elderly in New Cross where she was expected to do the decent thing and die.

Four years on and fitter than ever, she came to live with Joanna and Bob. She had not liked the Restview home. During the early months, she was regularly apprehended by the night nurse as she made her way off down the corridor, dressed in her coat and nightie and clutching her favourite china cat. (Pip had been put down. Joanna had taken him to the vet in a wicker cage singing *Alleluia* all the way. She had always hated that dog.) When Bob and Joanna visited she sat in the television room and told them loudly that the other residents were crackers. She made racist remarks to the sister in charge and reduced a nursing auxiliary to tears by listing her physical deficiencies, one by one, to a passing vicar. Joanna went to see the social services and arrangements were made to transfer Mrs Hawthorne to the spare room in their house, where she promptly took to bed and refused to move. Mrs Hawthorne had spent a long time fed up about being old. Safely ensconced in her daughter's home, she was now going to make the most of it.

'I'm tired,' Mrs Hawthorne announced. 'I'm going to have a kip.'

'It's only half past eleven,' said Joanna. 'You haven't even had lunch.'

'I'm tired,' she repeated, and yawned unconvincingly, showing two rows of bare gums around which saliva glistened. 'Stay till I go to sleep.'

This was something she had started recently. So far Joanna had conceded, sitting by her bed until the old lady started snoring. Sooner or later, she was going to have to put her foot down. She had not spent sixty-six years growing up to have to do this for her own mother. It was the wrong way round.

It was also painful. It reminded Joanna that she too was a mother, and that her daughter was a thin, stupid, middle-aged woman who had achieved nothing and wanted even less. They did not get on.

How is it, Joanna wondered sometimes, that I turned out to be such a good daughter and wife and such a failure as a mother? How come I got the small things right but not the big one?

She stared at the picture on the opposite wall. Her

granddaughter had bought it for them, from the Tate gallery. 'Some Russian geezer,' Bob had muttered as he hung it. It was a print framed in glass, a coloured swirl of rainbows and splodges. Joanna found it a comfort, sitting next to her mother. This was how she imagined death; not as something black but as a mad pattern of coloured shapes which mingled and collided: the strands of your life which – after years of messing about – would finally coagulate and blur. The painting reassured her. It was true. All things met and ended, one day.

Back at work, William sat at his desk and drew doodles on his spiral notepad. The place was deserted. Richard's office was locked. Everyone else seemed to be at lunch. William had sandwiches in his desk drawer but he had eaten two large sausage rolls in a café by Surrey Docks station. He had waited for his train gazing out over the stark greys and browns of Rotherhithe. There is more to life than this, he had thought gloomily. There is more to life than visiting mad people in ugly places.

Annette arrived back from lunch. He wandered over as she was unbuttoning her coat. 'You're wet,' he said conversationally. Her cream-coloured mac was peppered with dark spots of rain. 'When is Richard back?'

'Didn't you know?' she said, sitting down and rummaging through her bags. 'He was in that awful accident in Surrey last night. He's alright, but it was really close, apparently. His back is bad but he said he should be fit by next week. He'll be ringing in for messages.'

'Nothing trivial I hope.'

'Do you want to see what I bought?' Annette pulled a lemon-coloured blouse out of a plastic bag and held it up. 'In the sale, look. For the summer. To cheer myself up.' The blouse was sleeveless, with a small white collar and large round buttons. The light from the window shone through it. 'The assistants in there drive me mental,' Annette said as she folded it up. 'They're so slow. *How would you like to pay?* One of these days I'm going to say, *Oh, with rawlplugs.*'

Suddenly, William shivered. Annette chattered on but he was not listening to what she was saying. He was listening, rather, to the sound of her voice. It tinkled against his ear. While she talked, she pushed her bags under her desk and lifted up her handbag. She withdrew a small can of hairspray and a round brush. Her hands were small, her fingernails immaculate. 'Won't be a mo,' she said, and breezed past him.

He stood for a moment, watching her empty chair, as if he was surprised to find that she was no longer in it. Then he turned and went back to his desk. The office was still empty. He sat down and stared straight ahead.

William had only been in love once, some years ago, during his first year as a probationary surveyor. He was working for the borough of Hammersmith and Fulham; external repair works. He had bounced out of Thames Polytechnic ready to take on the world and found, to his surprise, that the world was not interested in a fight. He had his first job within two months and it was easy. He used one tenth of the knowledge he had gained while he was training and promptly forgot the rest. He was still sharing a flat with student friends who remained unemployed, apart from one who was going on to do an MSc. Now that he was a member of the working majority, their ideas irritated him. He was a grown-up. He was moving on.

He took two secretaries from work out to lunch, on separate occasions. One was very pretty but silent and awkward. The other was plain and wouldn't stop talking. He had no intention of seeing either on a regular basis but felt he should do it for the practice. There was no one else at work he was remotely interested in, but sooner or later they would come along and he had every intention of being ready when they did. Grown-ups were.

The months passed and the person he had prepared himself for did not arrive. He started taking Linda, the talkative secretary, to the cinema on Friday nights. Then he had sex with her and stopped. The next week, during an emotional scene in a pizza parlour, she accused him of losing interest the minute he had got what he wanted. This was not true. He had never been interested in the first place. He had talked her into sex because he felt it was expected of him. Telling Linda the truth would have hurt more than letting her believe the lie, so instead he looked at her sympathetically and said, 'I'm sorry.' She slapped his face.

For a few weeks, things were a little tricky. She refused to do his typing. She kept bursting into tears unexpectedly and rushing to the toilet. Word went round that he was a bastard. He was invited to join the staff football team.

One Saturday night, he and his flatmates were at their local, drinking soapy beer and trying to have a discussion. Towards closing time, Bob, the MSc student, came back from the bar rubbing his hands. 'Just met a mate, lads. Party.' A party was the last thing William felt like but it was easier to trot along than it was to make an excuse and go home on his own. The party was in a large terraced house just round the corner from the pub. William's heart sank as soon as he entered. He had spent his three years as a student doing this kind of thing. He was not in the mood for regression.

They headed for the kitchen which was bright with yellow light. There was a table that groaned with the weight of booze. He helped himself to a can of lager and then left the lads poking around the bottles. There was only a handful of people around. Those not standing in the kitchen had congregated on the stairs. He stood by them listlessly for a few moments until it was clear nobody was going to speak to him.

In the front room, there were two couples sitting in opposing corners, talking quietly. Untouched bowls of peanuts and crisps were scattered here and there, on the mantelpiece, the window sills. He went straight out again. A heavy beat was booming from the back room. Above the door was a handwritten sign which read, 'IN HERE TO FUNK'.

The room was stripped of furniture and the carpet had been rolled up to reveal bare boards. Large sheets of tin foil had been hung on the walls. Inside, two huge speakers were blasting out a beat which hurt his ears and vibrated beneath his feet. A bare red light bulb hung from the ceiling. It was so gloomy that at first he thought the room was empty.

She was standing against the wall, close to an open sash window. Her body was turned away from him and she was gazing out into the darkened garden. She was holding a can of beer in one hand, clutching it to her chest. In the darkness he could just make out an untidy bunch of hair and a long, dark cardigan over leggings and boots. He walked towards her. She turned, still clutching the can. She looked him up and down. She smiled. He took the hint and fell in love.

They saw each other two or three times a week, as often as William dared to suggest. Her name was Ellen. She was twenty-four, two years older than him (although as far as William was concerned it could have been two decades). She liked films and driving fast and take-away Chinese. She laughed easily. One night, in the bathroom of his shared flat when everyone else was away, she gave him his first blow job.

She had her own place just off the Caledonian Road, an airy maisonette furnished by a few artfully arranged pieces of junk. It wasn't really hers, she explained, she was just looking after it for her father. She was a production assistant for a film company. Every now and then she would disappear 'on shoots' and he would be rigid with jealousy until she returned. He hated her job, although he never told her so. He also hated her postman, and the man in the corner shop where she bought milk. He hated anyone or anything that claimed her time or attention, attention that by rights belonged to him.

For four months, everything was fine. They met each other's parents. They met each other's friends (he hated hers). They spent every weekend together, except when she was away.

The change began just before Christmas. He was desperate for them to spend it together. She insisted on going to stay with her family and he was hurt not to be invited. 'It isn't *you*,' she said to him, stroking his forehead as he lay with his head in her lap. 'It's just, we've never brought boyfriends home, any of us. It would be strange, that's all.' Boyfriends. Boyfriends plural. I am A Boyfriend, he thought.

Christmas stretched into New Year. She was taking time off, she told him on the phone.

'Time off from me?'

'No, silly. Time off from work, everything.'

He rang her every day.

When she returned, he knew that things had changed. He could sense her slipping. The more she slipped, the more he clung. The more he clung, the more she slipped. Eventually he said to her one night, 'Things aren't working out. I think I need more space.' To his horror she replied, 'Yes, you're right.'

They clung on for another month, out of habit, picking fights with each other so they would have a concrete explanation to give their friends. All through this terrible time he had an ever growing sense of unreality. Two forces ruled his life: the inevitability of what was happening and his inability to do what he wanted most: reverse the process. At last, in a final attempt to take control, he let himself into her flat while she was out and removed his belongings. He put the key in an envelope and dropped it through the door. She rang him a week later and he told the lads to say he wasn't in.

For six months, he wanted to die. After that, he was merely miserable. He went back to Linda who accepted him with good grace, knowing she was no more than a consolation prize. He despised her for not being Ellen, so he treated her badly and then despised himself. On Saturdays, he went out with his flatmates and drank himself stupid. One night, he got into a fight. On the Sunday morning he woke up with a sore nose and realised that self-destruction was no fun. It was time to be honest with Linda and cut down on the booze.

He only saw Ellen once after that. It was nearly a year after they had broken up. He was sitting on the tube, the Piccadilly line, between Green Park and Piccadilly Circus. The train had come to a stop in the middle of a tunnel. It made a few half-hearted chugging noises, then there was silence; the weird unearthly silence that comes deep underground after a great deal of noise. The passengers pulled faces, not meeting each other's gazes. William sighed and sat back in his seat. He was thinking about the Planned Maintenance report on Shepherd's Bush market. He wondered if he should add a sum for repair of external cladding.

Then he heard her voice.

'Shall we eat first or later?'

All at once, he felt his stomach fold in on itself. His scalp seemed to shrink. It was her voice, so close and clear he felt tempted to lift his head and respond.

Shall we?

She was the only person he knew who used the word 'shall' so frequently. He looked around. Most of the seats were full and there were several people standing nearby. In front of him was a woman in a red coat and a man and boy in matching baseball caps. Where was she?

To his left there was the glass panel that divided his row of seats from the area between the doors. He looked up. She was just the other side of the panel, facing away from him. Her back was pressed against it. She was inches away. He had been hurtling along a tube tunnel with her only inches away. If the train hadn't stopped he might never have realised she was there. Her head was leaning back against the panel. Her brown curls were crushed against the glass. She was wearing the green coat she had bought in the New Year sales after that awful Christmas. 'Shall I have the green or the blue?' she had asked him, holding them both up, one in each hand. 'Which one shall I have?' He had been so terrified of giving the wrong answer he had merely shrugged.

Then he saw, next to the crushed brown curls – just above the right shoulder of the green coat – a hand.

The palm of the hand was pressing the glass, the fingers splayed. It was a rough hand, a large hand. It was a male hand.

Oh God, he thought. Not this. Not now. He couldn't bear to look and he couldn't bear not to.

68

The man had not answered her question. William listened. He knew those pauses, the slow conversations, the lingering looks. Then the man spoke. His voice was deep, with a slight lilt, Welsh, perhaps. He spoke warmly, slowly, a smile in every syllable.

'Come here girl.'

William closed his eyes. He felt sick and hot. When he opened them again he looked resolutely ahead, at the man and boy in front of him. They were both looking over at Ellen. Then the man looked down at his son and grinned. William looked at the other passengers. Several were glancing over in Ellen's direction. Inches away from him, separated only by a panel of glass, the only woman he had ever loved was being kissed by someone else.

All at once he was overwhelmed with fury. Why should that stupid man in front of him grin down at his son in that stupid, knowing manner? How could Ellen make a spectacle of herself like that? He wanted to stand up and say to those nearby, 'I was with her when she bought that coat. She hasn't told him *that*, I bet.'

The train started with a jolt. The standing passengers staggered. He heard Ellen giggle.

They hurtled down the tunnel. The noise was deafening. As they pulled into Piccadilly Circus, William was already pushing his way through the other passengers, away from Ellen and her growling Welsh companion, as far away as he could get. At the door he stumbled against a Japanese woman and kicked a large box at her feet. 'Sorry,' said the woman.

He joined the other passengers jostling along the

platform. Half-way to the yellow exit sign, he realised that his legs were shaking. She was there, a matter of yards behind him. Perhaps she was settling down into the seat he had left, still warm from his body. He could have spoken to her, touched her even. Now she would never know. She would carry on, her evening undisturbed when his had been torn apart. He sank into a nearby seat. The other passengers rushed by. By the time they had cleared, the train had started to move. He watched it, trying to work out when Ellen's carriage would pass, willing Ellen to see him. The train picked up speed. The windows flashed past. The people inside became momentary images, then coloured blurs. The train disappeared into the tunnel with a rush of wind and a huge rattling sound that echoed down the empty platform.

He sat on the plastic seat, alone. He gripped the edge of it with his hands. He thought, I am in pain. I am in so much pain I can't stand it. All the achievements of the last few months seemed nothing. His promotion, his new car, the evening class he had started to get himself out of the flat: nothing; worthless.

He knew then that this small incident had set him back months.

He rose from his seat, breathing deeply. Then he turned slowly, as if he was an old man, and began the seemingly endless walk down the platform.

It was three years before he got seriously involved with anybody else and when he did he married her. Alison was tiny, efficient, funny. She wore neat little trouser suits

70

with high heels which would have looked old-fashioned on another woman her age but she somehow carried it off. Her hair was very short. She made jokes about looking like a pixie. Everyone (i.e. his parents) agreed; she was just right.

He was careful not to rush things. They went out for six months and were engaged for a year. They bought a small two-bedroomed terrace in Bromley and moved in four months before the wedding. He was so swept up with the business of purchasing property that he almost forgot they were getting married as well. Luckily, Alison had it all organised. She showed him the wedding list one night and asked if there was anything he thought she had left off. He cast his eye down it: crockery, cutlery, china, a yoghurt maker (he liked yoghurt), a pine hat stand . . . He shook his head in wonder and thought, we get all this just for having sex?

In the fortnight before the event, Alison disappeared altogether into a miasma of bridesmaids, car hire, disco equipment and unexpected aunties. He felt deserted and duly had an attack of last minute nerves. This, it turned out, had also been planned for. Alison took him out to dinner and told him she would be worried if he *wasn't* having last minute doubts. The next time he saw her alone was at Gatwick airport, when they had bid the best man goodbye and gone to join the check-in queue. They were on their way to Portugal. They were man and wife.

I have a wife, he said to himself as they handed over their passports. At the boarding gate, he waited for her outside the Ladies. There is my wife, he thought, as she emerged. On the plane, he said to the stewardess, 'My wife would like some orange juice.'

The novelty of having a wife lasted well through the first year of marriage. By then, he also had a son.

Paul was a boisterous boy who rarely cried and played with whatever he was handed: a wooden spoon, a holepunch, a piece of lettuce. By the time he was three, it was clear that he would be handsome and good at sports. William felt overwhelmed with gratitude. Paul was exactly the sort of boy he had spent his childhood wanting to be: unanalytical, good natured, not overly clever. He felt grateful to the child. He also felt grateful to Alison. How well organised of her to produce this neat little thing for him to care for. How considerate of her to give him all this certainty. Occasionally, he went drinking with other men who complained about their wives and children; the demands, the expense. William was hard put to come up with any complaints about Alison and Paul, although he did his best.

Sitting at his desk in John Blow House, William bent down and pushed a hand into the inside pocket of his jacket, which was slung over the back of his chair. He pulled out a small leather wallet – maroon-coloured – and flipped it open. Behind a square of plastic was a picture of his wife and child. Alison was smiling brightly. Her teeth gleamed. Paul was frowning and looking over to the left. William had been there when the shots were done, at a photographer's in Bromley High Street. Later, they had taken Paul for a burger and chips. He was up all night vomiting.

William closed the wallet and put it back into his pocket. Then he rose and went round the office divide, to Annette's desk. She had not yet returned. He sat down in her swivel chair and, for the want of anything useful to do, swivelled.

He turned and looked up as she returned. Seeing him sitting at her desk, she looked slightly startled. Then she smiled. She approached and lifted up her handbag, which sat next to her computer keyboard. She opened it and replaced the hairspray and brush. As she did, her hair fell forward. He gazed at her.

'Well?' she said, a little awkwardly.

He could not interpret the word. Well. Did that mean, *Well what now?* Maybe it meant, *Well get off my seat, I have typing to do.*

He stood. She was an inch or so taller than him.

He reached out and placed his hand around her upper arm. Through the thin softness of her jumper, he could feel how slender she was. His hand seemed large and rough by comparison. She did not move. He could not bring himself to meet her gaze in case it held reproof, so he stared at her throat; her pale, fragile, immaculate throat.

Then he felt the lightest of touches, her hand on his shoulder, resting her fingers there for a moment. The feel of them burned through the light cotton of his shirt.

There was a pause during which the air caved in, the clouds collided, and the stars burst into fatal showers that set the sky alight.

They both heard it at the same moment: the unmistakably prosaic sound of Raymond whistling to himself as he strode down the office, the chink of loose change in his pocket. They broke apart. Annette dropped down into her chair and lifted her hands to the computer keyboard. William reeled away, wondering, as the world righted, how on earth he was going to find his way back to his desk.

3

The only parts of school that Helly had enjoyed were taking up smoking and her history project. Their teacher, a thin Scottish man they called The Beard, had asked them all to think of a local topic. Helly, along with four others in the class, had come up with *The History of Stockwell Tube Station*. It had been one of the first to open, on the fourth of November 1890, as part of the City & South London Railway. There was a display in the local library.

She had started the project with some zeal, drawing the front cover before she had even written the introduction. The earliest tubes had distinctive domed roofs which housed the lifts. She drew her dome with great care. The rest of the station had been built with red bricks and decorated with white tiles. She bought a tin of Lakeland pencils specially for the task and drew three Victorian ladies, complete with bustles and parasols, promenading in front of the station. They held their parasols at an angle and their faces were smudgy, like the one in a Degas painting she had seen in the school secretary's office. At the end of two weeks she had the best drawing she had ever done and a contents list.

One day, The Beard asked them all to get out what they had done so far and lay it on their desks so that he could come round and check on their progress. He worked his way round the class.

Next to Helly was Marhita, the sulky girl who had joined the class last term after her father had pulled her out of her previous school, because of trouble with some boy. Marhita ran to the toilets at the end of each day to wash off her make-up. She was a year older than the rest of them and determined to leave at Easter. When The Beard got to her desk she sat back in her seat and shrugged. In front of her was a lined pad with two sentences scrawled on it. The Beard did his best to be angry but his heart wasn't in it. Marhita was already a lost cause.

Then he turned to Fola, who sat in front of Helly. Fola was the class brains. He did all his homework. He had never been late. The other kids thumped him around and called him a clever dickhead but Helly knew they were mistaken. He is not clever, she would think, in scornful silence. He just works hard. The Beard was soft on all the black kids because he was scared of being racist but he was particularly encouraging to Fola. Here, after all, was a black kid who worked hard and enjoyed his classes. He would do well at exam times. In the staff room he could be pointed to as a success. Fola was The Beard's insurance policy.

Fola had also chosen *The History of Stockwell Tube Station* as his project. Spread out on his desk were the two chapters he had already completed and summaries of the rest. Helly leant forward and caught a glimpse of the first chapter heading: *The Problems: Tunnel Construction and Train Propulsion.* The Beard picked it up and flicked through it. He paused for a respectful period. Then he put it back down and said, 'That looks very promising Fola. Very promising indeed.' Fola gave a rare shy smile. Mostly, he was a solemn boy.

The Beard paused in front of Helly's desk where her picture and her contents list were laid out.

He picked up the contents list and read out loud, 'Contents: Introduction, Transport in General, Stockwell Tube, Conclusion.' He paused, then lifted an ironic eyebrow. 'That it?'

Helly sat back in her seat and shrugged, like Marhita. 'Yeh.'

'Where is the rest of it?' The Beard had begun to talk very slowly. The rest of the class sat up and looked round. When The Beard started speaking slowly it was a sure sign that he was about to lose his temper.

Helly narrowed her eyes, looking at him. She knew that he would feel obliged to lose his temper with at least one of them during the inspection and she was damned if it was going to be her.

'At home,' she replied calmly.

'At home?'

She held his gaze, defiantly. 'I forgot it.'

The Beard wavered. The class waited. 'See me afterwards,' he said at last – a cop-out. The class relaxed.

They were supposed to work on their projects for the rest of the lesson. While Fola sat writing earnestly, head bent, Helly picked a blue pencil from her Lakeland set and drew a spaceship floating over Stockwell tube and the Victorian ladies. In the window of the blue spaceship she drew a blue alien, with two tentacles and a beard. She drew a speech bubble coming out of the alien's mouth and wrote in it, *We will be landing shortly, Headteacher.*

At the end of the afternoon, Helly packed up her things slowly while the other members of the class leapt to their feet and stampeded out of the door.

The Beard was standing and sorting through his papers, shuffling them around. As Helly approached him he sat down again and looked up at her. The skin around his eyes was saggy. His hair was unkempt. He was wearing a navy blue V-neck pullover over a grey shirt. She felt sorry for him.

'I'm not going to do Stockwell,' she said.

He looked at her, grateful that she was not expecting a bollocking. 'Why not?'

She shrugged. 'No point.'

He sighed and leant back in his chair. 'Well, we'll have to come up with something else then. There must be something. You'll have catching up to do.'

This was not true. Most of the class hadn't even started yet. She would have some catching up to do if she wanted to pass, like Fola. She shrugged again.

'It doesn't have to be local,' he said. 'Anything, really. Why don't you do something else about transport, seeing as you've made a start?'

She looked at him.

'How about this?' he said, leaning forward and flicking

through some notes on his desk. His voice had taken on an eager tone. 'This really tickled me.' He slid over some photocopied pages from a textbook. 'See here,' he pointed to half-way down one page. 'Things got really out of hand in Victorian times. It was almost as bad then as it is now. By 1875 London's trams were taking forty-nine million passengers a year. But even before then, before they got the trams going, they had a Parliamentary Select Committee to decide what to do. This guy came up with an idea about London's streets being built on three levels, one for horses and carriages, one for people and one for trains. It was all going to be built out of glass, like the Great Exhibition. It was going to be called the Crystal Way. That's what you could call your project, The Crystal Way . . .'

He looked up from the pages to see that Helly was observing him. He was slightly embarrassed. 'Well, I thought it was interesting, anyway, the crackpot ideas these Victorians had. Just imagine it – all built of glass.'

Helly hesitated. She knew that any minute now he was liable to sit her down and have a little chat. Teachers did this to her, on average, once a term. They told her that she was a bright girl and asked her, what did she want to do with her life? What did she *really* want? They were hoping she would reply, 'Oh, do you really think I'm clever?' as if she didn't know, as if they had given her some vital piece of information that would transform her life. Henceforward, she would attend classes on time, work on her essays, give up smoking and generally metamorphose into a useful member of society. They were asking her, in fact, to validate their last remaining glimmer of optimism.

She resented their demands. They were paid to be teachers, weren't they? Nobody made them do it. Why lean on her?

If she didn't say something quickly then The Beard would start to tell her how she could produce a very interesting project, if she really tried. The Crystal Way. Who the fuck did he think he was?

'Could do something on disasters,' she suggested, standing back and folding her arms.

'Disasters?'

'Yeh, you know, where lots of people get killed.'

The Beard looked deflated. 'Well, I suppose, research would be relatively –'

'Yeh, I could get quite into that, buses and train crashes. Accidents and that.'

The Beard lifted his hands, to indicate defeat. 'You had better start at the library. There must be a book. But don't just take it all out of the book. Go to the newspapers section. They keep old journals, you know.'

'Yeh, I know,' said Helly as she slung her bag over her shoulder. She was still holding her picture of Stockwell tube in one hand. She had folded it into four, with the contents list inside.

On her way out of the class room, she dropped it in the bin.

Helly's project was called *The Sinking of the Princess Alice*. A trip to Brixton library had indeed produced a book, coincidentally of the same title. It informed her that on the third of September 1878, the passenger carrier Princess Alice was making a routine trip across the Thames when

80

it met unexpectedly with another ship called the Bywell Castle. They collided just off Woolwich. Seven hundred and eighty-six people were killed, the highest death toll of any disaster other than in war time.

Helly thought it a pretty impressive figure. She decided to do a comparative study of contemporary death and disaster. She listed the numbers of people killed in recent transport accidents. Fires, wrecks, crashes – the figure only just topped a hundred. Are we to deduce, Helly wrote in the conclusion, that the Victorians were more accident prone than us? Of course not. You only needed one big bad piece of luck to add up to the same as a lot of small pieces.

One of her appendices was a survey which she carried out amongst her class, entitled, *Are You Afraid of Accidents*? It listed recent disasters, including bombings, and asked people who they thought responsible; the Government, the IRA, the Capital Transport Authority, Nobody, God. The Government took a clear lead, with Nobody and God tying for second. Not all her friends took the survey entirely seriously. Some added their own suggestions at the bottom of the list, including: Saddam Hussein, Norman Tebbit, the gnomes of Elsinore and my pet rabbit, Kenneth.

Her marks were good. At the end of the appendix which included the questionnaire, The Beard wrote: *Interesting use of primary research method*.

On the last day of the summer term, two of the boys in Helly's class set fire to The Beard's class room. The projects, returned from the external assessor and waiting to be collected by pupils, were sitting in a pile on The Beard's desk. They went up in smoke. Helly was at first annoyed, then amused. It seemed rather appropriate.

Along with the rest of the class, she received a visit at home from the police. She had no help to give them and would not have given it if she had. The boys later got youth custody for criminal damage.

After the police had gone, her mother came downstairs. It was a summer afternoon, a Wednesday. Her mother had been asleep.

'Who was that?' she asked Helly as she passed into the kitchen.

Helly followed her and went to the freezer compartment for two slices of bread. 'The police,' she replied.

'Oh. What did *they* want?' her mother said, sitting down at the table. 'Make us some toast too Hels.' Helly's mother was slumped forward at the table with her chin on one elbow. She was wearing a cream-coloured towelling robe with a tea stain on the left lapel. The robe was loosely tied and the pale swoop of her right breast hung forward. Despite her love of self-abuse her face had stayed attractive, but her body showed clear signs of strain.

Helly turned back to the grill. 'They aren't after me anyway. Make your own fucking toast.'

'Stupid little slag,' her mother replied neutrally, as she withdrew a cigarette packet from the pocket of her robe.

A six month period of secretarial training followed. Helly's scheme involved three days a week work experience at a painting and decorating firm off the Black Prince Road,

82

combined with two days at Vauxhall College. She learnt that pencils should always be sharpened, that paragraphs could – nowadays – be either indented or blocked and that office juniors were the repository of all the boredom, grief and egotism that other employees could muster.

When she left for her first proper job interview, with the Capital Transport Authority, her mother advised her casually, 'Plenty of lipstick and don't forget to stick your tits out.' It appeared to work.

There was a honeymoon period at the CTA. She had been interviewed by Richard and Annette, whom she thought were probably at it. Helly had met women like Annette before – in school, at the job centre: women who would organise your entire life but never tell you anything about themselves; women who never let go. They weren't particularly likeable but neither were they very offensive. You knew where you were. Richard was a prat, that much was obvious, but once appointed she had little to do with him. Joan was alright – good for the occasional laugh. The other men were stiffs. By the end of the first day, Helly could foresee the progress of her employment with the CTA. The job itself would be interesting for as long as it took her to learn where things were put and kept. It would be easy to tell lies, as long as she didn't make anybody feel stupid. She and Annette would eventually get on one another's nerves. It would always be tolerable, never more. It got her out of the house.

At home, things deteriorated. Now that she was earning, her mother expected a contribution. As soon as she got it, she took it down the pub. She was seeing a dentist called Jonathan. He was one step up from the usual bus drivers and labourers so she started stealing Helly's underwear. Jonathan came round for dinner one night and Helly was instructed to stay out of the way. She heard wild laughter from the kitchen, where a bottle of sparkling white wine was chilling in the fridge and Marks & Spencer dips were laid out on the table. Helly pulled on a jacket and crept down. She made it out of the front door just after she heard her mother shriek, 'Jonathan, put me down!'

She had a boyfriend of her own, briefly. He was the brother of one of her friends from school. Jamie was a rangy lad with bright blue eyes who wore vest T-shirts over baggy trousers. He was good-natured but hid it well. She discovered sex was over-rated. On Saturday nights, they drank with their friends and played pool in the Russell Hotel on Brixton Road. Occasionally they joined the landlord and the other oldies singing karaoke. Mr O'Brien was seventy-five if he was a day and did a great 'Lucille', swivelling his creaky hips and tossing the microphone from hand to hand between verses.

The Russell Hotel had a late licence and stayed open until one in the morning. Sometimes Jamie would borrow someone's car and they would drive up to Clapham Common. More often, he walked her home and they would kiss wet open-mouthed kisses in the alley behind her house and fumble with each other's flies. There was no need to be quiet. Her mother was rarely at home, although Helly never mentioned this to Jamie. Afterwards, she would let herself in and make a cup of tea. She would sit in the kitchen in the dark, drinking, staring out of the uncurtained window at the partially-lit concrete tower blocks of Lambeth, creating starships in the sky.

She had only been at the CTA for a few weeks when she found out about the letter. She arrived home from work one Tuesday. She hated Tuesdays: well into the week, ages from the end. It had taken her an hour and twenty minutes to get home, longer than it would have taken to walk. The Victoria line was down so she had gone to catch the 36 bus, along with everybody else who worked in SW1. After three of them had come and gone and the crowd had continued to swell, she went back down into the tube to get the District line to Westminster and pick up the 109. When a 109 came it was only going as far as County Hall. She stepped back, knowing that she was breaking the cardinal rule of travelling on public transport: go as far as you can on whatever happens to be available. The next 109 was full. She gave in and walked across the bridge, then down the Albert embankment to pick up a number 3, a sleek modern bus with furry seats that smelt of car sickness.

Her mother was watching television. Helly stormed past the sitting room door.

'Helen!' her mother called out.

'*What?*' said Helly. She had paused in the hall but did not go back to the doorway.

'You've just missed your gran . . .' Helly spelt the word 'fuck' with her lips. 'She said she couldn't stop. They were going out or something. They brought a letter round. The kitchen table!'

On the kitchen table Helly found a letter on Capital

Transport Authority headed notepaper, addressed to her grandparents. It came from Richard's office but was signed officially by the general manager of the property division. Beneath *Dear Mr and Mrs Appleton* were the words: *Rosewood Cottage, Sutton Street: Notice to Treat*.

It was her gran who persuaded her not to ask around at work openly. 'Don't get yourself into trouble,' Joanna Appleton had said. 'I only brought it round because you work for them and I thought you could find out how long we've got. But don't tell anyone you know us. It'll make things tricky for you.'

Helly decided not to ask but for a different reason. By then, she was working out her own solution. By then, she knew that Richard was bent.

Benny loved horses. He dreamt of them nearly every night as he lay in fitful sleep in his car-tyre igloo in the works yard of Robinson Builders Limited. In Venezuela, he had once performed a Caesarean section on a thoroughbred mare whose foal had not turned, saving the foal's life. The tiny horse was healthy, beautiful, perfect. Señor de Angelinos had been duly grateful. Benny's future looked bright.

After a day or so, the mare began to sicken. The wound putrefied. Benny fought to save her but within a week the battle was lost. Señor de Angelinos sent two *campesinos* round to break Benny's legs, but he was out playing draughts at the Hotel Colon with his neighbour's uncle. His brother Luis was in, so the *campesinos* broke his legs instead. Benny left town.

When he first came to England he had sought work

in the country, but the farmers thought he was a gypsy. Hunger forced him to London. Arthur Robinson had tripped over him as he huddled in a railway arch in Kennington. Benny had stared up at the fat white man and fought with his pride. He had not eaten for three days and was filthy; still he could not bring himself to beg. Arthur Robinson had looked down at the small proud Venezuelan and seen another opportunity to be adored. He took Benny into his yard, let him build the igloo, gave him work, saved his life. Benny was the loyal type. While Benny was alive, Arthur Robinson could have no breathing enemies.

Now Benny was in another railway arch, this time in Deptford. He was at the end of Sutton Street. He was watching Rosewood Cottage. Benny did not know why Mr Robinson wanted the cottage watched, but it was something to do with the smart-faced man who turned up once in a while. Benny could read faces. The smart man looked at him and thought that because he didn't speak he couldn't understand. Benny's English was fluent but in this wet grey city he had generally found it wise to keep that to himself. Benny sighed and withdrew a tube of Smarties from his pocket. He flipped the plastic lid and tipped the last remaining few into his mouth. Eating sweets was a habit he had copied from Mr Robinson. It was ruining his teeth but visiting a dentist was out of the question. Benny tossed the tube back into the arch disconsolately, peering out at the deserted street. It was windy and damp, although the rain had stopped. Benny sighed again. He had been in England too long. It was an armpit of a country. An armpit.

Benny had been in the railway arch since four o'clock.

His vigil was rewarded just after six p.m. A girl was strolling down Sutton Street, towards him. He withdrew into the shadows of the arch. She had to be visiting the cottage. There was no other reason to come down Sutton Street, unless you had a body to bury. The girl had a bag slung over her shoulder but it wasn't big enough for a body and she was too small to carry one anyway. She was wearing a brown mini-skirt and a huge grey cardigan that swamped her and made her seem dwarfish. Her light brown hair was pulled back into a long bunch that curled down her back. She was chewing something.

Benny watched the girl as she approached the cottage. She paused on the step and fumbled in her bag. Then she pulled out a bunch of keys and let herself in.

'Come on you girls,' Bob said, 'get out of my kitchen.' He eased past Helly who was seated on a tall stool by the fridge.

'What are you cooking?' she asked.

'Fettucine al dogshit. Now get out of my way.'

Joanna tugged at Helly's sleeve. 'Come on Poops, let the Maestro do his stuff or we'll be sending you out to the Deptford Tandoori.'

Helly and Joanna took their wine into the sitting room. They settled on the sofa and sipped for a moment, the silence companionable.

After a while, Helly asked casually, 'Had any more visits from the Transport Authority?'

Joanna levelled her gaze at her granddaughter. 'You know damn well we have. Don't you?'

Helly looked up, wide-eyed. 'Why do you say that?'

Joanna chuckled. 'Listen, Poops. Your mum may fall for that but you can't fool your mad old granny. We had some young fella round here last Wednesday telling us it's been suspended. Indefinitely.'

'Just suspended? Not cancelled?'

'Well, I don't know. He said suspended in a way that sounded like cancelled but I wouldn't trust those buggers as far as I could throw 'em. He said his name was Bennett. Do you know him?'

Helly nodded. 'William. New guy. Gets the dirty work.'

Joanna put down her wine glass and leant forward. She rested both her hands on Helly's knees. 'Poops, have you been up to something?'

Helly bit her lip.

'Look, just tell me this. Is this going to get you in trouble? I don't care what you do as long as you're okay. We're grateful of course, but the last thing I want is you getting the boot.'

'Gran, if I *was* up to something, don't you think I'd cover myself?' Helly took a sip of wine and sat back in her seat.

Joanna shook her head. 'You're a clever kid. Always were. But sometimes it isn't enough to be clever, Poops. There are some people out there you can outwit and do you know what they'll do? Turn round and smack you in the gob, that's what. I know you've had it tough with your mum, but you don't know yet how tough some men can be . . .'

'Oh *Gran* . . .'

'I want you to promise me one thing. Just this one.' Helly rolled her eyes. 'Now listen, for once. Just promise me this: if you get in an argument with someone, you'll do it somewhere public, okay?'

'Alright, Gran.'

'I mean it love, please.' Joanna's face had become tense and sad. She leant forward. 'Just don't let yourself get cornered, that's all.'

Helly put down her glass and grasped Joanna's hands in hers. 'I know what I'm doing.'

Joanna smiled. 'You know as soon as your great-gran pops off you can have her room, don't you?'

Helly returned the smile. 'Oh come on. Nan Hawthorne isn't going anywhere.'

'How's your mum?'

Helly bent and picked up her glass. 'Same as ever.'

'Joanna!' Bob's voice called from the kitchen.

'What?' Joanna called back.

Bob appeared in the doorway. He was wearing a plastic apron printed with the images of a lacy bra and lacy pair of knickers. He was holding a large wooden pepper mill. 'Where did you put the sun-dried tomatoes?'

The next morning, Helly woke on her grandparents' sofa. She would have walked to New Cross and got the bus, but it was dark by the time they had finished Bob's fettucine and Joanna had insisted she stay the night. She had slept in one of Bob's old shirts and her grey wool tights, under a sleeping bag they had dug out from the attic. The cottage had no central heating. It was freezing.

The rest of her clothes lay in a heap on the armchair. She unbuttoned Bob's shirt and pulled on her bra and T-shirt, then slipped into the brown mini-skirt she had been wearing the previous day. Her huge grey cardigan lay on the floor like a slug.

Joanna was in the kitchen, dressed in a pink kimono, making tea.

'You must be freezing,' Helly said as she came in, running her hands through her hair and fastening it back with a band. 'You didn't need to get up, I can let myself out.'

'I've been awake since five,' Joanna replied. 'Didn't you hear the racket?'

'What racket?'

'The wind. One hell of a noise, blowing half the street down, it sounded like. I don't know what was going on.' She opened the fridge door and lifted out a carton of orange juice. 'Here,' she said as she passed it over. 'If your hangover's anything like mine you'll need this.'

Benny had fallen asleep with his eyes still open just before dawn, crouched inside the railway arch, his head leaning against the brickwork. All night the wind had flung rubbish at him; no rain, no thunder, no lightning, just whispered secrets one minute and shrieked demands the next.

He woke as Helly slammed the cottage door behind her. He watched as she made her way past, picking through debris from the skip which had scattered itself across the street in bizarre attitudes. Then he stood up and stretched. He was stiff as hell and had run out of Smarties. He worked his shoulders backwards, trying to loosen up, then peered out at the sky: crisp, cold, a little smokey. He pulled a face, then he slipped out of the railway arch and began to follow.

Joan awoke to the ringing of bells. There were several, all clanging frantically in different pitches, a small mad cacophany that seemed to be growing in a corner of her head. She reached out a hand to touch the 'off' button on their bedside alarm. Her fingers brushed the plastic. The ringing didn't stop. She struggled upright on one elbow and peered at the alarm resentfully. It wasn't making any noise at all. Nor was it showing the time. Her fingers scrambled for her watch. Eight fifteen: the alarm should have gone off over an hour ago.

Next to her, Alun stirred briefly, snuffled once into his pillow and continued to sleep. In the early days of their marriage, his shifts had caused problems. After all these years, they now slept soundly through each other's routines. Whenever Joan cooked dinner, she made a double portion and left the rest in an ovenproof dish in the fridge. The food always went, although she would often not catch sight of Alun for days, other than as a bulk beneath the blankets, a heaviness that made the mattress slope, a male smell, a warmth.

She swung herself heavily out of bed and went to the window. The room felt cold. She placed a hand on the electric storage heater beneath the sill. It had not come on.

She pushed the curtain aside with one finger. The street below was in chaos. A wild wind was blowing a huge cardboard box down the road. It tripped and tumbled past a small ash tree which grew opposite their house and was now snapped half-way down the trunk. The branches were whisking to and fro, blocking half the road. Number eight's metal bin had blown over and several empty catfood tins were pirouetting in mad swirls a foot above the pavement. The ringing sounds were coming from the direction of Denmark Hill – shop burglar alarms, several of them.

Joan went to the door and pulled her dressing-gown off the hook. She tied the belt as she went downstairs. In the hall, she dialled her neighbour's number.

'Lydia? It's Joan. Have you got any electricity?'

Nobody in the street had electricity. It had gone down an hour and a half ago, setting off the alarms and causing mayhem. Lydia was surprised Joan had not woken earlier. She had been up half the night with tiles slithering down her roof. She was worried sick about the chimney.

Joan ate cornflakes for breakfast and drank a small glass of orange squash. Then she splashed her face with cold water and dressed quickly, feeling cold and grimy. She was going to be terribly late. She left a note for Alun in case he woke up and wondered what was going on.

Denmark Hill looked a riot. A tree and a signpost had come down and the police had cordoned off one side of the road. The burglar alarms were still ringing, some of them flashing like demented Christmas decorations. She saw the red hulk of a bus stuck at the traffic lights and began to run. Half-way there, she realised the bus wasn't moving. The traffic round the Green was blocked solid. Some drivers had got out of their cars and were wandering around, shaking their heads.

As Joan approached, she could see that the bus platform was packed with passengers. There appeared to be a fairly high turnover; some were crowded round trying to get on while others were crowded round trying to get off. As she got nearer she heard the conductor calling over their heads, 'Vauxhall only. I'm only going as far as Vauxhall.' A woman in a red mac was standing in the road and questioning him. He was shaking his head. 'You won't get anything going over the bridge,' he was telling her. 'Nothing's going over the bridge at the moment. The bridges are all closed.' Joan turned away. She had walked to work once before, during the bus strike. It took nearly an hour, through Kennington and over Lambeth Bridge. Anything was better than trying to get a bus.

The same madness held sway all the way up Camberwell New Road; cars stalled, dustbins in the street, clutches of traffic followed by empty stretches where the road was too dangerous to negotiate. Children were gathered around outside the Sacred Heart secondary school, jumping for joy at the chaos as though it was a trick they had performed on a world of unsuspecting adults. As she approached Kennington, three fire brigade lorries came steaming and swaying down the Brixton Road, sirens joined in a vicious whine.

Half-way across Lambeth Bridge she paused and looked out over the chopping, frothing Thames. The wind charged about her head, freezing the end of her nose and whistling icily in her ears. The whole of London paralysed, she thought, by a stiff breeze and a sense of confusion, and cut in two by this – this strip of brown sloshing water. A businessman staggered past, one hand grabbing furiously at his raincoat and the other clutching a briefcase to his chest. Few pedestrians had braved the bridge and those that had were taking it slowly, stopping now and then to pause and lean into the wind. Joan caught her breath, put her head down and carried on. She felt like having a good laugh. She wanted to stop on the middle of the bridge, throw her head back and roar with laughter.

At CTA, there was great excitement. Only half the staff had managed to get in. Annette had made it. Helly was nowhere to be seen. Richard was running around consulting. Everyone had a story to tell. It was the worst storm since 1987, they all agreed. Even worse than that, perhaps. At noon, Richard stood on a table and announced that, bearing in mind the atrocious weather, the view of the management – with whom he had consulted – was that staff should be allowed home early. Gentlemen could leave at four thirty p.m., ladies at four.

This was tantamount to declaring a national holiday. For the rest of the day, a party atmosphere prevailed. Joan spent much of it standing at the window with Annette, pointing out bizarre, detached objects which hurtled around in the street below: a man's hat, a blanket, a pair of dancing newspapers which, as Annette observed, were obviously in love.

By mid-afternoon the office was nearly deserted as

everybody made for home. Those commuting out of London had sloped off one by one. Richard, empowered to say who should leave and when, had been sidling up to individuals and giving them the nod, enjoying his munificence. At three o'clock he had come round to their desks and said, 'Not much point in hanging on I don't think, girls.' Annette had jumped to her feet. Joan had said, 'I'll just finish up.' With everyone else gone, she settled down to updating the list of Approved Contractors.

It was only when she started working on it that she remembered why it was taking her so long; it was boring. After twenty minutes she gave up and wandered over to the window. Perhaps she should go home too. She didn't fancy walking. If she was going to try for a bus she ought to leave.

The storm was nearly over and the street below was quieter now. A scattering of office workers was walking swiftly by. An ambulance swayed silently past. A small branch lay in the middle of the road, blown there from a distant tree. Joan watched it as it suddenly moved a few feet down the street, seemingly of its own accord. Then a van drove past and the branch was flipped over and blown into a gutter, where it stuck.

The wind is ordinary now, Joan thought, not wild. It is pretending again. After the mockery and mayhem of the morning, she found the sudden stillness sinister. She frowned to herself. We thought we were safe in the city. We didn't think it would come this far. Storms happen between hills, not concrete. Well, we were wrong again. Puny men and women. She shivered suddenly. What was wrong with her? This morning, crossing the Thames, the storm had made her want to roar like a medieval witch. Now she was frightened. She shook her head and turned away from the window, pulling her cardigan across her chest protectively and holding herself. All at once, a thought had come into her head, very clearly and distinctly: something bad is going to happen soon.

Annette had scarcely seen William for a whole week. He had spent most of the time on site visits. The day of the storm, he didn't make it in at all. When they had seen each other, they had smiled uncertainly and talked as always. Annette was puzzled. The afterglow of their odd moment had lasted for several days, then she began to doubt what had happened. More to the point, had anything happened at all? The memory seemed blurry: the briefest of touches, the feel of cotton, a catching of breath. She knew nothing about this man.

The day after the storm, he came around to her part of the office carrying a sheaf of paper, the specification for the refurbishment works at Harrow. She looked up at him. He came to a halt beside her desk, and looked down at her.

Joan came pottering around the office divide holding a cloth.

'You wouldn't believe the state of the cupboard.' She shook her head. 'You're going to have to speak to the cleaners, Annette. If we took all the cups out one Friday then they could get at it. Nobody has for years . . .'

Annette had always been fond of Joan, but now she

felt an overwhelming desire to lever her out of their second floor window.

Joan paused in front of her desk. She put down the cloth, then reached over and opened a drawer, 'I don't know . . .'

William was shifting from one foot to another. Annette wondered how long he would stand there without feeling impelled to say something for Joan's benefit.

Joan had finished rummaging. She stood up, clutching her handbag. 'Won't be a mo . . .'

William watched Joan leave and then handed Annette the specification. 'It's like this Phil in Commercial left the Dayworks out I can't believe it can you do you fancy a drink after work?' He gave a sharp intake of breath.

Annette wanted to giggle. 'Yes. Okay.'

William scratched his scalp. 'I've got the car, you see. I'm going straight to Fairlop in the morning so they've lent me the car. I could run you home afterwards. If you like.'

'Yes. okay.'

'A quick drink mind, you might be busy, I don't know. Whatever you fancy really.'

'Yes.'

'We could stay local or we could drive over your way – Lewisham, perhaps Greenwich?'

Annette nodded, biting her lower lip to prevent herself from standing, grasping him by the lapels of his jacket and shouting in his face, *I said YES!*

'Well, fine then,' William said.

He turned and was gone.

*   *   *

The rest of that afternoon took on a weird glow. William went out on a site visit. Annette put the specification to one side and tried to work as normal, but suddenly every detail of the office became invested with significance. At one point, she looked round to see that a smear of dirt on the filing cabinet next to her had inexplicably formed itself into an oblong shape that was almost a heart. The leaves of Joan's beloved ivy caught the light from the window and bounced it in her direction. When she heard a woman laughing in the street outside, she nearly joined in.

She picked up a tape of dictation that Richard had left. The letter she began to type seemed bizarre. Richard was explaining to a contractor that the tender documents would be forwarded to him as soon as possible. How sweet, she thought. Language had dissolved. Phrases had become like shards of coloured glass from a broken ornament; pretty and intriguing, but it was impossible to stand back and picture the whole. She typed, *I will contact you on Monday 15th with my findings* and giggled. He will contact them with his findings? Why doesn't he just use the phone?

The situation did not improve when she moved on to a Schedule of Dilapidations that Raymond wanted by the end of the afternoon. The contractors were instructed to infill ducts with trowelled cement. Poor ducks, she thought. Each duck had an approximate length of eight metres. Further down the page, the words *bitumous macadam* conjured up an image of half a dozen burly lads around a massive steaming cauldron, stirring with a wooden spoon and adding eye of newt or leg of toad. Some of it, she typed, was causing severe ponding in isolated areas. I bet it is, she thought.

A few minutes later, Raymond strode past. He stopped, turned back and frowned at her.

'Annette,' he said with a mixture of amusement and irritation.

She removed her headphones and looked up, wide-eyed.

'You're humming,' he accused.

'Oh, was I?' asked Annette. 'I had the audio phones on. What was it?'

'I'm not sure, but I think it might have been "I'm a pink toothbrush, you're a blue toothbrush" . . .'

William felt sick. He was waiting in the Capital Transport Authority's works car on the corner of Greycoat Street and Rochester Street. He and Annette had agreed to drive down to Greenwich and have a drink there. 'Greenwich is nice,' Annette had said. *And we don't want to bump into anyone from work*, she might have added.

William wanted this. He had wanted it all week. It had taken him four days and much careful planning to ask her. But right now, this minute, as he sat in an unfamiliar car down an unfamiliar side-street, he couldn't imagine what on earth he was playing at. What would they talk about as they drove? It was the middle of the rush hour, for Christ's sake. Well William, he thought, you sure know how to show a girl a good time. Twenty minutes getting past the roadworks on the Old Kent Road. That'll sweep her off her feet.

He turned on the radio. It was tuned to a music station, golden oldies of some sort. What did Annette listen to? Golden oldies wouldn't do, she'd think he was a prat. He fiddled, trying to find Radio Four, but was unable to escape from a harsh judgemental fuzzing sound. He turned it off. He felt sick; truly, deeply, comprehensively sick. He wished he had never set eyes on the woman. He wished he had gone to the toilet before he left the office.

In the office, in the ladies' second floor toilet, Annette was being sick.

She was ten minutes late, the longest ten minutes of William's life. He watched her as she walked down Greycoat Street. He liked her walk, a slow-swaying glide; funny that he hadn't noticed that before. She was looking at each car in turn. He raised his hand but realised that she was still too far away to see. Now she was making her way towards him. He sat back in his seat and relaxed, enjoying the moment: gazing at an object of desire about to return the gaze.

He started the engine as she approached, then leant over to open the passenger door.

'Sorry, I got held up,' she said, smiling, as she climbed in and turned to pull at the seatbelt.

'That's okay,' he said, returning her smile. He noticed that she had applied fresh lipstick, a soft peach colour that toned with her pale skin. She did that for me, he thought, swelling with pride. A traffic warden was making his way slowly down the street as they pulled out.

'Just in time,' said Annette, her voice low and warm.

'Greenwich here we come.' William accelerated away from the kerb, smiling all over his face, for suddenly, being in a car with Annette, driving away from work, seemed like the most natural thing in the world.

They drank in the corner of an empty riverside pub and talked about work and Perthshire. They both had relatives there. Annette entertained him with the history of personalities from the office. As their laughter died after one anecdote, William reached across the table and placed one hand over hers.

Annette had nearly finished her second half of lager and was dying for the loo, but stayed there for another twenty minutes rather than break the contact.

Neither of them raised the topic of dinner. It seemed enough to be sitting there, like toddlers who had just learned to sit at all. To go any further forward that night would be foolish.

At a quarter to nine, Annette checked her watch. She didn't want to leave but thought that William might be getting anxious and wondering how to break it to her.

'I'll drop you off home,' he said.

They pulled into her cul-de-sac and she pointed out her house. 'That's it,' she said, 'the one with the red numbers. I thought I'd be different.'

They sat in silence for a few moments.

'We must do that again,' Annette said, and knew instantly that she had said the wrong thing. To say that they must do it again implied that there was a possibility they would not.

'Yes, if you like,' William replied quickly, his tone carefully casual. The intimacy of the pub had been dissolved. They were back to square one.

Annette undid her seatbelt. 'Thanks,' she said. 'Goodnight.'

As William drove home on automatic pilot, euphoria fought with confusion, caution with desire. I am on a road, he thought, something like a motorway. No stopping. As he pulled out of Hither Green Lane, a roadsign informed him that there were 'CHANGED PRIORITIES AHEAD'.

His house was in a wide, quiet street with small square gardens in front of tall tight terraces. On the corner of the main road was a row of shops: fruiterers, off licence, launderette. As he approached, he realised that he could not possibly arrive home just yet. He pulled in by the shops and undid his seatbelt. He sat back, his head on the headrest. Unreal. It was all too unreal.

It began to rain, softly, the scarcest of noises pattering on the car roof. A neighbour walked past – Mr Greenly from number eighteen – turning up the collar of his sheepskin jacket. William was momentarily panic-stricken. Had Greenly seen him? What if he and Alison bumped into him at the weekend and he said, 'Hello William, what were you doing parked outside the shops on Thursday night?' Unlikely. Possible. William jumped out and trotted over to the off licence, where he bought a four-pack of lager and a packet of mints.

Back inside the car, he tossed the four-pack onto the passenger seat and opened the mints. He had been driving home when he had had a coughing fit, so he had stopped to get mints. He had bought the four-pack on impulse. He fancied a lager. Yes, it sounded perfectly plausible.

He sat back in his seat and sighed. Already, he thought. It has begun already: the lies, the excuses, watching my step, having an answer ready for any question no matter how insignificant or accidental. Already. And I've hardly touched her yet.

The next day was Friday. He drove out to Fairlop in the morning and rushed through his meeting with the contractors. He was desperate to get back to John Blow House before lunchtime.

He arrived at just gone one o'clock, as Annette was standing up from her seat and reaching for her coat. She shrugged it over her shoulders as he approached and lifted her hair free from the collar. Joan was wandering around a few yards away, but he was breathless and reckless by then.

He went up to Annette. 'Green Man? Ten minutes?' he said softly. She nodded.

After lunch, they walked back to the office side by side, together but carefully apart.

In the tiny mirrored lift, they had their first snog.

Saturday in Bromley. William was lying on top of his bed, dressed in jeans and a T-shirt. Alison was down-stairs, cleaning the kitchen before she went shopping. He could hear the clatter of the floor mop, Paul's reedy voice enquiring, followed by her softer tones telling him to get his shoes on because they were going out.

The previous night, they had had friends round to dinner. William was full of Annette – their lunch, their kiss, their future – so he had been more jovial and talkative than usual, to cover up the fact that he didn't feel like talking at all. This morning, after breakfast, he had feigned a hangover. He had to get Alison out of the house.

He waited tensely until he heard the front door slam. Then, every muscle relaxed. 'I won't be more than an hour,' Alison had said. A whole hour. A whole hour to do nothing except think about Annette. He lay on his back, gazing up at the ceiling. He thought through the rights and wrongs of phoning her, making a mental list. Rights: I want to talk to her; I am desperate to hear her voice; I'd do anything to be with her right now; I'll go crazy if I have to wait until Monday morning. Wrongs: she might not be in; she might be in but not want to talk to me; I will probably make a complete berk of myself. He picked up the phone.

The answer machine clicked on after two rings. He listened to her message, her cool, efficient, measured voice. As the beep went, he slammed down the phone.

Where was she? Out at the shops, probably. Probably. Maybe she was in. Perhaps, if he had spoken, she would have picked up the phone. Or maybe there was someone else with her. She had left the machine on and turned the ringer volume down, so that they would not be disturbed. The thought made him crazy, so he thought it some more. During their lunch, he had carefully avoided asking her what she was going to do that night. If he went too fast it would scare her off. If she was unattached, what *did* she do on Friday nights? How many friends did she have? She was beautiful; she probably had hundreds. He was probably the seventh man to ring her that morning, anxiously, and hang up without leaving a message. He should have left a message.

Already, he felt humiliated. Here he was, on a Saturday morning, with a whole precious hour to himself. Normally he would have been gardening or watching television or sleeping. Instead, he was staring at the ceiling, thinking about Annette. Beautiful Annette. Bloody Annette. She wasn't thinking about him. She was in bed with someone else with the answer machine on and the ringer off. She was saying to him, 'You'll never guess. There's this bloke at work who fancies me. I had lunch with him yesterday but just for a laugh. He's such a jerk. He's called William.' Henry – the man she was sleeping with – was replying, 'William? Really?' They were having a good laugh.

Then he thought of how she had looked the second before he had kissed her in the lift, the slow lowering of her eyelids. He groaned at the recollection. He had lifted his hand and placed his palm on her cheek. Her arm had encircled him, underneath his jacket. He could still feel the soft, insistent pressure of her fingertips.

He rolled over onto his side, wrapping his arms around himself, drawing himself in. His penis began to fill, pressing against his boxer shorts, causing a small ache to grow and blossom in his pelvic region; an unlocated pain, as if an animal was growing inside his groin. He uncurled, rolling onto his back and stretching out. Annette, Annette – the feel of her fingers on his spine.

He reached out and took the phone off the hook. As he rolled over, his T-shirt rode up from his jeans. He rubbed his stomach with the flat of one hand, imagining it was Annette's hand. Then he allowed the hand to wander of its own accord, downwards. They were in a hotel room in Paris, or Vienna or Rome – anywhere except England. (Anywhere a good long way from Bromley.) The hand fiddled around the top button of his jeans, unsure of itself. It twisted the button open. Then it paused. He groaned. Don't torment me, he thought. Torment me, he begged. The hand wandered over the top of his jeans to the fat full swelling underneath. She was lying on top of him, wearing a transparent white blouse. The hand began to flip open each button on his flies. She was sitting astride his legs, pinning them to the bed. He raised his buttocks slightly so that the hand could push his jeans down. As it did, he heard a soft chinking sound as some loose change slipped out of his pockets and onto the bed. At last, the hand slipped inside his boxer shorts. He was hard as a rock. Annette was underneath him. She was raising her knees. She was all pale warmth and wide eyes and her even, measured voice was saying in an even, measured way, 'Yes . . . '

He finished curled up on his side, clutching himself. For a moment he lay, feeling the small sweet throb, the ebb and flow. Then he uncurled and reached over for the tissues that Alison kept on her side of the bed. His hand was dripping. He wiped it then turned to scrape at the duvet cover. As he moved, he saw that he had managed to spurt over the loose change that had fallen from his pocket. The coins lay in a small pile with a large dollop of spunk spread across them, two sins tangled into one. He counted. There were several pound coins, two fifties and other small silver – nearly six quid. He wiped himself, sat upright and did up his flies. Then he scooped the coins up with the tissue and took them to the bathroom. He dropped them in the sink and ran some warm water over them. Then he pulled off a strip of loo roll and laid it along the side of the bath. When he had washed the coins, he placed them one by one on the loo roll to dry. He went back to the bedroom, to double check the duvet.

Annette stood over her answer machine and glared at it. She replayed the message. There it was, an unmistakable click. She had only taken the rubbish out to the bins at the end of the cul-de-sac, and in the ten seconds she had been out of the house someone had rung. Her mother? Her mother never rang on a Saturday morning. Saturday morning was her appointment at the hairdresser's, which held the same importance for Annette's mother as confession for a Jesuit. No, not her mother. Annette bit her lip, then began to smile. She strutted round her living room in a neat circle. *Got him*, she thought. I've got him.

Alison and Paul were back after only twenty minutes. Alison had got as far as Superdrug and then remembered that she had left her chequebook behind. She had enough cash for the toiletries but not the supermarket.

'You'll have to take him later. I did it last week,' she added defensively.

William had come downstairs in a hurry. 'Alright,' he said quickly, and went over and gave her a hug. 'Shall I make a cup of tea?' he said cheerfully.

Paul had broken away from his mother and charged up the stairs to take off his jumper.

'On the chair Paul!' Alison called after him. 'Not on the floor. Neatly on the chair! Any post?' she asked William.

William indicated an envelope on the kitchen table. 'The insurance people.'

Alison sat and began to open it. 'What did you do with Tanya's card? I haven't read it yet.'

'I'll get it,' William said. He plugged in the kettle and went through to the living room.

While he was gone, Paul came downstairs. He had taken off his jumper and, while he was at it, his trousers and one sock. He had two fingers in his mouth. He came and stood by Alison's chair while she opened the letter.

'Mummy,' he said, wrapping his naked limb around her chair leg and putting three fingers in his mouth.

'Yes darling?' Alison replied. She reached out a hand and stroked his hair while she read the insurance company's letter.

'Why has Daddy left money in the bathroom?'

'Has he?' asked Alison absently.

'Yes. On tissues. He's left money on the bath on tissues.'

'Don't know darling,' murmured Alison, 'why don't you run and ask him?'

Understand why, Richard thought. Then work out how.

It was Saturday in Surrey, too. Richard put down the phone. Arthur Robinson had rung first thing with the news. Benny had done well.

He went back into the kitchen. He was wearing his navy tracksuit and an Aran sweater. It felt good to be free of his suit, to be somewhere where he was not expected to make decisions. Gillian had gone out a few minutes ago, with her friend Janice, to check the storm damage at the riding school. She had left a pot of coffee on the hob and brioches in the oven.

Newspapers were scattered across the table. He sat down and picked one up, scanned the front page and dropped it down again, frowning. He didn't like Arthur Robinson having to ring him at home. He resented the intrusion – but then this business had intruded, there was no doubt about that. Still, everything was turning out as he wanted. It would be fine.

Two of the dogs, Goldie and Petal, padded into the kitchen in procession, heads down and tongues lolling. They had been out galumphing round the garden.

'Here . . .' Richard patted his knees with both hands and whistled lightly. Goldie pottered over and landed her chin in Richard's lap. 'There, girl . . .' Richard scratched her roughly behind both ears, the way she liked. 'Thirsty now, eh?'

Richard stood and went out to the utility room. A cold breeze was blowing in from the garden, through the door the dogs had pushed open. He closed it, then bent to pick up their tin water bowls. Gillian had written Goldie and Petal on the sides with indelible black marker. 'Come on girls! Here you are!' Richard called out over the sounds of the water splashing into the tins. Goldie bounded through.

As he walked back into the kitchen, Richard tripped on the step. He caught himself before he fell, landing against the door and giving a small cry as his back wrenched. It was still tender from the after-effects of his near miss on the M23. As he righted himself, Petal lunged past him. Richard swore, swung round and kicked the dog full in the ribs, flinging her back into the kitchen. Petal let out a yelp and then skittered back against the pine dresser, where she lay shaking with terror, panting in startled breaths, wide-eyed.

Richard leant against the doorpost, breathing more evenly. When he had recovered himself he went over to where Petal lay cowering and kneeled down beside her.

'Stupid old dog,' he murmured, his voice soft and coaxing. He raised the flat of his hand and stroked the dog's trembling side, feeling for where he had kicked her, shaking his head slightly from side to side. 'Stupid . . . old . . . dog . . .' His hand found the place. Petal whimpered. He stopped stroking.

Then he pressed – gently at first, then harder – until the dog let out a strangled, choking sound; a long, slow, inarticulate cry of bewilderment and pain.

4

*B*enny had followed the girl for two hours.

From Sutton Street she walked through Deptford to New Cross Gate, to a row of bus stops around which a disconsolate but mostly philosophical crowd was milling. She pushed through them and got on a bus. Benny could tell the bus was going nowhere and simply waited on the pavement, hidden amongst a crowd of macs and denim jackets and duffle coats. Being small had its advantages – and being dark. The one thing about London that Benny appreciated was that it was impossible to stand out in a crowd. Eventually, the girl got off again and joined the others. Benny watched her from behind the safety of a woman's bulky shoulder. The girl stood glancing around, rolling her eyes and pulling faces, then extracted a sweet from her pocket, popped it into her mouth and worked it round her cheeks, peering down the road to see what was happening and tapping her foot to keep warm. A few feet away from the crowd, a smartly dressed woman in her middle years was haranguing a lamp-post.

'Think yer big, don't you?' she was calling up at it, pointing with a raised bony finger, 'yer big bastard, think yer big.'

Eventually, the girl turned on her heel and began to walk. Benny followed. The girl kept her head bent, broke into a trot once in a while, then slowed down again. The wild wind seized her hair and wrapped it round her head like a bandage until she stopped, put down her bag and tied it back with a rubber band. Even then the wind pulled strands free which flapped upwards illogically, making her look like some small demon.

He lost her somewhere between Camberwell and Brixton. They were making their way down Coldharbour Lane, a long road full of crumbling terraces set back from the street, with stone steps and railings leading up to doorways or down to basement flats with iron bars over the windows. Many of the houses were boarded up, the windows blinded eyes of brick. One of them had been occupied by squatters who had hung bright banners from the first floor. Another had a damp, yawning Rottweiler chained to the railings, unenthusiastically guarding an open front door.

They came to a row of shops: newsagent, butcher, junk shop. Helly paused to tie back her hair again and Benny stopped and looked in the butcher's window. Apart from a plastic tub of mince, the only product was an obscenely long protrusion of bone and bloodied gristle which lay diagonally in a metal tray: *Frozen cow's tail, 75p/lb*. Benny shook his head in disbelief. In his country, poor people had some dignity. When he looked up again, Helly had gone.

He stepped out into the road and peered ahead. She

was nowhere in sight. Even if she had broken into a run, she couldn't have reached the curve in the road.

The junk shop had windows filled with rusting gas cookers. In front, on the pavement, was an assortment of seventies furniture, wood veneered tables and chairs with orange plastic seats from which fleshy yellow foam protruded. Just beyond it, Benny could now see an entrance.

The alleyway was long and gloomy, then broadened out at the end into the white light of a street. Dustbins and doorways lined either side and in the doorways lay bundles. The girl was already half-way down. He began to follow, but cautiously. If she turned round now he would be spotted.

Then, suddenly, two things happened at once. Benny had the sensation of treading on something small and unyielding, and there came the loud hollow yelping of an animal in pain. He jumped back. As he did, a brown shape at his feet metamorphosed into a skinny snarling dog – muzzle black, eyeballs huge and shiny, lips drawn back over tiny pointy teeth. The dog performed a neat frantic circle, then sank its teeth into a filthy grey coat which lay on the floor beside it. The filthy grey coat leapt to its feet. Underneath it was a man with wild brown hair and a sand-filled beard.

'Spot!' the man screamed in fury.

Benny withdrew swiftly behind the safety of a bin.

'What did you do that for?' the man hollered at the dog. 'Spot!' Then he began to beat the dog with the flat of his hand.

The noise roused the other bundles which lay in other

doorways. Several grey coats sat up, scratched their heads and began calling out to know what the hell was going on. Two more dogs started to bark. Benny stepped out from behind the bin and sidled swiftly down the alley.

The commotion was still going on as he reached the street. He scanned both ways, but the girl had disappeared.

As she neared home, Helly's feet slowed down. She had decided not to go to work about an hour previously, as she had been walking through Peckham. It was already mid-morning. The storm was still raging. No one was going anywhere. As she neared Stockwell, she realised she didn't want to go home either. Her mother would be there.

The wind had dropped slightly. She was walking down a deserted street which the storm seemed to have passed by. Small sturdy trees lined the road on either side. On her left were white-painted terraces with stripped wooden doors and coloured blinds. As she passed one, opera could be heard playing from the basement. Next to it was a Montesorri nursery. On the other side of the street there was the solid dark brick of a council block. London in microcosm. All at once, she felt unutterably depressed. She stopped and sighed. If only it wasn't so cold, then she could go up to Brockwell Park and walk around, or just walk around anywhere. There weren't even any decent cafés in Stockwell, none in which she could sit without being stared at by groups of wet-lipped men sucking roll-ups.

She paused for a moment, then turned and took a side-road that would lead up to Vauxhall. She wasn't going home or to work. She was going to go to the only place which was warm and free and quiet.

She had been going to the Tate for years. To start off with it was just somewhere out of the wind. Then, it was a place to hide. Nobody she knew would go to the Tate. It was anonymous and, at the same time, cosy. All the other people in that building, they had chosen to go there too. Even though she never spoke to any of them or even liked the look of them, these strangers and her had something in common. They all wanted to be inside.

At the entrance she handed over her bag to be searched by the security guard. It was quiet and he was bored so he took his time, rummaging around through her woollen gloves, make-up bag, box of mini-tampons, cigarettes. The inside of her bag was filthy. A biro at the bottom had leaked and blue ink was seeping through a seam. There was no Semtex but there was a label which said, *Luxury leather imitation, Made in Taiwan.* She sometimes felt as though that was the real purpose of the search, as if the guard might look up, shake his head sadly and inform her she was barred until she could afford a better handbag.

Inside, she took a left turn and trotted down the stairs to the toilets. To the right was the coffee shop. She paused and glanced through the glass door. It was almost empty. A small scattering of people sat at wooden tables punctuated by shiny dark green plants in terracotta pots. At one there was a fair-haired woman with a forkful of cake held carefully in front of her face. She was looking down at her Tate plan which was spread out next to her plate. With her free hand, she was pushing and pulling at a baby buggy next to her. The toddler in it was asleep.

At a table nearby, two young men in suede jackets were smoking and talking quietly, gesturing lightly with their hands. That is what being educated means, Helly thought. Talking quietly. Quiet talk has no real function, like taking a long bath.

She wandered over to the entrance arch and looked at the menu in its glass case on a stand. Blackcurrant and almond tart sounded nice: one pound eighty. Coffee was ninety-five pence. That was what having money meant: wandering into an art gallery café to have tart and coffee, sitting at a table on your own for as long as you liked without being bothered. For a man, money meant you could go to nice places. For a woman, money meant you could go to places where you would be left alone. It's all for sale, Helly thought: warmth, blackcurrant tart, personal safety, peace. It's all on the market. Every day of my life I will be reminded that I don't have the money to buy it, but it will never go away.

The woman rocking the buggy looked up, her forkful of cake still suspended, and glanced at Helly. She put down her fork quickly. A poor kid, thought Helly, that's what I look like. She was not intimidated by class. She knew what people thought of her and didn't care. Fuck 'em. She never tried to smarten up her accent – on the contrary, she put it on. Sometimes, she would work her mouth while she talked, as if she was chewing gum, because she knew it annoyed people. She would lounge against bus stops with her arms folded, glaring at passing drivers who looked her

117

way. You want Cheap Slut, her gaze would say? Fine, you've got it. I can do that one in spades. Eat your heart out, Pig.

The toddler in the buggy had woken and begun to grizzle. The woman bent to lift it out. As she did, a curtain of straight fair hair fell forward over her face. Rather you than me love, Helly thought. Why did upper class women always have straight hair? How boring could you get? She turned away to the Ladies. Thank God pissing was free.

Upstairs, she went straight to room seventeen, to make sure her favourite painting was still there. It would probably be coming down soon. She had bought Bob and Joanna a print of *Cossacks*. It wasn't really their kind of thing but that somehow didn't matter. She just wanted them to have it. She had laughed when she found out they had hung it in Nan Hawthorne's room. What on earth did the old lady think when she woke up each day and saw all those mad coloured swirls? Like the tube map gone bananas. She probably thought she was going sane. With any luck, Helly had mused, it will give the old bint a coronary, then I can have her room. If Kandinsky didn't do the trick, maybe she would try a Surrealist.

After the cold wind outside, the rooms felt light and warm. Helly wandered round for half an hour, looking up at the vaulted ceilings from time to time, loving the space and air, listening to the soft echoes of footsteps and murmuring voices. Room twenty-three contained *Abstraction, 1945–65*. She paused in front of a picture called *North Sound*. The plaque next to it told her, *Hoyland's paintings have proclaimed their self-sufficiency*

118

as visual facts or events. While she had been in the Ladies, she had peered at herself in the mirror and seen what the wind had done to her hair. She stood back from the painting. I am pretty abstract, she thought. Some people might think I'm a bit on the scruffy side, but I'm just proclaiming my self-sufficiency as a visual fact or event. Then she went to the shop.

Sometimes, she enjoyed the shop more than the gallery. It was easier, more concentrated. It could fit inside one glance – the rows and rows of great works of art all reduced to postcards, like a universe shrunk down to a rug. She could spend hours flicking through the racks of posters, listening to the metallic clicking of the frames, losing herself in each picture one by one, the slow fall of an individual world as she passed on to the next. Her room at home was full of rolled up posters representing the different phases she had been through. She had catalogued by subject matter rather than artist or movement. Landscapes, for instance, were gathered together in a small forest next to her stereo. A couple of ballerinas were stashed under the bed. She was a bit embarrassed about the ballerinas now. They had been purchased in the early stages, when she was thirteen or fourteen. These days, she wasn't into people.

Today, she went over to a pile of glossy hardback books in a carefully arranged pyramid by the entrance; the latest arrivals. She scanned it quickly, then picked up the largest – at last, something new on German Expressionism. She glanced around. An assistant was lounging behind a nearby till, picking at her fingernails.

There were only two other customers. It was too quiet. She would have to come back when the shop was more busy and nick it then.

At work the following day, nobody referred to Helly's absence. The office was agog with tales of the storm. She grew sick of hearing about greenhouses that had taken wing and flying garden gnomes. She didn't seem to have missed much work. Joan told her that Richard had sent everyone home early.

The next day was Friday. After lunch, she returned to her desk to find a pale yellow form lying on it. She picked it up, scanned it and then took it round to where Joan and Annette sat. Annette was nowhere in sight. Joan had her handbag on the desk in front of her and was counting out ten pound notes, folding them neatly one by one and placing them in the back of her purse.

'What's this?' Helly asked, proferring Joan the form.

Joan took it from her. 'It's a leave form,' she said, handing it back. 'Haven't you taken any holiday yet?'

'No,' said Helly, 'and I'm not planning to either.'

'It's for Wednesday,' said Annette, as she swept round the corner. She was holding a cup of tea. She swung herself into her chair and took a sip from it. Her face was slightly flushed and she was wearing a soft silk blouse with full sleeves that fluttered like butterfly's wings. She seemed unusually bright and cheery. She put down her tea and looked up. 'You've got to take a day's leave for not coming in.'

'I told you,' said Helly. 'I couldn't get in. No buses.'

'The rest of us made it,' Annette replied.

'Bollocks.'

Annette sighed. 'You didn't even ring in.' She turned to her computer.

Helly continued. 'Only half the surveyors came in, Joan told me. And Richard didn't get in till lunchtime. I don't suppose anyone is making him take half a day, are they? And you all went home at three.'

Annette began to type, speaking as she did. 'What those people who made it did is nothing to do with it. You didn't turn up and you weren't sick, so you take a day's leave.'

Helly stood glaring. She pursed her lips. She drew a breath. Then, slowly, she tore the leave form into two, screwed it up for good measure, went over to the bin by Annette's desk and dropped it in.

Annette looked up and met her gaze. 'Fine,' she said. 'Do what you like. I'll let Personnel know and they'll dock your salary.'

'Do what the fuck you want,' said Helly as she turned and went back to her desk.

After she had gone, Annette and Joan looked at each other.

'Oh dear,' said Joan.

'It's not my fault. Richard told me specifically this morning, anyone who didn't come in was to take a day's leave. It's not my fault.'

'What about the surveyors?' asked Joan.

'I don't know about them,' Annette retorted. It would be up to Richard to tell the surveyors to come to her for leave forms. It wasn't anything to do with her. The surveyors weren't her responsibility. She lowered her head and continued to type.

Joan shook her head. She hated arguments, even when she was only an innocent bystander. Arguments made her want to put the kettle on or tell a joke – or suggest they all discussed the weather. She folded the last tenner, placed her purse back in her handbag and put the handbag underneath her desk, just by her feet.

The incident with Helly preyed on Annette's mind. She knew she had been in the right but at the same time she knew how she must have appeared – the school marm, the office harridan, a dried up old boot. She wouldn't have bothered with the leave form but Richard had insisted. He was a stickler for all that stuff. And now she was going to be responsible for Helly losing a day's pay. She would have been horrified if something like that had happened to her. She budgeted each month down to the last penny: mortgage, standing orders, insurance, savings account. She was not well off but she managed, and she always knew exactly where she stood. No treats, no disasters – that was how she handled her own finances. An unexpected loss or gain would be equally disturbing. It was so important to be organised about these things.

But how else to handle it, she thought as she sat on her train going home that evening. Richard would have only told her to dock Helly's pay anyway.

She had come back from lunch with a head full of William and their kiss in the lift, feeling like somebody light and graceful. In the pub, she had gone to the Ladies just to look at herself in the mirror, to glance at the peculiar beauty she knew she would see. Her spat with Helly had put an end to all that. She felt heavy and responsible and old. Rationalising usually helped, but not this evening. Perhaps she was just tired. Perhaps Helly would get over it soon and not hate her after all. Perhaps, Annette thought, I could just go to sleep tonight and never wake up, then I wouldn't have to think about any of this any more.

She stared at her own reflection in the train's grimy window, the thin translucent picture of her features over the passing landscape of suburban London: factories, office blocks, building sites – wastelands. Her watery face passed over them all, each image sliding through the dark of her eyes.

It was Friday night and she was babysitting for Sarah and Jason. They lived in Lewisham, in a basement flat filled with toys belonging to their ten-month-old daughter, Dawn. Dawn was a placid, cheerful baby, large for her age, who could already crawl and stagger and wave her clammy fist in an entertaining variety of gestures. She loved Annette.

Sarah and Annette called themselves best friends. They had been secretaries together during Annette's first job, at an engineering firm in Beckenham. The job had been awful – the people they worked with even worse. Annette and Sarah had bonded. They went out to the pub together after work and talked about the rest of the staff. They took up smoking. Then together they gave it up. Annette was with Sarah when she met Jason, in a wine bar in Forest

Hill. When she and Jason split up, Sarah spent the night at Annette's house and cried until four in the morning. Annette was the first to know when, three weeks later, Jason proposed. At their wedding, Annette had been the maid of honour, resplendent in peach-coloured satin and holding a bouquet of floppy sweet peas. Her main task had been to look after a host of tiny bridesmaids, also in peach, who spent the day losing their tiny gloves and tiny handbags and tiny shoes. Sarah's gown was raw silk, off-white, and appeared to be built up in a profusion of frills and layers. Annette cooed and aahed along with the best of them, although her candid opinion was that her friend looked like a meringue.

Not long after the wedding, Annette went to work for the Capital Transport Authority and, six months later, Sarah moved to an estate agent's. They still saw each other regularly. Sometimes Annette went over to dinner and the three of them played cards until late. She never felt the odd one out. She got the vague impression that maybe Jason did. At the same time, she began to realise that she and Sarah had little in common. They had become friends because they had even less in common with the people around them. Sarah seemed not to realise this and still confided in her, still rang Annette when she and Jason fought, still begged her to come with them when they went out to wine bars or parties.

Their relationship reached a nadir when they went through a phase of introducing Annette to Jason's friends. It happened so often that Annette began to suspect they were working their way through his address book, one by one.

'There's someone else coming, by the way,' Sarah would say to Annette, over the phone. 'Timothy. Nice bloke. Friend of Jason's.'

Annette's heart would sink. She would imagine Jason saying over the phone to Timothy, 'There's someone else coming, by the way. Annette. Nice girl. Friend of Sarah's.' Timothy's heart would be sinking. Often, when she actually met Timothy (or David, or Rakesh, or Paul) they would turn out to be perfectly presentable. Friendly. Moderately interesting. Nice blokes. They would shake hands or smile at her and their eyes would meet. A moment of mutual understanding would pass between them. *No, I don't fancy you either but we might as well be pleasant to each other, to humour Jason and Sarah.*

The phase passed with the arrival of Dawn, as Jason and Sarah realised that single women friends were actually rather useful. Annette forgave their unthinking change of heart, just as she forgave their tactless jokes about maiden aunts and sell-by dates. She settled for the comfortable knowledge that she and this family would know each other for the rest of their lives and their relationship would always be a gentle cosy mixture of fondness and exasperation.

For some reason, Jason and Sarah's baby daughter fell madly in love with Annette. It was not reciprocated. Annette found babies sweet but liked to hand them back when they got sticky. Dawn was stickier than most. She grabbed at Annette's hair or earrings with plump, jammy fingers, making a sort of low throaty sound which, had it come from a corpse in a thriller novel, would have been called a death rattle. She was slow to pick up full words and for many months the death rattle was all her parents got. When she eventually said, 'Tur-tur,' Sarah and Jason went into paroxysms.

'Oh *darling!*' shrieked Sarah, pushing past Annette to grab her infant daughter and sweep her up into her arms. 'You said *turtle*. Aren't you *clever!*'

Annette sat on the carpet while Sarah and Jason whirled their daughter round the room. She was holding the green and yellow plastic turtle in her hands. She turned it over. It was a bulbous little creature, with a sadistic grin and wheels where it should have feet. Dawn had begun to cry.

Sarah later confided that Jason had been a little upset that his daughter had given her first word to Annette. Jason loved Dawn with the fierce, illogical passion of a man experiencing an emotion of which he has previously believed himself incapable.

Annette got off the train at Lewisham and went straight round to Sarah and Jason's flat. She let herself in with her own key. They were going out at seven, for dinner with Jason's parents, but would have bought her a microwave meal and bottle of wine to have with it. In the living room the television was on and the carpet scarcely visible for toys. Annette picked her way through a menagerie of rubber hedgehogs and purple plastic dolphins. She sat down in an armchair, picked up the remote control and flicked over to the news. Jason and Sarah were running round the flat in a frenzy. Once in a while, they passed the living room door and called out to her.

'The number's in the book,' called Jason.

'Go to sleep if you want,' cried Sarah.

Annette said yes she knew, and yes she would.

She did. She ate the microwave meal, she drank the wine, and a Clint Eastwood film finished her off. She was slumbering in the armchair with the television still churning softly when Sarah came into the room.

'Hi . . .' Sarah whispered. 'How was it?'

'Fine,' Annette murmured, pushing her hair back from her face. Her neck was stiff. 'What time is it? How was dinner?'

Sarah pulled a face. 'Gone twelve. Jason's checking Dawn. Let's sneak out and take you home.'

Ah, thought Annette, another row. When the evening had gone well, Sarah and Jason would come in together. Annette would turn off the telly and they would all drink beer. If Sarah wanted them to sneak out it meant she had some complaining to do.

In Sarah's Mini, on the way to Catford, Sarah began to cry. She kept her hands tightly on the wheel and looked straight ahead, sniffing and snuffling. In the darkness, Annette could see the tears streaming down her cheeks. 'I'm sick of it,' she sobbed. 'I don't know what I'm supposed to do. I've done everything I can. I thought this was all sorted out before Christmas but now it turns out he still expects me to make allowances. It's so unfair. My parents are in Wales, for God's sake. *He* doesn't have to make allowances . . .' Once in a while, Annette prompted her gently with questions. 'So what did he say then?' or, 'What do you think she meant?'

As they turned the corner into Annette's cul-de-sac, Sarah, still sobbing, said, 'It's such a nightmare, this whole bloody thing of being married. You don't know how lucky you are. You don't know how jealous I am.'

Annette felt suddenly cold. She had always known that Sarah was jealous of her; that came as no surprise. But all at once she thought of William. William – was his marriage a nightmare? Had he been out to dinner with his in-laws that night? Had he and his wife argued in the car coming home? At the thought of the word, *wife*, a jolt of pain went through her, as real and as physical as if someone sitting crouched in her stomach had poked her with a knitting needle. William did not just exist in the lift of the Capital Transport Authority. He had a context, a whole world that she knew nothing about, was not a part of. Nothing. She was a moment, that was all. She had no idea how he felt about her.

Sarah was still talking as she parked the car. 'Do you know what my first thought was in the hospital when they gave her to me?' she was saying. 'Thirty-six hours in labour, and they gave me this red-blue screamy thing with a pointy head. And do you know what my first thought was? I looked at her and thought, so you're what's put me through this . . .'

She pulled a man-size tissue from the box that sat beside her and blew her nose noisily. Then she said, 'Are you coming bowling on Thursday?'

One of the neighbours had organised a trip. Annette knew most of the group who would be going: Sarah and Jason, Winston and Paulette – maybe Paulette's step-sister

Jayne, who was a social worker. They were always good for a laugh.

'Yes, probably.'

'Okay, I'll ring,' Sarah said, wiping make-up from underneath her eyes.

Annette got out of the car. As she turned and waved goodbye, Sarah blew her nose again and gave a bleak little smile.

Annette let herself in, pushing at the front door because a clothing catalogue had been dropped through the letterbox and was in the way. She picked it up and closed the door behind her. In the darkness she could see the two tiny red rectangles on her answer machine: no messages. She flicked on the light and then went to close the curtains. The central heating had not come on – the thermostat was on the blink. Her house was cold.

The phone rang at five o'clock the following day, Saturday afternoon. Annette was expecting her mother to call. She picked it up and said hello in the tense, friendly way in which she always said hello to her mother.

'Annette? It's William.'

Annette's stomach folded in on itself.

'Listen, I've only got ten pence. Can you ring me back?' He reeled off the number.

She didn't even hear the phone ring at the other end before he answered, 'Hi.' In the background, there was traffic. The phone made the regular peep-peep noise that public call-boxes made on incoming calls.

'How are you?' Peep-peep.

'Fine. How are you?'

'Fine.' Peep-peep. 'Listen, I'm sorry, you're probably busy,' Peep-peep. 'But are you doing anything tomorrow afternoon? Are you going out to lunch or anything? I don't know what you do.' Peep-peep.

Annette kept her tone casual. 'Nothing special, no, nothing really.'

'It's just could I come round. Oh God.' In the background a dog had started barking. The peep-peep sound chimed in with its high-pitched little yap. 'There's a dog!'

'What?' shouted Annette. She could hardly hear William above the racket. She had automatically raised her own voice, as if that would help.

'Dog. Outside. Waiting to make a call.'

'What?' Peep-peep.

'No, the owner, not the dog,' William started to laugh. 'Look, about half past one. Can I come over?'

'Yes.'

'Is that okay?' Peep-peep.

'Yes . . . yes . . .'

'Okay.' The dog was going frantic. 'See you then.' He rang off.

Annette put down the phone. She sat down on her sofa in her suddenly silent house and wrapped her arms around herself. She smiled a very large smile.

William waved off Alison from the doorstep. His final image was of his son's face watching him out of the back windscreen, white and cheery, his little hand flapping. As

130

soon as they were round the corner, he sprinted upstairs to take a shower.

Bowling down the A21 to Catford, he began to worry. What on earth had Annette made of his call? He hadn't made it clear whether he was expecting lunch or not. He hadn't made anything clear.

In less than an hour, everything was clear. In less than an hour, he and Annette – having skipped the preliminaries of eating or drinking – were in each other's arms on Annette's sofa. William was leaning up against the corner, two cushions supporting his back. Annette half leant against him. His arms were round her from behind and her head lay back against his shoulder. They were talking quietly. He was moving one hand up and down her left forearm, very slowly, while her hand rested on his thigh. He had an erection like a rock.

'I had a navy blue blazer and a grey pleated skirt,' Annette said. 'They tried to introduce straw boaters in the summer term but they never really took off.'

'Sounds posh.'

'It was. My parents paid for me. I was the only one in our road. I hated it. Walking home each day I used to go past a row of kids from our estate – the local comp got let out half an hour earlier than us. They used to sit on the low wall outside the dental surgery and throw stones at me. They never threw very hard. I think they were just bored.'

'So how come you ended up at the Capital Transport Authority?'

Annette laughed. 'Thanks.'

'I didn't mean it like that.'

She turned in his arms and smiled up at him, a wry smile. 'Yes you did,' she said. 'You meant, how come I'm only a secretary if I went to a posh school?' She pushed herself up and kissed him lightly on the lips. Then she turned back to her original position. He could not see her face. 'The thing about being a secretary is,' she said, 'it makes things so straightforward. People ask you what you do and you say I'm a secretary and people say oh, and that's it. End of conversation. They think they know then. And actually, you've told them nothing, nothing about yourself at all. It's like saying I have fair hair or brown eyes, less even.'

William was frowning and thinking, that doesn't answer the question.

'My parents had high hopes, I suppose,' Annette continued. 'My mother sometimes says at least my father died at the right moment.' She paused. Her voice was still light. 'Downward curve, I guess. Row of As at O level, then English, Geography and Maths A levels; A,B,C, the kind of result you can sing. I didn't even apply to college or anything. I didn't want to read anything any more. I wanted to be out there; the real world.'

'Okay,' William said carefully, 'that's the version that goes on your CV. Now let's have the real one.' He wanted to know. He wanted to know what had turned a clever young girl in a grey pleated skirt into this careful woman.

She turned again and pulled herself up until her face was very close to his. 'Hey,' she said softly. 'What is this?' She smiled. Then she brought her mouth onto his. First, there was the soft plump dryness of it. Then, as their lips parted, there was the wetness of her tongue as it moved against his, the grazing sensation as the differing textures of their mouths met; the mingling until – very soon – they tasted the same.

William moved so that he could wrap his arm round her. The vestige of a question was still in his head. She had told him that her first job in Beckenham had lasted five years. She had been at the CTA for two. What had she done between the ages of eighteen and twenty-four?

She lifted her mouth away from his and laid her cool smooth cheek against his rough warm one. 'I don't want to talk,' she said, the words slurred.

He slid a hand underneath her jumper and began to pull her top gently up through the waistband of her skirt. 'Is it okay?' he whispered.

She looked at him and raised a hand to stroke his face, her eyes wide with amusement at his question. 'Yes.'

As he drove home, William rehearsed his story. When Alison got back from lunch with her Aunt Willie and Uncle George, she would be tired and bad-tempered. Paul would be over-excited. Alison would be happy as long as he took Paul off her hands and let her sit down and read the paper. She probably wouldn't ask what he had been doing, so there would be no need to explain that he had driven all the way to the new DIY centre at Surrey Docks only to find he had left his credit cards at home, so he hadn't been able to buy that shelving for Paul's room that she had been on at him to get for weeks.

'What do you mean, you've lost it?' Alun Hardy did not look up from his Weetabix. His wife was standing in the kitchen door.

'Oh Alun, what do you think I mean?' Joan turned away, back to the handbag which was sitting on the telephone table in the hall. 'What do you think I mean?' she muttered again, into the bag, but quietly this time because she had begun to cry and she didn't want Alun to notice. If he saw her crying he would start to realise it was serious.

She opened her purse again. It was useless going through the bag. She had gone to the building society in her lunch hour at work the previous day, Friday. Then she had folded up the sixty pounds and put it in the back of her purse, the way she always did. Now it was gone: sixty pounds. The weekend was ruined. She opened her passbook again, just to check. Yes, she had taken out sixty. She looked through the crevices of the bag, her make-up pouch. I knew it, she thought furiously, the day of the storm. I knew that bad things were going to start happening, that it was all going to blow up in our faces. It started yesterday, when Helly and Annette had that row. That was just the beginning. Now this.

Oh pull yourself together Joan, she thought, taking a neatly folded tissue from the purse and wiping her cheeks. Silly to cry over money. Where on earth could it have gone? She had folded it up and put it in her purse. Helly and Annette had watched her do it.

When she broke the news to him, Alun agreed that it was silly to cry over money. He thought it more sensible

134

to shout. He thought it particularly sensible to shout, repeatedly, 'In heaven's name, woman, how could you? How could you just *lose* sixty pounds! Nobody *loses* sixty pounds. How could you?'

Eventually, she put on her coat and told him she was going up the Walworth Road. If she got a move on she could get to the building society before it closed. She was going to withdraw another sixty pounds and carry on with the rest of the weekend as normal. The missing sixty could be sorted out on Monday. She refused to spend the entire weekend discussing it.

This solution did not please Alun. The money was gone and sixty pounds was a lot to lose. It had been in Joan's care and was now no longer in her possession. If she was capable of losing the sixty pounds she got out on Friday what made her think she could hang on to the same amount the following day?

'I have to go to the chemist, dear,' she responded, gritting her teeth but keeping her tone meek. 'And we need some frozen puff pastry for tomorrow, and I want to look at swimsuits.'

Alun raised his eyes heavenwards. We've just lost sixty quid and the woman wants to buy a swimsuit, his look said.

Oh say it, Joan thought in response. If you don't want me to buy a bleeding swimsuit then say so. But Alun would never say. Joan did all the cooking and cleaning and brought in a third of the household budget. She sent Christmas cards to their friends and visited Alun's father at the old people's home. In addition, she had to interpret his extensive vocabulary of glares, scowls and sighs and behave accordingly. Alun could shout, but only to express rage. The words he shouted never contained any information, they were just noise. He might as well shout their telephone number or postcode.

She wrapped a tartan woollen scarf around her neck and fumbled in her pockets for her mittens. 'I shan't be long,' she said in a conciliatory tone.

As she walked down Denmark Hill she thought, I'm going to pay for this. Boy am I going to pay.

Camberwell was in Saturday mode. Bert the flower-seller had set up his stall at the entrance to the alley next to KwikSave. He stood in his flat cap and overcoat between buckets of red tulips, blue iris and white carnations, the usual small globule of snot hanging perilously from the end of his nose. She usually stopped for a chat with him but he had two customers waiting, so she waved as she went past. She would get some daffodils on the way home, perhaps, at the risk of angering Alun even more. 'The main thing is that they last,' Bert always said as he wrapped them in tough pink paper and handed them over. 'That's the main thing. As long as they last.' They never did. Bert's flowers were cheap old rubbish and dead before the end of the weekend. On the other side of the road, outside the post office, a young man with a microphone was informing passing shoppers that God was great. If He is so great, Joan thought grumpily, then he can find my sixty quid.

At Camberwell Green she caught the 68. It was crowded. A young woman next to her had two small children on her lap. A collapsible double buggy lay across the luggage hold. Next to it were four carrier bags, bulging misshapenly with groceries. One of the children was making a thin moany noise, like a small mammal caught in a trap.

The bus ground slowly through the weekend traffic. Joan sat staring straight ahead. Half-way up the road, she suddenly became aware that there was some commotion at the front of the bus. They were waiting at a stop and eight or ten passengers were climbing on board. A group of old ladies had paid for their tickets and were muttering to each other as they came down the aisle. 'He didn't stop,' one was saying excitedly to another, 'he didn't stop.' Two settled in the seat behind Joan and craned their necks to look out of the window to the right. Joan was sitting nearest the aisle. The woman with the children had got off and another old lady pushed past Joan to take the window seat. Then she sat looking out at the road, like her companions.

The bus began to move. After a few yards it slowed down to edge past some sort of blockage in the road ahead. 'Look, look,' said the old lady sitting next to Joan, although Joan was not sure who she was addressing. As the bus became stationary, Joan saw an ambulance parked on the other side of the road. Its back doors were open and she caught a glimpse of bedding and equipment. Next to the doors were two paramedics in green uniforms. One of them was kneeling down next to a tiny, splayed figure which lay in the road.

The child was three, four perhaps, and dressed in blue jeans and a red anorak. Joan could not tell what gender it was because it was lying face upwards with its head covered by a large wad of bandage dressing. One of the paramedics was kneeling beside it and holding the dressing in place. The dressing was soaked in blood.

'It was a silver car,' the old woman next to Joan said, her face still glued to the window, 'a big silver car. It didn't even stop.'

Standing in the road next to the child was a woman of about twenty. She was wearing pale jeans and high heels and had untidy blonde hair. The other paramedic had his arm around her shoulders. She was bending slightly and reaching one arm out towards her son or daughter, as though she wanted to help but did not dare. Her other hand was over her mouth. The paramedic was holding her tightly.

On the opposite pavement a group of people had gathered, standing staring, silent and still.

As the bus pulled away, the old lady leant backwards so that she could see the spectacle for as long as possible. When it was out of sight, she turned to her companions who were sitting behind Joan and said, 'Isn't it awful? Awful, awful . . .' They all shook their heads.

Joan thought of the huge solid power of a car. Then she thought of the soft flesh of a young child, the silky vulnerability of skin. What chance did the eggshell skull of a toddler stand against implacable, speeding metal? She felt sick. Next to her, the old ladies gossiped and crooned.

She got off the bus at the building society and then went to Marks & Spencer where she wandered aimlessly around a small selection of swimwear. She had lost heart for the purchase but bought a black and gold contraption with a ruched effect around the neckline. She wanted to go home, but there was still the puff pastry. She wanted Alun to be nice to her. She was prepared to give in, do or say anything, if only he would be kind. Perhaps if they had not argued and she had not come out at that particular time, the accident would not have happened. If she had not seen it, it would not have occurred.

By Sunday lunchtime, a sullen silence had descended.

Joan could cope with many forms of marital warfare but not silence. Alun could raise his voice. He could throw a mug of tea at her (he had done that once, but only once). He could walk out and slam the door. To each of these she was prepared to weep then shrug, feeling herself to be no more than a part of that vast community of wives whose husbands shouted or slammed doors. Silence, however, was Alun's ultimate weapon; his nuclear capability. They had never discussed it (how could you discuss silence?) but he knew she hated it and she knew he knew. For the rest of the weekend they occupied the same house, often the same room, and Alun serenely read the papers or ate or watched television, all with a wordless demeanour which was tantamount to placing her in a straitjacket, blindfolded and gagged. Joan sat opposite him, trying not to think about the child whose death their row had caused, up to her ears in Alun's corpse-like fury and her own dumb guilt. The atmosphere was so thick she could hardly breathe. It was as thick as pea soup.

On Sunday evening, Alun went out to do his shift. When she heard the door shut behind him, she sank into her armchair in the corner of the sitting room and began to cry. She cried for the child and for the young mother's innocence, for the sixty pounds that had been lost or stolen – for everything that was gone and would never return. She cried for herself.

On Monday, she was questioned closely by Annette. Yes, she was sure the handbag had been at her feet the whole of the afternoon. No she had not, at any time, left it open on her desk. Joan quelled her irritation. Annette just wanted to get the story straight, that was all.

'We'll have to tell Richard,' she said eventually. 'If you're sure. We'll have to make it official.'

Joan sighed. 'Is that really necessary?'

There was a pause. Annette knew what Joan was asking. There was an obvious candidate for culprit. Once the theft was reported, the matter was out of their hands. 'I think so,' she said. 'If we don't do something then things could get difficult. I don't think we should try and handle it by ourselves. There's everyone else who works in this building to consider after all, it's not just us.'

After Annette had gone in to Richard's office, Joan sat at her desk with her head in her hands. Everything was horrible. Everything.

'Cheer up Joan!' said Helly as she swept past, twenty-five minutes late for work and not at all bothered.

Joan sat up quickly. Helly had gone straight past her, to the coffee machine. She had promised Annette she would not mention the theft to anybody else. She had to pull herself together. She sat up and reached for the pile of correspondence sitting on her desk, waiting to be opened and stamped. It was as bad as being at home with Alun. She couldn't say anything to anyone. Now she would have to be pleasant to someone she liked whom she had just accused of theft – as good as – and who might be completely innocent. Nobody liked Helly much. She would probably be sacked. Office juniors were ten a penny.

'Office juniors are ten a penny, so he says,' Annette shrugged. 'It's not a very nice way of putting it but it's true.'

'Oh dear,' said Joan.

It was lunchtime before Annette had taken Joan on one side to tell her what Richard had said. It had been a busy morning and Helly had been around.

'Listen, don't feel bad, it's not just this.' Annette took a sip from her coffee. 'Richard said there are other things. Even if this wasn't her, there's things that have been building up for a while. I'm not supposed to say.'

'He's probably just saying that to make me feel better,' said Joan.

Annette shook her head. 'He had a word with me a couple of weeks ago. Personnel have told him something about her that he can't tell us. Really. It's not your fault.'

'So what's going to happen?'

Annette shrugged. 'Nothing, immediately. He's got to clear it quietly with Personnel. He'll probably have a word with Marjorie. She can sort out the paperwork. Officially Helly will resign, as far as all that is concerned – in a fortnight or so.'

'I think it's awful. We have to carry on talking to her even though we know she's going to get the sack. It's awful.'

'It's not your fault,' Annette repeated. 'And Richard said he would much rather you got your money back quickly and quietly than have a whole great rigmarole. It's much better for her this way too; she's lucky Richard's handling it so discreetly. If it went upstairs they'd get the police in, and it would all be much more serious. She should be glad.'

Joan looked down into her tea. It was very pale and milky and almost cold. 'I still think it's awful.'

Richard's coffee was hot, black and very strong. Marjorie knew just how to make it. He was sitting on the edge of her desk, in the personnel department. It was the lunch hour and the office was quiet.

He and Marjorie had known each other for some years now. She was a neighbour's sister-in-law. Richard had helped her get her job at the CTA. She owed him one.

Marjorie was explaining to Richard how bored she was with life. As she did, she rubbed the side of her neck with her left hand, leaning back in her seat and looking up at Richard, sleepy-eyed. Marjorie was thirty-eight years old and married to a man who bought her garden centre vouchers for her birthday. She had very fine brown hair that lay in a flat sheen across her head and flopped down onto her shoulders. She was the only woman Richard knew who still wore false eyelashes – a walking museum piece.

'Now Marge,' Richard was saying to her. 'I know you're having me on. I don't believe all this nothing to do at weekends. I know what you're up to. Soon as your old man's asleep, you shin down the drainpipe in a leather mini-skirt and head for the nearest nightspot. I know you. I bet you drive them wild.'

Marjorie reached out her hand and cuffed Richard's arm. 'Oh Richard!'

Richard leant towards her across the desk. 'You can't fool me, you little hussy,' he said softly.

Marjorie glanced from side to side. 'Really . . .' she murmured, fiddling with a tiny gold lizard which hung on a fine gold chain around her neck. 'Honestly . . .'

Richard sat back and took a sip from his coffee, surreptitiously glancing at the clock above Marjorie's head. Another ten minutes of chatting her up, that should lay the groundwork. Some women would do anything if you flirted with them. Silly bitch.

It took slightly longer than ten minutes, nearer twenty in fact. Marjorie was subtle but voracious. When other members of staff started drifting back from lunch, Richard said goodbye and headed for the lift. Before pressing the button, he paused. He could go down to Finance on the ground floor and have a chat with Dave, or he could go back upstairs. He pressed the up button.

The lift was just about to pass. Almost straightaway, there was a whoosh and clunk as it came to a halt and the doors jolted back. It was empty except for a small figure in one corner.

Richard stepped inside. The doors slid shut behind him.

The lift was very narrow. It carried a maximum of four people and even that was something of a squeeze. Its walls were lined from top to bottom with dark mirrors which made skin look greyish. There was a large round bulb set in the ceiling which cast pale light down in an indistinct beam.

As Richard stepped in Helly stood up straight, looking up at him. He met her gaze, blankly.

Helly looked to one side. The mirrored walls reflected a dozen other Richards standing in the lift, inches away. They were all looking at something small tucked away in the corner.

The lift moved slowly and smoothly upwards. Richard did not speak or move. He stayed facing her, staring calmly, his back to the door. Helly bit at her lower lip and kept her face turned to one side, refusing to look up at him.

The lift reached the second floor and jolted to a halt. The doors slid open.

Richard turned and left.

When Helly came back from lunch, Joan could not meet her gaze. She could not escape the feeling that she had something to feel guilty about, however much she reasoned with herself. Helly seemed unusually quiet. Perhaps she is feeling guilty too, Joan thought. The thought made her feel a little better.

It was mid-way through the afternoon when Helly came round the corner and gestured at Joan's filing tray. 'Are we going to give it a go then?' Monday afternoon was filing time, the sorting out of the previous week's chaos before that week's had a chance to build up. At the end of each day the surveyors would drop copies of their correspondence into the red plastic tray on Joan's desk. By Monday afternoons, the pile had usually started to slither.

Joan and Helly had developed a routine. The huge grey multi-filing unit was behind Joan's desk. Helly would sit cross-legged or kneel in front of it, while Joan would spread the filing over her desk and hand pieces to her one by one. The sites were filed according to the alphabetical order of the tube station to which they were nearest. Rosewood Cottage, for instance, was filed not under R for Rosewood or S for Sutton Street or even C for Cottage. It was filed under N, for New Cross.

The office was quiet. Annette had gone to spend the afternoon at the Perfect Secretary exhibition at Earl's Court. The boys were out on site. Richard had been in his office all afternoon with the door closed.

They filed in near silence for almost an hour. Then Joan handed over a memo Raymond had sent to all the security supervisors concerning general site access. Contractors who wished to use the CTA's toilet facilities must always sign in before doing so. Helly shook her head.

'What the hell do we do with this?'

Joan shrugged. 'Oh stick it under Miscellaneous, love.'

Helly turned to the cabinet and kneeled up to 'M'. Then she stopped. 'Which Miscellaneous?'

Joan frowned. 'How many have we got?'

Helly pushed her fingers between the files. 'Miscellaneous Arches, Miscellaneous Offices, Miscellaneous Residential and Miscellaneous Sports Grounds.'

'Isn't there a Miscellaneous Miscellaneous?'

Helly shook her head.

'Oh well,' Joan said, 'we'd better open one up.'

Helly began to laugh. Then she began to cry.

Joan was silent. Helly sat back on her heels. Tears rolled down her cheeks in rivulets, as if a year's worth of crying had suddenly spilled over. Her shoulders shuddered. Every now and then, she gave a small gulp.

When Joan deemed the moment right, she reached into her skirt pocket and handed over a lilac coloured tissue, neatly folded. Helly took it, nodding her thanks, and blew her nose.

Raymond's memo had fluttered to the floor. Joan picked it up. 'A bit soggy for its own file,' she said. She turned it over. Then she crumpled it into a ball and tossed it into a nearby bin. 'There. That's filed that eh?'

Helly smiled damply. 'Sorry Joan,' she said, small-voiced.

'That's alright, love. I've always hated filing too.'

Helly smiled again. She drew the tissue underneath her eyes and then looked at it. Mascara and eye-liner had appeared in dark smears. 'Oh God,' she said. 'Is my face red?'

'Beetroot,' Joan replied.

Helly lowered her hands to her lap and bowed her head. She twisted the tissue round her fingers.

Then, Joan said very gently, 'Look love, is there anything you'd like to tell me about?'

Helly looked up. Joan smiled. 'I'm not daft you know, though most people round here treat me as if I am. If you don't want to tell me that's fine. But I don't mind.' She must know what I'm talking about Joan thought, unless there's something else as well. 'Are you in any bother?'

'Joan . . .' Helly said.

'Never underestimate the old ones,' Joan said, getting to her feet. 'Now you stay there while I make a cup of tea.'

When Joan got back, Helly was sitting on her chair. She had wiped her face and was peering at herself in the dark screen of Joan's computer. Joan sat down in the spare chair next to her desk and put down the tea.

'What have you got in the M&S bag?' Helly asked. Next to Joan's desk was a bulging green plastic bag.

Joan looked at Helly, then said, 'Swimsuit. I worked the lunch hour so I'm off early and I'm going to take it up to Marble Arch. I got it Saturday at the little branch on the Walworth Road. They didn't have my proper size and it's not really the type I'm after.'

Helly took her tea. 'What type are you after?'

'One I can get these knockers of mine into. Now what about you?'

Helly put her tea down. 'I think I'll go to the loo and have a fag.' She paused, then said briskly, 'Thanks Joan.' She turned and went to her desk for her cigarettes and lighter.

Joan stayed sitting where she was and looked at Helly's steaming cup of tea. She shook her head.

Night was falling over Rosewood Cottage. Under the framed print of Kandinsky's *Cossacks*, Helly's great-grandmother Mrs Hawthorne slept, and dribbled. Joanna Appleton sat beside her.

When Joanna was sure her mother was asleep, she rose softly and crept out of the room. It had taken over an hour. The old lady kept drifting off then waking again, muttering madly through her gums, something about a man watching the house, out there in the dark, waiting for the chance to get in. She had seen him from the window, she claimed. Joanna was sceptical. Her mother hadn't looked out of the window for years.

When she had closed the door to her mother's room, Joanna tiptoed carefully to the room next door which she shared with Bob. Without putting on the light, she went over to the window. She parted the curtain and peered out. It was almost dark. A solitary street-light cast a pale pool. Beside it, the rubbish skip glowed yellow. The railway arches opposite the cottage were dark open bottomless mouths.

Joanna shivered. There was nothing out there.

The old bat gets more barmy by the day, she thought. Gives me the creeps.

5

On the footbridge at Hither Green station, Annette hesitated. It had just been announced that the eight eighteen to Charing Cross was running four minutes late. The eight seventeen to Cannon Street was about to pull in on Platform 3 but if she got that she would have to change at London Bridge. She was one of a group of twenty or so commuters on the bridge, hovering uncertainly, looking down the line. As the eight seventeen became visible in the distance, most of them broke off and began to clatter down the steps. She watched them as they trotted down to the far end of the platform, where the train would be least crowded. It was a Wednesday. She was tired. She didn't feel like changing at London Bridge. She wanted to get a seat and stay in it all the way to Charing Cross. She wandered along the bridge to Platform 1, to wait for the late-running eight eighteen.

When it arrived, it was more empty than usual; most of the regular passengers had been sucked in like plankton by the previous train. She found a corner seat in an end carriage and slumped into it, her handbag on her lap. She carried a paperback novel each day but rarely opened it.

Reading made her feel dizzy and sick but she didn't like to be without something in case the train got stuck somewhere (she always urinated just before she left the house for the same reason and carried mints in case she had a coughing fit). The woman sitting opposite Annette was reading. She caught a glimpse of the title, *Living God*, black letters on a bright yellow background. The woman was wearing black patent shoes with thin straps and buckles. Underneath them, she had white cotton socks. Her feet looked like little hooves. A red mac was belted loosely around her small frame. Her face was shiny. How, thought Annette with some distaste, can any woman get to the age of thirty and not have discovered translucent powder?

She was staring out of the window as the train pulled into New Cross and it was then that she saw Helly, smoking fiercely, her bag slung over her shoulder. As the train pulled to a halt, she dropped her cigarette onto the platform and opened the door to the carriage in front of Annette's. I didn't know she lived out this way, thought Annette. She would have to wait a while at Charing Cross, to let Helly get ahead of her. They still weren't speaking to each other after their argument over the leave form. It was the week after Annette had reported the theft of Joan's money to Richard. She was expecting to turn up any day and find that Helly had gone. The last thing she wanted was to bump into her on the way to work.

The carriage filled up. A business couple in identical beige macs squeezed in next to the *Living God* woman and sat in silence, staring straight ahead, holding hands.

As the train began to lurch forward, Annette saw that

someone had tied an orange balloon to the New Cross sign at the end of the platform. It had a grinning stick-on mouth, a stick-on nose and one, off-centre, stick-on eye. It was caught in the train's slipstream as they passed and fluttered madly, banging against the post, its open mouth an obscene chortle – as if it knew something they didn't.

They pulled in to London Bridge. The man from the business couple kissed his wife lightly on the mouth and got off the train. The *Living God* woman continued to read. A few other passengers got on. The eight seventeen pulled in next to them at an adjoining platform, a minute later than them after all. Annette congratulated herself on having made the right decision as she had hovered on the bridge at Hither Green.

They sat.

Then, from somewhere towards the front of the train, there was a bang.

The sound was unmistakable. Annette knew the quality of it from the explosion she had heard at work some weeks ago. It was not the volume of the noise that made it so distinctive – although it was very loud – it was the density. There was no echo, no reverberation. The entire compass of the sound had been compressed down into one short, omnipotent blast.

The passengers sat in the carriage, frozen with doubt. Nobody met anybody else's gaze, although they all glanced around. Annette fought a battle of logic with herself. It was a bomb. A bomb had gone off inside the station. It could not be a bomb. This was a Wednesday morning and she was on her way to work. She was a secretary for the

151

Capital Transport Authority: slogan, *Organising Transport All Over The Capital*. It could not have been a bomb.

The door to their carriage opened and the man who had just left got back in. His wife looked up at him. He sat down next to her. Then he said simply, 'I think there's been a bomb.' They took each other's hand and sat as they had before, staring straight ahead.

Now that the knowledge of what they had heard had been articulated, the passengers started to shift in their seats, look at each other, shrug. Outside the train, Annette could see other passengers standing on the platform, bemused.

Then a voice came over the tannoy, speaking in the same flat nasal tones that habitually announced a platform alteration or a delay in the Maidstone service. 'This is a message to all passengers. We are evacuating this station. Please leave in an orderly fashion by your nearest exit. We are evacuating this station.'

The familiarity of the announcer's voice seemed reassuring to some of the passengers. They got to their feet, picking up cases and coats, muttering. The *Living God* woman, who had sat frozen up until then, closed her book and rolled her eyes.

The announcement was continuing as Annette stepped down from the train. 'We are evacuating this station . . .' She looked around. She was at the far end of the platform, furthest from the exit. To leave, she would have to walk towards the blast. She joined the crowd of commuters making its way slowly down the platform. Nobody spoke; all were orderly and silent. Then the tone of the announcer's

152

voice altered to something slightly more imperious. 'Please leave by the nearest exit. Do not cross over to platforms 3 and 4. Repeat, do not go near Platforms 3 and 4. Leave by the nearest exit.'

We *are* on Platform 4, Annette thought, as she continued to walk. This is really happening, and we are walking towards whatever it is that has really happened. She glanced around. If any of the other passengers shared her thoughts they showed no sign. Instead, they all continued their ghost-like, silent walk. The bodies around her seemed to be moving slightly up and down with each step. After the density of the blast, the collective clatter of their footsteps sounded muted. Already Annette was thinking, this is what will haunt me, this walk. We are all so slow and steady and quiet. Our pace is regular. We do not speak. Nobody is crying. We are walking towards what has happened. The air in her throat felt trapped. 'We are evacuating this station. Do not cross over to Platforms 3 or 4. Please leave by the nearest exit.' We are walking towards what has happened.

As they neared the stairs that led up to the exit, Annette saw a man collapsed next to a telephone stand. He was in a slumped position. A briefcase, umbrella and newspaper were scattered nearby. He was sitting turned away from Annette but his breathing was audibly laboured. Three people crouched round him, one with an arm around his shoulders.

Then she saw that walking alongside, to her right, was a tall young man in a navy blue suit with an older man beside him who had a hand on his arm and was talking quietly. The young man was nodding. He did not appear to be in any way distressed or in pain; they might have been discussing that morning's meeting. The young man had blood trickling from his left ear.

Just beyond the stairs, from the corner of her vision, she could see someone lying on the platform, with two people gathered round. She kept her gaze straight ahead, mounting the stairs briskly.

As they spilled out onto the station concourse, her group dissolved and mingled with the hundreds of people coming up from other platforms. The announcer continued to intone his directions. Still, there was no panic. As Annette reached the entrance, the first emergency services were beginning to arrive. An ambulance swung silently into the station and pulled to a halt. No sirens, Annette thought. Even the ambulance is calm. Two policemen ran past her.

Outside the station she hesitated. To her right, passengers were pouring down into the Underground, like vermin. She could not believe that any of them were capable of boarding another train. Anyway, the mainline stations and their adjoining tubes would be closed down soon. She wandered out of the station.

On the bridge, commuters rushed past. Two police vehicles came charging over from north of the river, sirens wailing. Other traffic continued. She gazed at it, bemused. Beyond the trafffic was London, a vast ignorant world which did not know what had happened; a world in which people were, bizarrely, continuing their normal lives. She wanted to stop a passer-by and say, do you not realise how oddly you are behaving? Something has happened. A thing that always happens to other people somewhere else is happening here, now. It has happened to me. Her legs buckled. She felt a concrete paving slab strike her knees.

She kneeled on the pavement for several moments, trying to breathe, trying to make her arms and legs regain their normal strength instead of the jelly-like uselessness they had suddenly acquired. The word *shock* came into her head clearly and distinctly. She imagined that she was standing next to herself, looking down and saying, *you are in shock*.

Then she felt a hand on her shoulder. 'Annette,' a voice said.

She looked up. Helly was standing above her, leaning slightly. Her hair was hanging forward on one side of her face, which seemed in shadow. She looked expressionless. The air behind her was white. There were acres of space above.

'Annette,' she said again. 'It's me, Helly. I was on the station. You've collapsed. You're in shock.'

Annette shook her head. Her mouth would not work. I know, she thought, I know I'm in shock.

'Here.' Helly pushed her lightly on her shoulder and made her sit back on the pavement. Then she put her hand on the back of her head and pushed it gently forward. 'Put your head between your knees. Breathe a bit. Just relax.'

Annette felt the rough cotton of her coat graze her cheeks. The enclosure of the material around her face was comforting.

'Does she need an ambulance?' She could hear a deep male voice beside them.

'Nah, don't think so,' Helly was saying. 'Thanks all the same. Thanks.'

Footsteps moved on.

Then, Annette felt Helly leave her side and call out loudly, 'Here! Here, over here!' Helly returned. 'You got money on you?' she asked.

Annette lifted her head. She frowned.

'Oh never mind, you'll have a chequebook indoors. Listen, be careful.' Annette became aware that Helly was lifting her by her arm and that a man was at her other arm, helping.

'She won't be sick will she darling?' the man was saying to Helly.

'I'll tell you to stop if she's going to be,' Helly was replying. As they walked her gently across the pavement she said, 'Annette, listen. It's Helly. Where do you live, just the area for now. Tell me where.'

'Catford,' said Annette.

Helly and the taxi driver helped her into the cab. As the driver got back into his seat Helly said to him, 'Not too fast.' Then she turned to Annette and said, 'Here, lie down.' She swung herself onto the pull-down seat which had its back to the driver. Then she took off her coat, a long tweedy jacket several sizes too big for her. 'Lie down,' she repeated. As Annette lay down, Helly placed the coat over her and said, 'Don't think about anything. Just lie there.'

The taxi driver had slid back the plastic partition. 'What's up?' he called back to Helly as he drove.

'Bomb,' Helly said. 'In the station.'

The driver shook his head. 'Rotten bastards.' He leant forward and turned on the radio. The sports news was on. He turned it down and sat back. 'Friend of yours?' he asked, jerking his head back towards Annette.

'Not exactly,' Helly replied. 'Can I smoke?'

By the time they reached Catford Annette was sitting up, Helly's coat still over her knees. She felt comfortable. She did not want to speak or move. She did not want the taxi to stop.

At Rushey Green she said to Helly, 'Next left, after the petrol station.'

Helly tapped on the driver's partition. As he pushed it back, the sound of his radio became audible. 'Next left, after the petrol station,' said Helly. A news summary was in progress; initial reports suggested two dead, forty injured, three critical. As they swung into her quiet cul-de-sac, Annette rummaged in her handbag and handed Helly her purse.

The driver pulled up, leapt out with the engine still running and opened the door for them. He helped them both out. Helly paid. As she counted out two notes, the news announcer was saying, 'No terrorist group has as yet claimed responsibility, but police sources are already saying that the attack bears all the hallmarks of the provisional IRA.'

The taxi driver nodded towards the radio as he handed over their change. 'Bright lot, our coppers,' he said. Then

157

he leapt back into his cab and swung round in a neat circle, pulling away.

As the clutter of his engine faded, Helly turned to see that Annette was standing with her back to her, a few yards off. She was being sick, carefully, into a grey wheely bin which stood amongst several bins opposite the houses. On the side of the bin were the white painted numbers 1 and 6.

Helly lit a cigarette and waited.

As Annette walked back to her, she nodded at the purse Helly was still holding. 'Key's in there,' she said. 'Number sixteen.'

Helly let them in. Annette went straight over to the sofa and sank onto it. She dropped her handbag to the floor. Helly closed the door behind her. 'Loo upstairs?' she asked. Annette nodded.

When Helly came down, she went straight over to the kitchenette and plugged in the kettle. 'Neat place,' she said. 'One up, one down. Not much of a home but a great love-nest. You on your own?' Annette nodded slowly. 'Lots of natural light,' Helly said appreciatively. She was opening and closing cupboard doors as she spoke, looking for mugs. 'Quite well-designed when you think how small it is – that big skylight up there, above the bed – but with the gallery you get the light down here as well.' She poured boiling water into a cup. 'I'm not too keen on modern housing myself but I can see why you bought it. Clean. Nothing needs doing.'

She came over to the sofa holding a red mug. 'Here.'

As she was walking back to the kitchenette, Annette took a sip of tea and grimaced. 'I don't take sugar,' she said softly.

'You do today,' Helly replied, without turning back. She made herself an instant coffee, then came and sat down on a round wicker chair opposite the sofa. 'This is nice as well,' she said. 'But you could do with some cushions. And pictures. Very bare.'

They drank their drinks in silence.

Eventually, Annette said, 'Do you want to use the phone?'

'Work?' said Helly. 'They'll know why we aren't in won't they? You could ring them later I suppose.'

'I was thinking more of home,' Annette said. 'Isn't there someone who'll be worried?'

Helly shrugged. Then a small smile twitched across her face. 'Are you going to tell me to take a day's leave for this as well?'

Annette smiled wanly – only her mouth moved. 'I don't think even I would be that much of a cow.'

Helly raised her eyebrows and smiled in similar fashion. 'Oh, I don't know.'

Annette put her mug down. Helly got to her feet. 'Well, I suppose I should be off.'

'Sit down a minute,' Annette replied, standing up and going over to the stairs. 'I've got to brush my teeth. I want to explain about all that.'

When Annette came back down, Helly was making herself another coffee. 'Want more tea?' she asked.

Annette shook her head as she walked slowly back

over to the sofa. 'No thanks, the last one was disgusting.'

'Got any biscuits?'

'Sorry. Marmite.'

Helly pulled a face.

When they were both settled again, Annette said, 'I wasn't just being an old cow about that, you know. Richard had been very specific. I don't know why. He's tightening up on all sorts of things lately. I flew off the handle a bit, but he would have told me to dock your pay anyway.'

Helly did not reply. Then she said, 'The surveyors?'

Annette shrugged. 'Is that relevant?'

Helly got to her feet. She went over to the patio doors which looked out over Annette's tiny square garden, an evenly mown postage stamp of grass. There was no border. The wooden fencing surrounding it was very low and she could see over the side into the adjoining postage stamp. Annette's neighbours had erected a plastic line where washing flapped lazily: two blue shirts, a sheet, a row of nappies. Beyond it could be seen the backs of neighbouring houses. In one of them, a sleeping Alsatian was sprawled in a wire cage. In another, a child's tricycle lay on its side. Over all lay the stillness of a weekday suburb.

Helly turned and leant back against the window frame, cradling her mug of coffee. She looked down into it, then back up. 'Funny, isn't it?' she said. 'Two people died, just a few yards away. It could've been us. Dead easy.' Annette did not reply. 'You know Richard's bent, don't you?' Helly said.

Annette frowned. 'What do you mean?'

'You know, bent. Crooked. Skimming the cream off the top.'

'He's not. Really? Backhanders and so on?'

Helly nodded.

'How do you know?'

'Remember that time you sent me to Victoria? Raymond had forgotten his bleeper and was going to be in Chiswick all day. He rang up from South Ken, nearly having a cow. He was expecting that architect to ring back and confirm something or other and you had to be able to get hold of him. He came back on the District line and I had to meet him at the barrier and hand the bleeper over. Stupid git didn't even say thank you. Just made me toss it over and then ran for it as if the place was on fire. Self-important arsehole.

'As I was coming out of the tube, I went to get an apricot croissant from that place near Platform 5. It was ten o'clock, I was bleeding starving. Anyway, as I'm turning away, I thought I'll go for a little walk up the plaza, eat my croissant, no hurry to get back – you know how it is when you get let out unexpectedly. As I'm going past the payphones tucked round the corner, who should I see but Richard, making a call from a public phone on his way to work. Ten in the morning.' She paused to sip from her coffee.

'Is that it?' said Annette.

Helly sighed. 'Listen will you? At the time I thought oh, that's odd, and then I didn't think anything more. Except later that day he was running round in a big state saying where was his jacket? Do you remember? He'd had a meeting upstairs and left it and they got Karen to come down; meanwhile he'd gone back up. I thought blimey, two people having a cow in one day. Two cows. I don't know where you were but anyway you weren't around, so I took it off her. As I did, this notebook falls out. Well, it didn't exactly fall out, it was sort of poking out the inside pocket, so I had a little look through it, as you do.

'In the front was a list of the main contractors and their phone numbers, with ticks next to their names, some with three ticks, some four. A couple with asterisks. Then inside, there's a page for every job Richard's been in charge of going way back, and lists of numbers, all in pencil. At the bottom, he's put a contractor's name and a question mark. Then after that, pound signs. Next to one he's written a list of things, conservatory, wooden floor tiles, garden shed . . . It looked like nothing much. Towards the end there were some notes on the Ealing refurb job, remember that? Went to Robinson's eventually, twenty-four grand.'

Annette frowned. Helly looked at her.

'When did that job go out?' she said impatiently.

'Oh I can't remember,' said Annette. 'End of November?'

'December second,' Helly continued. 'The tenders had to be back by the eighteenth. I checked.'

'So?'

'So Richard has a note in his little book of who is going to get the job, and how much, a clear month before the bids come in. What is he, psychic or something?'

Annette got to her feet. She picked up her red mug

from where it sat on the carpet and took it into the kitchenette. She filled it with water from the tap and put it down to stand in the washing up bowl. Then she poured herself a glass of water from the nearby filter jug.

'How could he be taking bribes without upstairs knowing? That's what the tender envelopes are for.'

'It's easy. Dead easy. Even I could do it. You have to have at least three companies tendering for any contract over ten thousand, right? The bids come in sealed tenders. Except Richard has the keys to the stationery cupboard, so he has his own supply of envelopes in case he needs to check a tender and then re-seal it. Either that or he has someone inside a company who tips him off what they're going to bid. Then he tells the other company to bid under.'

'Do you think it's a ring?'

Helly shrugged. 'Might be. Or maybe it's just one bloke on Richard's payroll in two of the companies and the boss of the one who's funding the whole thing.' She gave a small smile. 'I think I'm a fucking genius.'

Annette went back to the sofa. 'Have you got any proof of all this? Are you going to report it or what?'

Helly's smile disappeared. She drained her coffee cup and took it over to the sink, placing it next to Annette's. She paused; turned away. When she turned back, her voice had taken on a guarded tone. 'I shouldn't really have gone into all that. You're probably not even interested. Anyway I could have got it all wrong couldn't I? Look, I'd better go now. Are you going to ring the office and straighten things out?'

163

'Yes, of course. Helly . . .' Annette paused. They were both standing in the kitchenette. Annette glanced out of the window, then back. 'Do you notice everything that goes on, I mean . . .'

Helly opened her mouth and tipped her head back, giving a small hoot. 'You mean have I noticed you and William are knocking each other off?' She shook her head from side to side. 'Course I bleeding well have. I'd have to be a complete berk not to notice that one.'

Annette glared at her in alarm. 'How did you know? Does everybody else?'

'Everybody else did before you, probably.' Helly rolled her eyes. 'Look, you two were all chummy and flirty from the minute he arrived. Pretending to have little bust-ups about typing. Then all at once, it stops. One day you both come in and you are suddenly *very* polite to each other. Couldn't be more proper. It's a dead give-away. Nobody flirts in public once they've actually started *doing* it.'

Annette sighed. She lifted her hands, then dropped them again. Eventually, she began to smile. Then they both smiled.

Helly looked at her watch. 'Listen, I'd love to stay and get the details but I'd better push off.'

'Are you sure? How will you get home?'

'I'll go and see my gran. They don't normally listen to the news but you never know. I can get a 36 on Rushey Green can't I?'

Annette nodded. 'If you're sure. Or anything going into Lewisham. Helly.' They paused at the door. 'Thanks for bringing me home. Considering we don't really get on, it was nice.'

She shrugged. 'Beats going into work.'

Annette opened the door, then watched as Helly walked away down the cul-de-sac and turned into the main road. She closed the door and went over to the window. She lifted a hand to her mouth and bit lightly at a finger. It's obvious, she thought. It really is that obvious. William won't like that much. The thought sobered her. She could have asked Helly about Joan's purse, but that would have meant warning her that Richard was going to get her sacked and she clearly didn't have an inkling about that. She turned on the tap and reached for the washing-up liquid, to wash their cups. She thought about what Helly had said about Richard. She wondered if any of it was true.

When she had finished the cups she went back to the sofa and sat down. She put her face in her hands and rubbed up and down, suddenly overcome with a wave of deep, chilling exhaustion. Then she stood up and went over to the phone.

Her mother's number was engaged. She was probably ringing all the emergency numbers to see if Annette was among the casualties. She would be doing that even if the bomb had gone off in Watford.

While she waited for her mother's line to become available, she listened to the radio reports. The two dead were a woman in her thirties – married, two children – and a younger woman believed to be in her early twenties. Helly was right, Annette thought, it could have been us. Their names had not yet been released. Relatives had yet to be informed.

William had been on a visit to Baker Street station that morning. He had to be there at eight o'clock to meet the station supervisor and an engineer, so he had caught an early train. The first he knew of the bombing was mid-morning, as he was sitting in the supervisor's office having a cup of tea. The supervisor, a thin man with pale eyes, was taking a phone call. 'You'll be alright getting back now,' he said as he put the phone down. 'Victoria's open again.'

'Alert?' William asked.

'Nah, they closed all the mainline stations down because of the bomb at London Bridge.'

William finished his tea and left.

When he got back to the office, he found Joan sitting in solitary splendour, tapping carefully at her computer. He ran a hand through his hair and gave a little laugh. 'Morning Joan, morning.'

'Dreadful, isn't it?' said Joan, without looking up from her keyboard. 'Two people. A woman with two little girls as well. Dreadful.'

'Where is everybody?' he said lightly.

Joan looked up. 'Oh, you've only just got in. That's right, you've been at Baker Street. Richard was asking and I couldn't remember. You forgot to put it in your diary. He gets a bit cross when you do that, you know. You should watch it.'

William persisted. 'You're the only one here then?'

'Raymond's in. A lot of people got held up. And we won't be seeing Helly or Annette. They were ever so close you know. It must have been awful. I said to Annette she should have gone to hospital.' William sat down on a nearby chair, while Joan continued. 'She and Helly were on the train. They saw some of the people that were hurt. They got outside the station and Annette went into shock. Helly had to take her home. I don't think she'll be in tomorrow. I told her she should take the rest of the week off. That kind of thing really throws you even if nothing has happened.'

William got to his feet.

'There's two messages on your desk,' said Joan. 'One from Jefferson in Commercial, about the Grantham House Survey of Dilapidations. He said it's urgent. I don't know who the other one was.'

At his desk, William pulled up the two yellow notelets and re-stuck them on an envelope lying in his in-tray. He rested his elbows on his desk and put one hand over his mouth. Annette had been on that train.

He dialled her number. The line was engaged.

He sat for a moment, thinking. Then he rang home.

He and Alison discussed the bombing for a few moments, then he suggested that, as there was bound to be chaos on the trains that evening, he thought he might work late to let things calm down a bit before he tried to get home. Alison was less than pleased. That evening was her French class and they had an agreement that Wednesday evenings were sacred. Other nights, they could negotiate. Wednesdays were supposed to be hers.

Distraught at the thought of not seeing Annette

simply because he was married with a child, William had an uncharacteristic fit of sarcasm. 'Well I'm sorry, dear,' he said, with a slight emphasis on the dear, 'but it's hardly my fault if the IRA is renewing its mainland campaign. What do you expect me to do, come up with a Northern Ireland peace initiative?'

There was a pause. 'William,' Alison said gently, 'I think that's a pretty poor taste remark in view of the fact that there are two people who aren't going to get home at all tonight.' She hung up.

I hate her, William thought. She has a mind like a computer. She's like a wasp. She always goes straight for the main point. Supercilious cow. She has to be right about everything. The whole of her life, she's never put a foot wrong. He rang Annette.

'Hello?' Her voice sounded soft and distant. He was overwhelmed with warmth and tenderness. She was usually so efficient, so in control, and now she sounded like someone tiny, far away. His girl.

He wanted to come over, he told her, but he couldn't. He was so sorry. But if she was going to be at home for the rest of that week then he could make it tomorrow or Friday, during the day. 'Are you alright, my love?' he asked. My love. It was the first time he had used those words. They fitted.

As soon as William got to Charing Cross that evening, he realised that the disruption was so bad there was no way he would make it back home in time for Alison to leave for her class. He felt grim satisfaction. There was nothing he could do about it, and he had left work on time. Serve her right. He rang her from a call box and then joined the milling, stoical throng on the crowded concourse.

It was an hour before he was able to get on a train. Then it sat on the platform at Charing Cross for a further twenty minutes, followed by another half an hour at Waterloo East. As it pulled into London Bridge, the carriage fell silent.

The station had already re-opened. William was sitting next to the door and could see that wooden hoardings had been put up around the damaged platforms. The hoardings seemed so innocuous, the kind of thing he saw on building sites every day, yet behind them lay the site of the bombing, the spot where two women had died. Forensic experts would be hard at work. There would be a lot of cleaning up. The woman sitting opposite William was also gazing out of the window. She had tears in her eyes. A few silent, grim-faced passengers climbed on. The train waited.

Then, a young man in a business suit opened the door next to William and leapt on, slamming it shut. William looked up and saw that he was drunk. His face was red, his gingery-fair hair ruffled and unruly. His tie was loose around his neck and one of his shirt buttons was missing. As he stood above William, swaying slightly, his white shirt gaped.

There was no room for the young man to move further into the carriage. He was balancing unsteadily by holding on to the luggage rack above William's head as he looked around. His mouth was large and damp and his eyes very dark. He hung his head down briefly, then lifted it back up. He looked around again.

Then suddenly he called out, his booming young voice bouncing around the silent crowded carriage. 'Are there any fucking Irish here?'

The woman opposite William caught her breath. William sat very still. He could feel the pressure of the young drunk's leg against his knees. Nobody spoke. It was as if a temperature gauge in the carriage had been suddenly switched to zero.

'I *said*,' the young man bellowed, 'is there any Irish in this carriage? If there is, stand up, because I'm going to stick a knife in your face!'

The train lurched forward. The young man staggered slightly, bumping first against William, then against the woman sitting opposite. William looked at her. She had begun to cry with fear. She was blinking hard and biting her lower lip, trying to stop herself.

The train lurched again and then began to pull slowly out of the station.

'You Irish cunts!' the young man spat, as if he was addressing the carriage as a whole. 'I've just been to see my sister in hospital. My sister's lying in that hospital with fifteen fucking stitches in her face! You fucking Irish bastards!'

The woman opposite William had closed her eyes. Tears were streaming down her face. The young man standing between them was radiating hatred and violence in the same way that a burning torch would give out heat. William thought of Annette, shocked and frightened, alone

170

in her house in Catford. He thought of his son, Paul, and how smooth his skin was, how perfect the small features of his face. When Paul was concentrating on a drawing, the end of his tiny tongue would peek out from the corner of his mouth. Last weekend, he had been making orange coloured swirls on a piece of rough cream-coloured paper that Alison had given him.

'What is it?' William had asked, pointing at the picture.

Paul had looked up, his tongue still poking, and frowned. 'Crayon,' he had replied.

I want to be home, William thought. I want to be inside my own front door. I want it locked and bolted.

The young man had fallen into drunken, sullen silence, his head swaying from side to side as he looked round the carriage and his lips moving in a silent mutter. Still no one in the carriage spoke. The woman opposite had her face turned to the window and was gazing out at the dark, her eyes distant and vacant, still filled with tears.

For the rest of that day, Annette had the strange sensation of being underwater. Physically, she felt perfectly fit but the air around her seemed heavy. She moved carefully about her house. She turned her head slowly.

The feeling was still there when she rose the next morning. Outside, early spring sunshine had arrived ludicrously on her doorstep. She stood blinking at her kitchen window, drinking black tea, watching two sentinel yellow daffodils by the wheely bins, heads bobbing back and forth in the wind. Neighbours passed on their way to work. The postman came and went.

She did her weekend chores. She read a two-day-old *Evening Standard* from cover to cover. Each hour, on the hour, she turned on the radio and listened to the news bulletin. She had become addicted to it. The brother of the married woman who had been killed was on air saying that the lives of his entire family were ruined. The bomb had been planted in the ladies' toilet. A politician said that the men of violence deserved no mercy. The younger woman who had died had been changing trains at London Bridge, to go to Charing Cross. The previous day, she had celebrated her twenty-second birthday. Her boyfriend had bought her a furry giraffe. Another item included an interview with a psychologist who talked about post traumatic stress syndrome. Annette learnt that as she had not been in a prolonged situation of uncertainty or danger, she was unlikely to suffer from nightmares or flashbacks. It was possible, however, that she would spend the next month or so jumping at unexpected loud noises and swerving around litter bins.

In the summary that followed, the announcer added that the death toll following recent floods in Indonesia had now risen to three thousand five hundred.

Annette turned off the radio, lay down on her sofa and thought about William. She wanted him. She wanted him to buy her a furry giraffe. She wanted him to make the numbness go away.

He arrived on Friday morning with a bunch of orange lilies

172

and a tall glass vase. He handed them over awkwardly, while she smiled.

'I couldn't remember whether you had any vases,' he said. 'I couldn't remember seeing anything. I was in the shop and the vases were behind the woman's head on the counter and there were all these horrible pottery ones with flowers painted on them, which seemed a bit silly when you're going to put the real thing in them anyway. Don't you think?'

Annette laid the flowers in the sink. She held the glass vase up to the cold white sunshine that filtered through her window. 'It's beautiful,' she said. She put it down and kissed him.

When the flowers were arranged, she stood them on the counter where they could be seen from both the sitting room and the kitchenette, an ostentatious shock of orange in her plain beige house. She put her arms round William and said, 'You have brought colour.'

He moved his fingers through her hair, massaging the back of her head. 'Funny.' He kissed her. Then he put his arms around her and said, 'Safe.'

She held him. Then she said, 'I want to go upstairs.'

When William has an orgasm, Annette thought, he makes a sound like someone dying, a disbelieving sound.

Afterwards, they were hot. Annette threw back the duvet, pushed herself up from the bed and tiptoed naked to the skylight, her arms across her breasts. 'The heat rises in this house,' she said. 'It gets quite warm up here even when it's still cold downstairs. It's nice in the evenings, though.' She opened the skylight a crack, to let in the air. The small glimmer of sun had been covered by a thick blanket of cloud which was already beginning to darken. 'It's going to rain; a storm maybe,' Annette said as she went into the bathroom.

William pulled the duvet back up and lay on his back. Annette's sheets were a thick, crisp, lemon-coloured cotton, always spotlessly clean. The only items of furniture in her bedroom were a wooden wardrobe and a matching chest of drawers. On an unpainted shelf next to the bed there was a plain blue lamp. Through the bathroom door he could hear the small tinkling sound of urinating, then the noise of the flush and the tap running.

As she came back into the room, he lifted back the duvet for her to climb under and snuggle down, to get warm again. 'How long have you got?' she asked as they embraced.

'Ages,' he replied. 'I've got to go to the office this afternoon. Ages.'

They were quiet for a while, their cheeks pressed together. Outside, there was the gentle distant roar of an aeroplane passing overhead, its approach melting without pause into its departure. The neighbour's dog barked once, then was silent.

'What's she like?' Annette said. Her voice was quiet in the stillness. Neither of them moved. There was a pause.

'Physically, or do you mean character?' said William.

'Both.'

'Well . . . she's very short, with short hair. Pretty.

174

Very organised, I suppose. Dark hair, well not really dark, brown. Contact lenses, I don't know, what else?'

He shifted slightly in her arms. Annette could tell he was becoming uneasy. She regretted bringing it up but now she had, she knew she must see it through. She had to nudge him into saying something disloyal about his wife. He owed her that small victory.

'So what's she like?'

'Oh I don't know do I?' William drew back slightly. They looked at each other. He gave a half-smile, as if he had decided to get through this with an off-the-cuff remark. His expression was a little mean. 'She's the sort of woman who always has a tissue. Whatever the situation, you can guarantee she'll have a tissue.'

Annette returned his smile briefly, then pulled him back towards her so that he would not have the chance to examine her face. So am I, she thought. Oh God, so am I. Why couldn't William's wife be a sloven or a slut? Or just a party girl; that would have done. Loud-mouthed. Slightly fat. But no, she was a tidy, efficient young woman. She was a good mother. She rinsed the dishes. She always had a tissue. Like me, Annette thought, she is just like me. Then she corrected herself. No – *I am like her*.

William had done what she wanted but she still felt annoyed with him. So she said, quite brutally, 'Helly knows about us you know.'

He drew back again. She could tell that he was concerned but trying not to show it. 'You told her?' he asked, and his voice was careful.

'No. She guessed. She said it was blindingly obvious

– I had no idea – just from the way we were, then the way we changed. You wouldn't believe it, really. I don't suppose we're as clever as we think.'

William sighed. He rolled over onto his back and Annette turned and laid her head on his shoulder. 'Does that worry you?' she asked.

'Yes,' he said.

They fell quiet again. His honesty had made speech redundant. If he had tried to pretend he didn't care then she could have caused a scene. She could have asked if he was embarrassed about her and said, *What do you think it's like for me?* She suddenly smiled to herself. He hasn't done this before, she thought. He hasn't got the lines right yet. She was glad.

'Do you want to talk about it?' he asked reluctantly.

She was satisfied now. 'No, it's alright,' she said.

They lay, holding each other.

Gradually, the sky darkened. The clouds grew more dense. 'No curtain,' said William. 'Doesn't the light disturb you in the summer?'

'No I like it, look,' Annette replied, pointing up at the skylight. 'It's better than the telly.' She turned onto her back with William's arm still underneath her neck, so that they could lie side by side and watch. The clouds impacted together, rolling from white to grey. A breeze whisked underneath the skylight and rushed over to them before making a mad charge back out again. William shivered dramatically.

Annette giggled. 'Listen,' she said. 'Can you hear?' They listened. There was the distant meowing of a cat, cowering somewhere from the coming storm. 'It's next door's I think. It's really funny. Sometimes when the skylight is closed, it walks around my roof, over the window. I'm lying here and I might be thinking about something else, not really looking, then a bit of me thinks, that's weird, there's a cat walking across the sky.'

'Let's wait until it gets close,' said William, pulling his arm around Annette and snuggling up to her. 'Let's wait until it's on the bottom of the skylight, then we can sneak up and give the window a good yank.'

Annette spluttered. 'We'd send it into orbit.'

There was a scattering noise across the window. 'What's that?' William asked.

'Sycamore pods, from the trees,' Annette replied. 'The wind must be up.'

They heard a low distant grumble of thunder. The air in the room seemed tight. 'It's really building up for a big one,' William said.

Suddenly, a crash of lightning slashed open the air and filled the room with instantaneous, brilliant white light. The skylight banged open. They both jumped, grabbing at each other, and Annette gave a small yelp.

'God! God, that was close . . .' said William.

Annette jumped up and pushed the skylight shut, then leapt back onto the bed. Then they both sat, naked and clutching, and watched as the first few spots of rain on the window became a clattering deluge that danced against the glass.

'I love storms,' breathed Annette. William turned her

face with his hand. Their mouths met. They fell back onto the bed.

They kissed frantically for several minutes, then they lay and watched the rain. Annette's arms hung around William's neck. Once in a while, she kissed his shoulder. He stroked the inside of one of her elbows with a finger.

'When I was working at Hammersmith,' he said, 'there was a storm like this, one afternoon. Worse than this, not much rain but thunder and lightning. Amazing thing. Someone was nearly killed. It was a woman, one of the managers. She was sitting at her desk working when she decided to go and get a coffee. While she was out of her office, a bolt of lightning came through the window, the sixth floor I think. It melted the legs of her chair onto the floor and blew up the computer on her desk. Just imagine –'

'Really?'

'It was in the papers. Just imagine. If she hadn't gone for the coffee . . .'

'You know what that's like?' said Annette. 'It's like a god saying, watch it. Don't you think?' William shifted slightly. Annette pulled her arm out from underneath his head and they re-adjusted to a more comfortable position. 'It's like him saying, okay, I've let you off this time, but I can get you any time I like. In the office. At home. Anywhere I want. All I have to do is this. So watch it.'

William did not reply immediately. The silence was serious. We are both thinking about London Bridge, William thought, but neither of us wants to bring it up. We want to be alone together. He said, 'Yes.'

Suddenly, Annette rolled on top of him, grinning. She picked up his left arm and held it above his head. 'No one can get you though, William Bennett, because I've got you first.'

He brought his other arm around her neck and held her tightly. 'Help,' he said. 'Someone help.'

They held each other very hard and kissed, very softly.

As their mouths parted, he buried his lips against her left ear. 'Annette . . .' he whispered into it, and the words tickled. 'I love you Annette.'

Richard was the sort of man who liked to reward loyalty. Annette had always been a good secretary, although a little straight-laced. Ideally, he would have liked somebody slightly more flirtatious, someone who met his guests at the lift and flattered them as she walked them down to his office. But she had a good telephone manner and, most importantly, was both unsuspicious and trustworthy. These, he knew, were assets. There was plenty of the other sort.

He spoke to her at home the day after the bombing and told her to take the rest of the week as sick leave. He would get a temp in for Friday. After he put down the phone he went round to Joan and gave her a pound. 'Send Annette a card,' he said.

'Oh, that's a nice idea,' said Joan, looking at the pound.

'Can you ring Susan from the agency?' Richard said. 'I want someone for Friday. They've got to have audio.

179

Make sure it's not that mad Australian they sent when Annette had the flu.'

It was a mad New Zealander instead. Tara typed at ninety words a minute and talked at roughly twice that rate: simultaneously. While she whizzed her way through a pile of specifications she told Joan about her fiancé Adam, their flat in Dalston, her mother's sleepwalking problem and his father's kleptomania. Occasionally Joan said, 'Yes' or, 'Really?' By lunchtime, she had a headache.

Joan liked Antipodeans. They worked harder than British temps and didn't smoke. What she didn't like was the way their voices went up at the end of half their sentences as if they were always asking questions.

'It caused a real problem when she was younger?' Tara was saying. 'She used to walk around the house at night? One night, she goes downstairs and Grandma wakes up and there's a smell of burning? Grandma goes down to the kitchen? There's Ma, apparently, standing in the kitchen drinking a glass of milk in her nightie, still fast asleep, and there's smoke coming out of the oven?'

'Really?'

'Uh-huh,' Tara said, nodding. 'She was baking the budgie.'

Helly came round the corner and dropped a pile of papers on Joan's desk. Helly liked having temps in. It was the only time she was not the most junior member of staff. 'If Tara finishes those specs maybe she could do some filing,' she said to Joan.

Joan looked up, trying to manage a frown to indicate

that she disapproved of this kind of one-upmanship. Helly winked.

Tara was saying, 'Of course my fiancé reckons we should have an orchard instead of a sheep farm? Then we could call it Adam's Apples.'

As Helly turned away, Joan said, 'William was looking for you a minute ago.'

'I thought he was at Fairlop.'

'He's just got back.'

Helly wandered down the office. One of the other surveyors was celebrating a birthday and his desk was decorated with cards and balloons, but because it was early Friday afternoon, nobody was around.

She sat on William's chair. On his desk was a memo from Jefferson Worth in Commercial. She glanced at it: *As a result of our client's structural difficulties, it is essential that this Survey of Dilapidations is carried out as soon as possible. May I suggest . . .* Ah well, Helly thought, perhaps there are worse things than being the office dogsbody. At least I don't have to read that kind of shit.

'Helly?'

William was standing next to her.

'Yeah?' she asked.

He sat down on the edge of his desk and scratched his ear. He seemed ill at ease. 'Annette told me about you getting her home on Wednesday. She said you were really good, looked after her.'

Helly smiled. I bet that's not all she told you, she thought.

William smiled back. 'I just wanted to say thank you and, well, thanks.'

Helly picked up a pencil from William's desk and began to play with it, tapping it against the edge of the desk and leaning back in his seat. 'William . . .'

'Mmm?'

She tossed the pencil back onto the desk, grinning. 'Look, you don't need to worry. I know how to keep my gob shut. Nobody's talking about you two. It isn't common knowledge.'

William pulled a face, not unlike a Father Christmas with an empty sack. Her directness was clearly not his style. 'Oh, well that's nice to know. I suppose. Thanks.'

Helly stood up. 'Relax,' she said, 'you pair of egotists. People always think the same way. It's so important to you, you reckon it must be at least a little bit important to everybody else. It isn't. No one cares.'

Richard was coming back from a very nice lunch with a new architect called Brownson. They had been to an oyster bar near the station. Mr Brownson was very keen for work.

As he rounded the corner of the office, he saw Helly sitting at William's desk and William perched beside her, looking down and smiling.

Richard turned and walked back towards the lift. He would go down to the floor below, walk across and come up the stairwell. He didn't want them to know he had seen them together.

Of course. Now it all fell into place. How stupid of him not to have thought of it. That little tart didn't have the technical knowledge to work out what was happening with the contractors or Rosewood Cottage. Richard had seen the expression on William's face. He had been looking down at her as she leant back in his chair, her head thrown back. Richard knew that nervous, male look. He had used it himself a hundred times.

In the lift, he leant back against the wall, his arms folded, pursing his lips. Good, he thought. Now he knew everything. Now he could make his move.

Everything they said about Alison Bennett was true. She was trim and efficient and intelligent. She had been good at her job – a personnel assistant – and now she was a good mother to William's child. She also worked part-time in a local shop, a couple of hours here and there to help them out, when Paul was at nursery, and she was learning French.

She also knew that her husband was confused. William was the sort of man who was unusually kind to the people around him when he was miserable, because he felt guilty about resenting their happiness. When she had first identified this trait, not long after they were engaged, it had thrown her a bit. Whenever he did anything kind or pleasant, she found herself looking for the hidden motive. After a while, she began to love him for it, although she trusted him less. Alison had married with her eyes open. She was that kind of woman.

William had been confused for some weeks now but then it was March, a confusing month, she always found.

She was going to give him another fortnight before she sat down and tried to work it all out.

She was saying this to herself on a Thursday afternoon. Paul had thrown a tantrum for a solid half an hour, then fallen asleep. When she had explained to him that she could not mend his favourite truck he had told her he hated her. He loved his Daddy, but he hated her. She had resisted the temptation to say, fine, I'm not exactly wild about you either at the moment. After he fell asleep, she read a Sunday magazine; a few moments of peace.

When the doorbell rang, she went to the front door still holding the magazine. She opened it a fraction.

A man stood on the step. He was dressed in overalls and wearing a heavy jacket with the collar turned up. 'It's on the front here,' he said. 'Do you want it round the back?'

'I'm sorry?' said Alison. She looked past him. Parked on the pavement was a workman's van. Music tinkled from the cab, where a young man in the passenger seat was waiting for the older one. Then she saw that on the small square patch of grass in front of the house was a pile of wooden slats wrapped partially in tarpaulin and bound with rope. The top slat appeared to be a door of some sort.

'Do you want it round the back?' the man asked again. 'Only it's a bit parky and I'm in a hurry.' He was already backing away down the path.

'What is it?' Alison called after him.

'Garden shed,' the man responded, backing away towards the gate.

'What?'

The man paused, pulling a face. He fumbled around in

184

one of the pockets of his big jacket and pulled out a piece of paper. 'Bennett,' he said. 'Number fifteen.'

Alison nodded.

The man raised his hand in farewell, as if that settled the matter.

After the van had pulled away, Alison turned back into the hall, put down the magazine and slipped on a pair of loafers. She went out into the garden. Why on earth had William bought a garden shed? They already had one.

She parted the tarpaulin slightly. The door on the top had new chrome hinges, shiny bright. It looked like a nice shed.

She went back into the house, shaking her head. Now she knew for sure. Something was up.

6

'**S**end it back? Send it back?'
  'Yes for God's sake. You heard. Send it back. We don't need a garden shed. We don't want a garden shed. What's more we don't want to have to pay for it.'

Alison closed her eyes. She sighed, very slowly. 'William, where the hell are we supposed to send it back *to*? We don't know where it came *from*. There was no delivery note, nothing.'

William paused before crying out, 'Well for God's sake, how could you let somebody just dump a shed in our garden without asking for a delivery note!'

'Maybe it's a prize draw, maybe it's a mistake – I don't know. It'd be stupid to throw it away. It's much better than the one we've got.'

'You chose it, not me.'

'Yes, William, I know.' Alison's voice was strained. Her teeth were gritted.

At this point, the sound of Paul calling out from upstairs became audible. 'Mar-*mee!* Mar-*mee!*'

Alison sighed again, shook her head and left the kitchen. William picked up the newspaper that was on the table in front of him and threw it on the floor.

* * *

Arthur Robinson put down the phone. It was night-
time at Robinson Builders. His operatives had gone
home. He was working late, alone, in the rickety pre-
fab he used as his office. The only sound was the
wind outside and the companionable burble of his gas
heater. He was tired. He was stiff. His Opal Fruits
were finished and all that remained was an unchewable,
brightly coloured scattering of wrappers. Life seemed
grim.

Richard was asking for too much. It was one thing
wanting Benny to watch the cottage – although Richard
still had not explained why. What he was after now
was something else altogether. What if it went wrong?
What if they got caught? Arthur leant back in his seat,
trying to arch his back to ease the stiffness. The effort
brought his capacious stomach into contact with his
aluminium desk and pushed it forward, making a small
screechy-scrapy sound on the wooden floor of the pre-
fab.

The sound of Arthur Robinson's desk masked another
similar sound which occurred simultaneously in the yard
outside – but the wind carried it up over the wall and off
into the chill, smoky ether of Kennington.

Arthur heaved himself out of his chair and went over
to the heater. Standing over the warmth, his pudgy fingers
splayed, he waved at it with both hands. Perhaps it was sex;
perhaps that was what was absent from his life. He and his
wife hadn't had it for years but, truth to tell, he didn't miss
it. What was copulation when there were so many different
types of pastry in the world? And with pastries, you only

had to wash your fingers. Richard still had sex, he could tell. He was that kind of person. The world could be divided into two types, really. Those who had regular intercourse and those who preferred cake. He had infinitely more respect for the latter.

Then he heard the sound: a twisted wail which ended in a squeak followed by a choking noise, as if the voice making it had reached the limits of its pitch and was protesting. Arthur went over to the portakabin's grimy window, rubbed it with his sleeve (which made no difference) and peered out into the night. The lantern outside scarcely lit the yard but he could see the vague hulks of machinery, the sheds and – in the corner – Benny's igloo.

The cry came again. Arthur shook his head. 'Poor little sod,' he muttered to himself. He took his old sheepskin waistcoat from the hook on the back of the door and slipped his arms into it, then went outside.

It was not possible to knock on Benny's igloo – knocking on rubber produced no sound – so Arthur knelt at the opening and peered in. The interior of Benny's home was dark but he could hear squeaking and scuffling.

'Benny . . .' Arthur called softly, scared of waking him too violently, 'Benny . . . it's Senior Robinson. You're having a dream . . . perhaps you should try waking up.' There was no Junior Robinson, Arthur had explained, but Benny still preferred this term of address. Polite people, the Venezuelans.

There was another sharp cry, louder this time, followed by a sudden flurry of movement, then silence. Arthur Robinson waited, crouched by the entrance. He had never dared to venture into the igloo and had told his other operatives that nobody else should either, on pain of being sacked. Even the homeless deserve some privacy, he informed them sternly. What Benny did in there was anybody's guess: slept; dreamt; cried out. It was no life.

Eventually, Benny's small confused face appeared in the opening. He nodded, a little abashed. It was the only time that Benny smiled, when he was embarrassed.

Arthur felt sympathy for the man, so he did not mention the nightmare. 'It's like this Benny,' he said, pulling his waistcoat round him and holding it across his chest with his arms, although he was a man who never felt the cold. 'We need you to take a closer look at that cottage. You've done really well. We're very pleased. But we need you to actually get inside, that's why we asked you to check out the back and so on. He wants you to wait until the old couple go out. It shouldn't be difficult.'

Benny had mimed sash windows when Arthur had asked him about the Appletons' security arrangements.

'The man, I mean, my friend . . .' Arthur hesitated, 'he wants you to cause a bit of trouble. Not tonight. When he gives the word.' Benny frowned. Arthur Robinson frowned too. He found this difficult. 'You know, mess things up a bit, while they're out, mind.' Arthur could not bring himself to repeat what Richard had really said over the phone. *Tell him to piss on the carpets if he feels like it*, Richard had told him. *Crap on the sofa. Wank off into the breadbin. The works. I want a mess. I want it nasty.*

The thought of asking anyone to wank off into a breadbin was more than Arthur Robinson could bear.

It was a Tuesday night. Annette was in her house in Catford. She was lying on her bed, naked. It was half past nine at night and William had just left.

She lay for a long time, imprisoned by the texture of her skin. She felt too heavy to move. She could still feel the imprint of William's hands either side of her head, the feel of his fingers in her hair. Her skull felt fragile. Inside its brittle carapace, her mind turned. I am in love, her mind said. I love. At the same time, her body resented William's absence. The feel of the sheet beneath her naked back was insubstantial. The pillow did not move. She struggled to feel resentment but could only conjure warmth. I am lost.

She began to shiver, so she rose and pulled on her towelling robe. Then she padded lightly to the bathroom and leant her elbows on the sink, staring into the mirror. The robe was white, with a pale green trim and green belt, loosely tied. Beneath her throat, her fine skin plunged in a dark V-shape, an arrow between her engorged breasts, pointing downwards to the glowing regions of her thighs. She gazed at her face. Her skin was clear. Her eyes were bright. Her hair was ruffled into a light, fluffy mess. She was beautiful.

She did not bathe. She pulled the robe around herself and went downstairs. It seemed a shame to draw the curtains and turn on the lights. She hesitated, unwilling to make the room look as it always did. She put the television on but turned it off almost immediately – watching it seemed unbearably normal. Instead, she turned on the radio and fiddled with the dial until she found some classical music, then made herself a sandwich to the reassuringly unfamiliar tinkle of a harp. Afterwards, she left her plate and knife next to the sink and went to lie on the sofa with her arms folded behind her head and her legs dangling over the side. She gazed at the ceiling.

When she sat up to look at the clock on top of the television, it said eleven thirty.

She was running water over her sandwich plate when she heard the knock at the door. She froze.

She stood still for a moment, her mind computing possibilities. There were a lot of Jehovah's Witnesses in Catford but they wouldn't call this late. The only probability was William. No, that wasn't at all probable. Even so, she ruffled her hair and ran her tongue over her teeth as she crossed the kitchenette.

She went to the curtain which she kept across the alcove to the doorway and peered round. Through the wavering glass panels she could only see a dark figure, too tall to be William. She paused, then leant forward and slid the chain on. Then she opened the door.

The man standing on the step was in his fifties, tall, with grey-brown hair receding at the temples and a heavily lined face. He gave a half-ironic smile and the skin around his brown eyes crinkled. He pressed his lips together, shrugging slightly. *Ah well*, his shrug said.

He looked at her for a moment, then said, 'I know it's late. I was meeting a friend in Lewisham. I was going down Rushey Green. You can always tell me to get lost.'

She closed the door, unslid the chain, then opened it again. He stepped inside.

'Hello Girlie,' he said, and held out his arms.

*　　*　　*

William was home by ten o'clock. All the way home, he could feel Annette. As he parked his car outside the house he wanted to turn to her, as if she was sitting next to him in the passenger seat. As he put his key in his own front door he wanted to step back, and usher her in first.

Alison was in the sitting room, watching the news. He went and stood in the doorway. The top of her head was just visible above the sofa. He wanted to say hello but was worried that his voice would not sound normal.

'Hello,' she said.

'Alright?' he asked as he turned and went into the kitchen.

The kettle had boiled recently and steam was curling from its spout. He turned it on. If I smoked, he thought, now is the moment I would want a cigarette. He went back to the door of the sitting room. 'Tea?' he asked.

'No thanks,' the top of her head replied.

The kettle was already boiling as he returned to the kitchen. It clicked itself off as he pulled a mug from the pile of crockery sitting in the drainer, which collapsed with a small clatter. He tossed a teabag into the mug and poured on the water. While he waited for it to brew, he stared at the black square of uncurtained window above the sink. His face seemed distant and pale, the face of a man he had never met.

While Annette filled the kettle, the man sat on the sofa. 'So I finally got a decent price,' he was saying. 'Two years on the market. What a nightmare. I thought it would never go.'

'Will you go down to Southampton?' Annette asked.

'Oh I don't know Girlie,' he replied.

She plugged the kettle in and turned back to the sink, to finish cleaning her plate and knife from earlier. There was a moment or two of silence.

Then, she became aware that he was standing close behind her. He had removed his heavy coat. He lifted his hand and, with the backs of his fingers, brushed the soft towelling of her robe. 'Been a long time Girlie,' he said.

She stopped with her hands in the water. 'No Keith,' she said. 'No. It isn't what I want.'

'Eighteen months?' he asked. 'Maybe longer. We had that drink in Leicester Square.'

He lifted his other hand and, very gently, pulled her loose hair away from her neck.

Annette closed her eyes. Then she felt his lips soft and full against the back of her neck. For a moment she felt irritation with his persistence, then nothing, then – to her surprise – a sense of heat. Her breasts were still full and heavy from William's attentions, her vagina still damp. Sated, warm, relaxed, her body was responding to the familiarity of Keith's touch.

He moved his hand up to the back of her neck and began to massage it, strongly and slowly. Almost instinctively, her head fell forward. His other arm came over her shoulder and grasped her firmly across her chest. He pressed her forward against the sink unit. She could feel his erection through his thin trousers, pushing at her buttocks. Her hands were still in the washing up water. I don't believe this is happening to me, she thought.

I don't believe it. Tonight, of all nights. He turns up tonight.

All at once, she felt a rush of anger, not against Keith but William. Where was he? Why wasn't he here, preventing this? They had made love and then he had got up and dressed and gone home to his wife: burning, sweet love, the sort of love that leaves you clinging to another's body through the night, even in sleep. And he had gone home to his wife. He was probably in bed with her now, puking excuses. She owed him nothing.

Keith's arm withdrew slightly and his hand slipped into her robe, cupping the weight of her left breast. His thumb and forefinger moved to circle the nipple and then began to work it, gently.

He turned her round and she lifted her face, her damp hands resting on his shoulders. 'Still my Girlie . . .' he murmured as their lips brushed. I taste of William, she thought. Can he tell?

I taste of William, she thought, ten minutes later as he parted her thighs and lowered his head to her clitoris. He must be able to tell. She was lying on her back on the bed. Perhaps he doesn't mind, likes it even. He had carried her upstairs and laid her down, pushing the crumpled bulk of the duvet to one side. She and William had used a condom. Surely there would be the taste of that? There had never been any need for that with Keith – he had had a vasectomy when he was thirty. No accidents for Keith. He knew the purpose of sex. She reached out and tugged softly at his hair, lifting him up. As he rose, she searched his face for signs of distaste. She saw only the same, familiar, sleepy lust. He reached out one hand and picked up a pillow from behind her head. Then, lifting her slightly, tucked it underneath her buttocks, so that she was raised to him. As she continued to wonder at the unlikeliness of what was happening, he pushed into her.

Afterwards he lay on her for a long time, while she stroked his hair.

'Keith . . .' she said gently.

'I know,' he groaned. 'I'm sorry Girlie. It wasn't planned, I promise. I was passing, really. It was an impulse – I couldn't help it. Then you opened the door. I've never stopped feeling for you, you know that.'

'Keith. That is the last time. I mean it.'

He raised his head from her chest and looked at her. He pulled a face. She met his gaze. 'I mean it Keith. Don't turn up like that again. I don't care if you're passing or not. It's the last time.'

He lowered his head again. 'Oh well . . .' he sighed. She could sense that he didn't really mind, quite liked it in fact; same old Keith – pretending she was the one in charge while nudging her the way he wanted. It would always be like that.

He rolled off her and lay at her side. He groaned. 'I'm getting old . . .' he said. 'Look.' He prodded his heavy belly, the crumpled paunch against her smooth flesh. She smiled lightly. There were advantages to Keith. However worried she might get about the fine crows' feet around her eyes, she would always be twenty-four years younger than him. She knew he wanted reassurance but resisted the temptation to give it. He had seduced her, after all. She should feel some anger, or mild reproach at least. Instead, she felt a kind of gratitude. She had been unfaithful to William, the man she loved. The knowledge of this would protect her from loving him even more.

'I would die for a coffee . . .' Keith said cautiously, not wanting to push his luck.

Annette rose with good humour. She had given him a fuck for no good reason. Why not a coffee? Anyway, she was bursting for the loo. Her arms were still in her robe. She stood and pulled it round her, tying the belt. 'While you're down there,' Keith added, 'could you bring up my ciggies? They're in my coat pocket.'

As she reached the door he sat up and said suddenly, 'No come back here a minute.' She was a few feet away. He reached out and caught her hand, pulling her back. He knelt up on the bed and embraced her. 'You're a fine girl. Always were.'

She waited patiently while he kissed her, feeling nothing. She realised she was exhausted. He feels nothing either, she thought, but he wants to reassure himself this wasn't just sex.

He buried his head in her hair, then sat back, reaching out a hand to brush her fringe back off her face. 'Can I stay the night?' he asked.

She sighed. 'Keith I've got work in the morning.'

'I know, so have I. We'll just go to sleep now. I'll run you to the station in the morning. I'm over the limit. It's a long drive.'

She turned away, her silence acquiescent. She went into the bathroom, lifted her robe and sat down on the toilet. She knew that he would be lying down on his back, his hands behind his head, as he always had done.

'You've got this place spick and span I see,' he called out to her, chirpily. Now he was confident. 'I like to see you're still a good little housewife.'

'Piss off,' Annette called back.

'Ah, Annette. Is that any way to speak to your husband?'

William and Alison sat next to each other on the sofa, in silence, watching the advertisements which followed the news and preceded the weather report. Then, Alison rose and left the room. William picked up his mug of tea and looked into it. It was still half-full, and stone cold.

Alison returned ten minutes later. In her arms was a bundle of bedding almost as big as herself: the spare duvet, a folded sheet, a blanket, a pillow. She dropped the bedding down beside the sofa and said, 'Goodnight.'

She closed the door behind her as she left.

Annette woke to the solid unfamiliarity of another human being in her bed. She was hot. The duvet cover felt clammy. Keith had rolled over with his back to her and was snoring softly. She looked at the thinning hair against the back of his neck, his speckled back. He was a large man but loose, with a layer of soft flesh over his solid torso. It was strange to observe the ageing process in him with such detachment. When they had married she had been eighteen and he forty-two. Now, he was something more than older. He was old. Poor Keith, she thought sleepily, listening to his harsh breath. Poor Keith – he was bad for me, but only by accident. He had, in all honesty, believed that their marriage could last. When she had left him, he had wept. That was six years ago and he still turned up once in a while, all broad-shouldered and big-hearted. They were man and wife, he would murmur, in his heart, although he had not contested the divorce. Untangling her life from his had been a good deal less traumatic than moving in with him had been. She frowned to herself, remembering her mother's rage: the shrieking, tears in the supermarket – the strangled voice crying out down an aisle of tinned vegetables, 'Your father is turning in his grave!' – the other shoppers staring, grinning at the unexpected entertainment. No, she would not think of that. It was behind her now. She and her mother had not referred to it for years.

She lay curled up, trying to pull her mind towards the day ahead. Then she remembered William. She closed her eyes. William would never believe that she could be capable of having sex with another man immediately after him. The thought would be unimaginable to him, much as it had been unimaginable to her. She would never be able to explain.

She rolled out of bed and crossed the room swiftly. Closing the bathroom door gently behind her, she began to run her bath.

She was still in the bath, rinsing her hair, when there was a tap at the door and Keith came in. He had pulled on his trousers and shirt and was holding two mugs of tea in one hand. He put hers down on the edge of the bath. It was black, exactly the right strength. He perched precariously on the edge of her wicker laundry basket and raised his mug to his lips.

'Close the door,' she said. 'You're letting the steam out.'

As she took the tea and lay back in the bath he said, 'You want to be careful overfilling that you know. I can see from here. It's coming away from the edge on the window side. You should put some sealer in otherwise you'll get damp downstairs eventually.'

As they left the house he said, 'Why don't I run you all the way to work? There's time. I'm not in any hurry.'

Annette hesitated. It was exactly a week since the London Bridge bomb. She had commuted as usual for the previous two days. She had stood on the footbridge at Hither Green and watched the trains coming down the line. On both occasions, a picture had occurred: the people who had run for the eight seventeen that Wednesday, trotting down the platform to catch the train that would bring them in on Platform 3. 'The station will be fine,' she said, but her voice was uncertain. He glanced over. She had not told him about the bombing. He would have comforted her, like William had, and that would have seemed more of a betrayal than the sex had been.

'I don't have to be in Eltham until twelve,' he replied.

'It's miles out of your way.'

He shrugged, and started the engine.

As they pulled up at the front of John Blow House,

Keith said, 'So this is it, Girlie? You're a pretty grand sort of secretary now.'

'Office Manager,' Annette replied, 'if you want to be precise.'

He turned to her. She was undoing her seatbelt. He leant towards her and put one hand over hers as she struggled with the clasp. 'Are you angry with me?' he said.

She looked down the street. Jefferson Worth was walking towards their car. He turned and bounded up the steps without noticing them. She realised she was disappointed that it had not been William who had passed by as a strange man pulled up with her in his car at five past nine in the morning.

Keith reached out and tucked her hair behind her ear. 'You know you can call me anytime, don't you?' he said. 'If things get bad.' This was too much. If William were to walk past now there would be no mystery. A man tucking her hair behind her ear could only be another lover.

'I'm not angry Keith, honest,' she said, speaking quickly as she turned to get her handbag from the back seat. 'But I was serious when I said it was the last time.'

He let her go with good grace. 'You're a beautiful girl,' he said as she opened the door to climb out. As she turned to slam it shut behind her he called out, 'Don't forget what I said!'

Joan looked up as Annette walked past her desk. She watched her as she put down her handbag and removed her coat. Annette said, 'Morning.'

200

'Morning,' Joan replied.

Annette looked over.

Joan rose from her seat and came and stood next to Annette. 'In okay today?'

Annette nodded.

Joan reached out and pulled over a typist's chair to the left of Annette's desk. She sat down and pressed her knees together. 'You know I'm off on holiday next week?'

Annette sat down. Joan looked slightly anxious.

'Well, I know it's only a week,' Joan said, 'but I thought I had better talk to you before I went in case anything happened while I was away. I mean, about Helly.'

Annette pulled a face. 'I know. I've been wondering about that too. I thought Richard had it all sorted out. I haven't spoken to him recently but last time I did I had the impression she would be gone by now. It's all very awkward. I don't think he realises.'

'That's just it,' Joan said. 'I wasn't too happy from the start and now I really don't think, well, she's been walking around and we've been talking to her. She doesn't act like someone who's nicked anything. I mean, it's not as if she's being extra friendly or anything, she's just as bad-tempered as ever and her time-keeping hasn't improved. If it was you, wouldn't you be on your best behaviour?' Annette pulled a face and shrugged. 'Anyway,' Joan continued, 'I don't understand. It's over two weeks since my money went missing. If he really thought it was her she would have been out by now. And I don't know about all this doing it quietly. Why should he do her any favours? What's in it for him?'

Annette put her elbows on the table and leant forward, resting her chin in her hands. 'Oh I don't know, I don't really think it's up to us.'

Joan looked at her. 'I'm sorry Annette. But it is.'

Annette sat back up. In the whole time she had worked with Joan, Joan had never once disagreed with her or tried to alter her opinion about anything.

'We can't let it happen as if it was an accident and just hope we got it right. If she didn't nick my money then she shouldn't get the sack. If Richard wants to sack her on other grounds, then that's up to him.' Not long ago, Joan thought, I passed a child dying in the road; and it seemed wrong to be seeing it. There was nothing I could have done, then. But that isn't the point. 'When she took you home after the bomb,' Joan asked, 'didn't you get a feel for it? Didn't you want to ask her?'

Annette tried to smile. Perhaps she should have asked Helly about Joan's money when they were in Catford. All she had been thinking about was William.

'Is this a private party or can anyone join?'

Joan started. Annette sat back quickly. Helly had spoken as she walked past them on her way to the coffee machine. Her tone had not been pleasant.

'Did she hear?' Annette asked softly when Helly was out of sight. Joan pulled a face. Annette stood up. 'Go round to Richard's office and see if he's in. Then come over to the coffee.'

The coffee machine was in a small alcove in the corner of the office. It was cordoned out of sight by an office divide on one side and a huge cabinet with supplies on the other.

Helly was pouring a jug of water into the filter machine. She was still wearing her coat and had her bag slung over one shoulder. She glanced up as Annette joined her, then returned to what she was doing.

'Helly, look . . .'

'What have I done now?'

Joan stepped around the divide. 'Coast is clear,' she said to Annette.

'What you told me last week, about Richard . . . is it true?' Annette asked Helly.

'What?' said Joan.

Helly turned. She looked from Annette to Joan and back again. 'Yes it's true. Why would I make it up for fuck's sake?'

'What?' repeated Joan.

'Helly thinks,' Annette said, 'that Richard is taking bribes from contractors.'

'Helly knows,' Helly said. 'Helly has proof.'

'Oh,' said Joan. 'I've known that for years.' Annette and Helly looked at her. 'It's obvious, isn't it?' Joan said. 'Those three hour lunches? The way he gets all officious about tender procedure as if he really cares about everything being above board. The way he's so obsessed with paperwork. The surveyors can't even blow their noses without sending Richard a memo about it. It's obvious. He's covering his tracks.'

Helly was open-mouthed. 'You never said.'

'Didn't you want to report it to anyone?' Annette asked.

Joan frowned. 'What for?'

'Are you *sure?*' Annette said, looking from one to the other.

'Oh for God's sake Annette,' Helly hissed, 'you're so bloody straight you think everybody else is as straight as you. It's no big deal. Half the bloody managers here are on the take. They're in the business of awarding expensive contracts. What planet are you on?'

'I don't think that just because . . .'

'You don't like the idea because you feel bloody daft for not having noticed it yourself.'

'You said you had proof,' Joan said to Helly.

Helly hesitated. 'Well, that's what I told him.'

Annette stared at her. 'You mean Richard *knows* that you know?'

'Yeh.'

'You didn't tell me that.'

'You didn't ask.'

Annette rolled her eyes. 'Helly, this explains a few things.'

'Like what?'

'Like why Richard is about to get you sacked, that's what.'

'What?'

Joan raised the palm of her hand to indicate they should be quiet. Then she stepped back out of the alcove and peered around the office. 'Girls,' she said, as she stepped back, 'people are starting to wander around and Richard is going to be here any minute. Can we all get away for lunch at the same time?' She was looking at Annette.

'I don't know,' said Annette. 'Depends who's around.

I could get the switchboard to put my calls through to Lydia. I minded her phone last week when they all went out for her engagement.'

'Is The Green Man safe?'

Annette shook her head. 'We'll have to take a walk somewhere. Meet up separately.'

'What for?' said Helly.

'Because,' Joan replied, 'it is time we all swapped notes.'

Bob Appleton had taken up *découpage*. Joanna had given him a kit for Christmas but it had taken him some months to get around to it. He had a lot of jigsaw puzzles to finish first. Until they were put together, they could not be taken apart. Right through January and February there had been half a Spanish galleon in the dining room, a jagged 1950s Morris Oxford on top of his dresser and the frame and one corner of a flock of puffins on an ice floe lying in the corner of the bathroom. He had taken to putting the odd piece in place while he ate dinner, brushed his hair or went to the toilet. Joanna threatened to scramble the lot if they weren't done by the end of March and had hidden his new toy until the jigsaws were packed away. It was such a relief when they were completed and could be broken up.

He was in their bedroom in Rosewood Cottage, the electric fire on full to dry out the pictures more quickly. Next door, his mother-in-law Mrs Hawthorne slept. Downstairs, Joanna was watching a video of last Sunday's *South Bank Show*, some cello player she had taken a shine to.

The pleasures of *découpage* were proving elusive. The picture was done for you, after all. All you had to do was cut it out and lacquer it onto the rather tacky plastic plaques the kit provided. There wasn't enough art in it for Bob. He preferred the shrinking pictures Joanna bought him last year, the ones you painted onto a clear plastic sheet. You put the sheet into the top of a hot oven for twenty minutes and it duly shrank. Lo and behold, a perfect miniature. He had done one of Rosewood Cottage which now hung at the top of the stairs. Only problem was, you had to have your nose on it to see it.

Bob's current *découpage* picture was of a group of three horses all running out of the frame, towards the viewer. The first he had tried was of a bunch of flowers, blossoms bursting three-dimensionally. He liked the horses more. They were slightly scary – eyeballs all shiny and lips pulled back to reveal unnaturally large teeth. We can call it the three horses of the apocalypse, he thought. That would give us war, famine and pestilence – what was the fourth one called? We can nail it to the front door, as a warning to all staff from the Capital Transport Authority.

After he had finished lacquering, he left it to dry and went downstairs to make a cup of coffee.

In the kitchen, he found Joanna. She was crying. He went over to the table, drew up a chair and sat down next to her. He took her hand and squeezed it. She did not respond. He squeezed again, then said, 'The *South Bank Show* was that bad, huh?'

'Shut up you old fool,' she said moistly.

He sat beside her without speaking. Eventually, she

withdrew her hand and fumbled in her apron pocket for a tissue. He offered his hankie.

As she blew her nose she said, 'I don't think I can stand that poisonous old woman any longer, I really don't.' Bob rested his hand lightly on her shoulder. 'She knows we're just waiting for her to die,' Joanna continued. 'She knows we want Helly to move in. She doesn't enjoy living, she's as miserable as sin. She's just keeping it up to spite us, that's all.' She finished wiping her face and looked at Bob's hankie. 'Good God, what have you been doing into this? It's disgusting! Guess what she just said to me. I took her tea and she said, out of the blue, "No wonder Suzanne ran off with that good-for-nothing. She never got a decent cup of tea out of you. Mind you, what's a good-for-nothing husband when you've had parents like you two." I wasn't going to say anything, I wasn't going to rise to it, you know what she's like. Then she said . . .' Joanna drew breath. 'She said, "Maybe you two messed around with her, like it says in the papers these days. Something must have happened. Maybe you two interfered with her when I wasn't looking".'

Suzanne was their daughter and Helly's mother. Somehow, she and Joanna had never got on, not even when Suzanne was small. At the age of fifteen, she had dropped out of school. By seventeen, she was married. By eighteen, she was a mother. By twenty-one, she was divorced. Helly had never known her father, although the odd birthday present arrived. She had got to know her mother's friends, though. And her mother's drinking habits.

'Oh come on,' Bob said, 'last month your mum accused

us of putting peppercorns in the raspberry jam and blocking up the outlet in her bedroom in the hope she'd be poisoned by the fumes from an electric fan heater. She's mad as a hatter.'

'But did we, Bob? Maybe we did.'

'Did what?'

'Interfere with her. Suzanne. Not in the way she means, but she's got a point, hasn't she?' Bob shook his head. 'Our daughter doesn't give a damn about us,' Joanna continued. 'Here we are, all smug with our little cottage and our pensions and our Italian cooking, and we think we're one better than all the other people like us that we know because they don't cook Italian. But luckily we have my mad mother upstairs just to remind us when we get too smug. Our daughter thinks we're crap.'

Bob leant forward and took both of Joanna's hands in his. Outside, it was gloomy and dark. The kitchen was cold. 'But our granddaughter loves us,' he insisted gently. 'Nobody gets everything right. Granted, something went wrong with Suzanne and we'll never know for sure whether it was us or just her. But we've got Helly. And she'll come to live with us some time soon and that'll get her away from Suzanne and then we can start to make up for all the things that have gone wrong.'

Joanna sat back in her chair and sighed. Then she turned to her husband. 'Maybe it's too late.'

Bob shook his head but did not argue any further. They sat for a few minutes, holding hands. He ran his thumb over the back of her gnarled fist. The purple veins, the brown age spots, the yellowed fingernails – he knew her hands better than he knew his own. She had developed a touch of arthritis in the right one last year, just a touch, and he had been able to see it in her fingers even before the pain had begun, before Joanna knew herself.

From upstairs came the dull thump of Mrs Hawthorne's stick on the ceiling. 'She'll be wanting the toilet,' said Bob, getting to his feet.

'Oh let her wet the bed.'

He kissed the top of Joanna's head. 'If we could send her down the launderette, my little chicken, don't you think I would?'

Upstairs, Mrs Hawthorne was half out of bed already. When the door opened she frowned. 'Oh, it's you. Where's Joanna?'

'Busy,' Bob replied firmly as he went to help her up.

'I don't like you taking me to the lavvy. It's not right.' He ignored her. 'You'll be doing my sponge bath next, mind you you'd probably make a better job of it than that daughter of mine. Why's she busy?'

'We've been doing things, things we like doing,' Bob explained patiently as he inched her towards the bedroom door. 'She's been watching telly and I've been doing a new picture.'

'What of?'

'Horses.' Then he added, a little grimly, 'I'll show you later.'

'Horses!' the old lady spat, as if he had said lepers. Mrs Hawthorne thought that large animals carried diseases and that horses were – adding malice to malady – psychic.

'Yes, horses. And by the way Mum, I think it might be a nice idea if you don't go on about Suzanne. It upsets Joanna, you know that.'

'Upset? Upset?' They were still only half-way to the door. 'She's not upset. It's just her time of the month, that's all. Always made her blub, ever since she was thirteen. Her father got so fed up he belted her for blubbing once.'

'She doesn't have periods any more,' Bob said evenly, as they neared the door. 'She's sixty-six years old.'

Mrs Hawthorne leant forward, nearly tipping, and grabbed onto the door handle. When it had been gained, she shook Bob off her elbow and paused for a rest. Bob stood next to her while she caught her breath. Surreptitiously, he glanced at the back of her pyjama trousers, wondering if they would make it to the bathroom in time.

'Don't know what all the fuss is about periods these days,' Mrs Hawthorne grated on, catching her breath. 'The curse? Load of nonsense. Have you seen the adverts? Things you stick up you, things you stick on. How stupid can you get? In my day, we used cake.'

Bob returned to the kitchen half an hour after he had left. Joanna was still there. She had lit a cigarette. They had both given up years ago but kept a packet in the back of the kitchen drawer, for emergencies. Bob sat down next to her and passed a hand over his face. 'You're right,' he said. 'She's only hanging on to spite us. Give me a fag.'

Joanna passed the packet over. 'What are we going to do?'

'I don't know, but we need a night out. I'll go over

210

to Jill's tonight and arrange something. A Wednesday like we did last time – next week or the one after if they're busy.'

'Last time we had that fight over dominoes.'

'Well we'll play something else then, anything. Cards. Scrabble. Group sex.'

'Scrabble,' said Joanna.

'What if he'd called your bluff?' Annette asked.

Helly shrugged. 'Then I'd have been stuffed.' They were sitting in the back of a coffee bar on Horseferry Road. They all had tea. Annette had said she wasn't hungry but, once in a while, helped herself to Joan's plate of chips. Helly had a piece of gateau which she was chopping into large chunks with a fork. 'But if he'd got it wrong,' she continued, 'he would have lost a hell of a lot more than me.' She stopped chopping her cake. She looked down at it. Joan and Annette watched her. Helly looked back up. Annette thought, she is only seventeen.

'Don't you see?' Helly said quietly. 'People like me, we're the most dangerous of all. That's why people like Richard are so scared of us. We have nothing to lose.'

There was a pause. Annette sighed. Then she said, 'So what now?'

Helly shrugged. 'God knows. Looks like I'm going to get the boot.'

'Unless we report him,' said Annette. 'All of us.'

'Great, then we all get the boot.'

'Not if we can prove it.'

'I have a better idea,' said Joan. 'It's simple.' She

211

plunged her fork into a chip and dabbed it in the puddle of tomato ketchup that lay on the side of her plate. 'They put vinegar in this, I can tell.' She looked at them. 'I go to Richard and tell him I've found the sixty quid. He has no grounds for dismissing Helly. Not unless he can come up with something else which means that you, madam, start coming in on time and keeping your nose clean.'

'But that will mean you don't get your money back,' said Annette.

Joan shrugged. 'I don't like him. I never have.' She stabbed a second chip. 'Never.'

Helly shovelled gateau into her mouth and grinned. 'Well it would be fun seeing what he does next.'

'I'll do it on Friday,' Joan said, 'then I'm off all next week. Will I miss anything?'

Annette shook her head. 'I don't think so. I would go off and enjoy your holiday. I hope the weather is nice to you.'

'For the first week in April!' said Helly. 'Why didn't you go after Easter weekend?'

'That's when the prices go up,' said Joan. 'I can't wait to see his face. If he did nick my money then me telling him I've found it is going to come as a bit of a surprise.'

Richard did not like surprises; of any sort, not even nice ones. One of the reasons he had married Gillian was because he had sensed she was the kind of woman who would never throw him an unexpected party.

He was not an impulsive man. He could have taken the risk of sacking Helly on the spot when she had first confronted him, but he had taken the time and the trouble to tie up the loose ends, to make sure the whole thing was watertight and – if he was honest with himself – to teach her a lesson. Then there were all the other little players to be dealt with. He had enjoyed that. He had surprised himself just how much he had enjoyed it.

He had never considered old Joan to be a player, little or otherwise. In fact, he had never considered her much at all. She had tapped on his office door the Friday before she went on holiday, stepping inside as diffidently as if his carpet was an ice rink. Her face was bright red. She was holding one hand tightly clasped in the other, as though she was afraid it might drop off.

'Richard,' she said. 'Fact is, I'm such an old goose. I'm a bit embarrassed.'

Richard had just finished concluding some very satisfactory business on the phone and was in an expansive mood. He liked being courteous to Joan. She was a woman who had nothing to offer, after all. It pleased him to be more polite and attentive than was necessarily warranted.

'Take a seat,' he said, indicating the chair in front of his desk.

'No, I won't thanks, Richard, fact is I'm off shortly. I've taken a half day so that I can get things ready. I just thought I should let you know so you aren't thinking about it while I'm away. Annette said she'd deal with it, I've already told her, but I was so embarrassed I thought I ought to apologise for causing all this trouble.'

Richard was beginning to have a slightly bloated feeling somewhere in his lower intestine. It often happened when he sensed that life was about to become more unpleasant and complicated than it needed to be.

'Fact is,' Joan continued, 'I found that sixty pounds. I didn't put it in my purse after all. I put it in a little pocket in my handbag. Can't think why. Annette told me you offered to replace it and everything. I can't thank you enough, but it won't be necessary. I'm so sorry to have put everyone to all this bother, and I'm sorry if it maybe made you jump to conclusions about certain other people that weren't really right.' She was already backing out the door. 'It would be awful if anyone got dealt with unfairly after all, wouldn't it? I would've died if there'd been any misunderstanding. I'm so sorry . . .'

Richard did not reply but waved his hand in an all-purpose gesture of dismissal and farewell.

After she had gone he sat back in his seat and looked up at the ceiling.

There were several possibilities. Their likelihood depended on just how soft Joan was. It was not inconceivable that, realising Helly was about to be sacked, she would pretend there had been no theft because she did not want to see the little baggage out of a job. Richard's mother had been like that and Richard had despised her since he was a toddler. She had died of breast cancer when Richard was twenty-two, her tumour contracted weeks after her sister had been declared finally free of the same disease. He had hated her for getting ill, unable to shake off the conviction that she had deliberately taken the growth from his aunt so that his aunt might live. It would have been just typical. The other possibility, and one that he had to consider seriously, was that Joan was in on it. He chewed at his lower lip. This was getting rather complicated, even for him.

So: Helly, William. Probably Joan. Annette? He could not sack all his staff at once but it was time for a clean sweep, there was no doubt about that. Richard leant down, opened the bottom drawer of his desk and took out his cigarettes. He did not normally smoke in his office, but he felt like one now. Unlike other people, he did not smoke in moments of stress or tension but in ones of triumph. He liked exhaling. He liked doing that very much. Many a man would be intimidated by the forces arrayed against me, he thought. But I like a challenge. He drew on the cigarette deeply. He closed his eyes. So they are all in on it. So be it.

'Helly . . .' Annette's tone was contemplative. They were alone in the office. Joan had reported back to them, then left to go home and do her packing. An hour later, Richard had come out of his office, locked it and departed for the afternoon. They seemed to be the only two people around.

'Yeah?' Helly looked up from Joan's desk where she was making a start on the filing so that she didn't have to do it all on her own on Monday.

'You haven't got proof, have you.' It was not a question.

Helly bit her lip and moved her head from side to side. 'Not *exactly*. No.'

'What have you got?'

'I photocopied the tender result sheets, those I could find in the files – but they don't really add up to proof. They look too regular. It's clear the contractors are taking it in turns. It's odd, but it isn't proof.'

'So basically we hope he doesn't call our bluff?'

'Yes,' said Helly with a small smile. 'We do.'

They continued working in silence for a few minutes more. Then Helly said, her voice casual, 'Course, if one of us was friendly with a surveyor, then we could probably get proof.'

The terminology of the building profession was something it had taken a while for William to pick up. He could look at a damp elevation and tell exactly how long it would be before it crumbled – but he still wanted to call it a wall. He had only just passed his surveying degree, not because he was incompetent but because his verbal aptitude was not equal to his other skills. He had never managed the knack of throwing technical words around with the airy confidence of Richard or Raymond or any of the other surveyors. Things were as they were, and to him it seemed futile to call them something else.

Guano, for instance; guano was a term he had not come across before he came to work for the Capital Transport Authority. He first saw it on the Schedule of Dilapidations for Grantham House in Soho, a deserted and dangerous building which the company was hoping to knock down or refurbish. *Section Two: Roof. Clear large quantities of dried guano from roof area and make good.*

'What is guano?' he had asked out loud, standing in

front of Joan's desk, where she and Helly were filing. 'Do either of you two know?'

'Something not very nice,' Joan had replied.

'Pigeon shit,' said Helly.

Pigeon shit was what he found when he went to update the survey with Jefferson Worth from the commercial department. They had taken over the job from Raymond three months previously and it should have been done weeks ago. Sooner or later, there would be trouble.

As they approached the rotting building, Jefferson chatted to him amiably. 'It's our side of the CTA that brings the money in you know,' he informed him as they unlocked the doors. 'Our lot pays your lot's wages.' Jefferson Worth was twenty-two and loved his job. His speciality was muck; any kind of muck, he wasn't fussy. When Simon from Technical Services found a dead fox on wasteground behind the Hammersmith site, he called Jefferson. When there was a problem with rats dying and going mouldy in the tunnel between White City and East Acton, Jefferson offered to sort it out. When Jefferson Worth was a small boy, William thought, as the lanky lad shouldered the door open and trotted up the staircase, he probably made mud pies out of excrement and pulled the legs off beetles.

The roof of Grantham House looked like the surface of the moon. Over the years, the excrement had dried and built up in layers, caked in dull white with a grey, flaky surface. A flock of birds lifted off the roof as Jefferson flung back the iron trap door and they clambered out. Here and there were clumps of dead ones; the corpses dotted around in little groups, in various stages of decomposition. Some were only skeletons.

And everywhere, there was the thick smell of pigeon; live pigeon, dead pigeon, pigeon somewhere in between. Pigeon shit. William looked up at the London sky. It was white with cloud. He shook his head. Why hang around here all day when you could fly off anywhere?

The birds were roosting on the parapet wall above the gutter. William and Jefferson scrunched across the guano to take a look. Jefferson rested his hands on the parapet and grimaced. 'Look at this coping. It's really cracked.'

'Is the brickwork damp?' William asked.

'Hard to tell.'

Jefferson leant over the parapet. 'Careful,' William said.

'I want to take a look at the tiles,' Jefferson replied, 'see if the fixings are rusted.' William heard a scrape, then a slither, then an, 'Oh shit,' as Jefferson jumped back from the parapet.

'What happened?' asked William. As he spoke, there was a small crash from the street.

'I dislodged something.' Jefferson leant back over the parapet. 'It wasn't a whole tile, only a piece of slate. Don't think it hit anyone. No pedestrians down there at least. Well not any more, anyway.'

William pulled out his notebook. 'We'd better make a note to get the pavement cordoned off.'

'Nah,' said Jefferson derisively, 'it was only because I wiggled it.'

William made the note anyway. 'I'm amazed you haven't had a serious accident by now.'

Jefferson tucked his hands in his pockets. 'People like me never have accidents. Let's take a look at the south elevation.'

As they crossed the roof, Jefferson stopped. He frowned. 'Here,' he said. 'This roof feels bouncy.' He bounced up and down on the balls of his feet. 'Does that feel like damp to you?' He moved off the patch.

William went over. Suddenly, he felt the bitumen give way beneath him, its fibres pulling apart like a damp tissue. He gave out a cry. Jefferson whooped and flung himself over. William's hands hit the roof and grasped at its rough surface. Instinctively, he tried to push his weight back up. His legs were flailing desperately, in thin air.

Jefferson grabbed his arms. He was swearing, over and over again. He hauled William towards him and William heard his jacket rip. He managed to swing one leg back up onto the roof and push himself round.

When they were both clear, they collapsed. Jefferson was still swearing but had started to laugh. Shock and relief combined in William and he began to laugh as well. 'I lost a shoe!' he gasped.

'A what?'

'A shoe!'

Jefferson began to crawl towards the hole that had opened up in the roof. 'I can't believe it,' he said, peering down into the room below. 'Look at this. The beams are completely rotten. It's only the bitumen holding this roof together. Jesus, we could have both gone through.'

'Come away from that hole, you idiot.' William levered himself onto his feet. 'We can go down and get the shoe.' He looked at his hands. They were grazed badly. He had scraped the skin off the side of his left hand, and most of the thumb. It was bleeding. The right sleeve of his jacket had pulled away at the seam. He breathed deeply, looking at his blackened, bleeding hands.

'You alright?' Jefferson asked.

'Yeah . . .' said William, still breathing deeply. Jefferson had probably caused the accident with his stupid bouncing, but then he had probably saved him from falling through the roof.

'God, we're going to have a lot of forms to fill out when we tell them about this one,' Jefferson said. 'You could have broken your neck. Sit down. You're white as a sheet.'

William shook his head. 'Let's get my shoe and get out of here.'

At Leicester Square tube station, they waited on the platform. 'We could've got a taxi, I reckon,' Jefferson said. 'With you being injured and everything.' Two blonde tourists passed and glanced their way. 'Thought our luck was in for a minute,' he added, 'but I think they're wondering what a couple of dossers like us are doing wearing suits.'

William looked down at his filthy torn jacket. 'I look like a tramp out of that Judy Garland film.'

'Maybe they'll make you go to Casualty.'

William chortled without humour. 'I shouldn't think

so. More likely to give me a tube of antiseptic and tell me to get on with it. Who's the first aider on our floor?'

'Annette.'

Annette. Their train pulled in. Annette. He hadn't been able to see her properly all week. It was Thursday. They took their seats. William had a handkerchief wrapped round his grazed hand. He smiled to himself. He and Annette would be able to touch in the middle of the office, with people walking past. She would caress his hand. He sat back in his seat, imagining. It was like having money in the bank.

Opposite them, a businessman in his forties sat staring gloomily into the middle distance. He was wearing a thin, navy blue tie with a very neat knot. His hair receded slightly at the temples. His eyes were milky, as if he was blind.

I want a divorce, William thought, and the idea came to him as fresh and clean and shocking as if somebody had tipped a bucket of cold water over his head. I want to be with Annette. I want to take her to the cinema. I want to go for walks on Sundays and introduce her to my friends. *I want a divorce*. He blinked hard, as if the carriage and Jefferson and the businessman were all a mirage which would disappear if only he could see straight. He drew breath and exhaled sharply.

Jefferson leant forward in his seat. 'You sure you're alright?' he asked. William nodded. 'Delayed shock,' Jefferson said. 'Take it easy. If you feel sick, put your head between your knees.'

William shook his head to indicate that he was okay, but found himself unable to speak, as though his powers

221

of speech had been channelled instead into that thought, that realisation – the vast swimming enormity of it.

Just before Green Park the train slowed, crawled, then halted. Jefferson muttered an oath. The businessman opposite sat up and looked around in alarm.

After a few moments, the driver's intercom crackled into life. 'We apologise for this delay, ladies and gentlemen. This is due to the knock-on effect of a person under a train at Earl's Court. I hope we shall be moving shortly.'

'Not, "person under train" again,' said Jefferson. 'I had that going home last night. I always think when they say that, what they're really saying is "listen, it's one of you lot that's caused the problem, not us". Mind you, can't say I blame them. Last night I was stuck at Harlesden for half an hour. You'd think if someone was going to top themselves they'd at least have the consideration not to do it during the rush hour.'

William nodded, dumbly. He looked at his watch: eleven thirty-two a.m. April the first. His whole life had changed. Jefferson's voice was loud in the stillness of the carriage. The businessman opposite glared at them.

In the middle of the office, in full sight of everybody, William and Annette held hands.

'Will it hurt, nurse?' William asked, as Annette withdrew a tube of antiseptic from the red plastic first aid box sitting on the desk beside them.

'No dear. It'll feel a bit cold. Are you sure you washed it properly?'

'Yes miss.'

Raymond came briskly round the corner. Thursday's bow-tie was a jaunty tartan number, blue and green. Raymond looked concerned. He came and stood over them with his arms crossed, gazing down at Annette's efforts contemplatively. 'I told Richard you should have gone to Casualty,' he muttered.

Oh piss off, William thought.

'I don't think that's really necessary. He says he had a tetanus three months ago . . .' said Annette, her head bent over William's hand as she – slowly and carefully – smoothed in the antiseptic cream.

'I know that,' Raymond snapped. 'I'm thinking of insurance purposes. You know, our legal position. He lost a shoe. He should have his leg X-rayed.'

William kept his head lowered. He knew that if he met Annette's gaze they would both begin to laugh.

'Don't imagine you can sue us in three years' time young man,' said Raymond as he strode away.

William moved his head a fraction closer to Annette. 'I need to talk to you,' he said quietly. She glanced up at him. 'I have to talk to you now, as soon as possible. It's important. There's something I want to ask you.'

She lowered her head again. 'Actually I want to talk to you as well. I've been wanting to all week but we just haven't had the opportunity. It's been really busy with Joan away.' She stood up. 'We won't put a dressing on for now,' she said, 'give it a chance. But if it's weeping then we'll have to cover it up.'

She picked up the first aid box and he handed her the tube of antiseptic which she had left lying on the desk next to them. 'Basement in fifteen minutes?'

She nodded and said, 'The main thing is to keep it clean.'

Richard was in his office, making a list. He enjoyed doing that, although he often destroyed them afterwards. It helped to order things. He liked to see it down in writing, in black and white. He liked things to be real. Physical proof was important.

When his mother had died, he had wanted physical proof. He had asked to see her body, in the private hospital room where she lay. The nurse had left them alone together and closed the door. Richard had gone over to his mother's corpse. Beneath the crisp white sheet, he knew it to be mutilated – one breast missing, irradiated, full of chemicals. There was no doubt about it. She was dead. Richard stood over her, then bent down to her heavily lined face. Illness had aged Marion Leather beyond her years. The face was sagging, helpless. Richard spat in it.

Afterwards, he stood back, breathing heavily. No one would ever know what he had just done; no one would catch him. He was going to get away with it. When the nurse came in ten minutes later, she found him sitting by the window, weeping.

The list he was making in his office went thus: Helly, the old couple, William, Joan, Annette. Annette's name had a question mark beside it. He still wasn't sure about Annette. Still, the rest was well on its way to being sorted out. Timing was important. He wanted it to work out right

– it was like being the conductor of an orchestra. The cymbals had to crash at exactly the right moment or the entire symphony was ruined. The way he had worked it out, the cymbals would crash some time around the end of the following week, before Easter. He and Gillian had planned a weekend away together over the holiday, their first for some time. Sailing in Norfolk, just the two of them, he with the full knowledge that this business was all sorted out. Perfect.

He was smoking – he smoked a lot these days. He had made the list on a piece of paper torn from his notebook. He put it into his ashtray, a large, square-shaped one made of heavy smoked glass. The list fitted neatly in the bottom. He went to stub his cigarette out on it, then paused. He picked up the piece of paper between his fingers and, carefully, began to scorch small holes in it with the end of his cigarette. The flimsy paper browned, frizzled, dissolved. He spaced the holes evenly, so that the list became a piece of fragile lace, blackened around the edges. Eventually, it collapsed and fluttered helplessly into the ashtray.

William was sitting on a stack of cardboard boxes. They were only just taking his weight. He could feel a slight sag beneath him and the muscles in his thighs were tense, ready to stand up quickly if it collapsed. Annette was kneeling on the ground in front of him. He was holding her face in his hands.

'So,' Annette was saying, 'it's very simple really. We need proof. We need proof or Helly will probably get the sack. We've got to do it quickly. If he sacks her or any of us we can't make accusations then because it just looks like sour grapes.'

William took his hands away from her face and sat back. Annette moved back on her heels. The distance between them doubled.

William was thinking. They were probably right. It all fitted together, the way Richard had behaved over Rosewood Cottage. Technically, there was no reason for it to be demolished but that hadn't struck him as particularly odd. Properties were often compulsorily purchased as a precaution. Surveyors or project managers taking money from contractors was commonplace. Then there were the lunches, the golfing trips, the cut price conservatories. It was a grey area.

He sighed. 'You know, what Richard is up to is really very ordinary. It goes on all the time. That John Summerton took me out for drinks after a site visit last week. I've never taken a bribe but, strictly speaking, nobody's whiter than white in this business. You could make almost anyone's behaviour look bad if you wanted to.'

Annette was looking at him. 'I know that,' she said quietly. 'Helly doesn't give a damn about what Richard takes off the contractors. She probably wouldn't have said anything to anyone if it wasn't for her grandparents. And now he's trying to get her sacked but he's being sneaky about it. He took that money from Joan, he must have done, it's him that's involved the rest of us.'

'He hasn't involved you.'

They held each other's gaze.

Annette stayed quiet, calm, although she could feel

the walls of her universe folding in, gently, like a collapsing soufflé. This is how the world ends. *Of course*, she had thought, when Helly had mentioned it, *William*. William, of course. He loves me. He's one of us. But William was not one of them. He was a man, a surveyor, a breadwinner. Helly could scheme and plot. Annette had a low mortgage and only herself to consider. Joan had a husband who brought money into the household. They were all so small and unimportant. But William was married with a child – he could not afford to join the game. She tried to reason with herself. She tried to say, there is more at stake for him. What she was thinking was, he isn't one of us. He never will be. He's on a different side of the barricades – and he doesn't love me enough to clamber over.

She sighed, then she got to her feet, turning and brushing some dust from her skirt. She looked around the store cupboard. Metal ladder shelving held boxes of supplies: envelopes, staples, indelible markers. This was their life, their job – to work their way through these supplies, a little more each day. What had they been thinking of? She and William. Helly and her schemes. Joan and her surprising bravado. They were all trying to pretend that they were not little people doing little daily activities. How pathetic they were. Grand schemes – they should be so lucky. It's over, she thought, glancing round. Dirty, dust-filtered light came from the fluorescent strips above them. William and I can see each other too clearly. This is how the world ends.

'What was it you wanted to ask me?' she said.

William looked up at her. His eyes were like lakes.

He looks as though he is swimming in doubt, she thought, a pool of doubt. Perhaps he does understand, after all.

William opened his mouth to speak. As he did, the stack of cardboard boxes beneath him buckled with a small sigh. He sank by a few inches. He stood up.

'What's in the boxes?' Annette asked, her voice rich with misery.

He looked down at them. 'Paperclips,' he replied, his voice low and dull.

Annette turned to go. Then, as she reached the door, she paused. She waited for a moment, listening, deciding. Then she reached out and clicked the Yale lock. She turned back, leaning against the door. William was looking at her. He came to her. As her arms wound purposefully about his neck, he began to lift her skirt. She pulled him to the cold hard floor.

It was the first time they had made love since Keith had turned up on her doorstep. And she knew it was the last. He felt more hot and sweet than he had ever done. She did not touch herself or want to come – she wanted to be aware of him, to feel his need of her. As it grew, he hesitated. She pressed him to her. 'It's okay,' she whispered, 'it's alright, my period's due tomorrow, it's okay.' She wanted him to come. She hated him.

She hated him because it was the last time and he didn't realise it. She hated him because she had been unfaithful and he didn't know that either. She hated him for all the things he did not know.

Afterwards, he looked at her, bewildered. She drew him in and stroked his head, murmuring, comforting. She

228

could feel a trickle of semen down one buttock so she arched her back slightly and, still stroking his head, used her other hand to pull her skirt clear, so that it would not stain.

Annette was leaning forward over the sink and peering into the mirror when Helly walked into the ladies' toilet. Hastily, she tipped her head forward to hide her face and began combing her hair. 'Hi,' she said lightly.

Helly did not answer. She went over to the window sill and hitched herself onto it. She paused, observing Annette's attempts to repair herself. Eventually she said, 'I take it he said no.'

Annette burst into tears.

Helly jumped down from the window sill and went into one of the toilet cubicles. She detached a gigantic roll of loo paper from its metal fixing and brought it over to Annette. She unwound a long streamer of it, then handed it to her. When Annette had finished crying, she said, 'I'm not entirely surprised.'

'I am,' sniffed Annette.

Helly smiled. 'You got a lot to learn, glasshopper.'

Annette turned and peered in the mirror. Her face was red and smudgy. It was going to take work. Helly put the giant loo roll down on the edge of the sink and leant against the wall, her arms folded. She watched as Annette fumbled around in her make-up bag, withdrawing mascara, eye-shadow, liner and blush.

As she inspected the damage, Annette said, 'So what now?'

Helly shrugged. 'What we should have done in the first place, I guess. Go and see the boss, take the risk. Do you know anyone up there?'

Annette shook her head. 'I met Gregory Church once.'

'Which one is he?'

'He's the one who had his papers biked to his house in Surrey when the lift was out of action. Somewhat corpulent.'

'Oh, the fat git.'

Annette was trying to dry her eyelashes with a tissue. 'Let's talk to Joan when she gets back on Monday.' She stood back from the mirror. The glass had a slight greenish tinge. It was difficult to tell what she really looked like.

'Look,' said Helly. 'Thanks for trying but really, don't fuck up your relationship with William over this.'

Annette shook her head. She was still looking at herself in the mirror. 'It isn't just this. And I haven't fucked up anything. I'm not upset because it's over. I'm upset because I've realised it never began.'

They stood in silence for a moment or two. Annette was looking at herself.

Helly was looking at Annette. 'You want to know what I reckon your problem is?' she said gently.

Annette did not turn from the mirror. She stayed observing herself, and gave a half-smile. 'What?'

'You don't know what sort of woman you are.'

Helly went on her lunch break. Annette went back to her desk.

She picked up a pile of typing from her in-tray and opened up a file on her computer.

She had only been typing for five minutes when William came over to Joan's desk and picked up a cardboard wallet lying amidst her pile of filing. 'I've got to go over to Fairlop,' he said, without looking at her. 'Will you tell Richard if he's asking after me? He wanted a word about something but he isn't in his office and I've got a contractor waiting.'

Inside herself, Annette felt something collapse, leaving an empty cavity in her stomach, as if an extra space had been created that wasn't there before. 'Okay,' she said, her voice perfectly neutral. He glanced over at her and she looked down at her keyboard, as though she was trying to concentrate on something. There was a pause, both momentary and eternal. Then he left.

After he was gone, there was a period of time when she felt he might come back. Five minutes, say, in which he could be in the toilet and popping back to pick something up, or getting to the lift and remembering a phone call he had to make before he left. For this transition period, she remained sitting stiffly at her desk, typing with her back rigid and her fingers flying over the keyboard, making it rattle like a machine gun. Then the moment came when she knew that he must by now be out of the building, walking down the street, going down the steps to the tube, whistling away from her on a train. He was gone. There was no chance that this scene was going to turn out differently.

She knew she was about to cry again. Raymond was standing a few yards away, talking to a surveyor.

A post lady ambled past, dropping Richard's afternoon correspondence onto Joan's desk. There were too many people around for Annette to run to the toilet without someone noticing. Her only choice was to stay at her desk and wait for them to wander away. She prayed that nobody would come over and speak to her. If they did, she would be finished.

She picked up her audio headphones and put them on so she could at least keep her head down and look engrossed in her work. She returned to the schedule Richard had given her that morning, forcing her mind to concentrate on building construction. But language itself seemed against her, falling apart in the same way it had in the early days, when she had first loved William. *Minor amendments to the layout will be required to comply with racking and benching requirements.* Racking and benching. She was being racked and benched.

Her eyes were so brimful with tears that she could not see the screen. The lines on the schedule swam and wavered. She typed furiously, unable to see the numerous errors she must be making, determined only to keep working, to work as hard as she wanted to run. Richard's voice continued evenly. *Repair cladding. Stop. In addition, comma, ensure prevention of water leakage from gutter down front elevation. Stop.* Her leg began to tremble and her foot caught on the pedal of the audio machine. She pressed and her foot slipped. She pressed again. Richard's voice repeated solemnly, *stop, stop, stop . . .*

She bit her lips. She drew breath. Tears streamed

down her cheeks. She kept her head down and kept typing.

That evening, Annette arrived home as dusk was beginning to gather over Catford. She walked from the station through the small residential streets, where flowers were showing off in the neat terraced gardens. Early evening, spring, the beginning of things. The end.

Her house was the same as it always was.

She made tea, still wearing her coat, feeling too tired to take it off and hang it up. She took the mug and sat on her sofa, staring out of the patio doors onto her small square patch of garden. She sipped gently at the hot drink, with her coat still on and her handbag on the cushion beside her. It was like being in a waiting room.

She tried to tell herself it was peaceful, while knowing it was merely silent.

When the phone rang, she jumped so hard that tea slopped over the edge of the mug and onto the sofa. She was lifting the receiver before she even had time to hope.

'Annette?'

It was her mother.

'Hullo, Mum.' Her tone of voice was chirpy, the stock reaction whenever her mother called. No matter how tired or upset or annoyed she might feel, she was always chirpy.

'Is that you, Annette?' her mother repeated.

No, thought Annette, it is a burglar talking falsetto. Annette is upstairs tied to the bedstead with the cord from her dressing-gown. I am about to do unspeakable things to her.

'Yes Mum, it's me.'

'How are you? Are you alright?'

'Yes, I'm fine.'

'What have you been doing?'

It was the same every phone call. What have you been doing? This question did not mean, what have you been doing that was interesting or worthy of note? It did not mean, has anything happened that you would like to tell me about? It meant, give me a full account of your week. Tell me from start to finish: how work was, whether you went anywhere, if you spoke to anybody, what television programmes you have watched and, most of all, how the weather has been in London on each of the days since we last spoke.

Annette drew breath. Then she began. 'Monday was okay. Things are rather busy at work at the moment. Joan, the other secretary, is on holiday this week and the new budgets are being prepared so I've had to . . .' She told her mother about her week. It took twenty minutes, slightly shorter than usual because it was only Thursday. Annette's mother usually rang at the weekend, to get a full account.

'How are *you?*' It was always a relief to get to this part of the call.

'Fine, dear, as well as ever. I was just wondering whether you'd made your mind up about Easter.'

Ah, Annette thought. Now we are getting to it. 'No Mum, I don't think so. I think I'm going to stay here. I've got things to fix. The house. There's some stuff I've been waiting for a chance to get at.'

'Oh . . .'

Annette had learnt by experience that the worst time to visit her mother was at the expected times: Christmas and Easter, the festivities. It allowed too long a period for a build-up. When she arrived, they would both be so full of dread it was sometimes hard to speak. Visits home were easiest to get through when they were spontaneous.

'What about this weekend?' Annette said, in a moment of inspiration. What else would she do? Sit wondering if William would call?

'Oh . . .' Annette's mother always pronounced *oh* in exactly the same way, whether she was pleased or disappointed. 'Oh, yes. Yes alright, dear.'

By the time the phone call was over, the remainder of her tea was cold. She went back to the sofa. I am nothing, she thought. I am a dirty little liar who never tells her mother anything. My life is something that I hoard away like a squirrel hoarding nuts. Squirrels are also vermin.

The following day after work, Annette caught the train from Victoria. The unfamiliar route was a pleasant variation: *Oxted, East Grinstead, Uckfield* – hardly an adventurous itinerary, but different at least from *New Cross, Lewisham, Hither Green*. Such is the detail of my life, she thought, sitting against a window with her weekend bag on her lap. Small change.

She visited her mother roughly every two months. The last time had been in February, when she had brought a bag of old tights, for stuffing cushions. Her mother was fond of collecting objects to use in some way to change or decorate her home. One of her favourite activities was tearing out advertisements from colour supplements. Last time, she had shown Annette one for a collection of china butterflies. She was paying a monthly subscription. Every other month, she received a butterfly through the post. There were a dozen to collect. *So lifelike, so real*, the advertisement said in curly letters above a glossy picture of a hand painted fine bone china Cabbage White. Below it were the words, *Butterflies of the World*. Annette had been seized with the desire to grab a biro and add the word, *Unite*.

By the time she arrived at her mother's house, she was tired and hungry. Her mother would have a ready-made pie in the oven. When she heard Annette's knock, she would turn on a ring on the electric cooker, on top of which would be sitting a saucepan of peas. They would have an early night.

The door opened. There was her mother, again. The same, again. Annette leant forward and pressed her cold damp cheek against her mother's, which was warm and papery.

'I've got a pie in the oven,' her mother said. 'Minced beef and onion. I thought we'd have an early night.'

Later, Annette vomited the pie neatly into her mother's clean white toilet. There was a heavy smell of disinfectant and the water in the bowl was slightly blue. Annette pulled the flush, then added some more bleach from a green plastic bottle that sat on the floor, and flushed again.

As she came out of the toilet, her mother passed her on the landing. 'Night night dear,' she said.

'Night,' Annette replied.

Her mother knew about the vomiting – she could not help but know. Their house had been built in the sixties and the walls were thin as greaseproof paper. Ever since it had begun, when Annette was thirteen, the sound of her puking and choking must have filled their small semi, sometimes for nights in a row, then sometimes not at all for several months. She imagined her mother lying in bed and listening. She imagined her ironing downstairs,and listening. She imagined her turning the telly up.

Her father had known about it, known consciously, in a way that her mother had not. Annette was sure of that. She saw the way he looked at her sometimes, half questioning, half annoyed. The start of the vomiting coincided with the early years of her adolescence, the years when her father had begun to follow her around. He stood in her bedroom doorway while she did her homework, most evenings, and asked her if she wanted any help. He would not allow her to go shopping on a Saturday afternoon unless he gave her a lift to the high street, even though it was only a ten minute walk. He would not allow her out of the house at all unless her coat was buttoned and she could prove she had gloves in her pocket.

When she was twelve, she demanded to be allowed her first trip to the cinema. She wanted to go with her friend Bridget. Bridget's mum would pick her up, drop them off and bring her safely back.

Later on that evening, she overheard her parents arguing in the kitchen.

Bridget's mother had hair which was the most beautiful colour Annette could imagine for hair, a thick glossy mass of orange. 'She puts mud on it,' Bridget had confessed, in tones which suggested she wanted to die of shame. As Bridget's mother drove them to the cinema she shrieked with laughter and said, 'Your parents, Annette! Dearie me, you poor love! I thought they were going to ask to see my licence!' As she parked the car outside the cinema she said, 'What on earth are they going to do in a couple of years' time when it's boys you want to go out and see?' She was shaking her head.

'I'm sorry about my mum,' Bridget muttered as they waved her off from the cinema steps. 'She's so embarrassing.'

'I like her,' said Annette.

They were early. There was no one at the ticket desk although the sweet counter was open. 'I'll get some,' said Bridget, 'but we're not allowed to start eating them until we're inside.'

By the time the ticket desk woman had ambled back, a small queue had formed. The people behind them were mostly children of their age, some a little older, a couple of adults. It was as they were turning away with their tickets that Annette saw – standing by the cinema entrance a few feet away – her father.

Their eyes met. He made no attempt to greet her. He

did not smile. She wondered momentarily if he could have a double, but no, this man was wearing her father's heavy coat. As they wandered slowly away from the ticket desk, he stepped forward to take his place in the queue.

'Here,' said Bridget. 'I want a drink as well. Do you?'

Annette shook her head. 'Let's go in.'

'In a minute.'

She felt her father walking behind them as they followed the usherette's torchbeam down the aisle. As they edged along a row of seats, she sensed him edging along the row behind them.

The cinema was two thirds empty. The bright rectangle of the screen threw out flickers of pink and grey. Bridget sat down and slumped back with her knees up against the seat in front of her. Annette removed her anorak, folded it neatly and put it down on the seat beside her. Then she sat down too. Bridget pulled their sweets from her jacket pocket. As she opened the packet wine gums popped out, sprang into the air and dived down into the darkness beneath their knees. 'Oh bugger,' giggled Bridget. Behind them, Annette heard a cough.

The film began; an adventure. Annette forgot about her father. Once every few minutes, Bridget's clammy hand would sneak over and drop a wine gum into hers. They both chewed noisily. When a spider dropped down the heroine's neck, Bridget leant over and said, 'Yuck . . .'

It was approximately half-way through the film. Annette had slid down in her seat and put her knees up, like Bridget. She had lifted her long hair clear so that she could lean her head back on the top of her seat. She went to sit up. And found that she could not. The man sitting in the seat behind her had leant forward and had rested his forearms across the top of her seat, on top of her hair.

Perhaps she had made a mistake. If somebody was leaning on her hair accidentally, then when she tried to move again, they would get off. Experimentally, she lifted her head. It was only possible to move an inch or two. The man was leaning firmly on her hair and he had no intention of moving, although he must realise that she was trying to lift her head. She sat back down. Bridget passed over a wine gum and Annette put it in her mouth, chewing automatically. It seemed flavourless.

The man did not move. Her neck became more and more stiff. She was desperate to shift her position. She hardly saw the rest of the film. Instead, she concentrated on her physical discomfort.

Towards the end she suddenly sneezed, and found that she could move. She sat up and glanced behind her. The man had gone.

When she got home, she found her parents in the sitting room. They were both reading newspapers. Her mother looked up. 'You got home alright, then?'

'Yes. Bridget's mum brought me.'

'Good.'

Her father looked up as well. He stared at her. She left the room.

*   *   *

240

For the first week after he died, Annette hardly noticed he was gone. He had had a heart attack at work. She was fifteen. His boss had come round to the house in the middle of the afternoon, just after Annette had arrived home from school. She had opened the door in her grey pleated skirt. The boss stood there, clutching a plastic bag to his chest with one hand. The other hand hung down by his side, clenching and unclenching. He looked at her and said, 'Is your mum in?' She nodded, not moving. From somewhere inside the house her mother called out, 'What is it?'

The boss looked at Annette as if it was she who had asked the question. Then he said solemnly, 'It's your dad.'

Within hours, the house was invaded. It stayed that way for days. Then there came the unequivocal glamour of the funeral. Annette's Aunt Alice took her out and bought her a new dress, soft navy blue wool with a tea-coloured lace edging around the cuffs and collar. It was from a boutique in East Grinstead called *Young Lady*, which was full of middle-aged assistants with gravity-defying hairdos who followed Annette around the shop twisting their hands together and saying, 'Oh that looks lovely on.' Annette had never had anything so old fashioned. She was enchanted. She was less enchanted when, the following day, she found her mother in the sitting room with the dress clasped on her lap. She was unpicking the lace with the end of a fruit knife. Annette sat down on the sofa and watched her in silence. Eventually, the lace lay curled next to her mother's feet, like crumbled biscuit. Her mother held the dress up, proudly. 'There, now you're decent.'

At the graveside they stood close together. Annette in her new dress with the tiny pin-prick holes around the cuffs and collar, her mother in an old brown coat, her face red from weeping. Their next door neighbours, Mr and Mrs Dobson, stood either side of them and held umbrellas over their heads. Mrs Dobson was on one side, with her arm around Annette's mother. Mr Dobson was on the other, next to Annette. Once in a while, he squeezed her shoulder protectively. She liked the feel of the Dobsons either side of them. It was like having bodyguards. She stared at the coffin and thought, Mum and me, we are the stars. For days now, people had been coming round to the house and telling her how wonderfully well she was coping; complete strangers, some of them.

The following week, all the people disappeared. Her father had been buried. The house was silent. It became apparent that he was gone.

The only person who hung around was Mr Dobson. He was an electrician, self-employed. He started fixing things for them. 'Might as well,' he would murmur from underneath the sink, his voice echoing. Annette understood that this was because her father was no longer around, although she couldn't remember him ever having fixed anything even when he was. A week after the funeral Mr Dobson came with a bunch of carnations for Annette's mother and a book for Annette. 'Just to cheer you up a bit,' he said, a little bashfully, looking at Annette's mother. After he had gone, she swayed softly from side to side in the kitchen, and said to Annette, 'He's such a thoughtful man, and that wife of his leads

242

him a merry dance. She doesn't deserve him. What's in your book?'

'Poetry.'

Upstairs, later, Annette opened it: *Palgrave's Golden Treasury*. Inside Mr Dobson had written, *To a brave and lovely girlie*, and signed it, *Keith*.

Her mother did not find out about Keith for eighteen months. By then, he had left his wife and moved into a flat in a new development on the edge of Uckfield. Mrs Dobson had come round and wept in their kitchen. 'I don't know why . . .' she had sobbed. 'He won't talk to me even . . .'

Later Annette's mother said, 'That put me in a rather difficult position you know.' Then she added with a secretive little smile, 'Not that you'd understand.'

The first time Annette removed her clothes for Keith, she was standing in the bedroom of his new flat. Except for the bed and a wardrobe, it was completely bare. The walls were covered with woodchip wallpaper, painted beige. She stood in front of him. He sat on the bed and stared. She was wearing the knickers that her mother regularly bought for her, cream-coloured ones which came right up to her waist. Keith was staring at the knickers. Oh God, she thought. How awful. I must look about twelve years old. I've got to chuck these out and get some new ones. How embarrassing. Keith took her wrists and drew her towards him. He gazed up at her. Then he buried his face in the palms of her hands.

Eventually, Annette plucked up the courage to tell

her mother she was moving out. She was going to live with Mr Dobson. He wanted them to get married. Her mother looked up at her, disbelievingly, from where she sat on a wooden kitchen chair. It was a Sunday. 'Don't be ridiculous,' she said.

Annette went upstairs and began to sort through her things. Later, her mother came and stood in the doorway and began to shout. 'That man is married! He's the same age as your poor father! They were almost best friends! He may have left her but he's still married! What about your A levels? Think of his poor wife!'

The shouting continued for several months, whenever Annette or her mother met, which was not often and usually accidental. Once, they bumped into each other in Gateways. Her mother had shrieked, from one end of the aisle to the other, 'Your father is turning in his grave!'

It was Sunday afternoon. Soon, Annette would leave to catch her train back to London. She and her mother sat in the kitchen. They had eaten lunch. They were drinking tea. Alternately, one of them would lift their cup to their lips, as if they were figures on a rain or sunshine weathervane. In the back garden, cloud and sun were also alternating. Shadows moved about.

There was a pile of brochures and leaflets on the kitchen counter. Annette saw them as she rose from the table and went to refill the pot. She picked one up while the kettle boiled and began to flick through it.

'You can put crazy paving wherever you like these days you know,' her mother said. She was sitting with her back to Annette. She didn't turn around. 'Not just paths. In the front, down the back, up the walls. Except if you put it up the walls it's called something else.'

Annette read: *It is important that crazy paving is laid level. Pegs should be placed every nine feet, alternately on each side of the path. Stones should be placed adjacent to the pegs* . . . Opposite the instructions was a glossy colour picture of a man in early middle age wearing jeans and a lumberjack shirt, grinningly handsome. He was standing in a front garden and holding a broken concrete slab. Behind him was his house. Standing in the window of his house, was his wife. His wife was holding their baby. She was also grinning. They were both looking towards the camera and the wife had her hand raised, as if she wanted to comment on proceedings in some way. *The joints between stones must be between one quarter and one half of an inch and should be filled with mortar.* 'I had no idea it was so complicated . . .' Annette murmured.

'You have to do it right,' said her mother. 'You can't just do it anyhow.'

Annette looked out of the window. *You know what your problem is* . . . Helly had said. Perhaps Annette did not know what sort of woman she was, but she knew what sort of woman she was not. She was not the woman in the crazy paving picture. She was not her mother. She was not Mrs Dobson – or William's wife. Perhaps, she thought, as I get older and older, all the other women I might be will get eliminated, one by one. Perhaps, eventually, there will be one final option. Then I shall know. 'Funny thing is,' her mother was saying, 'the man said if there's any pattern, then it isn't crazy paving. Which strikes me as a bit illogical, if you think about it.' Annette was thinking of all the different types of women she might or might not be. She thought about her childhood and words ran round her head. In particular, one word – abuse.

She read the papers. She knew the meaning of the word. She knew about two-year-olds being felt up by their uncles, adolescent girls made pregnant by their fathers, children of all ages beaten, buggered. Throughout her childhood, all her awakened years, her father had never once touched her improperly.

It was simply that, throughout those years, she had felt that at any moment without warning, he might.

7

The weather was not kind. Alun said they were unlucky.
April was often fine this far south, he said. That's
what it said in the brochure. Joan knew that they were
not unlucky, they were average. They were mean, that's
what they were. If they had come a month later they would
have had sunny afternoons, all the shops open, warmth.
Instead, they got the special offer with twenty per cent
off, a brisk breeze and plenty of cloud.

Torrievieja was perched on the coast a few kilometres
south of Alicante. Their apartment block was outside
the village, a custard-coloured edifice built around a
central courtyard with a restaurant and kidney-shaped
swimming pool. It was built to house a couple of thousand,
by the size of it, but the only guests at that time
were their tour group and three teenage girls in the
room below Alun and Joan who played pop music in
the middle of the night and did their make-up on the
balcony.

Most of the other travellers in the group were women.
On the bus from Alicante, Joan had allowed herself a glance
round and a moment of perverse satisfaction that she was

one of the few people on the bus whose husband had not yet dropped dead.

Once they were settled in they kept themselves to themselves. Joan tried to feel pleased. She had prepared herself for mucking in, exchanging life stories, the spirit of the blitz. She had come ready to tolerate people she did not really like. Instead, the group seemed to keep in its pre-arranged order, mixed and single sex couples and the odd lone female. Joan and Alun were among the youngest. The exception was a group of four women who were sharing an apartment on the same floor. They knocked on Joan and Alun's door the first morning and said they were going on an adventure down to the beach and did they want to come?

'Oh,' said Joan. 'It is rather windy . . .'

After they had gone, Alun said, 'What did they want?'

'They wanted to know if we wanted to take a walk with them to look at the beach. They said nothing ventured nothing gained.'

Alun grunted and said, 'Teapot.'

The restaurant was wood-panelled and served cheese and ham sandwiches at lunchtime and steak and chips in the evening. It was staffed by two young waiters in white shirts and black waistcoats. They had brown eyes and heavily loaded accents which they practised on the teenagers. 'Hallo,' they would say, as the girls slid themselves up onto the tall thin bar stools. 'Would you like somet'ing to eat or drink or shall we talk about t'ings?'

They ignored Alun and Joan, sitting at a table in an

alcove. Alun was relatively patient to start off with, tapping the table with the end of a teaspoon and waiting for one of them to amble over. Eventually, he went up to the bar and gave their order in a voice that boomed around the little restaurant and out into the courtyard.

'I,' (pointing at himself) 'would like steak and chips. My wife,' (pointing back at Joan) 'would like egg and chips. We would like them pronto. Quickly.'

The waiters looked at each other and pulled faces. Then they shrugged and lifted their hands.

Alun sighed, picked up the plastic-covered menu and pointed at the pictures of what they wanted. '*I* . . .' he began again, pointing at himself.

The young women watched, giggling.

Eventually, one of the waiters said, '*Aah*, Señor,' as if Alun had explained the meaning of the universe, 'I understand. Cheeps!'

At that, there was great rejoicing. The other waiter threw his hands up into the air and beamed with joy. 'Yes! Cheeps!' They both ran around behind the bar calling, 'Cheeps! Cheeps!' Then one of them lifted the hatch behind him and shouted into the kitchen, 'Luis! The Eenglish! He want cheeps!'

The girls nearly fell off their stools.

The four women were there. They clattered in together just after Joan and Alun, talking in high-pitched voices in a mixture of London accents. 'Old hens,' Alun muttered as they nodded a greeting on their way past. They dined in the alcove next to them, talking loudly and playing cards. They started off with whist and rummy but by the time Alun and Joan had finished eating they had degenerated to snap. Every now and then, one would bang the table and they would all scream 'Snap!' in unison. The level of hysteria rose gradually. One of them shrieked at the waiters, ' 'Ere, Pedro, let's have another bottle of vino!' When he brought it over, the same voice cracked, ' 'Ow about a kiss?' More shrieking. Alun rolled his eyes at the ceiling.

Alun and Joan went back to their apartment, Joan dawdling to breathe in the cool, clean night air. Inside, Alun sat down to read the day-old paper they had bought in Torrieveja that afternoon. Joan sat in the chair with a puzzle book on her lap and stared out of the sliding doors which led onto their balcony. Funny to think it's a Monday evening, she thought, and that somewhere else, my ordinary life is carrying on, as if there is another Joan who went into work today and talked to Helly and Annette and asked them if anything had happened with Richard and watered plants and filed correspondence. I wonder how my impersonator is getting on. She tried to think of it the other way around, that her perspective of the world had merely shifted from London to Torrieveja, but it was hard to grasp: the one thing we never manage to get hold of, she thought – a sense of our own absence.

Their curtains were open. She gazed through the patio doors out onto the balcony and beyond. That blackness out there, she thought, that is the sky, and the sea.

The days remained cloudy. Each morning Joan woke, left Alun's silent bulk in bed and padded into the little kitchen to put the kettle on. This was the best bit, being alone in the tiny room with nothing familiar around. All was new and white and clean, a fresh start. She went to the toilet while the kettle boiled, then tiptoed into the bedroom and pulled a cardigan on over her nightie. She returned to the kitchen and filled the stainless steel teapot they had brought from home. While it was brewing, she went over to the patio doors, slid them quietly back and stepped outside.

It was chilly. The sky was white, with clouds here and there which folded into grey. A light morning breeze whisked across the courtyard, ruffling the surface of the swimming pool. Sun-loungers and plastic tables were piled high at the side, waiting for the peak-season hordes. She imagined how it must be in July and August: rows of girls in coloured bikinis, tanned boys diving into the pool, hot blue sky, bottles of cold beer, radios blasting out.

The only figure she ever saw was a cleaning man in a blue overall who wandered around with a garden fork. One morning, she saw him saunter over to the deserted pool, reach out and drag a large white plastic bag over to the side. It had been floating there for two days.

They read a lot: Joan her puzzle book, Alun his papers. Most afternoons they went for walks along the deserted front, past the little supermarket and the boarded up souvenir shop. The main beach was a huge strip of sand ten minutes' walk from their apartment block. Pale gold, dusty, empty, it stretched into the distance. One afternoon they met an elderly Scandinavian walking his dog. He invited them to have a cup of coffee in a sea front café. Joan looked at Alun, expecting him to say no, but he

251

merely shrugged. The café was the other side of the road from the beach and made of wide windows and blue-washed stone. Inside were two other couples from the group and Joan nodded to them. They drank coffee and ate cake and the Scandinavian said he came from Norway and his name was Bill. He had lived in Torrievieja for thirteen years. He spoke such good English because his wife was English. She was a belly-dancer from Newcastle-under-Lyme. They had married just after the war and divorced two years later. He had fought in the Navy, in a ship that was sunk by a U-boat. Only he and four others had survived. They were sitting by the window and Alun stared out at the sea while he talked. Every now and then, the wind chucked a light handful of rain against the glass.

The day before they left, the weather brightened. Joan rose and found the sky a brilliant blue. Out on the balcony, she breathed deeply. The cleaning man was whistling as he did his rounds. She waved to him.

At lunchtime, the waiters set some plastic tables outside the restaurant and served sandwiches there. Joan and Alun had just begun theirs when they were joined by two of the four loud ladies.

'Do you mind?' one of them said. 'It's just, we're dying to have lunch outside and there aren't enough tables.'

Joan smiled nervously and said, 'No . . . of course . . .' glancing at Alun. To her surprise, he put down his paper and said, 'No of course not ladies. Why not? Now what will you be having?' He got to his feet and rubbed his hands together. Joan looked up at him.

The ladies beamed. 'Sangria!' said one, 'as it's our

last day. Here . . .' she began fiddling in her hand-bag.

'No, it's okay,' said Alun, 'this one's on me. Two sangrias. Usual, Joan?' Joan nodded.

When Alun had turned away, one of them pulled a packet of Fortuna cigarettes from her bag. 'These are pretty disgusting,' she said chummily to Joan, 'but in for a penny in for a pound, that's what I say.' She offered one. Joan shook her head.

'Nice, your husband,' said the other. 'Quite a surprise. I said the other night he looked like a miserable old git.'

'Glenda!' said the other.

'Oh, she doesn't mind . . .' said Glenda, laughing.

Joan said stiffly, 'I think I should go and give my husband a hand.' As she left, the woman with the cigarettes was saying, '*Glen*da . . .'

Later, the other two arrived. They had just climbed a hill, they said, and they were knackered. They dragged chairs out from the restaurant and plonked themselves down. Noisily, the four women decided that a whole jug of sangria was called for. Glenda went to organise it.

After a while, Alun said to Joan, 'Think I'll go back for a kip.'

'Oh,' she said, 'I'll just finish up then,' indicating her drink.

'No, it's alright. You stay if you like,' he said.

'What about a game?' said Glenda. The other women groaned.

'Do you play games?' she asked Joan.

'Puzzles,' said Joan. 'I do puzzles.' When she looked round, Alun had gone.

They played poker. The afternoon sun grew so warm they called one of the waiters over and asked him to fetch an umbrella. There was much hilarity as he tried to insert the metal spike into the hole in the middle of the plastic table. Glenda told him what he needed was more practice. When he had finished, they gave him a round of applause and he responded with a smile and a bow.

When Joan next checked her watch she saw that it was nearly four. She rose from the table. 'I should just go and check on Alun,' she said to the women apologetically. Glenda opened her mouth to say something and one of the others shot her a warning look.

'I'll see you later,' Joan said firmly.

She hurried back to the apartment. Alun must be wondering where on earth I am, she thought.

The apartment door was unlocked. In the living area she found him, asleep on the sofa. She took her shoes off so that she could walk around without disturbing him. She filled the kettle very slowly and plugged it in. Then she sat down on a kitchen chair while she waited for it to boil.

Joan observed her husband. He was not attractive when he slept. It made him look older. The skin on his face seemed grey and his mouth loose and slack. He looked vulnerable.

All at once, she was overwhelmed with a rush of tenderness. She remembered their honeymoon, in Devon. It had been a hot summer, that year. The hotel had been wonderful, the staff so polite. Everyone loves a honeymooning couple. She had never been treated so well. On their first day on the beach they had got sunburnt. That evening Alun had laughed at her red face and dabbed cold cream on the end of her nose. Then he had smoothed some on her forehead, very gently, and said, 'Do you know, Joan, it's very odd. Has anybody told you? Sunburn or a tan makes your eyes look more green.'

She watched him on the sofa, watched the skin on his throat as it rose and fell with his breath. His thin hair lay across his speckled scalp. I love you Alun Hardy, she thought, I really do. Not for what you are but for what we have been through together, all these years. Not exciting years, perhaps, not filled with noise or fun or children, but *our* years. After all, we have been through our lives together. She resolved, there and then, to try and understand him more. When he wakes, she thought, I will tell him. I am going to be more pleasant and lively. We will enjoy our lives.

She brewed the tea and went to the bathroom. She combed her hair in the tiny mirror, peering at herself. She opened her mouth and examined her teeth. She had good teeth. I am not old yet, she thought, not by a long chalk.

When she went back into the kitchen, Alun was awake. He was sitting up and reading the newspaper.

'Did you have a good sleep?' she asked, as she poured the tea.

'Not bad,' he replied.

She looked at him. He looked exactly the same.

'So what do you think of our new friends?' she asked brightly.

He pulled a face. He shrugged.

She took the tea over to him and stood in front of him. She felt quite desperate. 'Alun . . .' she said.

He lowered the paper. He took his tea. 'Thanks,' he said.

She returned to her seat. 'It's our last night,' she said.

He did not reply.

'What shall we do?' she said.

He shrugged.

'Shall we go back to the restaurant?' she asked. Her voice had taken on a slightly shrill tone.

'Whatever. If you like.'

The next day they woke early and packed their things. The coach was coming at ten, to take them to the airport. The weather had gone back to being dull and grey. Joan checked all the cupboards and drawers to make sure they had not forgotten anything, even though they had never put anything in them in the first place. Alun sat at the kitchen table with an old pencil and a smoothed out paper bag and made notes on what they could afford to get in Duty Free.

At Alicante, the Young at Heart tour rep showed them to the check-in desk, then ran off to meet the next group which was arriving shortly. The queue was huge. 'Bloody pain this is,' muttered Alun. 'There's no one in that queue there.'

He told Joan to mind their bags while he went to ask a young man at a nearby empty desk if they could check in there. Joan watched him while they talked. One of the turn-ups on his slacks had started to droop. It hung down slightly, just visible above his comfy shoes, the corduroy ones she had talked him into that time they went to Brent Cross. She stared at his back, where his polycotton jacket strained over his rounded shoulders. My life is hell, she thought. My life is hell.

Helly did not enjoy menstruating at the best of times. Now was not the best.

She woke on that Monday morning with an abdomen of mangled chaos: blood and guts and soft, under-developed flesh. She clutched at it beneath the sheets and resolved, as she often did, that she was going to take up exercise. One day. Aerobics. Tennis, perhaps. She kept her eyes closed and thought of a green grass court with perfect white lines, blue sky above, yellow sun. She pictured herself in a white pleated skirt, her body trim and tidy, her arm swinging gracefully above her head.

From outside her bedroom door there came a loud, 'Oh shit!'

Her mother was up.

Helly lay, absorbing the sound. Then suddenly, she sprang out of bed. She grabbed her towelling robe from where it lay on the floor and slung it around her shoulders as she ran out of her room.

Too late. Opposite her bedroom, next to the loo, was the airing cupboard. The doors stood open. There were some folded sheets and a faded yellow pillowcase. Otherwise, it was empty. 'I'm going to clock her one,' Helly muttered as she turned on her heel. She paused to tie her robe before crossing the landing to her mother's room.

The door to her mother's bedroom was closed. Helly knocked on it, loudly. There was no reply. She knocked again. 'Mum!' she called. '*Mum!*' she hollered.

After a pause, her mother's muffled voice replied. 'What? What do you want?'

Helly opened the door. Her mother was sitting on a small stool in front of her dressing-table, the one with the scalloped wooden trim and angled mirrors. She was wearing a straight brown skirt over a slip. She had one arm raised and was holding her curling tongs. Wrapped round the tongs was her fringe. She scowled at Helly in the mirror but did not turn around. 'What you yelling for?'

Helly folded her arms and glared. 'Have you got my knickers?'

'Oh for God's sake Hels.'

'You have, haven't you?'

'I didn't get down the launderette this week.'

'Give them here.'

'What?'

'You heard me. Take them off. I handwashed them last night because I needed them this morning. What do you think I washed them for?'

'I didn't know you needed them, I thought you had some in your room.'

'Bollocks. You probably set your alarm so you could be up before me and nick 'em.'

'Oh piss off.'

'Mum!' Helly's voice had reached a shriek of outrage. 'I *need* those knickers. I'm *on!*'

'Helly!' Her mother unravelled the curling tongs from her fringe and slammed them down on her dressing-table. 'How many times have I got to tell you I'm sick of you screaming round the house and slamming doors. I've got to go and see someone and I didn't know they were your only clean pair and if you think I'm taking them off you've got another thing coming. Now piss off. If you don't like it, go and live somewhere else.'

Now that it was curled, Mrs Rawlin's fringe appeared to take a rash dive off the top of her head, change its mind just above the eyebrows and spring back up. As she shouted at Helly, it bobbled merrily about.

Helly looked at her mother and took a deep breath. 'Slag!' she spat, then left the room, slamming her mother's bedroom door behind her and sprinting for the bathroom.

She managed to shut the bathroom door and lock it just as her mother caught up with her. Mrs Rawlins hammered on the door with the flat of her hand. 'I'm going to rip your head off you foul-mouthed little bitch!' she screamed. 'I mean it! No fucking daughter of mine talks to me like that!'

'You and whose army . . .' muttered Helly to herself, as she upended the laundry basket and started sorting through the underwear to find the least dirty pair of knickers.

She waited in the bathroom until she heard her mother leave the house. Then she crept out and dressed hurriedly. She was going to be late. Joan was back from holiday today and she had promised her that she would be on her best behaviour.

Half-way through dressing, she suddenly stopped and sat down on her bed. She put her head in her hands. A slow spiral of pain was twisting its way down her lower intestine. She always bled heavily for the first two days. She sat up, breathing deeply. Then she rose and walked around her room in two small circles. Walking seemed to help a little. Perhaps she should walk to work. If she was going to be late, she might as well do it properly. She pulled on her cardigan, went over to her window and drew back the curtains. There were no nets and her window looked out directly onto the back alley, so she usually kept the curtains closed. It was a grey, heavy day. Two school children walked solemnly past, like little monks, the straps of their satchels across their foreheads and the bags hanging down their backs. A dog was sniffing around the rubbish bins. Helly leant her face against the cold window pane. Nothing to lose, she thought. Nothing. She would walk.

On Lambeth Bridge she paused. Funny how different the view was, depending on which way you looked. Towards Westminster, there were the Houses of Parliament, St Paul's, the glamorous buildings. Look the other way and there were the ruins of industrialisation, the muddy sludge of businesses and people gone bust.

At the roundabout just before Horseferry Road, there was a roadblock. Pedestrians were walking through but vans or large cars were being stopped. There was a

handful of civilian police directing the traffic and two
soldiers in navy blue combat gear holding machine guns.
Helly stared at them as she went past. They had stopped
a small white van and the woman driver was giving details
to a WPC who was relaying them into a walkie-talkie. The
roadblocks had been stepped up in recent weeks but they
usually took place in the City. It was the first time Helly
had seen one on Lambeth Bridge. There had been talk on
the telly last week that there would be random checks on
all bridges following a series of security alerts.

As Helly passed the derelict Westminster Hospital
an elderly woman, even smaller than herself and dressed
in rags, approached her with a filthy hand outstretched,
mumbling. Helly shook her head and walked on. Behind
her, she heard the woman curse. Never mind love, Helly
thought, I'm going to be homeless too, the rate I'm going.
If only old Mrs Hawthorne would hurry up and die. Thinking
about the old bat reminded her of her grandparents Joanna
and Bob, Rosewood Cottage, Richard. Now that William
had refused to help them, the prospects did not look good.
Annette meant well but she had her own mess to deal with.
Helly regretted involving Joan. Her job was probably on the
line as well now. It was four weeks since Richard had stared
her down in the lift. She had managed to avoid him mostly –
he seemed to be out of the office a lot these days – but she
knew now that he wasn't the kind of man to let bygones be
bygones. He would keep going till he got her. And if he
couldn't get her, he would simply make her life hell. There
were plenty of ways he could do it. Either way, Helly
thought with a bitter sigh, my days there are numbered.

Good riddance. But how could she protect Joanna and Bob if she got the sack?

When she had been twelve, there were some problems at school – a woman teacher had taken a dislike to her. Her mother had said, 'What do you expect me to do about it? She's the Deputy Head.' Her grandmother Joanna had put on her best mac and polished her shoes and turned up at the school one afternoon. She had taken Helly into a deserted class room and listened carefully to her side of the story. Then together they had gone to see the teacher concerned. Joanna had made Helly wait outside the staff room while she went in.

As they walked away from the school, Helly asked, 'What did you say?'

'I was very polite,' Joanna had replied grimly.

Later that afternoon, Joanna and Bob had sat either side of Helly in their kitchen. Bob rested his arm across the back of her chair and Joanna put both her hands on Helly's knees. 'If anybody ever bothers you,' Joanna had said, 'whether it's a teacher or some other kids or some bloke, you tell us. We can't wave a wand and do miracles, but you tell us. Okay?'

Half-way down Horseferry Road, Helly paused to withdraw a tattered tissue from her jacket pocket and wipe her nose. She looked up at the sky, white with cloud. If they get chucked out of the cottage, she thought calmly, I'll knife that evil bastard. So help me, I'll kill him.

Joan frowned as Helly approached her desk. 'If this is your idea of timekeeping, my dear, I would hate to see what happened if you ever decided to be late.'

'Ah lay off,' said Helly, smiling. 'How was your holiday? You're not very brown.'

'Yes well,' Joan replied.

'Where's Annette?'

'Talking to Raymond about a spec. I'm glad you're here at last, I've been dying to know what's been going on while I've been away.'

'Not much,' said Annette as she rounded the corner, a bundle of specifications flopping over one arm. 'Except Raymond saving up specs for me to type like they're going to go out of fashion . . .' She dropped the pile onto Joan's desk. 'Hang on while I have a look-see who's around.'

The door to Richard's office was open. It was empty.

'He's been very quiet,' Helly was saying to Joan as Annette rejoined them. 'Too quiet really, gives me the willies.'

Joan looked a little disappointed. 'I thought I'd be coming back to high drama. What do we do? Just keep our heads down and hope nothing happens, or go upstairs and spill the beans? Who to?'

'Mr Church, I guess,' said Annette, 'I get the impression they're quite chummy though.'

'What's he like?' Joan asked.

'He's a fat git,' said Annette.

Helly smiled. 'What Annette means,' she said, mimicking her accent, 'is that he is not the kind of gentleman who is likely to take the word of an office junior over the chief surveyor of his technical services department.'

'I think it would be better coming from me,' said Annette.

Helly looked at her. There was a pause. 'Are you sure?' she asked.

Annette nodded, 'Yes, I am. But I think we should lie low for this week. It's a short week anyway, not much can happen. I think it would be better done after Easter.'

'Don't you think it would be better done after Easter?' said Mr Church.

Richard frowned. It had been bad timing to come and see Church on a Monday morning. He had forgotten that Monday morning was not his best time.

'Well, in addition,' Richard said, examining his fingernails, 'I'm afraid there's the matter of the youngster. I can't prove she is implicated in what he has been up to but it seems likely. Anyway, there are problems with her timekeeping and her general work performance. My secretary's been keeping records.' Richard sighed, as if this was all terribly difficult. 'Of course, it will help with the budgetary problem in my section. There's also an elderly secretary that I think we could move sideways and frankly I think the rest of my staff are due for a pay freeze. We haven't had an overhaul for a while. How's Jennifer?'

Mr Church smiled broadly. 'She did terribly well in her mock exams. Always nice to have an artist in the family.'

Richard pressed his lips together in a regretful expression. 'Must be wonderful to have a lovely daughter. Of course, my wife and I, well we've not been able to . . .'

Mr Church shook his head sympathetically. His plump

face wobbled slightly as it moved. 'This surveyor, what's his name?'

'Bennett,' said Richard. 'William Bennett. Young family as well.'

'Humph,' said Church, and his bulk heaved an inch or two up from his chair. 'Well he should have thought of that before he decided to try and pull the wool over our eyes. I don't believe in being soft over this sort of thing.'

Richard raised both hands and then clapped them down on his knees, as if to indicate that neither did he but, all the same, it was a terrible pity.

After Mr Church there was the dreaded Marjorie, in Personnel. After Marjorie there was Simone in Accounts, who had been pulling the figures he had asked for, the ones that showed it might be necessary to reduce the number of staff in his unit, maybe move a couple of people sideways. The figures weren't ready, she told him, but they would be by Wednesday. The accounts department was always trying to produce figures showing that the staff needed rationalising. He had the strong feeling that old Simone couldn't believe her luck.

The following day, Tuesday, Richard spent out of the office, visiting some of the contractors that he hadn't seen for a while, tying up a few loose ends.

On the Wednesday, he went down to Simone and picked up his figures. When he got back to his office, he phoned Arthur Robinson. He didn't normally ring people from his office phone – you never knew when the switchboard might be listening in – but on this occasion he knew he could handle the topic of conversation obliquely. 'Arthur, about that job . . .' he began. Arthur was prevaricating. What a joke this whole business is, Richard thought. I should be able to hire people specially for this kind of thing, not have to rely on two-bit weirdos belonging to soft-headed contractors like Arthur Robinson. I'd do it myself if I thought it was worth the risk. Do my own dirty work. He thought it prudent to remind Arthur, obliquely of course, of the extent of his obligation. 'I want it done by the end of this week, Arthur. There must be an opportunity. Or the weekend at the latest. Come up with an alternative if necessary. I mean it. It's important for my schedule.'

Next, he buzzed Raymond, who came striding round to his office in his usual brisk, officious manner, the loyal lieutenant. Raymond was slightly bow-legged – couldn't stop a pig in a passage, as Richard's mother would have said – consequently, when he was being brisk he bobbed almost imperceptibly from side to side, like a child's toy which would wobble but not fall down. Richard had dwelt on the possibility of including Raymond in his arrangements with contractors but had come to the conclusion that it wasn't worth the risk. Raymond was a greedy man, with ideas above his social station, but he had a Calvinist streak which probably would have baulked at a little honest give and take with building companies. Anyway, Richard didn't like to trust anybody.

'Raymond!' he said, leaning back in his chair. 'Look I know it's short notice but I need you to do something for me. Thursday afternoon. The Croydon meeting. Don't think I'll be able to make it. It's on your way, and it'll only take half an hour and then you could go home afterwards, it being Easter. Would you mind?'

Raymond looked pleased. He liked to deputise for Richard. He insisted on signing all outgoing mail when Richard was on holiday and informing Annette what Richard might want her to prioritise. Richard knew that the women in his section disliked Raymond intensely, which suited him very well.

After he had gone, Richard began leafing through his surveyors' work plans for that week. Most of them were already sorted out. He was going to leave William to the last minute. By four o'clock on Thursday afternoon, the whole floor would be deserted.

He was really doing very well indeed.

'You're doing terribly well.' Gillian's voice was coaxing, but stern.

'Am I?' Richard pleaded, his own voice a schoolboy squeak. 'I do mean to be a good boy, I really do.'

It was evening. Richard's plans were made for the following day. He had come home with a Chinese take-away for them both, feeling tired but pleased. Afterwards, they had cleared up together, then had a drink while they watched television.

The ten o'clock news had finished half an hour ago and they were now in their bedroom. They were on the bed lying towards the opposite end to the headboard. Gillian was wearing the uniform of a hospital matron. A watch was pinned to her chest and her hair was in a bun. Underneath the uniform, she wore stockings and suspenders. These were visible because the polyester skirt of her outfit had ridden up over her thighs. It had ridden up over her thighs because she was straddling Richard, her knees on either shoulder. On the floor beside the bed lay a thermometer and her sensible shoes.

Richard was blindfolded. His arms were spreadeagled either side and his hands grasped the wooden bedposts at the bottom of the bed. 'I *want* to get better . . .' he squeaked, and thumped the heels of his feet against the pillow.

'Stop wriggling!' Gillian hissed viciously.

'Sorry . . .' Richard wheedled.

Afterwards, Gillian pulled on her kimono over the polyester dress and went downstairs to fix drinks. She returned a few minutes later with two whiskies and dry ginger and a cut-glass bowl cradled in the crook of her arm. In the bowl was a small heap of crinkly, low fat crisps.

Richard was sitting up on the bed, smoking. 'Goody,' he said. 'What flavour?'

She handed him the drinks and put down the bowl on the bedside table. 'Cream cheese and chives. Your favourite.'

'Mmm.'

Richard stubbed out his cigarette and took a sip of whisky as he gave Gillian her glass. She passed over the crisps. He snuggled down and rested the bowl precariously on his taut, hairless chest. 'Feed me?' he suggested impishly. He was naked but for the unfastened blindfold which hung around his neck. He wasn't cold because,

268

before they had settled down to watch the news, Gillian had taken the precaution of turning up the radiator. Gillian thought of everything.

She settled next to him, loosening her robe. Then she cradled his head underneath one arm and began to slip crisps, alternately, between her lips and his own.

'I spoke to Mum today,' she said, crunching. 'She wanted to know if we would go over weekend after next and help her and Dad with the greenhouse.'

'Of course we will,' said Richard, crunching too. 'Tell them not to even start it. We'll do it for them on the Sunday. Then we'll take them out to dinner at the carvery.'

Gillian bent her head and kissed the top of his. 'What a nice idea. They'd love that.'

As Richard and Gillian were munching their crisps, Joanna and Bob Appleton were sitting up in bed in Rosewood Cottage, tossing a coin. They were tossing a coin to see whose turn it was to come last.

'Heads,' called Joanna.

Bob lifted his hand up, peered at the coin and pulled a face. 'Best of three?' he suggested.

Joanna shook her head. 'You lost, sunshine.' she said, as her arms went around him.

Afterwards, they lay in bed and held each other in the semi-dark, listening to a low wind which was looping round the cottage. Once in a while, it rattled a window pane.

'I love you,' said Bob.

Joanna smiled. 'Me too.'

They kissed. Bob pulled her closer into his arms

and said, 'Do you know what I found really sexy, doing, this time?'

'What?'

'When I took my finger out of you and drew wet little circles on your backside. My damp Joanna.'

Joanna laughed. 'I think you'll find the dampness was the K-Y jelly, not me. I am sixty-six.' They kissed again. Joanna drew her head back and gazed at him. Then she lifted a finger and gently, smiling, drew it around the lines in his face. 'How ridiculous we are,' she said softly. 'I don't think we should ever forget it you know, any of us. How ridiculous we all are.'

'Look on the bright side my love, we've had our bi-annual sex session, so no danger of anything untoward happening when we go round to Jill and Tom's. They're quite safe.'

'The thought!'

Then she frowned.

'What?' Bob asked.

'Oh, I don't know. I'm a bit worried about leaving Mum on her own tomorrow night. She keeps raving. Somebody after her, she says. Seen his eyes, through the window.'

'She's always been raving. You just feel guilty after all those things we said about her,' said Bob, stroking her head.

'I suppose so.'

Bob placed his hand under Joanna's chin and tipped her face upwards. As his lips met hers, he slipped his forefinger gently into her mouth, and their two tongues and the finger met together, all three slippery as eels.

270

As Bob was sliding his finger between Joanna's softly parted lips, Arthur Robinson was tucking into the fourth of his fresh cream éclairs. Worry always sent Arthur straight round to the bakery. Éclairs were his favourite. Arif's, opposite the yard, did them with a liquid chocolate topping in which there was just a hint of lemon juice. It was slightly inappropriate, and quite delicious. He was being careful not to gorge himself, though. He was on his fourth but he was rationing himself to one per hour. Darkness had fallen long ago but paperwork and worry about Richard kept him occupied in between each treat. He had rung his wife earlier, to explain that urgent business was holding him up. He might be very late.

As Arthur Robinson's fourth éclair made its way down his gullet, Annette's chocolate cake was coming back up hers. She had bought the cake on her way home from work, from the little shop on Hither Green Lane. She had gone in for teabags, then she had seen the cake and found herself reaching for it with all the slow, solemn purpose of a Dalek. From that moment on, the rest of her Wednesday evening had been defined.

She sank down into a sitting position beside the toilet. So, she thought, it wasn't just going home last weekend that did it. It's back. Each time it went away, she thought that she would not do it again. Each time it returned, she felt sure it would never stop. It was this that made it so unbearable. Full blown anorexia, one hundred per cent madness; at least if she had either of those she would know what she was. She had had this problem since early adolescence, but every time it reached the point where she thought she should do something about it, it stopped – as if there was a small ghost in her stomach. She did not even know what the ghost was called.

She laid her bare arm on the cool enamel of the toilet seat. The rich smell of vomit rose up from the bowl. She sat there, the hot stink in her nostrils, and thought of William, last week, and their scene in the basement. They had not spoken to each other all week, so now she knew that he knew it was over. She was relieved, and miserable. She thought about his hands, the bitten nails, the slightly crooked left thumb. She thought of how he had felt inside her on the cold hard floor of the Capital Transport Authority's store cupboard, next to the battered boxes full of paperclips.

William did know that it was over with Annette, but he was pretending that he didn't. He was also pretending that he wanted sex with his wife. They were in bed. His sojourn on the sofa had lasted only one night, but the silence with which Alison had allowed him back into their bed had indicated to him that he was on probation.

They were both wearing pyjamas. His were brushed cotton, hers silky. She was wearing her reading glasses and was seemingly intent upon an orange book called *Cours illustre de français*. William had his hand rested on her thigh and was turned sideways, looking at her. He did not know why he was doing it. He had a vague idea that if he pretended he wanted sex, then whatever conclusion she had come to about his behaviour over the last few weeks would be somehow confused. He thought that, perhaps, he would get away with whatever she had guessed him to be guilty of.

'William . . .' Alison said slowly, without taking her eyes off her book. 'You are touching me safe in the knowledge that I will say no, and I think that is despicable.' He removed his hand. 'Touch me again,' she said, turning a page, 'and you can go downstairs to the sofa again and stay there.'

Helly was on the sofa in her house in Stockwell. Wednesday night was the night her mother usually went out bonking the dentist, a source of great relief to all concerned. They hadn't spoken to each other since the incident over the knickers. As soon as her mother had gone, Helly had turned off the telly and gone upstairs to her room. Hidden in a box beneath her bed was the book on German Expressionism which she had, at last, managed to pinch from the Tate.

She took it downstairs because there was a standard lamp in the sitting room with a good strong bulb. She brought it over and balanced it on the arm of the sofa. On the coffee table beside her was a cup of tea and a packet of biscuits which she had also stolen, from a health food shop in Brixton. The book was the prize, though, the biscuits could wait. She sat with her feet up on the table and the book on her lap. She sighed, and smiled. Then, slowly, she lifted the cover and began to turn the thick, glossy pages. She passed her fingers lightly over the prints, relishing the silky feel of the paper, the fresh smell of a virgin book – light and beauty and knowledge. Sod her mother. Sod the dentist. Sod them all. Helly knew the definition of the word sex. It was here, resting in her lap, clean and glowing in her hands.

Joan was already in bed. She usually got an early night during the week. As it was the first week back after their holiday, Alun was on shifts and already upstairs in bed when she got home from work. That Wednesday, she joined him around ten.

For some reason, that night she couldn't sleep. She turned over several times, trying to get comfortable. Alun stirred and murmured, 'What . . . God . . .' Thinking that she should try not to disturb him she rose, pulled on her dressing-gown with her big wool cardigan on top, then tiptoed downstairs.

The sitting room was gloomy and dark. She felt her way across to the sideboard and turned on the heavy lamp with the floral lampshade. Then she turned on the television and stood in front of it, flicking from channel to channel. There was some news programme on two; politicians arguing about terrorism. She turned it off. She stood in the cold and half-lit room. Why couldn't she sleep? What was wrong? On the sideboard, a wooden clock with gilt edging ticked surreptitiously. Next to it was an Easter card that had arrived early, written in her cousin Gilda's spidery hand. On the front was a glowing golden cross. *He died and rose again*, said the inscription. Cousin Gilda had found God two years ago and sent them cards on every occasion which had a remotely religious significance. Funny that it's called Good Friday, Joan thought. Why good, when something so bad is supposed to have happened? She shivered. No re-births for her or Alun – for any of them. No rising again. Just blackness. The end.

What *is* wrong with me? she thought again. She rose to her feet and went over to the sideboard. She picked up Cousin Gilda's card. As she did, the bulb in the floral lampshade made a small pop-pink sound – and she was plunged into darkness.

In Benny's dreams, the horses came galloping towards him across a wide open plain. The sound of their hooves was like water rushing in his ears and sometimes the large palomino at the front let out a wild, joyous braying sound. He would awake, then lie in the darkness, confused, listening to the steady hum of traffic on the Kennington Road and the dying fall of a passing police siren. Benny loved his dreams. Even the nightmares were better than the dead moment that came after he awoke and realised where he was: damp, cold, far away.

On that particular Wednesday night, he woke blearily, turning himself over onto his front with the sensation of having rolled over onto a small warm animal, a bit like a hamster. He rolled back and opened his eyes. The interior of his igloo was completely dark. Then he felt the slight dampness in his groin. He closed his eyes again and groaned. The last time he had had a wet dream was the night before the men had come and broken his brother's legs. It was a bad omen.

He groped for the small, battery-powered torch which Arthur Robinson had given him and turned it on. A weak golden crescent flickered over the large dark loops of the car tyres which formed his home. Moon shadows hung around. Benny crossed himself.

The next day was Thursday, the day before Good Friday. Benny woke early and put his extra set of clothes on, on top of the ones he had slept in. It was time to go down to the little house and wait, again. It was nearly three weeks since Señor Robinson had told him what he wanted doing to the little house and Benny was beginning to doubt the opportunity would occur. He had seen the man go out, and the woman, but never together. Still, today maybe. He always went prepared. He slipped a hammer into the pocket of his jacket, before he pulled on his coat.

Outside, it was only just light. The yard was cold and empty. Benny was always up before the other workers arrived. He trotted across to a pile of lumber covered in tarpaulin which sat against one wall. He swung himself up on top of it, then reached up to grasp the top of the wall. Some time ago, he had chipped away the broken glass which was embedded in cement along the top, to make a space just big enough for him to clutch with both hands and haul himself over. That way, he could come and go as he pleased.

Pictures, pictures, this whole damn cottage is full of pictures of one sort or another. And what good do they do? What are they for? Mrs Hawthorne was standing in her bedroom in Rosewood Cottage, her nose a few inches from the Kandinsky print. What did it mean? That

276

Bob – she blamed him. It didn't come from her side of the family.

It was early evening. She had got up as soon as she had heard Bob and Joanna leave the house. She had watched them walk down Sutton Street and be swallowed up by the gloom at the end of the road, hand in hand like a couple of silly teenagers. She couldn't believe her luck. It was ages since they had both gone out together and given her a bit of peace and quiet. They were always spying on her. Grown people; you'd think they'd have more important things to do. But now, at last, they had left her to her own devices for a whole evening. She was going to make the most of it. She was going to have a good nose around, each room systematically, one by one. She was going to find out what they were planning. They thought she was virtually immobile, helpless. They were wrong.

First she did the box room; nothing much there. Then the bathroom, and the cabinet she never got to look in because there was always someone fussing around when she wanted to go to the toilet. There wasn't much she could make sense of: some bottles of pills and lotions and what looked like a large tube of toothpaste, but when she squeezed a little onto her finger, it was a clear substance.

Their bedroom also proved to be something of a disappointment. Mrs Hawthorne inspected the sheets, but the light from the stairs wasn't bright enough to see properly and she didn't want to turn on any more in case they came back unexpectedly and caught her at it. In the corner was Bob's desk, where he did all his silly jigsaws and suchlike. She groped her way over. By the thin landing light she could just see, in the middle of the desk, his new picture, the one he had been telling her about. She picked it up. Then, grasping it as if for support, she made her way over to the door, to take a proper look.

She was standing at the top of the stairs peering at it when she heard the noise. It came from downstairs, from the kitchen. She froze. Then it came again. It sounded like the slow, harsh scrape of a sash window being lifted.

The first game was over by seven and Bob was the clear winner. He had managed to rid himself of all seven letters and scored the extra fifty. His word had been *ablative*. After that, the others had lost heart.

Jill rose from the table, good-humouredly considering she had been in the lead until Bob's unexpected coup, and offered to fix another drink. 'Shall we put the news on?' she asked over her shoulder as she went across to their well-stocked booze cabinet. 'We haven't heard it yet today.'

'Nah . . .' her husband Tom replied. 'To hell with that old rubbish, I want to beat this bastard at something.'

Bob stretched out his hands and rubbed them together, grinning. 'You'll have a fight on your hands mate, I'm on form tonight.'

'Listen to him,' said Joanna. 'I think we should bring him down a peg or two.' Tom rose from the table to help his wife. Joanna turned to Bob. 'Don't get too big for your boots sunshine, or you'll have me to deal with when we get home.'

Bob smiled and put a hand on top of her head. 'Isn't it great to have an evening out?'

'Not half.'

In another life, Benny might perhaps have been a lawyer, or a brain surgeon. He had intelligence and he had guts. He had instinct. Thus it was that, when something came hurtling at him through the half-gloom of the Appleton's small kitchen, he knew that he had got it badly wrong and that the cottage was not empty after all. Strangely, he saw horses – paper horses, their heads hanging from an indistinct rectangle. He turned to one side and tried to duck but even as he did his heart caved in and he resigned himself to darkness. Benny knew a nemesis when he saw one.

Mrs Hawthorne had not always been a barmy old lady. She had once been a single mother, a widow, a capable woman with a young child called Joanna. One day, the small Joanna had tripped and landed on her head. Mrs Hawthorne had taken her to the local doctor who had said, 'As long as she fell on her forehead she'll be fine. Back of the head or behind the ear, that's when we'll worry.'

So it was that as Mrs Hawthorne stood stock still just inside the kitchen door, the picture in one hand and a cast iron saucepan in the other, she knew exactly what she was going to do. She waited as Benny eased himself over the windowsill. The picture first, to make him duck down, then the saucepan. Behind the ear, the doctor had told her, and she thought it strange that she had not realised all those years ago how useful that information would one day be.

Bob and Joanna stood in the kitchen for a full three minutes before either of them spoke. They had taken in the situation but stood in silence still, taking it in some more. The window was open. A hammer lay beneath it. Face down on the floor beside the hammer was a small dark man in scruffy clothing with blood seeping from the back of his head. He was dead. The blood had spread in a puddle and was leaking down into the cracks in their speckled linoleum. On the other side of the corpse lay Bob's new *découpage* picture: the Horses of the Apocalypse they had indeed proved to be.

On a kitchen chair next to Benny sat Mrs Hawthorne, clutching the handle of a cast iron saucepan. She was gibbering. Her eyes were glassy and spittle ran down her chin. Her pink hair-net was hanging from one ear. 'Half a farthing . . .' she burbled. 'Half a farthing, threepence ha'penny for a twist. Twist, you used to get. Paper bags. They used to stick together. Jam or biscuit, not both. We chose each night, jam or biscuit.'

'What are we going to do?' said Bob, eventually. Joanna glanced across at her mother, then at Benny's corpse. 'Bury him in the wasteground?' she suggested.

'Joanna!'

'Oh why not?' grumbled Joanna. 'Look at him. It's obvious what's gone on. He's a burglar. And a tramp. Just look at him. Probably thought we were easy pickings. Now my mum's going to get done for murder.'

'He's still a person love.' said Bob. 'Poor little sod.'

'Oh, I know.' Joanna folded her arms. 'Do you know what they do, the tramps, or at least what Tom said they do? I don't know if it's true. He said they steal dogs, to use as hot water bottles. They cuddle up to them at night, then when the dogs die and get cold they go out and get another one.'

'Maybe that's why he wanted your mum.'

'Well he got more than he bargained for,' said Joanna. 'Here, pass me that tea-towel. Let's see if we can soak up some of this blood before it ruins the linoleum.'

'Odd grapes,' gibbered Mrs Hawthorne, 'from Surrey Docks. Half an hour, you could have a bag. Jam or biscuit.'

'Oh shut up you mad old bat,' said Joanna.

Bob put his coat back on and went to ring for the emergency services. 'Which one do I ask for?' he said to Joanna, stopping at the door on his way out. 'I've never done it before.'

'The one that deals with violent, psychotic old ladies,' said Joanna, tying his scarf round his neck for him. 'They probably have a specialist service for that these days.'

After he had gone, Joanna went back into the kitchen and gazed down at Benny. He had fallen on his front but his head was turned sideways. His eyes were open and his face wore a resigned expression. He had dirty, stubbled cheeks, as if there wasn't enough nutrition in them to grow a proper beard – a face like a wasteground, Joanna thought. Bob's right, you are a poor sod. I wonder what your name was. I wonder if there is anyone who'll even notice you've gone, let alone care. She sighed. The sash window was still open and there was a cold breeze blowing in. It was only when she turned to close it that she realised that Mrs Hawthorne was now stiff and silent on the kitchen chair. Joanna stopped and stared. Then she said, out loud but softly, as her lower lip gave the faintest tremble, 'Oh, Mum . . .' She leaned over and prised the bloodied saucepan from her mother's rigid fingers.

The heart that had withstood a world war, widowhood, a hysterectomy, the amputation of a finger and the loss of her beloved dog Pip – had finally given out. Mrs Hawthorne's last words had been, 'Cake. Fruit cake. More absorbent than Victoria sponge.' But Joanna and Bob had been in the hallway so there had been no one there to hear.

When Bob returned, they made a cup of coffee and sat at the kitchen table to wait. Bob sat in his usual place, near the window. Close to his feet was Benny. Joanna had covered him with the old rug from the hall cupboard, the one they had bought in Walton on the Wolds. Joanna sat opposite her husband, sipping her drink, while her mother's rapidly cooling corpse sat at the end of the table, sagging slightly in its chair.

'Another cup of tea Mum?' said Joanna.

'Joanna!' scolded Bob.

Eventually, the police arrived. Bob let them in. Two young officers followed him into the kitchen, regarded

Mrs Hawthorne and nodded sympathetically at Joanna, who was dabbing her eyes with a tissue.

'I thought the ambulance would be here first,' Bob remarked, neutrally. 'Thing is, the old lady's copped it too in the meantime.'

One of the policemen went over to Benny and lifted the rug to peer underneath it. He winced.

The other police officer removed his peaked hat to smooth his hair back over his head. 'I'm afraid the ambulance service is a bit stretched tonight sir,' he said. 'They're mostly up at Victoria.'

Joanna lowered her tissue and looked at him. 'Victoria?'

'Middle of the rush hour, day before Easter.' The policeman was shaking his head.

Joanna looked at Bob. 'Oh God . . .' she said.

The last day before a bank holiday always had an end of term feel, but to William that Thursday afternoon on the second floor of the Capital Transport Authority's Victoria offices felt more like the end of the world. All the other surveyors seemed to be out on visits. Even Raymond, who was mostly office-based, had disappeared after lunch wearing a self-important smile. It was towards the end of the afternoon that Richard came out of his office and beckoned him over. William was a little startled. Richard had been so quiet that he hadn't even realised he was in the building.

Richard had a little job for him. William sighed inwardly, glancing out of the office window at the light rain which speckled the glass with white and silver.

'Richard, I'm not sure anyone will be there. There isn't a site phone so I can't check. Can't it wait until Tuesday?'

Richard looked at William coolly. A word came into William's head. Blank. Richard's face was completely blank. 'I need it done this afternoon. I know it's late. I'd like you to go now.'

Annette was also thinking about the bank holiday weekend. It was not going to be easy. Holidays never were. She would sit at home and picture William buying a chocolate egg for his young son. How they must draw parents together, those small acts of giving, the mutual treats. Very bonding, they must be. She had no plans. It would be like four days in the wilderness but perhaps, at the end, she would emerge whole: redeemed. At least, for four days, she would not be sitting at a desk wondering whether or not William was about to walk around the corner.

William walked around the corner. 'I've got to go out on site,' he said. 'I've put my phone through.'

Joan was sitting at her desk, opposite Annette. She looked up. 'Have a good Easter, if you don't come back.'

'Thanks, you too,' William said. 'Bye Annette.'

'Bye.'

After he had gone, Joan picked up her handbag and said, 'I've just got to nip over the road and get a pint of milk. I won't be a minute.'

'Take your coat, it's raining,' said Annette.

Annette pushed herself back from her desk. Less than an hour to go. The phone rang. It was Reception. The third floor was empty and everyone in Finance had gone as well. Their department was the only one with people left in the building. They were going to lock up and close the front door. After she put down the phone, Annette realised Joan would have to use the code to get back in. She began to tidy up her desk, put her stapler and holepunch away, gather up scattered biros and drop them into the red plastic carton next to her computer. Half-way through, she remembered that she had borrowed a calculator from Dennis round the corner. She took it round but their section had all gone home. Their offices were deserted. They had turned the lights off. She took the calculator back to her desk and locked it in her drawer.

The telephone rang again. Annette answered. 'Good afternoon, building section.'

The woman's voice on the other end of the phone sounded strained, slightly distant. 'I'm trying to get through to William Bennett.' Automatically, Annette reached out for a biro. 'I'm sorry, he's out on site at the moment. Can I take a message?'

'When will he be back?'

The tone of the question – anxious, alert – froze Annette's hand, the biro poised above her notepad. 'I don't know, I'm not sure whether he's coming back this afternoon.' She allowed a slight pause then repeated, with an edge of insistence in her voice, 'May I take a message?'

The pause was echoed on the other end of the line. 'It's his wife.'

I know, thought Annette. I know who you are. And what's more, you know who I am too.

'I'm sorry . . .' Alison said, then there was a scratching sound as she placed a hand over a mouthpiece. In the background, there were muffled male voices. Then the high-pitched tones of a child. The hand was removed. 'I'm sorry,' repeated Alison, 'but I have to get hold of my husband. Now, as soon as possible. Is it possible to contact him on site?'

Annette thought her own voice sounded unnaturally normal. 'He's got a bleeper. I could try paging him. You can't send a message though, it just bleeps and he rings in to the office. I don't know if he'll have it turned on.' She allowed herself a moment of pleasure at her superior knowledge of William's habits. 'He forgets sometimes.'

'Will there be a phone where he's going? Can you tell him to ring me straightaway?'

'It depends. If he's on the tube it won't go off until he gets above ground. If he's still on route he might just turn round and come back to the office.'

'Well, when he does,' Alison's voice had become very measured, 'tell him to ring home immediately. It's an emergency. Tell him it isn't Paul. He's fine. We're both fine. But it's an emergency.' She paused, then added, as if she was afraid that Annette would not believe her, 'The police are here. Tell him to ring home straightaway.'

'Yes. Of course.'

There was a pause. Annette waited. Then she heard movement in the background. Alison said briskly. 'Thank you,' and hung up.

Annette put down the phone. She opened her drawer and drew out her list of pager numbers.

She had just paged William and put down the phone when she looked up to see Richard in front of her desk, standing very still with his arms by his side. She started slightly. She had not seen him all day. She thought he might have gone home without telling her.

He was glancing over towards Joan's desk. He turned back towards her. He was wearing a slight smile. Annette opened her mouth to explain that Joan had not left, only gone over the road for a pint of milk, but he interrupted her. 'Annette . . .'

'Yes?' She was trying to work out what it was about Richard that was bothering her. Then she realised. He was motionless. He was not gesturing with his hands or moving his head as he spoke. It was as if he was doing something rehearsed – very, very slowly.

'Time you were going,' he said, still wearing the slight smile. 'I've decided to close the office. No point in you hanging on here when everyone else has gone. Why don't you get off now?'

'Yes,' said Annette, uncertainly. She wanted to wait until William came back, to find out what had happened. She couldn't possibly leave yet. Richard was staring at her. She kept her voice calm and casual. 'Yes, I'll just make sure all the PCs are closed down.'

He stepped closer and leant slightly towards her. His voice sounded heavy. 'I would make a dash for it if I were you,' he said, 'the rush hour has already started.'

He turned and left.

Annette frowned. She looked around her desk. It was almost tidied away: not much excuse to stay. She opened her locked drawer and pulled a few things out that she could pretend to be tidying if he came back: her date stamp, her stapler, the ornamental paper-cutter that was used for opening the tender envelopes.

Helly looked up. Richard stood beside her desk. She leant back in her seat, trying to look relaxed to the point of boredom. Behind her rib cage, her heart thumped away like an Easter bunny metamorphosed into the mad March Hare.

'Do you mind if we have a little chat?' Richard said, not meeting her gaze. 'Nothing heavy. I just want to get a few things straightened out.'

She shrugged. He stepped back and lifted his hand in the direction of his office. She rose slowly from her seat.

Annette had re-arranged the items on her desk several times. She had cleaned the keyboard on her computer. She had over-watered the plants. There was nothing else she could think of as a delaying tactic.

She went round to Helly's desk. It was empty. She stood, rubbing her lips together. Helly would not have gone home without saying goodbye. She stepped out from the alcove and looked down the office. It was dark and deserted. The secretaries had lowered the blinds before leaving and turned the lights out, although there was still daylight filtering through in narrow stripes. The computers sat on their desks, vague hulks underneath grey plastic covers. Someone had gone round tucking the chairs in neatly, ready for the weekend cleaners. Behind the nearest desk was a small arrangement of sagging, deflated balloons which were Sellotaped to the wall, left over from somebody's birthday a few weeks ago. There was the eerie, unidentifiable silence of a place which was usually full of noise.

Slowly, gradually, she began to feel uneasy. Where the hell was Joan? She went back to her desk and picked up her coat from the hook on the wall. She slipped it over her shoulders and moved swiftly across the office to the back stairs.

In Richard's office, Helly was sitting in front of his desk while Richard stood with his back to her, looking out of the window. 'So,' he was saying. 'I just thought we might come to some sort of compromise. You're a clever girl, and you've got guts. I admire that.'

He had been talking for several minutes and the whole time, Helly had not responded. He turned from the window and looked at her.

'Richard,' she said, turning in her seat. 'This is bullshit. What did you really want to say? Get it over and done with because it's Easter and I want to go home.'

Richard looked at her, then raised a finger. 'Hang on a minute.' He crossed the office swiftly and opened the door. Very briefly, he turned the corner and glanced around the office. Annette had gone. The office was empty, and dark. He went back into his office and closed the door behind him. Helly looked up as he came back in. She had not moved from her seat. He came and stood very close to her and looked down. She froze. He bent down, so that his face was very near to hers. At the same time, he removed a large cotton handkerchief from his pocket and held it up to her face. 'Put this in your mouth,' he said.

Helly sat very still. Then, she began to hyperventilate. 'What . . . for?' she asked breathily, in a last ditch attempt to pretend that it was not about to happen.

'Because I'm going to hurt you,' he said.

She sprang up from her seat. But she had left it too late.

As Annette opened the front door to John Blow House, she saw Joan standing on the steps outside. 'Oh thank God you came out,' she said. 'I've been standing on these steps like an idiot. I didn't know they were going to lock up, did you?' She stepped inside, brushing rain off her shoulders. 'You wouldn't believe it, not a pint of milk to be found. I went all the way up Strutton Ground.'

Annette's voice was anxious, irritated. 'Couldn't you remember the lock code?'

Joan looked at her, pulling a face. 'How would I know that? I don't normally have to use it do I?'

'Did you see Richard at all?'

'No why? I thought he'd gone home.'

'So did I, then he turned up at my desk, and I can't find Helly.'

'She'll be in the loo probably, staying out of his way. Let's go and find her.'

The trick to causing pain without marking was to twist rather than press. Richard had worked this out at school and it had stood him in good stead ever since. There were other things he knew without ever having consciously developed them as theories. For instance, he knew that physical pain was compounded by fear and anticipation. The best moment of this encounter, the moment that he would treasure, had been the moment before he had jammed his handkerchief into Helly's mouth, grabbed her hair and pulled her over onto his desk: the look on her face as all the foolish bravado fell away – in her eyes the wild knowledge, she had let herself get cornered. She had lost.

Now, she was pinned down with her arms twisted up her back and her face pressed hard onto his blotting pad. He was bent over her, using his body-weight to keep her there. His face was very near to her left ear 'Corrupt surveyors are a real problem,' he was saying calmly. 'People write articles on how to deal with it.' Helly gave out a muffled cry. Tears were streaming down her face. 'The point is,' Richard continued, 'your lover-boy is going to be summarily dismissed either way, as of Tuesday. And he's going to find getting another job very difficult indeed. But then that's what you get for messing around with a bone-idle little slag like you. You needn't bother turning up next week, either. It's all arranged.' He pushed her arms up further and she made a choking sound. 'You stupid little tart. My God, are you stupid. You judge everybody by your own stupid standards and you think that everyone else is just as stupid. Even me. Well, you got it wrong. Oh, and the first thing I'm going to sort out next week? A little demolition job.' Helly gave another muffled cry. The handkerchief was still jammed into her mouth. With his body-weight still over her, Richard manoeuvred her arms further up so that he could restrain them with one hand. Then, with his free hand, he began to stroke the side of her face where it streamed with tears, gently, with slow rounded movements. 'Mind you,' he said coaxingly, 'you might find there's not much left to demolish.' He bent back down. His voice became a whisper. 'Take a good look next time you go round, and remember. You tell anyone anything about me or try to do something about it, and this is just the beginning.'

Richard drew back and made a small noise, like a demented donkey. 'You've got me all wrong. You thought I was doing it for money, because that's what you'd do it for. But you're wrong.' He leant forward again. His face was so close to hers that the rist of her body, still pinned beneath him, seemed blurred. Her loose, scoop-necked top had fallen open and, almost distantly, he glimpsed the pale curve of her collar bone, pressed against the blotting pad. She was struggling to move, a howl of pain thrashing inside her. He knew that some men would enjoy grabbing this small, fleshy girl but he was not attracted to a weak squirming thing like her, a helpless little heap. 'I'm not breaking your arm,' he said gently. 'I'm not that stupid. I'm simply making sure that you realise just how wrong you've been.' She was so formless there was hardly anything to break. She revolted him.

The ladies' toilet was empty. Joan and Annette stood looking at each other. 'You sure she's not upstairs?' said Joan.

Annette shook her head. 'Maybe she is now.'

'Hang on, I'll have a wee while we're here.'

When they got back upstairs, the office was still deserted. Annette pulled a face. Joan shrugged. 'We might as well be off then.'

'Hang on a minute,' said Annette, and walked round to Richard's office, Joan following cautiously behind.

The door was ajar. She stopped, and held her breath.

She could hear something, a gasping sound. She stepped forward carefully and pushed back the door.

Helly was sitting against the wall. Her arms were pulled up over her chest and her knees were bent with one leg drawn up and the other splayed at an angle. Her top was dropping off one shoulder and her tights were torn. Her hair was skewed half-way across her face. She was staring straight ahead and gasping, great heaving gulps of air which jolted her to and fro. She looked as if she was trying to speak or cry out but could not draw breath. Annette ran forward and dropped to her knees beside her.

As they helped her up, Helly winced with pain. They sat her down on the chair behind Annette's desk and Joan ran for a cup of water.

'Okay,' said Annette. 'This is very simple. We go straight to the police. Right now. We don't mess about. This is assault. It's a criminal offence.'

Helly was shaking her head. 'I've no . . . he didn't . . . nothing . . .' Joan returned. Helly took the cup of water from her and drank. Her face was red and bleary with tears. Her fringe was smudged across her forehead. 'He's mad,' she said, looking up at them. 'Completely mad. He'll do something awful to Gran and Grandad. If he had lived during the war he'd have tortured people. He's mad.' Every now and then she gave another gasp, like a small aftershock. Annette was shaking her head. 'You don't know the half of it . . .' Helly continued. 'William. He's stitched up William.'

'What do you mean?'

'He's made it look like it's him. He thought William and I were at it. He thought that's how I knew.'

'That's why – God!' said Annette. She drew breath. She took a step away and then back. 'The police – his wife rang. He won't have the faintest – what will they . . .?' Her voice withered to a breathy squeak.

Helly had stopped gasping. She looked up at Annette. 'Joan, do something,' she said quickly. Annette had her hand over her mouth.

Joan grabbed Annette's elbow and pulled her over to the coffee cupboard where there was a small stainless steel sink. Annette bent over it and gagged. A small amount of spittle dropped from her mouth. Joan picked up a cup and filled it with water. 'Here.' Annette took the cup from her and drank, then handed it back. 'Thanks,' she said. 'Sorry, it's really stupid. We have to think. We have to work out what to do.'

Joan rinsed the cup, then put it down on the drainer. 'Well let's get Helly out of here for a start. Find out where her grandparents are.'

They went back to Annette's desk. Helly had gone. So had the ornamental paper-cutter which was used for opening the tender envelopes.

* * *

294

William rose from his seat and wormed his way through the other passengers, so that when the train halted he could be first onto the platform. Annette would never have paged him unless it was urgent. What could be urgent at the end of the day before Good Friday? For some reason he could not justify, he felt sick with apprehension.

On Victoria Street, everybody else seemed to be as frantic as Joan and Annette. 'Excuse me, excuse me,' Annette repeated as they barged through the other pedestrians. A few irate commuters turned to look as she pushed past. They should have gone through the backstreets, which were quicker and quieter. That was probably what Helly had done. 'Excuse me.' Annette repeated it like a mantra, even when she wasn't elbowing somebody out of the way.

Joan was falling behind. As they neared Victoria station, Annette stopped and looked back. Joan had stopped and was resting her hands on her knees, panting hugely. She waved at Annette and gasped, 'Go on, go on . . .'

Annette turned. As she did, she caught sight of Helly's small figure disappearing through the huge vaulted entrance to the station. She sprinted forward.

Richard walked through the rush-hour bustle of Victoria Street. He wound his way through the crowds, his step firm and purposeful from habit rather than inclination. I am not a malicious man, he thought. I am not enjoying this. It is simply that I am right. Peasants – he exhaled, grimly – all of them. His staff were all peasants.

At the entrance to Victoria Station he paused by the kiosk and bought a packet of cigarettes. He put down his briefcase and dug a hand into his trouser pocket to find some loose change. A small queue built up behind him while he counted out the exact amount and handed it over to the assistant. A pretty girl, she smiled and said, 'Thank you sir.'

He smiled back.

The smile stayed on his face as he crossed the concourse towards his platform. The full extent of his triumph was becoming apparent. They were like schoolchildren, all of them. They had ganged up against him and he had skewered them all. He had covered everything, every option, every possibility. It had all been a game, of course, for him. He had never seriously thought that any of his activities were in jeopardy. A game. And he had won.

He paused in front of the departure board and checked his train time. He was slightly earlier than usual but the station was already packed solid with bank holiday commuters, all pelting around to add those precious extra minutes to their long weekend. Platform 8. He had nine minutes. He pulled his cigarettes from his pocket. As he removed the cellophane wrapper, he saw William from the corner of his eye, coming towards him across the concourse. Richard furrowed his brow. William seemed agitated as he crossed the concourse, hurrying back out towards the street. Last time I'll see you buddy, Richard thought. Goodbye. A clean sweep, that is what he would have, starting next week. New people, who would be so grateful in this climate they would mind their own business and do what they were damn well told. Temps, perhaps. Temps always knew how to behave themselves, particularly when Fridays came around and they needed their timesheets signed.

As he inhaled the first drag of his cigarette, he was suddenly overcome with an enormous feeling of exhaustion. The adrenalin of victory drained into his shoes. He looked at the people rushing past him. What was it all about? Here they all were, weaving in and out in this inelegant, pointless dance, some pausing for a moment like him, others rushing as if their lives were at stake. Pausing and rushing, pausing and rushing, the human traffic ceaselessly flowing in and out and around London. I never wanted to do this for a living, Richard thought. I never planned to work for the Capital Transport Authority. If I had had my choice, I would have liked to go out to Africa, like David Attenborough or one of those types of people. I would have liked to raise leopards for a living.

He glanced to one side. A few feet away, in the middle of the concourse, there was a mobile cleaning trolley with a small bin attached to the end. Its attendant had wandered off. He took a couple of steps towards the bin and tossed the screwed-up cellophane wrapper from his cigarette packet, but it sprang open again as soon as it left his grasp. He watched it flutter to the concourse floor. The nasal tones of a British Rail announcer started to say, 'This is an announcement for all passengers and staff . . .'

Richard heard a young female voice behind him shout, 'Hey!' The voice was bitter, furious. He turned.

Then the bomb exploded.

8

The acupuncturist was called Julia. She practiced in a white room above a flat in Tufnell Park. Hanging in the window of the white room was a mobile made of coloured triangles of glass.

'Do you like my seagull?' asked Julia, as she inserted a long fine needle into Annette's right elbow.

Annette was lying on her back on a high couch covered with a white paper sheet. From where she lay she could see the coloured patterns of light made by the triangles: purple, pink, green. 'It's not a very mobile mobile,' she said, feeling Julia smile in reply. Outside the window, poplar trees waved to and fro in a light summer breeze; beyond the poplars, sky.

'You seem more relaxed now,' Julia commented.

'Perhaps it was the – yinglan?'

'Yintang,' Julia corrected softly.

'The needle in my forehead.'

'Yes, also the massage helps I think. I only did your shoulder for today because that's where I'm putting most of the needles. Next time we can do your neck and back as well.'

'How long will it take to put the rest in?'

'Not long, then we leave them for twenty minutes. Are you comfortable?'

'Yes.'

After she had finished inserting the needles, Julia sat in an armchair next to the couch. It was covered with a fine cloth on which were embroidered tiny roses in various shades of pink. Julia sat among the roses, the pinks reflected in her white coat. She was just visible in the periphery of Annette's vision. Annette could see she that was holding a clipboard.

'Annette . . .' Julia said, her voice warm and coaxing.

'Yes?'

'I wonder if we could go through a few more questions. I know we've done your medical history and I've had the details from the hospital but I'd like to go a bit further back.'

'Yes of course.'

'There's something I'm not quite clear about.' Julia coughed. 'You made a reference to attacks of nausea that occurred before you were injured. You weren't very specific. Can you tell me a bit more about it?'

Annette did not reply. Instead, she watched the coloured triangles of light on the white ceiling.

Julia waited in silence. Eventually, she said, very softly, 'Annette, how old were your parents when you were born?'

Annette remained silent. From somewhere inside her chest she felt a swelling; she knew it was only emotional but it felt as real and as physical as if a loaf of bread was leavening beneath her heart. She began to cry.

Julia rose from her seat and stood behind Annette's head. She placed her hands on either side very gently, so gently that Annette could hardly feel the touch. She stayed there while Annette sobbed.

When Annette had finished, Julia said quietly, 'I think we have a lot of work to do.'

After the treatment, Annette asked to use the toilet. Julia showed her downstairs. The bathroom was also white, with a lilac patterned lino. A clothesline made of string hung from brass hooks in opposing walls and washing dripped into the bath; socks and T-shirts, two pairs of men's boxer shorts striped in white and candy yellow and pale green – ice-cream colours. Annette lifted up her skirt and gripped it between her teeth. Then she pulled down her tights and knickers. She had removed her tights so that Julia could put needles in her knee, then struggled back into them afterwards. She should have left them off until she had been to the toilet. Tights were the thing that caused her most difficulty. It would be more sensible to stick to loose trousers for the time being, as her physiotherapist had suggested, but that somehow seemed like too large an admission, too big and visible a change.

As she sat on the loo, she gazed at the T-shirt hanging directly opposite. It was grey, with purple lettering, the words beneath each other: *Absurdity, Anguish, Freedom*.

After she had finished going to the toilet and pulled her tights back up, she went over to the T-shirt and, leaning over the bath, peered at the other side. It said, *Paris Post War, Art and Existentialism 1945-55*. She thought of Helly and smiled, a little sadly.

Upstairs, Julia was folding the paper sheet which had been on the couch. She looked up as Annette came in. 'How are you feeling?'

Annette nodded. 'Fine. Tired.'

'You can expect to feel quite exhausted, that often happens. When you're in a relaxed state, all sorts of things come out.'

Annette was pulling on her light summer mac. 'Can I ask you something about the treatment?'

'Yes of course.'

'Why did you put needles in my hand?'

Julia put down the folded sheet on the chair and began to move towards the door. 'Well, you explained that you are still feeling sensations of pain from your missing hand. That is why I placed needles near to the amputation point, the wrist and elbow. But it's also possible to treat the remaining hand for pain felt in the one that is missing.'

'Really?' said Annette, as they made their way downstairs. 'You can treat the hand I still have and that will help the one that I don't have any more?'

They had reached the front door. As Julia opened it, Annette automatically tucked her stump into the pocket of her coat. 'Will I be able to cut down on the Tegretol? It's making me drowsy.'

'We'll discuss that in conjunction with the hospital,' said Julia, 'but naturally I would hope so.'

'Thank you,' said Annette, raising her left hand in

farewell and turning to go down the steps and out into the sunlit, tree-lined street.

'You're welcome,' said Julia. 'Have a good week.'

It was Janey, the physiotherapist, who had mentioned acupuncture. It was sometimes used at the hospital for pain management, although there was no official referral scheme. Annette liked Janey, a young black woman with large, doughy hands who had never once offered to pity her. The weekly appointments with her were an interim measure while she waited for her referral to the limb rehabilitation centre at Roehampton. Janey was just one of a group of professionals looking after Annette now. Although she knew they all had other patients, she couldn't help thinking of them as her team, her own private entourage. Individually, they had all been wonderful, although nobody in particular seemed to be in charge.

When she told the psychiatrist about going to see Julia she had the feeling that he disapproved, but then he was a bearded man in his fifties. There were no ice-cream colours in his consulting room on the hospital's fifth floor, just a dark wooden desk and metal filing cabinet. On top of the filing cabinet was a spider plant that ticked. By the end of her first session, Annette had worked out that it ticked because there was a clock hidden behind it which Dr Gibson could see but she could not. When she realised this she began to giggle. Dr Gibson had observed her, silently, which made her giggle even more.

He had come to see her a week after the bombing, at her bedside in the women's orthopaedic ward. For the first couple of days she had been in a mixed ward with several of the other Victoria casualties, along with a man who had come off his motorcycle the same day and was bandaged from head to foot like a patient in a *Carry On* film. He was the only thing she could remember clearly from that time – the only sharp picture. The rest had been a blur; greetings cards by her bedside, her mother crying, a nurse inserting a drip, all of these were vague hallucinations. Mostly, there had been pain.

The pain had come in several varieties. First, there was the variety which started at her wrist and made its way up her arm where it curled around her brain like an earthworm, burrowing. Then there had been the type in her shoulder. These were real pains, the doctors told her. But there was also the pain in the fingers that were no longer there. Phantom pain, they said, and gave her a drug which they said was for epilepsy and would make the phantoms go away.

Because of the pain, she was unconscious when she was first brought into Accident and Emergency that day. She had regained consciousness to find eight or ten people busy around her bed, a nurse cutting off her clothes. All about her was clatter and commotion, voices calling out, a woman shrieking, footsteps running past. The noises echoed in her head. There was a chemical smell. Although she was lying flat she felt as if she was reeling. A man gripped her shoulder lightly and bent down close to her ear. 'You're in the resuscitation area, St Thomas' Hospital. You're going to be okay. Can you tell us your name?'

She had frowned while the people buzzed round –

blurs of white and blue with featureless pink faces, all talking to each other. The reeling sensation seemed to be steadying, locating somewhere in the region of her right arm, re-defining itself as something more specific. From somewhere both near and distant she heard a voice shouting furiously, 'I want this corridor kept clear!'

'Neurological status?' said another figure on the other side of the bed. From out of the range of her vision a woman called, 'Triage!' and the figure turned away.

'Who are you?' she said to the man with his hand on her shoulder.

'I'm a surgeon,' he had replied. 'Can you tell us your name?'

It was only after she was transferred to the women's orthopaedic ward that the surgeon came to explain about the amputation. He was a broad-shouldered man with ginger hair and a scattering of freckles across his nose. The freckles made him look boyish but she could tell by his eyes that he was middle-aged. He perched himself on the side of her bed and talked to her slowly and quietly. She felt overwhelmed with gratitude, not for the kindness but for the information. She still did not know what had happened.

'You were caught by the second blast,' he said. 'As far as we can tell, when you heard the first bomb, the one actually on the concourse, you threw yourself back behind the pillar, but your hand was still round the corner, holding on.' The second bomb had been in a suitcase near the entrance. It had been timed and positioned to catch the people running away from the first bomb. 'Most of the people who were killed were killed by the second bomb. That was the biggie; the one in the cleaning trolley was just a decoy. You sustained a severe shrapnel injury . . .' The freckled surgeon paused.

'No, carry on,' said Annette.

'We're not sure but it was probably a largish piece of metal. Your hand was crushed against the pillar. Nails and ball bearings were packed around the bomb, that's what's caused most of the injuries but it must have been something a bit bigger in your case. It was a clean amputation and we X-rayed the arm just to make sure there were no other bits of shrapnel. We amputate very rarely these days. When your hand was crushed you lost the fingers but more importantly the middle of the hand, that's why we couldn't save the thumb. If there's anything at all we can save, we do.'

'So I was unlucky.'

The freckled surgeon raised his eyebrows and shrugged slightly. 'There's two ways of looking at it. Yes, you were unlucky. On the other hand, if even part of your torso had been round the corner of the pillar instead of behind it you almost certainly would have been killed. Unlucky and lucky. Both are true, I suppose. It's up to you to decide which one you want to choose.'

'How many people were killed, altogether?'

'Eleven. It went up to eleven this morning. We don't think it will rise. There are a lot of badly injured though. A lot of internal injuries. That's what shrapnel does.'

They were silent. Then Annette said, 'Lucky. I

suppose I should choose lucky.' She looked at her arm which was raised slightly in a sling and heavily bandaged. The loss of the hand was still theoretical, to her. The minor details were more actual – the discomfort in her shoulder, the constipation because she found using a bedpan difficult. The amputation itself was something she could describe but not feel. Would there be a moment, an all-consuming second, when she would know? Or would it dawn on her gradually, as if the hand was melting away? She blinked. 'If I give you some names,' she said to the surgeon, 'can you find out what's happened to them?' The surgeon looked at her. 'They're friends of mine. I meant to ask the nurse yesterday but I felt sick. If I tell you can you write them down and tell her or get someone to find out?'

'Yes,' he said, 'of course.'

Joan had been separated from Annette on the station concourse, when Annette had been swept up by the emergency team. An ambulancewoman in squeaky green overalls had taken her by the elbow and led her, stunned and shaky, to join a group of others waiting just outside the station. The group stood in dazed silence as the more seriously injured were rushed past them on stretchers. Beyond a rapidly constructed police cordon, sightseers were already gathering. Joan felt herself swaying in very small circles. Eventually the man standing next to her, an Asian businessman, asked her if she wanted to sit down. The ground felt cold and hard. The rest of the group remained standing. Joan felt silly.

At the hospital she was put in a side room, with a large

group who had been asked to wait while the emergencies were dealt with. After some time, an orderly came round with a notepad and pencil and asked them who they wanted the hospital to contact. Joan shook her head. 'He'll be on a shift,' she said.

'What about a neighbour?' the orderly asked.

Joan frowned. 'Lydia. I suppose she could put a note on the door.'

Finally, she was taken into a cubicle to be examined and they told her what she already knew. Her injuries were light: mild shock, and some bruising from where she had fallen to the ground. She had been outside the station when the first bomb had gone off and had stopped dead in her tracks, disbelieving. She was still standing there when the second bomb, much closer, had exploded – and after that the horror had been too loud and visible for doubt.

When the doctor had finished, a young nurse helped her down from the bed on which she had been examined and said, 'If you need anything to eat or drink there's the cafeteria round the corner. Perhaps a nice cup of tea?'

'I suppose I do feel a bit shaky,' said Joan, suffering instant guilt because this nurse was probably about to rush off and deal with somebody who was badly hurt. She wanted to ask about the others but the nurse was leading her out of the cubicle. 'The waiting room is round to the left, follow the signs for the Lambeth Wing.' As they made their way past a row of cubicles, they passed an orderly emerging from behind a curtain. He was wearing plastic gloves and holding a rubbish bag into which he was pushing heavily blood-stained clothing, a brown skirt and a cream-coloured top. Joan stopped and turned to the nurse. 'My friends,' she said. 'Annette Simon. Helen Rawlins – ' Suddenly, a group pushing a stretcher trolley came charging down the corridor. A doctor at the front gestured them out of the way and called to the nurse, 'We need a cubicle . . .'

'End right,' the nurse called after them. The group hadn't paused. The trolley's wheels rattled frantically. The nurse turned back to Joan and said to her quickly, 'Round to the left,' then turned away.

The waiting room was crowded. Nearest to Joan sat a young woman, clothes dishevelled but make-up immaculate, staring at a gauze dressing on her forearm. Next to her were a middle-aged couple, clutching each other's hands. Twin boys of around four or five squatted on the floor in front of them, bickering softly, too absorbed in their quarrel to register their parents' sombre mood. The only empty seat was at the far end of one row, next to a young man who sat bent over with his elbows on his knees and his head in his hands. Next to him was an elderly woman, sobbing softly. Joan knew she could not wait here.

The cafeteria was also crowded. A queue snaked along the empty glass counters. Most of the food and snacks had gone. I suppose all this has taken them unawares, Joan thought. She asked for a tea.

She paid at the till, then paused, holding her tea and looking around. The cafeteria was very large but nearly every table was full. Despite the quiet air of tragedy, there was the gentle hubbub that cafeterias everywhere seemed to make, regardless of geography or circumstance. Floor to ceiling windows afforded a view of the river, towards the golden glories of the Houses of Parliament. She was reminded of holiday camps that she and Alun had been to – the crowds, the stress. All at once she felt tearful, and very much alone.

To her left was an elderly woman sitting at a small table around which there were two other seats. One had coats and bags piled onto it. The other was empty.

The woman was rather odd looking. She was wearing a green cloth hat with a purple brim and huge owlish glasses. She was looking at Joan. Joan approached, tentatively, and indicated the free seat. The woman nodded.

As Joan sat, her hand began to shake. The cup of tea rattled in its saucer. The woman jumped to her feet and took the tea from her. 'Here,' she said to Joan, 'you sit down and make yourself comfortable. You look like you need it.' Joan nodded. 'Weird place this, isn't it?' the woman continued. 'Have you seen the gift shop over there? I had a look through the window. Flan dishes. They sell flan dishes, with primroses on. And St Thomas' Hospital tea-towels. You here because of . . .' she waved a hand loosely in the direction of the Accident and Emergency department. Joan nodded again as she raised her tea to her lips. 'Me too,' said the woman and her face became suddenly grim. 'My granddaughter. My husband's gone to find out. They wouldn't tell us anything. He wouldn't let me go. He knew I'd raise merry hell.'

The woman buried her face in her hands.

Joan put down her tea, reached out a hand and patted

the woman's arm, awkwardly. 'I'm sure . . . I'm sure she'll be . . .'

'Oh God,' the woman said. She picked up a paper napkin, took off her glasses and wiped at her eyes. 'Oh God, you wouldn't believe the day I've had. My mother brains a burglar and there's blood all over the linoleum, then she pegs out with a coronary, then I scream blue murder at two police officers until they put the siren on and bring us up here quicker than Concorde. Now we can't find Helly and nobody will tell us anything. It's been one hell of a day.'

'Helly?' Joan said. 'Helly Rawlins?'

The woman nodded. She gazed at Joan and then said, slowly, 'I know who you are. You're Joan. You're the only nice person in that awful office she works at. She told us.'

Joan tried to smile – and tried not to think about the blood-stained clothing she had seen in Accident and Emergency.

'Oh God,' said Joanna. 'I'm such a berk. You must have been there. Did you see her. Are you okay?'

'I'm fine, fine . . .' Joan said. 'I don't know anything about her I'm afraid.'

'Oh.'

For a moment, conversation died as they both thought about the reality of what was happening and, briefly, words became impossible. They looked at each other.

Funny, Joan thought, she looks so odd, but actually I have the feeling I am quite like her in some ways.

Odd, Joanna thought, she's a funny old bird, but she seems nice enough.

'Do you know what?' Joan said suddenly. 'Do you know what I really feel?'

Joanna put her glasses back on and looked at her.

'Jealous. Yes, that's it. I feel jealous of those people in there, even though they're lying there in their hospital beds, maybe terribly injured. I wish I'd been injured. They've discharged me already and I should have gone home. I could have got a taxi. Instead I'm sitting here where my husband won't be able to find me, wishing it was me getting all that attention in there. I always thought if anything like this happened to me I would be quite useful – you know, go back forty years to when I was a Girl Guide and stem somebody's bleeding. Somebody else did that for Annette, this other secretary that I was with, that is. One of the station staff got to her before I did. I can already hear myself talking to people about it, exaggerating how close I was, the things I saw. Truth is, I stayed by them until the ambulance came and kept my head down. I didn't see anything much.' She looked at Joanna. 'Now it's all over, for me, and I wish I had. Is that terrible?'

Joanna shook her head. 'We aren't frightened of injury in the way that men are. That's why we cope better with accidents and things like this. We bleed every month after all. And when we have babies we get torn apart. Men go to war I suppose, but what happens to us isn't unusual. It's part of who we are.'

Joanna's glance switched to further away, over Joan's shoulder. Joan turned round. A tall, white-haired man was approaching them. Joanna leapt to her feet as he came over. 'She's going to be fine. Fine . . .' There were tears in his eyes. 'Nothing broken. They're doing X-rays.'

Joanna sat back down, her hand to her cheek. 'Oh God, oh God.'

'They said they probably won't even keep her in overnight, they're just doing some other checks.'

'Did they let you see her?'

'No but we can in a bit, I thought I'd come and tell you straightaway. Oh Joanna!' Bob sat on a spare chair, clenched his fists and waved them in the air. 'We can take her home!'

Joanna indicated Joan. 'Bob, this is Joan. Works with Helly. Joan, this is my husband, Helly's grandad.'

Bob grabbed Joan's hand and shook it up and down. The motion rattled the flimsy table and Joan's tea slopped over the side of her cup and into the saucer. 'She was there at the station,' said Joanna.

Bob's face became more serious. 'I'm sorry. How are you?'

'Oh I'm fine,' said Joan. 'Helly?'

'Hardly injured, very lucky they said, considering how close she was. Some people further away got it much worse.' Bob was shaking his head. 'It was some poor bloke who saved her. Some bloke was standing between her and the bomb and took the full blast. She was a bit of mess though, splattered, and stunned of course. They took her clothes off and put her in a gown.'

Joanna was smiling and crying again. 'Oh God . . .'

'They said they'd get her some clothes from lost

property so we could take her home. I'll go over to her
mum's tomorrow and pick up her stuff,' said Bob.

'All of it,' said Joanna firmly.

'Yes,' replied Bob. 'All of it.'

Gillian Leather sat with her hands folded neatly in her lap,
like a good student waiting to hear her examination results.
The young policeman stood awkwardly in front of her. Two
nurses in plastic aprons rushed past. Opposite, there was
another row of seats. A man sat in one of them with his
head leaning back against the yellow hospital wall and his
eyes closed. Staff continued back and forth, the soles of
their shoes squeaking. The corridor echoed.

The young policeman bent down slightly and then
straightened up, as if he was trying to decide whether
or not to kneel in front of her. He was very tall and thin.
His trousers flapped around his stick-like legs. Eventually,
he reached out a bony, pale hand and laid it gently on her
shoulder. 'Please,' he said. 'Let me contact somebody for
you.' She was impressed by the simplicity of his request.
She looked up at him. His face was surprisingly round. The
mouth in the round face moved and said, 'You might find
this easier if someone is with you, I mean, even if they
just wait for you outside. I'm afraid it is going to be very
unpleasant.'

She shook her head, annoyed. She had seen a
Caesarean section performed on a horse. Did they think
she was a woman who was frightened of the red inside
of things? First of all, they had shown her the contents of
Richard's pockets, his season ticket and credit cards, and

requested confirmation that they were his. Then they had asked her if she would come down to the mortuary, for the official identification. Their sympathetic tones had made her angry. Did they think she would refuse? If they had tried to stop her, she would have screamed the place down.

'Can you tell me . . .' she began. Her voice sounded odd, a slightly higher register than usual. She cleared her throat. 'Can you tell me, you weren't there I realise, but somebody might – can you tell me, is there anyone who will know? I know you said he was unconscious by the time the ambulancemen got to him but had he been unconscious all along or do you think he knew?' In her mind, she was already picturing what she would see of Richard on the mortuary slab: blood, flesh, bone. Half the face was gone, they had said; *the* face, not his. But even that didn't mean that he had lost consciousness straightaway. She had to know.

'I'm sure,' the young policeman said, too hastily for honesty, 'I'm sure it was instant.' Gillian looked into his round, pale features and searched them for signs of truth, awareness, knowledge. He did not know. Perhaps no one knew.

It was two weeks before William was able to visit Annette. He too had been injured in the second bomb but had been much further away. He had sustained a collapsed lung but his chest had been drained successfully and the lung re-expanded. It might have been worse, they told him. There were also lacerations to his torso, two in his right upper leg and one to his face; all caused by shrapnel, all relatively shallow, none life threatening. He would be permanently scarred.

Joan had been to see him and told him that Annette was about to be allowed home. He had arisen the next morning and insisted to the nurse that he was well enough to walk around the hospital. He knew it was his last chance.

At the side of her bed, he wept.

He was wearing pyjamas and a towelling robe. Annette looked at him and thought that it was the first and last time she would ever see him in night clothes. Helly and Joan had already visited, early because they were on their way to the shops. They had chattered – Helly was going to be on television. Now Annette felt tired. She stared at the top of William's head where he was bending over her bed, weeping softly, his shattered chest giving small, shallow heaves. Eventually, he lifted his head.

'I don't know what to say,' he said.

'I know,' she replied.

He passed a hand across his reddened cheeks and glanced anxiously from side to side to see if anyone around them had noticed him. Annette lifted her left hand and indicated the box of tissues on the stand by her bedside. He took one. By the time he spoke again he had recovered but his words were fumbling. 'I wish I could . . . it's just . . . it's so unfair . . . what's happened. Terrible . . .'

'You were injured too.'

'Not like this.' He glanced up and down her still body, his eyes resting only briefly on the sling. Then he looked down at his lap. His voice was no more than a whisper. 'It was so short, Annette. It meant so little in comparison with this, this awful thing that was waiting round the corner for us. It was so tiny and I hate the thought that it was a passing, unimportant thing. I wanted it to be monumental. It was. But it's been eclipsed.'

Annette winced. She was having a problem with stiffness in her back from lying in the same position all the time. She was ready to start walking about more. She looked at him. He loved me, she thought. And I loved him. I could count the number of times we made love on the fingers of both hands. If I had both hands. She drew breath. It had been astonishing, the past two weeks, to discover just how much of the English language comprised of phrases which involved fingers or arms or hands.

He looked up at her and met her gaze. His face was still crumpled. He shook his head slowly and rested the length of his forearm against her uninjured arm. She gave a small smile in reply. His eyes were moving over her face, as if he was trying to record every last detail of her features. 'I would give almost anything to be able to look after you.'

'I know,' she said and her voice was kind. 'I know.'

In the days immediately following the bombing, it had been William's turn to lie in bed while a woman sat beside him. The woman was Alison, his wife. She had not wept.

For those first few days, they had been drawn together by the magnitude of what had happened. All that mattered was that he was alive and would continue to live. Then, as the immediate danger passed and the novelty wore off, so their ordinary lives were pieced back together in phrases and gestures. The first day that William was allowed to sit up, Alison brought Paul in to see him. Paul sat on his father's bed and held his knee with both hands and said, 'I'm being very good Daddy and I'm going to make you a card and a cake.' William and Alison had smiled at their son and loved him for all the things he did not know.

It was the day after he had visited Annette that William suddenly found himself blurting out something he had thought that he would never say. Alison had come in for her daily visit. Outside, it was spring-like. She was wearing a short-sleeved, lemon-coloured jersey and pearl earrings that twinkled. The doctors were pleased with his progress and had just told them he could be allowed home within a fortnight.

'There's something else,' William said quickly as the doctor left them alone. 'Something I want to say before I come home. About before the bombing. It's over now, but before it all happened I was . . .' he could not bring himself to use the words *unfaithful* or *affair*. 'I was seeing someone. Someone else.'

She looked at him. Her mouth twitched in a half-smile but her eyes were bright, brimming with pain. She looked down and appeared to see a piece of dirt or fluff on the body of her lemon jumper. She picked it up between two fingers, then rubbed the fingers together so that it would drop from her grasp.

'You'd realised anyway, hadn't you?' he said.

She nodded.

William closed his eyes. He had thought that telling Alison would be terrible because she didn't know.

Now he saw that telling her was terrible because she did.

The following day, he had another visitor. The visitor was Gregory Church, general manager of the property division of the Capital Transport Authority. It was the first time an official superior had visited William since the bombing and the man was clearly embarrassed. Still, I suppose he had a lot of people to get round, William thought. He sat up in bed and tried to look relaxed, manly. Lying down put him at too much of a disadvantage.

'About your little visitation, the day all this . . .' Mr Church waved his hand loosely about the ward and William understood that he was referring to the police search of his home the afternoon of the bombing. Church had brought a box of expensive toffees which sat open on William's bed. The two men had both taken one and removed the plastic wrappings which made loud crinkly noises. William popped his in his mouth and tossed the wrapping back into the box.

'I want to explain, between you and me of course, that that was not authorised by myself or anyone else in an executive position at the Authority. Richard . . .' at the word Richard, both men looked down briefly. 'Well, let's just say he was a little over-eager in some aspects of his work. It had come to our notice some time before the unfortunate . . . before he was . . . and in due course we would have taken action.'

Bit embarrassing, thought William, being in the position of having substantially accused a bomb hero of bribery and corruption. And the only way out of it is to blame another bomb hero who happens to be dead. Which is even more embarrassing. Poor old Mr Church. William's financial position was uncertain. There was compensation to be had. He might never work again, for all Church knew. No wonder the man had brought toffees.

William took another toffee, paused, then offered the box to Church who smiled, shook his head, changed his mind and took one anyway. I wonder if you will speak at Richard's memorial service, William thought. I wonder if you will stand up in a church or crematorium and talk about what a pleasure and an honour it was to work with a man of the ability and warmth of Richard Jeremy Leather. And I wonder if you knew that the man was duplicitous, sadistic and very possibly psychotic. And I wonder if you even care.

'Now don't forget you're miked up,' the technician said as he fiddled with the lapel of Helly's waistcoat. The microphone was attached to a small black clip. Helly peered down at it, pulling a face. It was like having a cockroach perched on her chest. 'At the end of the show,' the technician continued, 'don't leap up off your seat. Just stay put and we'll come and dismantle you.' He moved on to the person sitting next to her, a counsellor with expertise in dealing with the long-term effects of traumatic injury. 'Don't forget you're miked up,' the technician began again.

'Alright, alright,' said Helly, 'we get the point.'

The counsellor was called Cherry. She and Helly had

got talking in the hospitality room. 'What are you here as?' Cherry had asked.

'Bomb victim,' Helly had replied. 'How about you?'

They were both on the front row. All the front row contributors were miked. The rest of the studio audience sat on banked seats behind them. Along the row were ranged two other survivors of the Victoria bomb, one who was facially disfigured. There was also a Unionist politician, a Catholic priest and a florid, middle-aged man from an organisation called Victims For Action Against Terrorism. They had been given a rough running order. Helly would be the third or fourth to speak.

Opposite the banked seating were cameras, lights and more technicians, under a huge draughty roof not unlike an aircraft hangar. A producer stood with a clipboard and stopwatch. 'Where's Kilroy?' Helly asked, leaning over towards Cherry.

'There,' said Cherry, pointing.

Kilroy stood amongst the technicians, watching his guests settle in and fiddling with his ear. Joanna had made Helly promise to take a good look – she had always had a thing about Kilroy, she had said. Helly regarded him with distaste. His suit was sharp enough to chop the Sunday veg, in her opinion. His light grey hair was in lurid contrast to his hot orange tan, which looked as though it could be peeled off like the mask of the Invisible Man. He glanced their way. Helly leant over to Cherry again and murmured, 'What a ponce.'

'Ssh! Don't forget you're miked up!'

Kilroy was fiddling with his ear and frowning at them. 'Oops!' said Helly.

*   *   *

'That was just the start of it!' Helly screeched with glee. She was sitting on the sofa in Rosewood Cottage. She was holding a can of beer and wiggling her legs to and fro. 'They cut what I did at the end, well not exactly cut it, you can tell some sort of commotion is going on.'

Bob was on his knees in front of the television, trying to rewind the video. Joanna sat on the sofa next to Helly. She was also holding a can of beer. 'Another dream gone,' she said, shaking her head. 'He'll never marry me now.'

'Ah shut up, I brought you a signed photo.' There had been an elegant fan of black and white signed photographs on the table in the hospitality room. Helly had helped herself to one, which Bob had framed. It now hung in Rosewood Cottage's lavatory. 'And they sent a car for me,' Helly added to Joan and Annette, who sat in armchairs opposite. 'And it brought me back home again. The driver called me miss.'

'You've never been a miss in your life,' muttered Joanna. 'Annette, another cup of tea?'

Annette shook her head. She would have loved a beer but she had only been out of hospital for two days and was still on strong painkillers.

'Almost there,' said Bob, still bent down with his nose to the video recorder.

'Oh hurry up,' said Joanna. 'We've had enough of the sight of your arse.'

He sat back. As the music to the programme started, Helly and Joanna began to sing along. 'Da! Daaa!'

Bob rolled his eyebrows and gave Joan and Annette a comradely glance. 'Can you imagine what it's like *living* with them two? They were doing that over breakfast this morning. I'm ready to go after the bloke with a hammer.'

'Good morning!' said Kilroy from the television, with a beaming smile. Then his expression switched to tragic. 'Bombs are exploding all over London again. Nobody knows whether they are safe. In the wake of the latest outrage, I'll be talking to survivors and the bereaved, and to some people who think they know the solution. This is not a political programme . . .'

'You can say that again,' muttered Helly, caressing her beer.

'Ssh!' said Joan.

'On this programme, we'll be talking to people who have direct experience of what it's like to be a victim of terrorism.'

Helly had taken exception to the word victim, and when her turn came to speak she told Kilroy so in no uncertain terms. During the rest of the programme, the screen switched to catch her facial expressions even when she wasn't talking. There were a lot of expressions to catch. She had dressed up for the occasion, in a velvet waistcoat and one of Bob's floral ties, knotted neatly. Her hair was piled on top of her head and she was wearing bright pink lipstick. The camera loved her.

Towards the end she became engaged in a heated debate with the florid middle-aged man from Victims For Action Against Terrorism, who became more and more florid as the debate proceeded. 'For your information young lady, I lost my daughter in the London Bridge bombing in March. I don't intend to sit idly by and watch these murdering bastards – sorry about my language but that's what they are – I'm not going to sit by and just let them walk all over us. I want to see some of them behind bars or better still, strung up.' There was a smattering of applause from the rest of the audience.

'This bit! This is it!' cried Helly from the sofa. 'You watch. It's nearly the end.' Kilroy was looking over to Helly for her response. 'Well for your information, matey,' she was saying, 'I was on London Bridge when that bomb went off too, so I've had my fair share. I'm sorry about your daughter but you're an angry old bigot and you'd be an angry old bigot whether you'd lost your daughter or not and if you think stringing up a few Irish people is going to help you're bleeding mental. It won't stop someone else's daughter getting blown up.'

The florid man was apopleptic with rage. 'How dare you! How – how – '

Kilroy had sprinted across the studio to a white-haired woman sitting half-way up the seating who had her hand raised to comment. He thrust his hand-held microphone into her face.

'I would just like to say,' she began in quavery tones but Helly and the florid man were still arguing. At that point, Kilroy turned to a camera and said, 'Well, ladies and gentlemen, it's been a very passionate debate but I'm afraid that's all we have time – '

In a corner of the screen, Helly could just be seen getting to her feet and beginning to unclip the mike.

'Get this thing off me!' she could be heard saying as Kilroy continued his closing announcement. Her voice went muffled and then disappeared.

'What did you say?' shrieked Joan. She was on the edge of her seat.

Helly was grinning from ear to ear. 'I said, and get me away from this orange ponce and that red-faced prat over there who both have blancmanges where their brains should be.'

'You didn't!' said Annette.

'She did,' said Bob, philosophically.

Joanna shook her head. 'Our Helly,' she said. 'Well, that's the start and end of her career in television.'

Helly was beaming. 'It was fucking great.'

'Rewind it,' said Joan. 'I want to watch it again.'

Later, Helly gave Annette the guided tour. It was the first time she had been to the cottage. Joan had been several times already. In Helly's bedroom, Annette sat on the narrow single bed and looked at the walls. 'Helly,' she said gently, 'all these paintings . . . I didn't know you liked art.'

Helly sat cross-legged on the floor. 'It's still a bit of a mess, this room. I want to decorate – paint it white I think. This awful floral stuff is what they had for my great-gran, the one who died. Doesn't really go with Kandinsky.'

Annette rose and went over to the print. 'Hmm,' she said, 'not really my kind of thing.'

'No, you're more . . . Corot, I think.'

'I don't really know much about paintings.' Annette

324

sat back down. 'Haven't you thought about going to art school or something?'

Helly pulled a face. 'Nah. Not for me, that kind of place. Full of ponces. I'd be telling them all to piss off inside a fortnight.'

'It's nice,' said Annette, looking around. 'It's a nice room.'

'It isn't,' said Helly, 'but it will be.'

As they came down the stairs Annette said, 'Time for me to go.'

Joan was emerging from the sitting room. She looked up at them. 'Are you off? Maybe I'll come with you.'

'Nonsense you two!' Joanna appeared behind her, holding the tea-tray. 'Stay the evening. We've got plenty else on video besides madam here. Bob's going to do lasagne.'

Joan looked from one to the other uncertainly.

Annette said, 'I really wish I could. I've got my mother at home.' Her mother had come to stay for a few days following Annette's discharge from hospital and was sleeping on the sofa-bed in her tiny house. She was determined to do housework of some sort or another, even when there was nothing to clean up, and followed Annette round like a small dog, waiting for her to drop something.

'You stay Joan,' she said, automatically reaching for her coat with her right arm, remembering, then switching.

'Oh, there's Alun . . .' grumbled Joan.

'Stay. You can get a mini-cab later,' said Joanna, in a tone of voice that suggested it was all settled.

'I wouldn't argue with Gran if I were you,' Helly advised. 'Not unless you have a saucepan handy.' Joanna cuffed her granddaughter across the top of her head.

Helly ducked, straightened, then said to Annette, 'I'll walk you to the main road.'

They reached the end of Sutton Street in silence. 'This'll do fine, I know my way from here.' They stopped. 'You were great,' Annette said, 'really good.'

'It was a laugh. I wouldn't have minded doing it again but I think I blew it.'

Annette looked at the ground and then up at the sky. 'I hope we all get together again soon. I'd like to stay in touch.'

'Yeh.'

They looked at each other and there was a moment of sad, swift collusion. They would not keep in touch, not long term. They both knew it and both regretted it, slightly. Put together, their regret might be enough; singly, it wasn't quite.

Helly laughed. 'Well, we will if my gran has anything to do with it. She seems to be starting some kind of people-who-know-Helly society. She's already got Joan to agree to come to Windsor with us on Saturday. They're going to be as thick as thieves, I can tell. Joan and Joanna, sounds like a television series, doesn't it?'

Annette felt a twinge of jealousy that she had not been invited to Windsor, then thought how silly it was to feel jealous of two gossipy women in their late middle-age, then thought that actually it wasn't silly at all. 'I'm going to see an acupuncturist tomorrow,' she said, 'in North London.'

Helly pulled a face. 'Bleeding hell, they all want a piece of the action, don't they. When will you get shot of this lot?'

Annette smiled. 'Oh I rather like it, all this attention. Gives me something to do while I work out what comes next.'

'Well, I suppose that's what we've all got to work out now.' Helly had started to walk backwards. She waved. 'Are you sure you know the way?'

Annette raised her voice slightly. 'Yes, thanks. And thanks to Joanna and Bob, and you were great, really. Really good.'

Helly waved again, turned, and began to trot back down Sutton Street towards the cottage. Annette watched her until she reached the door. She continued watching as her small figure opened it, turned and waved for one last time, then disappeared inside.

While they had been talking someone had gone round the cottage turning on lights, although it was only early evening and there was no more than the merest hint of dusk. From where Annette was standing, the windows' pale golden rectangles lit up the cottage like a miniature, misshapen fairy castle, squatting solidly amidst the grey-brown patch of wasteground beneath a slightly purple sky.

It was a Thursday and Alison had gone for her mid-morning swim at their local baths. With William at home now there was no need to leave Paul with the child-minder. Instead, he minded his son and then drove over to the pool to pick her up. They were early, so he and Paul went up to the viewing gallery. They were the only people there among the rows of empty wooden seating. On the ceiling above them the reflected waves from the pool made light, shifting patterns. There was the clean, heavy smell of chlorine.

Paul clambered onto William's knee and William said, 'See if you can see Mummy.'

Paul leant out to look and William held onto him. 'There,' said Paul, his tiny voice echoing and his hand shooting out to point.

William scanned the water. There she was, half-way down the pool, swimming the front crawl with slow, measured strokes, lifting her head to the side every third stroke, her mouth an open 'O', to take in air. William watched her – Alison his wife – so clean and careful and calm. She hardly made a splash. 'That's right,' he said to Paul. 'In the water, there, just about to pass that stepladder with the man sitting at the top.'

Paul turned to him and frowned. 'That isn't Mummy.'

'Yes it is.'

'No it isn't. Mummy's *there*.' Paul pointed again, his face screwed up indignantly.

Standing on the edge of pool, at the deep end, was a woman in a red swimsuit with wet, slicked back hair. She paused, then lifted her arms, about to dive back in. It was Alison. I didn't know she had a red swimsuit, William thought.

*   *   *

In the water, Alison swam in slow sure laps, alternating one stroke after the other; front crawl, breaststroke, back-stroke. Every sixth length, she stopped at the deep end and did leg exercises against the edge of the pool, then climbed out and dived back in again. She liked coming on a Thursday morning. It was the quietest time. It was the only time she was able to think clearly.

Earlier that week, she had been to see William's counsellor. He had asked to see her, William said, to get an idea of the family support he was receiving following his trauma. She had sat in the counsellor's room at the hospital and he had talked of his concern. Six weeks on from the incident, William was still suffering flashbacks and night sweats. The counsellor wanted to refer him to a specialist who would take over his treatment long term. Alison had agreed readily, nodding, absorbing both what she was being told and what she was surmising on her own. Her husband was permanently scarred in more ways than one. Towards the end of the session, the counsellor had paused, looked at her and said, 'And what about you?'

Alison reached the deep end and paused to catch her breath. She breathed deeply, holding onto the side with her fingers and treading water. What about me? Am I supposed to be worried about my husband or resent him? Am I supposed to be endlessly supportive – or rage against the way in which a moral victory has been snatched away from me? He had an affair. He was unfaithful. (With a woman who is now an amputee. How can I compete with that?) He lied to me. But he has been injured and somehow in the great scheme of things that is supposed to make up for the wrong he has done. But he didn't get bombed because he lied to me. And the lie is still there; it's just undergone a little plastic surgery, that's all, and I am supposed to avert my gaze. More lies, but this time of the moral kind. The worst kind of all.

She rested her chin lightly on her fingers and continued kicking her legs, gently. *Pain*, she thought, and it was the only clear thought that came to her. I am in pain.

They waited for her in the entrance hall, sitting on lurid green plastic seats which were so clean and shiny that Paul kept pretending to slip off. After he had picked him up for the fourth time, William let him lie there on his back on the tiled floor, waving his arms and calling in mock distress, 'Help! Help!'

William placed his foot gently on the boy's stomach and wiggled him from side to side. 'Help!' called Paul, gurgling with laughter. Then he glanced over to the stairwell and saw his mother.

William looked up. Alison was wearing her black tracksuit and had her sports bag slung over one arm. She was towelling her short hair. Paul pushed himself out from underneath his father's foot and charged over, hurling himself against his mother's legs. Alison dropped her damp towel over his head and he squealed with glee. She picked him up and held him against her chest, pretending to growl.

William watched them. My wife and son, he thought. The perfect couple.

*   *   *

330

In the car going home, they were silent. Paul had screamed for ice-cream for five minutes, then fallen asleep. I wonder what will happen to us, William thought as they drove through Bromley's quiet, midday streets. I wonder whether we will stay together and have another child and watch them both grow up. I wonder if we will ever sit next to each other in a school staff room and talk to Paul's geography teacher. I wonder if we will split up, separate, divorce; if Alison will re-marry and move to a different part of the country so we can argue about visiting rights.

He didn't know. He had no idea how his life would turn out. It all depended on Alison, really. And Alison was unfathomable.

Alun Hardy was sitting in his kitchen, eating the dinner that his wife had prepared. He was holding his fork in his right hand, as he always did, and scooping it at regular intervals into the food that lay on the plate which was sitting directly beneath his nose. He always chopped up his food and ate using only the fork. He had done since he was a child. An open newspaper lay in front of him. He read it as he ate.

His wife was upstairs. She'd eaten earlier, she had said.

Alun Hardy's fork had just scooped a large piece of chicken when he heard his wife's voice behind him. She was standing in the hall.

'You know something Alun,' Joan said. He continued to eat. She often chattered away when he was eating. It irritated him. 'There's something I've been meaning to tell you ever since I got bombed. I should have explained before now but I wasn't sure how to put it and anyway I don't think I really worked it out until now.' It was a Sunday, around teatime. It had been a nice day. The sun had shone. 'I've been making a list.' The piece of chicken was in his mouth and he chewed slowly, his eyes passing over the TV page. 'It's a list of the things I want to take with me when I leave you.'

Alun Hardy froze, the fork suspended in mid-air.

'I've been making it for thirty-two years. It's got quite long. It started after that row we had over the rabbit hutch the first year we were married. After you'd gone round to Bill and Sally's I sat down and wrote a list of what I wanted to take with me when I left. It was quite small then: clothes, the tea service, the woodland picture Gilda gave us. My sewing machine.'

Alun slowly lowered his fork but did not turn round.

'It's grown over the years, of course. A list like that can get quite long in thirty-two years, as I'm sure you can imagine. Clothes, the tea service, the woodland picture, sewing machine, knitting needles, silver teaspoons, the red saucepan, velvet curtains from the back room, cuckoo clock we bought in Amsterdam even though it's plastic, vanity unit including all the bits and bobs, wellies. I tried not to let it get out of hand. Only the things I cared about, not things that were valuable, like that three piece suite we bought from Dalton's Furniture in 1975. It was a lot of money for us then, as you well know but then I thought, I never really liked the blue stripe. It was you wanted the blue, not me. Funny thing is, however long the list got, I never dropped anything off. It got so it was like that rhyme, you know, the old lady who swallowed a fly who swallowed a cat and so on. I never wrote it down. I never forgot a single thing. It just got longer and longer.'

She paused but still he didn't turn around.

'Well yesterday I realised something Alun. I didn't want it. Not any of it. The tea service has got those cups with the little spindly handles you can hardly hold and I never liked that woodland picture. I had to say so to Gilda of course and somehow I got to believing it myself. All these years I've walked past it, thinking I liked it.'

Joan took two steps back down the hall to the cloakroom. She took her favourite coat, grey wool with gilt buttons, from its peg. She put it on. Then she picked up the suitcase she had packed that afternoon and a plastic bag.

As she passed the kitchen on her way to the front door she stopped and said, 'So it's all yours Alun. Everything. I'm not taking any of it, except some clothes and toiletries of course.' She paused. 'Oh, and the cuckoo clock.'

Then she left.

Helly stood in the ladies' toilet and regarded herself in the full-length mirror. Around the mirror was the ornate gilt edging with which the hotel bar and lobby also appeared to be covered. When she had first come in she had thought it was posh, but on closer inspection it looked rather tacky. Baroque on the cheap. Beside each of the sinks on her left were little white china trays in which there were selections of coloured soaps. She had already slipped a set of those into her handbag.

She smoothed her short skirt over her slightly bulging

abdomen. She had just eaten a three course lunch, with wine, and it showed. They can't be after me as a nymphet-type, she reasoned. It must be earthy authenticity they want. Well that's no problem. She bent her head down and ruffled her hair which was freshly washed that morning, loose and chaotic. Then she flicked her head back up and pouted into the mirror. 'Well Ms Rawlins,' she said to herself softly, 'better not keep Rosylyn waiting.'

The call had been the first she had received after the telephone line was installed in Rosewood Cottage. (Helly had told Bob and Joanna that she would live with them on two conditions: one, a washing machine; two, a phone.) Rosylyn – 'That's Rosylyn with two ys' – James was a producer for an independent television production company called A-One-O-One. Helly said she had never heard of them. Rosylyn laughed in a twinkly, that's-alright kind of way and said, 'We make children's and youth programmes. We did that documentary on teenage fathers last year, you know, the one where we reunited a teenage father with his own father who was in his thirties.' Helly didn't have the faintest idea what she was talking about. 'Helen, it's like this. I saw you on *Kilroy* the other week. Now, we're about to start making a pilot for a new series where we get young people to interview other young people about what they believe. We're looking for a stable. Complete unknowns. That's the whole point, you see.'

The upshot of the phone call was, she wanted to buy Helly lunch in a nice, expensive, central London hotel.

By the time Helly returned to their table, their dessert

334

plates had been removed. Rosylyn had had cheese and biscuits. Helly had had three-layer orange cake with fresh cream. A coffee sat at her place.

'I went ahead and ordered coffee,' Rosylyn said, apologetically. 'I hope that's okay.'

Helly picked up her napkin from the gilded, heavily padded chair and sat down. Rosylyn was smoking. An open packet of cigarettes sat on a silver tray on the table. She gave the tray a small push in Helly's direction.

Helly had not expected to like Rosylyn, who, over the phone, had sounded like a git. She had been pleasantly surprised. Rosylyn wore a fitted purple jacket over black leggings and a silver bangle set with large bits of purple glass. The jacket was a mistake. It was slightly too tight across the chest and the buttons strained. Rosylyn was a bit of a fatty. Her nails were long but unvarnished. She would start a sentence full of bullshit – 'Helen, how nice to meet you I'm so glad you could find time to' – but by the time she got to the end of it, she would have lapsed into normal speech – '. . .anyway have a seat where's our blasted waiter.' Now that she had met Rosylyn, Helly could understand why she was so interested in her.

Rosylyn drew on her cigarette. 'Anything else you want to ask me?'

Helly shook her head. 'Maybe I should get this right, just so's I can tell my gran and grandad later. I get bombed, am rude to people on *Kilroy*, and end up as a television presenter.'

Rosylyn laughed. 'Well, it's not quite that straight-forward. It's only a pilot, after all. And there's all sorts of meetings to do first and then there's no guarantee that the series will be bought. But I do want to get you in to meet some other people at A-One-O-One as soon as possible.'

Helly helped herself to a cigarette. 'Well it looks like my side of the story is ending well enough. I'm happy.'

Rosylyn-with-two-ys leant forward and lit Helly's cigarette. 'This is not the end of the story, Helen, just the beginning.'

'Actually,' said Helly, 'I call myself Helly. Is that alright?'

Rosylyn leant back in her seat and smiled. 'Perfect.'

Annette knew that not all stories end happily.

It was the Sunday after she had been to Rosewood Cottage, the Sunday after her first trip to Julia the acupuncturist, early summer, midday, the first Sunday she had been for a walk since the bombing.

Mountsfield Park was not a pleasant park. It only came to life once a year for Lewisham People's Day, when local organisations set up stalls: the Catford Boy Scouts, the South London Mental Health Survivors Group, the Liberal Democrats. Most days it was gloomy and windswept, even at weekends, with no more than a handful of visitors. It was the place to take your dog when it needed to defecate or your child when it needed to scream; the park you went to when you couldn't be bothered to go to a more interesting one.

It was a light afternoon, flickered with sun, with the merest hint of a chill in the air, to remind everyone that the winter was not far behind them and would one day come again. At the entrance there was a single tennis court occupied by two muscular, middle-aged men in white shorts, taking themselves very seriously. As she approached the rise, there were two Alsatians who were sitting gazing around, enjoying the view and panting at each other. A small group of young teenagers hung around the bandstand, smoking. Three drunks were sitting in a row on a nearby bench and another was standing next to them, berating them loudly. 'Youse wouldn't know a good thought if youse fell over it!' The sitting drunks seemed disinclined to argue. They were gazing at him, nodding sagely.

Annette began a slow circuit around the perimeter. Towards the far side there were a few families, women pushing empty pushchairs while toddlers streaked ahead. Coming towards her along the path was a woman of similar age, wearing a long cotton top like hers and no make-up, like her. Like her, she was staring straight ahead. As she passed, they exchanged glances.

Annette turned and went over to a bench. The view from this angle was uninspiring: the distant bandstand with the teenagers and drunks, a lone dog with the characteristic rolling gait of a pit bull trotting along the path.

God, she thought, to think I used to do this regularly before the bombing; every Sunday almost. This is what I had become, a woman who believed in genteel suffering. I can remember myself, casting brave, sly glances at passing groups or couples, walking with my collar turned up against the wind and gazing into the middle distance, imagining that passers-by thought me lovely and wounded. *That woman, so sad. Not beautiful perhaps, but haunting. The eyes. I wonder what it is that makes her seem so wistful?* In fact, I was invisible.

She sighed. No more genteel suffering for her. Now she had the real thing.

She smiled to herself, thinking of the newspaper report of her release from St Thomas'. She hadn't seen it at the time but her mother had shown her when she had come to stay: 'BOMB HEROINE LEAVES HOSPITAL'. The photograph had been one she had allowed them to take the morning of her discharge, while she sat in a low-slung chair in the ward's television lounge. *Former secretary Annette is determined to smile through her tragedy.* Her mother was collecting her cuttings. It was a novel variation on china butterflies.

Former secretary, bomb heroine; what neat phrases, how sharp and distinct these definitions were, and how insignificant they seemed to make her vague, shadowy adolescence. Her friends Sarah and Jason were frightened of her disability but had made a point of asking her to a dinner party as soon as she came out of hospital. Once she had raised the topic round the table, the other guests had given an almost audible sigh. As soon as she had signalled that it was alright to ask her questions, they had been unable to stop. In social terms, a missing hand was almost as good as a baby.

Her physiotherapist Janey had warned her about what she called the honeymoon phase. It happened to some people, apparently. At first, an amputation seemed impossibly horrible. Then there was the slight lift as you came out of hospital and realised all the things you could still do, a kind of wild hope, a fierce, perverse belief in your own persistence and ingenuity. But the hardest bit was yet to come: the day-to-day struggle of incapacity, the fury and resentment. Acceptance would take months, if she was lucky, possibly years. The practical side was easier to deal with. There was the money from the compensation scheme, which would come in handy as the acupuncture did not come on the NHS and she was going to be seeing Julia once a week from now on.

And, she had put her house on the market. She was moving.

A breeze blew around her head, flicking her hair across her face, then back again, mockingly. Not all stories end happily, she thought. But stories end. And now it is ended, a whole phase. I can feel things turning, like the earth creaking round on its axis. Two pigeons strutted past her feet, one after the other. Then the first one stopped, turned and strutted back. The other pursued. As they strode back and forth, their speed increased. Annette smiled. Stupid birds. She placed her feet together neatly and with a small push of her legs, rose from the bench in one swift, efficient movement.

The pigeons took fright and flung themselves upwards, wings beating the warm light air.

Annette paused on the path and looked from left to right, unsure which way to go but enjoying the possibility of choice.

Acknowledgements

I would like to express my warmest gratitude to Merric Davidson, Denise Neuhaus and Roy Parker, each of whom helped enormously in their own particular way. I would also like to thank the many appalling bosses I worked for during my years as a secretary, men who made the writing of this novel not only possible but a psychological necessity.